see it
through
JULIA WOLF

Playlist

"STICK SEASON" NOAH KAHAN

"Pink Skies" Zach Bryan

"Small Town" John Mellencamp

"I Remember Everything" Zach Bryan, Kacey Musgraves

"Golden Hour" Kacey Musgraves

"You're Gonna Go Far" Noah Kahan

"Butterflies" Kacey Musgraves

"Lost Your Home" Mantra

"Sparks" Coldplay

"Meet Me In The Woods" Lord Huron

"Dawns" Zach Bryan, Maggie Rogers

"Light On" Maggie Rogers

"Stay" Gracie Abrams

"Take Me Home, Country Roads" Lana Del Rey

"I Lied" Lord Huron, Allison Ponthier

"Rivers and Roads" The Head and The Heart"

"Wildfire" Seafret

"I'm With You" Vance Joy

"Wildflowers and Wild Horses" Lainey Wilson

"Like A Stone" Audioslave

"Solid Ground" Vance Joy

"Big Black Car" Gregory Alan Isakov

"Coffee" Sylvan Esso

"The Story" Brandi Carlile

"Spotless" Zach Bryan, The Lumineers

"To Build A Home" The Cinematic Orchestra, Patrick Watson

Chapter One

Remington

Sugar Brush had shrunk in the thirteen years I'd been away. Or maybe I'd grown. Either way, it wasn't the same. Main Street no longer seemed like it went on forever. The stout buildings had lost some of their gleam. Brick and glass showed their age. Wyoming winters didn't go easy on anything, not even the structures built to withstand them.

I stopped at a red light and looked around at the heart of town. It belonged on a postcard. Hell, it *was* on postcards. Hazel's pharmacy had displayed them on a swiveling rack. As a kid, I'd gotten into trouble for spinning it too fast a time or two. I idly wondered if that same rack was still there. Or if Hazel was. She'd been old then, and time had kept turning.

I drummed my thumbs on my wheel, my patience wearing thin as I waited for my signal to go. There were two traffic lights on this street now, but they had to be more for show than anything. A town like this barely needed one.

There were businesses I didn't recognize, but a lot I did. Sugar Rush Bakery was new, while Joy's Elbow Room hadn't changed a lick. Not on the outside anyway. I'd left before I was old enough to drink, and Joy would have tossed me out on my hide if I'd tried to sneak in.

The plan had been never to return. The town held nothing for me. But now that I was here, I was hit with an urge to get out, stretch my legs, and walk the length of this street to see if it felt as different as it looked.

Another day.

Daylight was already waning, and I wanted to get to the house before the sun set. The last knock on my head was still doing a number on me and driving at night now tended to bring on headaches.

The light turned green, and I drove to the end of Main Street, navigating my way to the lone grocery store. There was a big-box store out in Cheyenne, but time was at a premium, and I didn't need much. I'd venture farther when I had the time and inclination. For now, The Grocery Warehouse would suit me just fine.

The name was apt for the square concrete building I walked into. No frills. Metal shelves and handwritten prices. There weren't ten types of bread. It was wheat or white around these parts, and something about not having to make a lot of choices was comforting.

I shook that thought away, replacing it with the memory of how stifling it'd been to live like this. Leaving was all I'd thought about. Making escape plans had been my source of solace.

The fluorescent lights made me flinch, and a sharp pain sliced my forehead in half. I slid my sunglasses from the neck of my T-shirt and slipped them on. I wasn't a man who wore shades indoors, but if I wanted to get through this, it had to be done. No way I could spend any amount of time in the bright, artificial lights without trying to claw my skull off my neck.

Grabbing a cart, I made quick work of throwing essentials in. Not only did I want to get out of here, but I also wasn't eager to run into anyone who'd recognize me. That time would come. Word filtered through Sugar Brush like summer brush fires. I just wanted a day or two to find my bearings before it happened. There would be opinions about my return—questions too. And I wasn't looking forward to answering them.

I made it to the checkout line before taking in the people around me. The cashier, about my age, was familiar in the way most people in a town this size were. We'd probably gone to school together, but I couldn't be sure. She was taking her time ringing up the man in front of me, and my attention diverted to the other customers in line, stopping on the woman behind me.

Her, I recognized. There was no mistaking the tall, icy blonde for anyone other than Mrs. Elena Kelly, my childhood best friend's mom. I'd spent a lot of my days out on the Kelly ranch with Caleb, getting dirty and making trouble. His parents had been firm but not strict, and they had welcomed me into their home for countless dinners and sleepovers.

Elena Kelly's gaze swept over me, pausing for a moment. I nodded at her, my mouth curving into a half smile.

"Good evening, Mrs. Kelly."

She cocked her head, taking me in. There was no flare of recognition, but it'd been more than a decade since she'd seen me. I pushed my sunglasses to the top of my head, giving her a better view.

Finally, she drawled, "I'm sorry, have we met?"

"We have, ma'am. Been a while, though. I was friends with Caleb back in school."

"Hmmm." She gave me a long once-over, her lips pursed. She had to be in her mid fifties, but she looked ten years younger. Caleb had once told me his dad called her Elsa, after a Disney princess, and even now if someone told me she ruled over an ice kingdom, I'd believe it.

"Well, you must not have been close, or you'd know I despise being called 'ma'am and Mrs. Kelly is my mother-in-law."

I had to clench my jaw to stop it from falling open. I didn't know what I'd expected her to say, but it wasn't that. I had distinct memories of this woman from my adolescence, of her laughing at how dirty Cay and I were, admonishing us for not wiping our boots on the welcome mat, taking me aside to ask if I was okay at home, and she had no recollection of me.

Reality slapped me in the face. I'd extricated myself from this town, but this town had done an even better job at exorcising me.

"Sorry, ma'a—" I stopped, correcting myself. "Elena, it's good to see you again."

Her icy eyes trailed over me once more, and her mouth curved into a polite if not entirely sincere, little smile.

"Caleb works on the ranch." She flicked her perfectly manicured nails in my direction. "But I'm sure you know that already."

I nodded. I hadn't known but I'd figured as much. Caleb Kelly had loved his family's ranch. His goal had always been to take over for his dad, who'd taken over for his dad, and his dad before him. It was the kind of legacy he'd been proud to continue, not one he couldn't wait to walk away from.

"Thanks. I'll get in touch with him while I'm in town."

I didn't know if I meant it. I couldn't be sure Caleb would even welcome hearing from me after all this time. But I wasn't going to say that to his mother.

She lifted her elegant chin. "It's your turn."

"Ah..." I twisted my neck to see the cashier had scanned and bagged my groceries and was now tapping her fingers, waiting for me to pay. "Thanks. I'll see you around."

"You're welcome."

Her cool politeness frosted over me as I paid my bill and followed me outside into the setting sun. Only as I got into my truck did it thaw.

I didn't linger in the parking lot. Putting my truck into gear, I went on my way. The house was on the outskirts of town, and I was running out of daylight. It's what I got for dragging my feet on the route to Sugar Brush, but there was almost nothing here I was looking forward to.

They said you could never go home again, but as I pulled onto the long drive leading to the house I grew up in, the same old dread pitted my stomach, just like it did back then. I could've been seventeen again for how little the feeling had changed.

Except it was all different now. Just an old, empty house. Nothing but echoes of my past waiting inside. Nothing to fear. Nothing to dread.

It was just a house.

Walls, floors, fixtures.

Nothing and no one else.

Just me and my memories.

I took a deep breath and climbed out, my boots hitting the dusty gravel.

This was it. It had to be done.

No way out but through.

Chapter Two

Hannah

I DRAGGED MY FINGER along the pastry case, practically drooling over the choices behind the glass. Muffins, donuts, cookies, lemon bars…ugh, how was I supposed to choose? I wanted one of everything, but it would be difficult to do my job in a sugar coma.

"Hurry up. You're holding up the line."

I straightened, pinning a narrow-eyed glare at the owner of Sugar Rush Bakery. "This is your fault."

My little sister put her hands on her curvy hips, her chestnut ponytail bobbing with the attitude she reserved for me. "And how is that?"

I gestured toward the case, overloaded with all kinds of temptation. My sister was the devil when it came to baked goods. "Are you kidding, Phoebe? White chocolate and raspberry donuts? Banana coconut muffins? Apple streusel? Making me choose is torture."

With a huff and eye roll, she slid the case open, plucked up a blueberry muffin, put it in a bag emblazoned with her adorable, sassy pink logo, and held it out to me.

"There. We both know this is what you were going to choose. It's what you always choose."

I took the muffin from her, indignant. "I might have changed my mind."

"We both also know that isn't true."

We did. I was a creature of habit. I'd eat the same breakfast every day until I couldn't stand to look at it then move on to a new food obsession. I was going strong with Phoebe's blueberry muffins, though.

She pointed to the opposite side of the counter. "Your coffee will be over there when it's ready."

I blew my sister a kiss. "Thanks, Phe."

She blew a kiss back at me. "Welcome, Banana. Now, get out of here, you."

Phoebe went back to her line of customers while I hitched my hip on the vintage linoleum counter, watching. Phe was good with people. She had a natural way about her, floating softly around them, cushioning anyone who needed it. She'd been sweet since the day she was born. I'd been all of three years old, but I still remembered her warm weight as our dad put her in my arms for the first time.

Our family was a little protective of her. She was our little cinnamon roll, far too sweet for this world. When she'd decided to open Sugar Rush, my two brothers and I had begun showing up in shifts. Caleb at opening, me midmorning, and Cormac in the afternoon. Ostensibly, we were here for the baked goods and coffee, but it went unsaid we were checking in on Phe. She knew it, we knew she knew it, but there had been no stopping us.

Us Kellys were like that. Hardheaded, tight-knit, uninterested in changing.

Phe's barista and friend, Camille, slid my iced coffee across the counter. "Here you go," she chirped.

I hopped down and grabbed my drink with a grin. "Thanks, Cam. You're the best."

I waved at Phe and eyeballed everyone in line on my way out. There were a couple guys who looked like some type of trouble in their backward caps and their T-shirt sleeves rolled just right to show off their pumped-up biceps. I looked at them extra hard. Some of these young cowboys thought they were God's gift and wouldn't hesitate to give my sister a hard time if they felt like it. I wouldn't have it, but Phoebe didn't love me threatening her customers, especially if their only crime was being too handsome for their own good.

One last hard, menacing look and I was off.

Rolling my truck windows down, I turned up the radio. I wasn't in a hurry to get to work. It was a heavy paperwork day—my least favorite. I'd done it to myself, though. Had I not put off everything I needed to do until the last minute, I wouldn't have hours of sitting in my office ahead of me.

I shrugged and sang along to the music. It was my fate, and there was no point getting upset about it. Tomorrow would be another day.

I still hadn't gotten used to unlocking the door to Graham's house. It didn't feel right for it to be locked up and deadly silent. It'd been a month. A month without *"Mornin', Hannah-girl,"* when I walked in, and *"Get conquerin' the world"* when I left. Sliding my key into the door shouldn't have still felt so wrong. It made me wonder if maybe it would always feel that way.

I walked through the living room, my blinders on so I didn't have to see Graham's recliner, which I knew from memory had his butt print in it. It was where he'd spent most of his time this last year. The first time I came here after...well, *after*, seeing it empty had almost been my undoing. Since then, I'd purposely avoided looking.

In the kitchen, I turned on the coffeepot. My measly iced coffee wasn't going to cut it. Not even close. I'd taken my meds this morning, but I was still going to need way more caffeine to get through my tasks without my mind wandering in a hundred directions.

I opened the fridge, surprised to see more than just the small carton of milk and bag of apples I kept at the house. There was deli meat, a pack of chicken, veggies, and a bottle of orange juice.

Strange. Henry must've been by. That had to explain it.

Henry was the groundskeeper who lived in a small cabin at the far edge of the property. Graham had owned ten acres, so Henry's place was pretty far off from the main house. He kept to himself, but I knew he looked out for me in his own way. He'd heard Graham reminding me to eat more than a time or two, and now that Graham wasn't here...

I pinched the bridge of my nose and squeezed my eyes shut to stave off the burning. Now wasn't the time for getting upset. There was too much to do, and I could almost hear Graham's disgust at me getting lost in my feelings over him. *"Find somethin' else worth cryin' for. It isn't me!"*

Grabbing a full mug of coffee, I headed to my office at the back of the house. What had once been used for storage was now a comfortable, if not fairly disorganized, space. When I'd started working here, Graham had kitted it out with a solid oak desk, filing cabinets, and a brand-new computer. And thanks to a satellite twinkling up in the sky, the internet was faster than it had any business being considering we were well off the beaten path.

Graham never said anything to me about it, but once I caught him reading an article about the best office design for people with ADHD. A week later, he'd had curtains and blinds installed to cover the large picture window overlooking the property. He'd done this quietly, without shaming me for the times I'd gotten lost in the view. Now I automatically closed the curtains when I needed my brain to stay on task.

I shook my head, but it was impossible to stop thinking about Graham when I was sitting in his house, surrounded by all the little things he'd done to show me I was important—not just as an employee but a person.

I picked up the phone to return a call. Dell Rivers answered on the first ring, like always, bypassing any kind of greeting.

"I need you out here, Hannah."

I tapped my pencil on my appointment book. "I understand, Dell. I have a spot for you, and I'll be happy to come out and take care of your horses, but I need to know you're going to let me do it."

His bluster was audible through the phone. "Of course I am. That's why I called you. To do your job. If I could, I—"

"You would. I know." I barely suppressed a laugh. Dell Rivers would run the universe if he could. He was the definition of a control freak. "Before I pencil you in, I need a promise from you, Dell."

More audible blustering. I was sure his face was bright red and the vein in his forehead was throbbing. If I didn't know he was a decent man, deep down, I wouldn't have bothered humoring him. He was too much trouble for that.

"Fine. Yes, I promise to leave you alone to do your job." He mumbled something too low for me to make out. "Is that good enough, or do I need to call Cleve? He's been after my business for a while now, and I know he'd be happy to come out tomorrow—"

"You can call Cleve." I tapped my pencil with a little more force. "But we both know he'll have your horses on a three-week cycle, and you'll be lucky to get that. If you want to get six weeks out of a trim..."

I didn't need to finish my statement. Cleve Jones had been a farrier for over twenty years. He might've taken pride in his work once upon a time, but these days, it was rushed and shoddy. I'd been called to clean up his uneven trims and loose shoes more than once, but he still had customers because of his lower prices and willingness to work with anyone.

Dell's horses didn't like Cleve. We both knew it. We also both knew his threats of going to Cleve were empty; I just needed him to stop breathing down my neck every time I showed up to do my job. Dell loved his horses and thought that made him an expert—more than my farrier schooling and dozens of certificates. Not to mention the years of mentoring I got from Graham and experience I had in taking care of horses on my own.

"Yes, all right. You called my bluff, Hannah Kelly," Dell admitted. "When can you get out here? Trixie's hooves need some serious TLC. If Cleve tries to get near her, I'm afraid he won't leave without a dent somewhere on his person."

We made an appointment for later in the week, and I got on with more phone calls, only stopping when my stomach started to growl. That was when I remembered my blueberry muffin was still inside the paper bag it came in.

I reached inside, licking my lips with anticipation. Before I could slide it out, my office door swung open, slamming into the wall behind it.

There, standing in the doorway, was a man.

A very wet, very naked man. Chest heaving, fists clenched at his sides, his wild eyes bounced over me. I backed up a step, and he tensed like he was about to pounce.

My spine iced over, and my limbs became heavy with the dread of what might come next, but I didn't let the fear paralyze me. Blindly feeling around on the desk beside me, paper crinkled under my hand. It wasn't much of a weapon, but it would have to do.

Before I could think better of it, I reared my arm back and threw my muffin at him.

Chapter Three

Remington

SOMETHING SOFT BOUNCED OFF my forehead, stopping me in my tracks.

"What the hell?" I bit out. The offending object rolled across my foot. "Why are you throwing muffins at me?"

"It was one muffin, and you have to leave. This is private property," the intruder commanded in a high, quavering voice. "If you need clothes, I'll throw them out the window once you're outside."

Next thing I knew, a desk chair launched toward me. The thick rug on the floor slowed it down. By the time it reached me, it was barely rolling. I gripped the back, keeping it between me and the woman now brandishing a keyboard like a baseball bat.

"Clothes? Why would I—?"

I looked down, shocked to find myself naked, though I wasn't sure why. I'd been getting ready to take a shower when I'd heard movement and a voice coming from downstairs. My instincts had carried me down here without a plan...or clothes.

Too many years of living and working in dangerous situations kept my guard up, even though the angry bull facing me down didn't strike me as a true threat. The longer we stared at each other, the more familiar she looked.

"Why are you still standing there?" she raved, the keyboard poised, ready to smash my head in. It wasn't a heavy weapon, but it might do the trick. The scar running along my temple twinged. "If you don't get out of here right now, I'm not going to bother giving you pants. You can fry your pasty ass off in the sun."

I kept the chair strategically in front of me—and not because I was modest. I didn't trust this woman not to make mincemeat out of parts of me better left intact.

"Seeing as this is my dad's house, and you're not him, I'm thinking you should be the one to get out."

She barked an incredulous laugh.

"Nice try, bucko. This is Graham Town's house. His son hasn't been heard from in more than a decade." Her fingers flexed, and those feral eyes roved over my face. "The asshole," she muttered.

Now that I had been able to take a nice long look at the intruder without adrenaline coursing through me, I knew exactly who she was. When I'd left town, she'd been around fifteen or sixteen. She'd done a lot of growing up since then, but there was no denying those chocolate-brown eyes. They were a Kelly trait through and through. Same as her height, which had to be nearly six feet. I remembered her being coltish, like a newborn horse getting used to its gangly limbs. She'd filled out since then. In a black tank revealing long, tan arms defined with muscle and well-worn jeans clinging to strong, endless legs, there was no doubt Hannah Kelly was all woman.

She was also the second Kelly who'd forgotten me in the span of twenty-four hours.

"Don't think it's right to call me an asshole just yet, considering I haven't been around to earn it," I said.

Her big brown eyes narrowed. "What are you talking about? And why are you still standing in my office buck naked?"

"Which question do you want me to answer first?"

Groaning, she let her eyes roll heavenward. "None of them. Get outta here right now before I call Henry. He might be old, but he's fast, and he's a prepper. He'll come down here with a cannon if I tell him some naked perv broke into the house."

Her office? Interesting. Now that she'd said it, this room did have a distinctly feminine touch. Not that there were any pink or roses, but it smelled slightly sweet and a whole lot fresh, and artistic pictures of horses and landscapes hung neatly on the wall. Graham hadn't been much of a decorator back when I was around, and I didn't figure that had changed.

"Didn't break in."

She raised her chin. "Yeah, you did. I remember locking the door behind me."

I winged a brow. "Do you?"

The tension in her arms eased as her eyes slid to the side. Like she was searching her memory, doubting herself.

Then she went taut again.

"Yes, I do remember. Which means you broke in. If you damaged the lock, I'm billing you for it. If you messed with anything else, I'll—"

"You'll what?"

"Let's just say you'll be wishing for the muffin."

I could have gone back and forth a while longer, but my presence was causing her stress, and I didn't like that.

Chuckling, I looked her square in the eyes. "I know it's been a while, and I have a couple more scars than I used to, but you really don't recognize me, Hannah Kelly?"

She gave me another long look. Something sparked in her gaze, and her mouth fell open. She'd managed to make her slack-jawed surprise look cute...before it morphed into tight-lipped anger and fiery red cheeks.

"Remington Town, you're about a month too late."

My hands tightened on the back of the chair. "That's one way to see it."

She tossed the keyboard on her desk and folded her arms over her chest. "We buried Graham four weeks ago—but I guess you probably know that from all the messages you received. I'm only guessing you received them since you're here, not because you bothered to return any of them."

Henry's voice had replayed in my head since I first heard it. *Yer dad's dead, kid. Guess you gotta come back and settle up.*

"I got the messages. You want to talk about it, I will, but not when my ass is in the wind."

Her eyes squeezed shut. "Oh my god, go get dressed, and please stop bringing up your ass."

Despite myself and where I was, I grinned at her holding her hand over her face like the sight of me was offensive. She'd been a wildcat way back when, and it seemed like that still held true. A lot had changed, and I was inexplicably relieved that wasn't something that had.

"If that makes you happy, Hannah Kelly."

She shooed me away, and this time, I went.

Hannah was in the kitchen when I returned, fully clothed. The second she saw me, her spine stiffened, and she eyed me warily, but she didn't offer a word of explanation for her presence in Graham's house.

I poured myself a cup of the coffee I assumed she'd made and added some of the milk she must have bought if her growl was anything to go by. Considering she was the intruder and I had every right to be here, I didn't let it bother me.

We were in a silent standoff while I drank my coffee and looked around the kitchen. Graham had done a lot of work on the place. The cabinets had been painted bright white, and what looked like a relatively new butcher block counter had been installed. The walls were painted too, and the light fixtures had been switched out. The only thing I recognized was the oversized farmhouse sink, and even that looked different. What had always been filled with dirty dishes was now empty and scrubbed clean.

Hannah huffed, bracing her hands on the island opposite from where I stood. "I was in a pretty foul mood before you came bumbling into my space, swinging your dick at me."

"Didn't swing it at you," I muttered, not bothering to raise my voice. She was on a roll and most likely wouldn't have heard me anyway.

"I don't know why you bothered showing up after all this time, but let me make something clear, Remington Town, we don't need you here. Everything that needed to be taken care of has been, and that includes seeing your father to the other side. You can go back to your adventurous, freewheeling lifestyle and leave the rest of us in peace."

My mug clunked as I set it down, but Hannah didn't flinch.

"Think you remember I go by Remi," I said softly.

She lifted one shoulder. "Things change. I figured since you're famous now, you're probably a little more formal. Isn't that what your byline says?"

I huffed a humorless laugh. That was the last thing I'd expected to be talking about right now. "I'm flattered you've been following my career, but famous is a stretch."

There were one or two photojournalists who were widely known, but for the most part, it was our pictures that became famous, which was all well and good with me. I didn't do it for the acclaim.

Her fingers flexed on the counter, turning white from the pressure. "Graham followed his son's career. He showed me your pictures every chance he got. I had little to no interest, but since I respected him, I paid attention."

It was incredibly hard to believe Graham had cared about me after I'd left since he hadn't bothered to while I'd been living in the same house, but this woman had no reason to lie to me. But I couldn't take what she was saying in, wrap my head around it. Not when a headache was sneaking in with all the anger I'd lassoed and left behind in tow.

"Funny, 'cause when I was here, the old man had little interest in me." I dragged my hand over my face, still tired after a restless night in my too-small childhood bed. It had creaked every time I shifted, which had been a lot since the mattress springs had kept trying to pierce me.

I raised my eyes to Hannah, finding her watching me intently. Neither of us was going anywhere, so I took a long pull of my coffee, hoping it'd perform a miracle and stave off my headache.

Hannah raised her chin the same way her mother had the night before.

"You're in pain?" she asked, seeing right through me.

"Got a headache coming on." I absently touched the scar that disappeared into my hair.

With a sharp nod, she swiveled away from me, marched to the cabinets, then returned to the island a moment later, thrusting a bottle toward me.

"Here."

A bottle of painkillers rested in her open palm. Something warm swept across my chest, there and gone before I could fully register it.

I took the bottle from her and shook out a couple pills, swallowing them with my coffee. It wasn't much, but it was better than nothing.

"Thanks." I rattled the bottle before setting it down. We'd danced around what we needed to talk about long enough. It was time to face what was going on here. "So, am I right that you work here at Graham's house?"

"Yep." She backed up until she could hitch her bottom on the counter behind her.

"Okay." I palmed the crown of my head, mulling it over. "I'm not gonna rush you to get out. It'll take a while to sell the place, so you'll have time to find another place to work. But you'll have to make those arrangements as soon as you can."

Her lips pressed together as I spoke, and once I was done, she burst out laughing, full and loud. Bending in half from the force of it, she slapped her thigh and everything. I'd have thought it was hysterics from the reality of having to find a new office, but that wasn't what this was. I didn't know *what* the hell it was other than Hannah being greatly amused by something I said.

Finally, she straightened, her laughter petering out. Her cheeks were rosy, and she swiped the tears caught in her thick, sooty lashes.

"Oh, Remington," she drawled. "You really have no idea what the hell you're talking about, do you?"

"Thought I did." I pressed my hand against the snakes slithering in my belly, sure I was about to hear how my dad had screwed me over one final time. "Care to explain what I got wrong?"

"You're going to have a hard time selling this house when it's not yours."

A curtain fell over what I thought I knew, the reason I'd come, leaving me in the dark.

"What'd he do?" I gritted out.

Hannah smiled at me, but it wasn't exactly cheerful. There was too much melancholy behind it for that. I could only guess she was sad over Graham's death, which I couldn't begin to understand. As far as I was concerned, there was nothing worth missing now that he was gone.

"He left instructions that Henry should be allowed to live in his cabin for the rest of his life or as long as he wants to stay. And this house...it isn't yours."

She shot me a mirthless smile, and I braced myself for the rest.

Chocolate brown eyes danced with mine. "It's ours, Remington."

My stomach bottomed out as my plan of getting in and getting out flipped on its head.

All I could say was, "Call me Remi."

Chapter Four

Hannah

I walked into my parents' house and took a deep breath. *Home.* My mother's cooking, aged wood, the remnants of a fire in the hearth, and something that had no name but belonged only here. If this scent was the last thing I smelled before I died, I'd be at peace.

Once I kicked my shoes off and made sure the hems of my jeans weren't muddy, I walked into the kitchen, greeted by a tableau that made me smile. My dad at the large farmhouse table, shucking corn. My mom chopping watermelon. Phoebe at the stove, stirring something in a large pot. I went straight for my dad, who put down the ear to tap his ruddy cheek. Bending, I gave him a peck, and he patted my arm.

"Good day, Han?" he gruffed gently. My father was a big man, tall and robust. Strong from manual labor and soft in the middle from genetics and the rich recipes my mom liked to test on us. He could squash a grown man's head in his baseball-glove-sized mitts, but he had never been anything but tender and careful with us kids. In his late fifties, silver traveled through the sides of his hair and crinkles lined the corners of his eyes, but he didn't seem old. As far as I was concerned, Lachlan Kelly was invincible and always would be.

"Weird day," I answered.

My mom popped a piece of watermelon into her mouth and walked over to pop one in mine. "Delicious, right?"

"Mmm. Like sugar."

She smoothed her palm over my hair and patted my cheek. "By your lack of dishevelment, I'm guessing today was a paperwork day."

I snorted. "You guessed right."

My mother was the girliest girl. Ultra-feminine, always wearing beautiful clothes, impeccably put together. Originally from California, she looked the part but fit in on the ranch like a fish in water. Sugar Brush River Ranch wasn't any ol' ranch, though. It was also a world-class resort. Our thirty-thousand acres had been in the Kelly family for generations, but the resort had only been added fifty years ago. Three presidents' children had been married in the chapel, and many more celebrities and billionaires had vacationed here.

My mother ran the resort's marketing department, though Dad was tempting her to retire with him sooner rather than later. Despite who she was—glamorous, fastidious with her image, a fashion maven—she'd never imposed that on me, letting me be myself. Sometimes that meant I was filthy and smelled like horse. Other times, I'd put on a dress, my best cowboy boots and add a bow in my hair. My mom might've teased me about it, but she'd never once made me feel like she'd disapproved of who I was and the choices I'd made.

In short, my parents were awesome. I understood enough about the world to know they were rare jewels, and I was a lucky girl to have come from this family. I certainly hadn't done anything to earn it, but I didn't take any of my people for granted.

Phoebe turned away from the stove, a wooden spoon poised in her hand. "What was weird about the day?"

I took a seat across from my dad and exhaled a heavy breath. "You'll never guess who showed up at the house."

My mom pursed her lips. "Remi Town."

I jerked in surprised. "Okay, I stand corrected. You guessed."

She flicked her manicured nails. "I ran into him at the grocery store last night. He acted like I should have recognized him, so of course I pretended I had no clue who he was."

"Ellie," Dad drawled. "Be sweet."

She went to him, and he snagged her around the waist as soon as she was close enough. Her lips met the top of his head, her hand, his cheek. "I'm always sweet, Lachlan. But the arrogance of a man expecting to be remembered when he's been gone without a word for more than a decade got me in a tizzy."

Phe laughed. "You've never been in a tizzy."

Mom gasped. "I can be and have been in plenty of tizzies, my darling daughter."

I cocked my head. "You were being a mean girl, weren't you?"

My mother had gone through a lot when she was younger, turning her into an angry teen. Fortunately for all of us, she'd worked through it in therapy then fell in love with my dad, who brought out the softness she'd had to hide behind armored spikes. At least, that was how they told it.

She tossed her pretty blonde hair behind her back. "It was instinct. That boy hurt Cay when he abandoned their friendship."

Dad's huge hand spanned the side of her hip. "He has his reasons. You know that as well as I do."

She hummed, lowering herself to his thick thigh, and twined her arms around his neck. "I do. And if I see him again, I won't be unkind. But I can't be the only one who remembers how Caleb felt when his best friend cut him off."

"Dad doesn't hold grudges," Phe said.

Mom slid her fingers through the side of his hair. "I know he doesn't. I hold them for both of us."

The sound of the front door opening interrupted our line of conversation, and my brothers' voices greeted us before they appeared in the kitchen.

Caleb was Dad's spitting image, except scruffier. That might've been because our parents had met in college and Dad kept himself put together for his wife. Caleb didn't have a woman to impress—though, from what I'd heard and seen, to my chagrin, my brother didn't have any trouble in that department. In fact, he had a ten-year-old son as a result of one of his one-night stands.

"Where's Jesse?" I asked.

"Shelby has him this week. I would've brought him for dinner, but Shel's parents are in town for a visit," Caleb explained, pulling his thick chestnut hair into a haphazard bun at the base of his skull. When it was down, it grazed his broad shoulders, and his beard ranged from heavy stubble to biblical. Today, it was mostly the former.

He stopped to kiss Mom on her head, ruffled Phe's hair after stealing a piece of watermelon, then slung his heavy arm around my shoulders.

I shoved him off with a fake grimace. "Dislocate my shoulder, why don't you."

His chuckle rumbled like rolling thunder. "You're always reminding me how strong you are. Can't take one brother's arm?"

"Not when it's the size of a tree trunk," I shot back.

Cormac clapped once. "All right, children. Don't get started, or we'll be hearing the two of you snipe all night."

"Hey..." Mom grabbed Maccie's hand and held it between both of hers. "Isn't parenting my job?"

He offered her a crooked grin. "I thought you could use a break after trying to keep Cay in line for thirty-one years."

Mom kissed the back of his hand. "My sweet baby, always looking out for your mom. Don't worry about me, honey. I'm giving free-range parenting a try. They can learn from their mistakes while I get to cease worrying about them killing each other."

I waved my hand. "Hello, I'm right here." Then I picked up Cay's arm and made it wave too, though it took a lot of strength to do it. "Cay's here too. His feelings are hurt."

"They're not," he added wryly, tucking his hands in his pockets so I couldn't use him as my puppet anymore.

Cormac cocked his head, exchanging a glance with our parents. "Are you sure about the free-range thing?"

At twenty-four, Mac was the youngest, and he was pretty wonderful. As much as we all doted on Phoebe, Mac was the baby, and even though it pained him, we all saw him that way.

In his finely-tailored suit, however, he didn't look like a baby. Maccie was as tall as Caleb and our dad but lean and rangy. His hair was similar to Cay's but slightly shorter and more refined, and he kept his light beard neatly trimmed. He was the only one who had Mom's icy blue eyes, and they were gorgeous. In fact, in looks and interests, he took after our mother more than the rest of us.

Maccie had gone to college for hospitality management and was now the assistant manager of the resort with plans to take over entirely in a few years. While I would be bored to tears working inside day in, day out, Mac was good at it. Empathetic to his core, people loved him because he was good to them. In that way, he was very much like our dad. Not that our mom lacked empathy, but she was sharper with a bark *and* a bite.

I folded my arms over my chest, putting on an offended pout, though I wasn't in the least. "I've been free range since I moved out of this house. Somehow, I manage to feed and clothe myself."

Phe nodded. "She hasn't even burned down her apartment."

I raised a finger. "Not even once."

Cay's huge hand landed firmly on my back. "Pretty sure the fire department has you blacklisted, so it's good you haven't needed their services."

I rolled my eyes, muttering, "Forget you're cooking noodles one time, and no one lets you live it down..."

"You started a fire," he stated.

I held my fingers an inch apart. "A small one, and that was at least a decade ago. You need to let it go."

Mom hopped up from Dad's lap and swept around us to return to cutting the melon. "Speaking of a decade, guess who rolled into town last night? Hannah was just about to tell us about it."

Caleb's head cocked. "A decade? What's that about?"

I blew out a heavy breath. "Remington is back."

He flinched like he'd taken a blow. "Back where? In Sugar Brush?"

"Yep."

Cay scrubbed his bearded cheek and turned away. His normally loose limbs were drawn tight, and his jaw moved back and forth as he processed this bit of news.

Remi leaving hadn't impacted me much. I wasn't one of those girls who'd paid a lot of attention to the boys my brothers hung around. For me, Remi had been here one day, gone the next. I moved on easily. But Caleb had moped around the ranch for months. He'd checked the mail for letters or postcards, his phone for texts or missed calls. Then, one day, he just stopped and never brought up his old friend again.

I'd thought he'd gotten over it.

Looked like I was wrong.

"What's he doing back now?" he asked lowly.

"We didn't share a heart-to-heart." I wasn't about to tell my family a buck-naked Remi had burst in on me. They wouldn't have taken too kindly to that, and it wasn't like the naked part had been a big deal. It was his existence in a house where he no longer belonged that had gotten under my skin.

"What'd he say?" he pressed.

"He was under the impression the house was his. I guess he came to sell it and collect his payday. I relieved him of that idea, though."

Mom huffed. "What did he think about that?"

I rolled my eyes. "I'm not sure he believed me. Said he's going to talk to Graham's lawyer."

"He doesn't even know who that is, does he?" Cay asked.

"Doubt it." I shrugged. "I'm sure he'll head right back out of town once he figures out he won't be getting a dime."

"I really doubt he needs money," Phoebe said.

When Caleb and I whirled around to stare at her, she raised her hands. "I'm not claiming to know his motives, and while I don't know what a successful photojournalist makes, I have a feeling it isn't pocket change."

"I don't care about his motives," Caleb grumbled. "Long as he gets outta this town as quickly as he arrived."

The corner of my mouth hitched. "He's certainly not going to like coexisting in that house with me."

"You're barely ever there," Phoebe reminded me.

"Well, things change," I stated. "I might need to make more appearances to check on my property. Since he's basically a stranger, you never know what he might be up to."

A rumble came from my father as he rose. Passing by me on the way to my mom, he touched my shoulder.

"Be sweet, Han. You don't remember how Graham was when you were younger, but I do. He wasn't always the man you came to admire. Must be difficult for Remi to be back here."

I wasn't one to argue with my dad, mostly because he was always right, but I wasn't too sure I agreed with him now. This was one of those instances where I'd have to wait and see.

Maybe Remi would be gone in the morning and I'd never see him again.

Maybe he'd stick around like a thorn in my side.

If he chose the latter, he'd better make sure he kept his clothes on.

After all, there were a lot more muffins where that first had come from.

Chapter Five

Remington

Turned out my father's will was with his lawyer, a nervous man with stark white hair named Dell Rivers. Dell wore a tweed sports jacket, bolo tie, jeans, and cowboy boots. I couldn't say I remembered him from my youth, but the second I stepped foot in his office, he yelped my name like he'd been expecting me.

Maybe Hannah Kelly had given him a call.

The other possibility—the one I didn't like to think about? Each day that passed, as I grew older and the world weighed on me bit by bit, I looked more and more like Graham. The one person I never wanted to emulate looked back at me in the mirror each morning, and that was a real kick to the teeth.

Either way, Dell recognized me and invited me in. I hadn't made an appointment, but considering Sugar Brush wasn't a bustling metropolis, I had a feeling Dell's calendar had more than a few open spots.

He handed me a copy of the will, but my head was aching something fierce, making the letters swim. Luckily, Dell volunteered to read it to me.

As much as I'd been hoping Hannah had gotten it wrong and the house was mine to get rid of, that wasn't the truth. Graham had left half the house and property to her—minus Henry's cabin and small plot. He'd also left her all his farrier tools and business.

"Now, don't get offended Hannah got the business," Dell blurted out, his cheeks flushing rosy. "She's been running Town Hoofcare for years on her own. Graham couldn't move without pain, but he taught Hannah everything he knew. The business has been hers in all but name for at least five years. She took it over and built it up, so you see, it wouldn't be fair for her to have to split any of that with you."

I nodded sharply, turning the name of the business over in my head. "Wouldn't want it."

It'd been called Town and Son Hoofcare since the day I was born. Graham had expected me to join him and take it over one day. Except horses had never been my thing—not as a career, anyway. Probably because they'd been *his* thing and liking something he liked hadn't been an option for me.

"Good, good." Dell shuffled some papers around on his desk. "Now, on to—"

"How'd Hannah Kelly get mixed up with Graham?" The question was out before I'd known I was going to ask it. But it'd been on my mind since yesterday, and I really doubted going to the source would yield me results.

Dell paused and scratched the side of his head. "You know, I'm not sure. Seems like Hannah started working with Graham as soon as she graduated high school. I remember her following Graham around back—she couldn't have been more than eighteen or nineteen— watching him work."

Two or three years after I left.

When I drove away from Sugar Brush for what I'd thought was the last time, Graham had barely been functioning. He'd worked—sometimes—but spent most of his days at Joy's and his evenings laid out on our couch, rotting away. Thinking of Hannah spending time with him in that condition sent a sharp spike through my skull.

Dell went right on talking, not seeming to notice me clutching my head. "Now Hannah's been trimming all my horses' hooves for a few years. They all like her, but Trixie's my temperamental girl. Anyone else tries to get ahold of her hooves, she goes wild. Not with Hannah, though. She has the magic touch."

He leaned forward like he was about to confide something he needed to stay between us. "It's like children. You're not supposed to pick a favorite, but Trixie...well, I call her my soul horse. We understand each other, and I want her to have the very best. She's barefoot, you know, so it's important to get her trims just right. Cleve Jones came out once to trim her after I made Hannah mad." He waved his hand in front of him. "Never mind that. The point is, Hannah's the best and deserves Town Hoofcare, free and clear. Graham did right by her. As for the house..."

My forehead crinkled. "You think he did right by me, splitting the house between us—making it so I can't sell unless Hannah can buy me out?"

He flattened his hands on his messy desk. The office was cluttered with piles of paper and filing cabinets, and his ancient computer wasn't even turned on. I idly wondered if all his business was still done on paper.

Not that it mattered. It was just easier to think about what Dell's life must've been like than focusing on my own.

"Listen, son," Dell began. "It isn't my place to say what's right or wrong. I can assure you Graham was in his right mind when he had me draw up this will. He knew Hannah would take care of the property and could use the land for horses of her own if she wanted, but he didn't feel right leaving you nothing in case you wanted to come back. Splitting it was the best he could do. I have it under good authority if you want to sell your half to Hannah Kelly, she has the resources to buy you out. Graham was well aware of this too, son. If you want to be done with all this, you have that choice. Let me know, and I'll be glad to get the ball rolling."

I didn't know what to say. Then again, based on the immediate search through his desk drawers, he wasn't waiting for a response.

"Ah, yes." He waved a thick envelope like a prize. "This is for you too."

He shoved the white envelope toward me, my name scrawled across it in my father's handwriting. I took it on instinct, holding it with both hands.

"What's this?"

"Not sure. Graham delivered this to me a few months ago, instructing I give it to you should you turn up here. If I knew him, he had some words he wanted to leave you with, knowing he'd never be able to in person. That might be what's in the envelope, but I can't say for sure."

My hands flexed around the envelope, crumpling it slightly. It wasn't even close to what my gut urged me to do. As soon as Dell had said this might contain my father's final words, knots had tightened my stomach and chest, and a voice inside me screamed to rip it up until there was nothing left but confetti.

I didn't, though, and not because I had any intention of ever reading what was inside. I was more circumspect with my emotions than that, and there was not a chance I'd be breaking down in Dell Rivers' office, even if holding this envelope felt like a live wire singeing my palms.

"Is that it?" I asked tightly. "No other surprises?"

"Nothing I can think of."

I signed a few papers and walked out of Dell's office, no idea what my next step was. I would've turned my truck toward home and driven until I reached it, but I didn't have one anymore. Before my last trip overseas, I'd been living with my ex-girlfriend, but she'd given me an ultimatum: her or my job. I'd headed out the next day. For all I knew, she'd burned everything I'd left behind. She sure as hell wasn't holding on to anything for me.

Graham's house wasn't a place I could stay long term, but I could stand being there as long as I knew I'd eventually be leaving. As evidenced by my splitting headache, I was still healing. It'd be some time before I could go back to work.

I climbed into my truck and pointed it toward Graham's house.

It wasn't home. Never would be again. But it'd do.

For now.

Chapter Six

Hannah

I WAS BENT IN half, ass in the air, when Remington Town showed up. He'd made a lot of noise walking up the driveway to the detached garage where I was, kicking up gravel and clearing his throat. Maybe he thought a warning of his presence would have me position myself in a more ladylike manner, but I had things I needed to do. If he got a look at my ass in my Wranglers, he was welcome to it.

"Hannah," he gruffed, coming to a stop next to where I was putting tools away in my rolling cabinet.

I took my time finishing the task before turning to face him. Some strands of my hair had come loose from my braid, so I brushed them off my face then tucked my hands in my rear jean pockets.

"You're still here?" I asked.

"Still here." His eyes were pinched as he looked me over. I examined him right back. His body was tightly strung, tension making his arms rigid at his sides.

Remington had grown into a tall drink of water. In any other circumstance, I might have gotten flirty with him. It wasn't often I came across men who were so much taller than me I had to tip my head back. But it wasn't just his height that appealed to me. I remembered him being cute when we were kids, but I would never use that word to describe the man in front of me. His features were powerful and striking. Observant hazel eyes, a strong Roman nose, a wide mouth bracketed by dark scruff. His jaw was sharp at the hinges, chin resolute.

I liked the way he looked, but that was as far as it went. Every minute in his presence was salt in the wound left by Graham's absence.

"I spoke to Dell Rivers today. He's a big fan of yours," Remi drawled.

Another strand of hair landed on my lips. I blew out a puff of air, sending it flying. "His horses like me." I narrowed my eyes. "Did he tell you anything different than I did?"

"Nope. I hadn't expected him to." He rolled his lips over his teeth, staring at a spot over my shoulder. "He tell you how he was writing that will?"

"Sure. We talked about what his death would be like a lot. He'd been facing the barrel of a gun the last two years; it was hard not to." I had to swallow down the wave of sadness, deciding to replace it with disdain for the man who hadn't bothered showing up for his own father's funeral. "I'm sorry he didn't leave you everything. If you'd checked on him once or twice, all this could've been yours, and I could've been out on my ass like you want."

His jaw rippled as he ground his poor molars to dust. "I get you don't like me. You see me as a bad son, maybe a bad man. But I'm going to be around for the next couple months, so it'd be appreciated—"

"You're going to be around?" I put my hands on my hips, reminding me I was still wearing my chaps. My hands went to the buckles, undoing the straps. "Why?"

It took Remi a while to answer as he watched me remove the heavy leather that protectcd my legs while I was working. I normally took them off when I was done for the day, but with everything else going on, it'd slipped my mind.

"Never seen a woman farrier," he muttered. "Surprised Graham worked with you. He had a lot of old-fashioned ideas about what women should do."

I tossed my head back and laughed. "Oh, I know he did. I quickly disabused the old man of those when I told him he was going to train me."

He raised his brows. "You *told* him?"

Walking over to the wall, I hung my chaps on the sturdy metal hook, smirking at Remi.

"I did. My gumption was what had gotten him to agree."

His mouth quirked. "That sounds like a Graham word."

"Gumption?" I rubbed my aching chest, missing my mentor and friend like a severed limb. "I think you're right. We spent so much time together, our speech patterns started lining up."

Remi didn't have a reply for that, but I could almost hear his thoughts. He was wondering how I'd been able to handle hanging around Graham for any extended period of time. I wasn't privy to the inner workings of their relationship, but Graham had made it clear he hadn't blamed Remi for not returning.

I didn't have any such reservations. I fully blamed Remi for not being here when his father died. I thought he was a selfish dick, and there wasn't anything he could say to convince me otherwise.

"Just so you know, I keep in touch with a couple instructors at the farrier school I went to in California. The last graduating class was ninety percent women." I hooked my thumbs in my belt loops.

"Your perception of who's a farrier is a little old-fashioned too. Like father, like son, huh?"

His hazel eyes shuttered. "I'm *nothing* like that man."

I raised my chin, pissed at his vehemence. "You might be right. You'd be lucky to be half the man Graham was."

Remi reared back so sharply, he stumbled a few steps. He shook his head like his vision was cloudy before finally focusing on me again. "You have no idea what you're talking about. You might think you know who he was, but what you got was one side. Sounds like it was a side *I* never got. Guess he saved all the goodness up for you, Hannah."

In the back of my mind, something screamed at me to pause, to take in what he was saying, but I'd been angry at this man for a long time. Their relationship might've been complicated, but to leave Graham alone in his final days was unconscionable.

"Not sure you deserved it with how heartless you are, Remington. You have no idea how hard Graham hung on to give you time to get here. He insisted he had to be at the house so you could find him when you came. Of course, you never did."

I shook my head, no longer seeing the man in front of me. I was back in Graham's room. Day after day, I'd begged him to take the morphine, to find *some* comfort, but he'd wanted to be conscious when Remi came, refusing any more than something to take the edge off, and going to the hospital had been out of the question.

"The cancer was always going to be a death sentence, but those last couple weeks were hell. He held on for you. He wanted to see you, tell you things, make sure you were okay. His body quit on him before he gave up. I can tell you without any doubt, you were his final thought, and you couldn't even bother to show up for an entire *month* after he was gone."

It was impossible not to cry when I thought about how I'd seen Graham through to the other side. That experience had marked me. Not that I hadn't been honored to be with him. Not that I wouldn't have been there even if Remi *had* shown up. I just shouldn't have had to do it alone. I had, though. I was the sole keeper of the memory of Graham's last breath, and that pissed me off. But being pissed off was better than giving in to the aching sadness swelling in my chest.

"Hannah—" Remi started.

I held up one hand, wiping my face with the other. "You got my messages, didn't you?"

After a pause, he huffed. "Got a lot of messages. It was Henry's that brought me here."

"You don't know how difficult it was for me to track down your phone number. It took me weeks, or I would have called you sooner." I shoved more hair off my forehead. "Maybe if I'd gotten it sooner, you would have come. That's what I think about. If I'd tried harder, started searching earlier, you would have made it in time."

"You don't need to worry about that anymore," he gruffed.

I looked up at him through bleary eyes. "It's not something I can help."

He shook his head, not meeting my gaze. "I mean, I wouldn't have been here. Nothing you can do to change what happened."

"Oh."

I'd sort of lied when I'd said I hadn't paid attention to Remi's career. The moment Graham had brought it to my attention, I'd looked him up on my own, becoming enthralled with the evocative and emotional images.

Remi had traveled all over the world, taking pictures during political coups, famines, uprisings, wars. He had a special talent for capturing heartbreak, showing the world the horrors other human beings were capable of inflicting on each other. A child covered in dust, tears carving paths down their face. A husband bent over the body of his broken, bloody wife. Soldiers who didn't look old enough to even touch a gun, let alone use one. His work was utterly haunting yet filled with empathy for the people and tragedy he'd witnessed.

The man standing before me, expressionless and indifferent after I'd poured my damn heart out, didn't seem capable of caring for anyone but himself. Maybe the empathy I thought I'd detected in his work had just been me projecting.

Remi took a step toward me. "What I mean is—"

"Nope." I swerved around him, done with this man. "I get what you mean. I don't need to hear anything else."

His heavy sigh was followed by his footsteps nipping at my heels. He let me get to my truck but put his hand on the door so I couldn't leave, pissing me right off.

"Hannah, listen to me." His voice dropped to something low and soothing. Not that I could have been soothed. Had I been looking for that, though, his soft tenor would have done it.

"It's fine, really. You're here for an indeterminate amount of time. I work out of the house. But we don't have to mingle. You stay out of my way, and I'll gladly stay out of yours. I don't have anything else to say to you, so..."

He dipped his head, trying to catch my eyes, but I wasn't having it. I gave the shoulder of his Henley more attention than a square inch of a shirt had ever received.

"I'm sorry you had to face that on your own. That shouldn't have been on you. I can only imagine it must've been incredibly hard. I know, without a doubt, you did right by Graham. His last thought might've been of me, but I bet his second-to-last one was of you."

He reached toward me, for my hair or face, maybe, but I flinched before he could touch me, and his hand fell to his side.

He sighed. "If I could change how things played out, I would, but there's no going back."

I swallowed hard, and his boot scuffed the gravel. I was done, but he wasn't.

"Like I said, I'll be here for a while, but not forever. You want me to stay out of your way, I'll do that. Just know, no matter what you think of me and my absence, I'm grateful you were the one who was here for Graham."

My eyes flicked to his, there and back. He was hurting me, being tender when all I wanted was a brick wall to wail on. I shouldn't have started this conversation at all, but I had a big mouth and didn't always clue in on when I should stop.

"If you want me to buy you out, I can get the money." I shifted on my feet. "My parents will help me. It won't be instant, but I can do it."

"Ah. Dell mentioned that."

"Think about it," I said. "It'll be easier for all of us, but especially you. You won't have a reason to stay *or* come back. Isn't that what you want?"

His boot scuffed the gravel again before he slapped the door of my truck. "I'm not gonna keep you any longer. Get on your way."

He stepped back just enough for me to squeeze by him. My back brushed his front, but he didn't shift away. I didn't know what he thought he was doing, but it wasn't working on me.

He lifted his chin, and I slammed the door.

I'd never driven away from Graham's house quicker.

Chapter Seven

Hannah

I drove straight to Sugar Rush. It wasn't as packed as it had been in the morning, but there were plenty of people getting their later-in-the-day dose of caffeine and sweets. Phoebe was floating behind the counter, looking pretty and put together even after working ten hours.

The shop closed at five, but Phe had trouble telling people to leave. Since I was here, I had no problem helping her with that.

I needed sister time—without all the nosy ears listening in.

Grabbing an iced coffee from Camille and a pistachio cream donut from Phe, I plopped down in one of the empty armchairs. I hadn't gotten that dirty or sweaty at work, so I didn't think my sister would mind me sitting in her nice chairs too much.

The relaxation I needed didn't happen. As soon as my butt hit the chair, Teller McDonald and her sidekick, Tina Klem, turned around from their table for two to stare at me. They were blatant about it, but I ignored them until I'd taken a long drink of coffee and a hearty bite of my donut, then I raised a brow.

"Did you need something?"

Teller crossed her jean-clad legs and leaned her elbows on her knee. "I heard Remi Town is back. Is it true?"

I nodded. "It is."

"Is he here to stay?" Tina asked.

I shrugged. "I don't know his plans."

"But you've talked to him?" Teller pressed.

"Sure," I replied.

Anyone else, I might've given them more, but Teller and Tina had been mean girls since elementary school, and at almost thirty, neither had grown out of it. They both lived by the motto "the bigger the hair, the closer to God," but there wasn't anything heavenly about the duo. Their fluffy blonde curls were all right, and I didn't have a problem with their bedazzled jeans or heavy makeup. It was their above-it-all attitudes. Like we all hadn't grown up in the same small town. Like any of us had forgotten Teller wiping her boogers on every hard surface all the way through middle school or Tina making out with everyone's boyfriends in high school. Gossip spread like wildfire in Sugar Brush. If these two hadn't caused the spark, they were fanning the flames.

"Well?" Teller's eyebrows raised, yet her forehead didn't move. "What did he say for himself?"

"Not much." I sipped my coffee.

"Do you think he's up for company?" Tina scrunched her nose at the massive bite of donut I took. "I could bake some muffins to welcome him home."

Teller rolled her eyes. "Please. We don't want to give the man food poisoning. I'll *buy* him some muffins from Phoebe."

"You can't welcome him without me," Tina blurted.

Teller cocked her head. "Were you planning to invite me along to deliver your atrocious cooking?"

Tina hmphed indignantly. "Of course. I would never go without you, Teller."

If Teller ever found out Tina used to regularly have sex with Teller's then-boyfriend, now-husband, Brady, back in high school, all hell would rain down on Sugar Brush. It had sort of been an open secret amongst our classmates and a wonder Teller had never caught wind. If there was any funny business still going on, I was not privy to it, but I wouldn't doubt it.

"He'd probably love a visit," I said, thinking how much Remi would truly *enjoy* these two.

Tina clapped her hands beneath her chin in excitement. "Oh, great. I was worried you'd try to keep us away from him."

Teller tapped her long fingernails on Tina's knuckles. "I had no doubt Hannah would see the good in our neighborly intentions. I'm sure Remi would love to catch up with us." She poked her bottom lip out, and her eyes melted with faux sincerity. "Just like I'm sure he's got the blues since he lost his father."

"Oh, yeah." Tina tossed her hair behind her shoulder. "We can cheer him up for sure."

My smile was as real as it got. I only wished I could be a fly on the wall when they went knocking on Remi's door.

"I would write him a nice condolence card too." I brought my coffee to my lips, considering what other mischief I could layer on. "Plus, he seems really lonely after all that time on the road. I'm sure he'd love for you to stay and share everything he's missed over the years—in full detail. And I remember Graham mentioning he adores listening to poetry. If you know any—"

Tina perked up. "I can take care of that."

Teller shot her a sharp look. "You've never read poetry in your life."

Tina wasn't deterred. "I have, and anyway, I know how to Google. I'll find the perfect poem to read to him."

I didn't know for a fact that Remi wasn't a fan of poetry, but the idea of these two bumbling through a reading tickled me so much I had to bite my cheek not to laugh. "He's so humble, he might try to turn you down—"

Teller took over. "Oh, I know exactly the type of man he is. I won't let him turn us down." She layered her hands over her heart. "I think he really needs us right now."

Tina nodded enthusiastically. "He does. We'll head out to the house first thing in the morning."

They left quickly after that, forgetting about me in favor of plotting their impending visit. My perverse satisfaction was only tempered by the bubble of discomfort still lodged in my belly from my confrontation with Remi.

Unfortunately, Phoebe caught me smirking before I could wipe it away. She was too busy to ask me what I was up to, but once the shop cleared out, she approached my table, cloth in hand and question in her eyes.

"What did you do to Double T?"

I yanked the rag from her hand and hopped up to wipe tables. "What makes you think I did something?"

She put her hands on her hips. "Because I know you. I know your *I'm-up-to-no-good* face, and that was it."

"They were asking about Remi, and I may have implied he would love their company...as well as a poetry reading."

Her inhale was sharp. "You sicced those two on him?"

I looked up from the table I was wiping. "They were going to visit him whether I encouraged them or not. I just nudged them along."

She swiped her forehead with the back of her hand and blew out a heavy breath. "That wasn't nice of you, and you know it. The man is probably trying to get his bearings after losing Graham and being back here. The last thing he needs is a visit from the Terror Twins."

I rolled my eyes. "He didn't lose Graham. He left him and only came back to claim the house. Remi is doing just fine. Trust me."

Phe's gaze stayed on me as I wove around the tables, cleaning coffee rings and crumb piles. Her judgment was silent but rang out as if she'd spoken it. My sister had always been too nice and forgiving for her own good. On the flip side, once I made up my mind about something or someone, it was nearly impossible to change it.

A therapist I used to see had called it rigid thinking. Maybe that was true, but I didn't think of it as a bad thing. I knew my own mind, and I wasn't easily swayed by empty words.

Despite that, Phe's unspoken disappointment weighed on me. I followed her into the back of the bakery, hopping up on one of her pristine stainless steel counters while she cleaned up. I knew better than to try to help her with this. She was laid back about a lot, but not her kitchen and there was no way I'd ever measure up to her standards.

I swung my legs, letting the rhythm of Phoebe's fluid and sure movements calm me. The thing about being calm, though? My thoughts quieted, allowing room for the image of how Remi's face contorted as I poured my low opinion over him like tar to come back full force.

He'd been stricken. Slapped into silence.

"I told him off."

Phe looked up from the gleaming mixing bowls she was stacking, a puzzled frown tugging at her lips. "Who?"

"Remi. I told him off."

Her brow crinkled. "What do you mean?"

"I mean, I let him know what I thought of him for not showing up for his dad. I told him he was heartless." I rubbed my thighs, not meeting Phe's eyes.

"Okay." She took her time, precisely choosing her words. "Do you regret saying that?"

My sister and I were opposite in many regards. Where I let my mouth get away from me more than I should have, she weighed and measured every word she said, careful not to step on toes or be misconstrued. That meant people often spoke over her, or she'd miss her chance to voice her opinion. We both could have stood to take lessons from the other, but we were who we were.

"I was...harsh." I sighed, scrubbing my palms harder on my thighs. "It felt good to get it off my chest, but the relief was only temporary. Getting mad at Remi didn't make anything better. It didn't bring Graham back or take away the hell he went through those last few weeks. But once I'd started, I couldn't stop."

"Are you going to apologize?"

"Nope." I hopped off the counter and shoved my hands in my back pockets. "Even if I was harsh, even if what I said fell on deaf ears, none of it was untrue. I have nothing to be sorry for."

Her brow winged, and the dubious look she gave me lingered long enough for me to squirm and throw out my hands.

"All right. Maybe I shouldn't have called him heartless. I probably should have kept my mouth shut entirely, but once I started—"

"You couldn't stop. You don't have to explain it to me, Han. I get it. It's only been a month. You're still grieving. Your emotions are raw, and seeing Remi in the house probably isn't helping anything."

I shook my head. "It's not. If he was going to come back, why couldn't it have been before Graham passed?"

It was a rhetorical question. Phe didn't know Remi's reasons any more than I did.

She put her hands on the counter and leaned toward me. "Did you think to ask him?"

"I—" My mouth opened and closed, nothing but a faint creaking sound coming out. "No. No, I didn't ask. I just assumed it was because he's a self-centered jackass."

"Graham wasn't mad at him for not being there."

I hadn't noticed I was pacing until I had to turn around to face Phoebe. "Yeah...well, he let me handle that. I'm plenty mad for us both."

"I think you should ask him where he was over the last month and why he didn't get here in time. So you know. So you don't have any doubts." Pushing away from the counter, she came to stand in front of me. "I'm all done here. Walk me home?"

My grin was crooked and didn't last long. "You know it."

Home was only a few blocks away. We shared a house that had been converted into a duplex long ago, my little apartment stacked on top of Phe's. She'd lived there for a few years before the unit above hers had become available. I'd been reluctant to leave the ranch, but the situation had been right. I was a family girl. Being close to at least one member of the Kelly clan was imperative to my happiness.

Plus, our proximity meant I got first dibs on bakery leftovers—not that there were ever many. Our town might have been small, but when it came to Phe's baked goods, we showed up big.

I paused outside Phe's door, one foot on the stairs leading to my place. "Any plans tonight?"

She rolled her eyes and smiled. "As if you need to ask."

I bumped her shoulder with my fist. "You could have plenty of plans if you wanted."

"Sure." She twisted the end of her ponytail around her fingers. "I could say the same to you. You could go out, meet someone..."

My stomach clenched at the very idea. "No thank you. I'd rather be a cool aunt to your future perfect little children."

She laughed. "Crazy aunt, since these kids are very much imaginary." Then she gave me a shove. "Go home. You smell like horse."

I lifted my arm and gave myself a sniff. Sunshine and the tiniest bit of sweat. More times than not, I'd left work smelling far worse. "Shut it. I smell fine. Not all of us can smell like cupcakes and lemon bars."

Her giggle and wave sent me off for the night, feeling a lot better than I had when I'd burned rubber leaving Graham's driveway.

As soon as I had the thought, a wave of dread struck. Today was over, but tomorrow was looming. I'd have to go back to that house and bear Remi being there while Graham never would be again.

I let myself into my place, shut the door behind me, and leaned against it, my fist pressed to my gut.

A month.

I'd gotten through a month post-Graham. It had been the hardest feat of my life, but I'd done it.

Getting through Remi's presence was nothing in comparison. All I had to do was wait him out. He'd be gone sooner than later. No doubt about that.

Chapter Eight

Remington

I'D HAD NO INTENTION of heading out to the Kelly ranch when I woke up in the morning. It'd been on my list of *eventualies*, but I hadn't worked myself up to doing it, and the dull ache in my head wasn't helping anything.

Yet here I was, the tires of my rented truck crunching over the gravel of the road leading to their property. I'd needed a reason to make an exit during a strange visit from two women bearing muffins and poetry. No idea what that had been about, but they hadn't seemed too keen on leaving, so I'd made my excuses.

Sugar Brush might've changed, but at first glance, things were the same. Crispy, yellow grass covered the prairie fields as far as the eye could see. Hand-constructed fences lined the road on either side. A few pronghorns grazed, unconcerned by my presence.

I'd spent a lot of days out here, riding one of the Kelly horses alongside Caleb, checking the fences and repairing weak spots. Mr. Kelly had paid me a sweet salary, but I would have done it for free. Spending time riding and bullshitting with my friend while giving me a solid excuse not to be home had been all I'd needed.

I couldn't be mad about the money, though. I'd socked it away, using it to buy my ticket out of here when I graduated high school.

Driving up to the house I grew up in had left me cold. Steering my truck under the solid wooden archway—the words *Sugar Brush River Ranch* emblazoned on it—gave me a feeling of coming home, as unfamiliar as it was.

Best times of my life had been spent on this ranch. I'd let myself forget all the good that had happened here—pushed it all away with the things I'd tried hard to forget. It had been a matter of survival. If I would have allowed myself to miss anything about this place, I wouldn't have been able to cut myself off so completely.

I pulled my truck into a makeshift spot next to a couple others near the barns. Ranch hands and other workers were around, doing their jobs, not paying me any mind as I climbed out, my boots hitting the dirt. I closed my eyes and sucked in the air. I'd been all over and had never found anything like the air in Wyoming. Even in the high heat of summer, it was crisp, filling my lungs with goodness.

Pushing off my truck, I made my way to the main barn. I had no idea where Caleb would be this time of day, but this was my best guess. Chances were just as good he was on the other side of the property.

I walked into the stable where the working horses were kept. At first glance, most of the stalls were empty, but a few had horses. In front of one, two men were in conversation. One average height and leanly built, a cowboy hat perched on his head. The other tall, broad as hell, with shaggy brown hair hitting his shoulders and a backward baseball hat.

Didn't know the first guy, wouldn't have recognized the second if he'd passed me on the street. But we weren't in some random location. Here, on the ranch, I knew my former friend, even if he'd grown half a foot and his shoulders had exploded outward, creating their own hemisphere.

The two stopped talking as I approached. The lean man frowned, but it wasn't unfriendly. Caleb, on the other hand, surveyed me, stark suspicion weighing down his furrowed brow.

"Hey," I started. "Caleb, it's—"

"Nope." He held up a hand. "Turn right back around and go back to where you came from. Not interested, and not welcome."

I stopped moving, my hands balled at my sides. The lean man's head swiveled between us. I hadn't been counting on a welcome home parade, but his anger was a surprise.

"Now, Cay, that's not neighborly. I—"

Caleb cut him off too. "I don't have any desire to be neighborly right now, Bill. This guy's not a neighbor, and he's not a guest at the ranch. That means he has no reason to be here."

I pushed through the heavy weight crushing my chest. "The reason is seeing you." I shoved my fingers through my hair, grazing the scar on the side of my head. "I'm assuming you recognize me."

He grunted, focusing on some point over my shoulder. "Know who you are, Town. That's why I'm telling you to leave. You're not welcome here."

I never contemplated what it'd be like seeing Caleb again. Those kinds of thoughts hadn't had any place in the life I'd created away from here. The truth was, I'd never planned on coming back. But if I'd taken any time to consider it, it wouldn't have gone down like this. Not even close.

"I'd like to talk to you." Lifting my chin at the horse nudging him from behind, I said, "I can see you're busy. I would've called, but I didn't have your number."

He scoffed. "Hasn't changed. Guess you erased it along with everything else."

Yeah, this isn't a good look for me.

The lean man strode forward, his hand out. "Bill Eddings. Pleased to meet you."

I shook his hand. "Remi Town. Nice to meet you too, Bill."

His eyes flared as he let go of my hand and smoothed his down the front of his button-down. "Real sorry for your loss, Remi. Graham will be missed around here. When I see Hannah driving her truck, I catch myself looking for him in the passenger seat. Can't get used to not seeing him." He shook his head sadly. "Anyway, I'll leave you two to it. Sounds like you have some catching up to do."

Silence stretched thick between us once Bill left. Not that it was true silence. Horses huffed. Shouts and idle chatter filtered in from outside. Wind whistled through cracks. Gravel got kicked up by trucks and ATVs. But it was all background noise, leaving Caleb and me face to face for the first time since we were eighteen. Kids, basically.

He broke the silence. "I'm working, Town. Not up for any re-unions."

"I figured." I nodded, forcing myself to push back the discomfort of not being welcomed back into the fold as easily as I was suddenly wishing I could've been. "I had to replace my phone years ago. Couldn't keep the same number and lost all my contacts. Losing your number wasn't a choice, but it happened. Like I said, I would've called first if I could've."

He grunted but didn't give me an inch to work with. I pushed forward.

"I'm hoping I can buy you a beer and explain. Catch up on what I've missed. I'm not asking for forgiveness, Cay. Just a beer and shooting the breeze."

He turned his head, but I didn't miss the way his nostrils flared. "Two beers," he gruffed.

It took me a second to comprehend what he meant. Once realization hit, the corner of my mouth hitched. I had no right to feel the swing of optimism, but I did all the same. Caleb agreeing to a beer didn't equal forgiveness, but it was better than I'd set out expecting.

"Think I can afford a couple beers."

His jaw worked back and forth. "I'm gonna need a burger too. Least you can do is buy my dinner if you're gonna fuck up my night."

I bit back a laugh. "Yeah, I could go for a burger too."

"All right then. I'll meet you at Joy's. It'll have to be early."

I nodded. Ranch hours probably had him rising with the sun. "Right. Five?"

"I'll be there." He turned his back to me, giving his horse his full attention. I'd have liked to stay, see the ranch, ask him a hundred questions, but pushing my luck didn't seem wise.

As I drove back to the house, I hoped I wouldn't have any more women with strangely tall hair popping by to read me poetry. I didn't think I could be polite if I had to sit through another sonnet. I just didn't have it in me.

Chapter Nine
Remington

Joy's Elbow Room was everything I thought it'd be when I was a kid peeking through the gritty windows from the sidewalk. Flickering neon beer signs on the walls, rustic wood tables clustered in the center, a long, curved bar taking up two walls. A few two-seater booths were tucked away, their burgundy vinyl seats clean yet worn. Two pool tables in the back surrounded by a few high-top tables, already filled with women who'd put in a lot of effort to make themselves look special from head to toe and men who looked like they'd come straight from a hard day on a ranch.

I scanned the flannel shirts and scruffy beards, landing on Caleb Kelly pretty quickly. His height made him hard to miss. That, and he was beelining toward me.

He stopped when we were almost toe to toe, brows dipping like thunderbolts. I braced to take a hit or a verbal smackdown. What I hadn't been ready for was him wrapping his huge arms around me in an embrace.

"Missed the hell out of you, Town," he gruffed next to my head. "Pissed as hell at you but missed you all the same."

The hug was over as quickly as it had started. When he released me from his stronghold, I stumbled back a step, and he caught my shoulder in his wide mitt, steadying me without a word.

"Got us a table. Come on." He turned and walked away like nothing had happened. If my ribs hadn't been slightly tweaked from how hard he'd squeezed me, I might've believed I'd hallucinated the encounter.

Cay was already seated at the table when I caught up, his body sideways so he could stretch his legs out, one elbow resting on the wood. I pulled out the chair across from him and flipped over the one-page menu, giving myself something to do with my hands.

He glanced at me, sniffed, then took a long pull from his beer. I looked around the place. Even though I'd never been inside, I was comfortable here.

A waitress came by and took my order. Her voice was so soft I barely heard her over the din of conversation and clinking glasses, but she scribbled down my request efficiently and scurried away without another word.

Cay lifted his chin. "That's Alice. Don't take it personal if she doesn't talk to you. She's shy."

"Got it." I nodded a few times, unsure where to go from here. This had been my idea, but the years between us were feeling more like an obstacle than they had this morning. One thing I knew was true: seeing his lively eyes and easy grin, I had missed him too. "It's good to see you again, Cay. Even if you're pissed at me, I'm glad I got the chance to see you all grown up. Kinda feels surreal to be in our thirties together."

"Yeah." Setting his beer down, he cocked his head to look me over. "Difference is I always expected to be sitting here with you at this age while you knew it was never gonna happen. You could've given me some warning. Told me you were leaving. Least I wouldn't have looked like a fool when I had no answers for all the questions lobbed at me from every direction."

"I didn't think I was going to do it until I was on the bus. I kept it to myself in case I didn't work up the guts to go through with it—and so I wouldn't be talked out of it." I rubbed my stubbly jaw and let my hand fall heavily on the table. "You knew I couldn't breathe here. I told you I wanted to get out of here and see the world. But I don't know if you ever got it. You were always happy to stay, to do what your dad did, what his dad did—"

"Ah." He drummed his thick, blunt fingers on his knees. "I understand. You couldn't talk to me because I didn't have big, worldly dreams like you, huh? I'm surprised you have the desire to talk to me now, seeing as I'm still here and you captured what you were looking for. The traveling, the fame—"

"Fame was never one of my dreams. And you're not hearing me, Cay. I don't look down on you for knowing what you wanted and sticking to that. I admire it. I was always jealous of how damn happy you were here while I was climbing the walls to get out."

He swallowed down the rest of the beer, and another appeared moments later, almost as if the little quiet waitress had been waiting for him to finish. She delivered mine at the same time, along with our burgers, then essentially ran away as soon as the plates hit the table.

Cay didn't seem interested in talking. His focus was on his burger, biting into it like he'd been waiting all his life for it. It was like stepping back in time. He'd always eaten like that. I almost laughed but held it in. Didn't think it'd be appreciated when we were on rocky ground.

So, I ate my burger. It was one of the best I'd had in my life, and the beer that washed it down was even better. I credited the hunger gnawing at my stomach and the fresh Wyoming air.

I wiped my mouth with my napkin and wadded it in my fist. "I try not to hold on to regrets, but I always regretted losing touch with you."

He swiped the back of his hand over his mouth and nodded. "Makes sense. I was the best friend you ever had. I imagine that still holds true."

That got a chuckle out of me. "It's true. I made a fair few friends in my time away, but none like you. I don't think buddies like us happen in adulthood."

"Nah, you're probably right. Gotta have dirt, skinned knees, and boyhood to form that kind of bond. At least, the kind I always thought we had."

"We had it," I said with adamance. "Never forgot it, and I missed the hell out of you too. I met a lot of people in my travels, but I haven't been close to anyone since you. I'm sorry for abandoning our friendship. Sorry for not sharing my plans. I'm even more sorry I lost your number and couldn't call to tell you all that when I got my head out of my ass."

He sucked in a deep breath, his broad chest rising toward the ceiling. When he exhaled, he looked at me, calm and unreadable.

"All right."

I cocked my head. "All right?"

"Yeah. I get it. You had to go. It wasn't personal. I'm not gonna waste any more time being angry at you. Not about that anyway."

My mouth twitched. "Appreciate it, but let's get it all out in the open now. Are you angry at me over something else?"

He polished off his last fry drenched in ketchup. "Can't say I'm pleased you left my sister to tend to your sick father and take care of everything when he died. Not that she wouldn't have been there had you shown up. Wild horses couldn't have dragged her away."

He folded his thick arms, and I braced for what I knew he was about to ask. "But you should've been there. It's messed up you weren't. Where were you? Why show up now and not then?"

Unthinking, I reached for the scar on the side of my head, dragging my fingertips over it. Caleb tracked my movements, his eyes narrowing like he was trying to piece together a puzzle dumped in front of him.

I wasn't going to leave him guessing. He wanted answers, and I owed it to him to give him that. "When I left, I was a kid. In my mind, I was never coming back. I didn't have the experience to think about what would happen to my dad when he got older. Didn't consider him getting sick, who might take care of him, none of that. When it comes down to it, I would've been here if I could have, Cay."

He jerked his chin toward my scar. "Your reason has something to do with you looking like shit warmed over?"

I laughed despite the seriousness of the subject. Leave it to Caleb to never pull punches—a trait that ran in their family.

"It has everything to do with it. I was overseas, documenting the coup in—"

Caleb winced. "Yeah. I've been watching the news. Ugly stuff going on over there."

"Right," I agreed, though there was ugly stuff going on in every corner of the world. It just so happened this coup had been getting the most media attention. "I can't tell you what exactly happened, just what I was told when I woke up. The vehicle I was in with three other journalists was inadvertently targeted by militia. We took fire, our driver maneuvered to avoid being hit, and we flipped into a ravine. Don't know how I survived it. Only me and two others made it out. The driver and one of my colleagues died immediately. They didn't think I'd make it either."

"*Fuck*," he gritted out. "Your head took the impact?"

"Among other parts, yeah. I was in a medically induced coma for a week, then spent a month in the hospital after that recovering. I was too out of it to be concerned about where my phone was or anything going on in the outside world."

His eyes darted around my face, almost frantic. "How are you doing now? Should you have even traveled?"

"Don't worry about me. My doctor gave me clearance to be here."

"But you're not all right, are you?"

"I'm as good as can be, considering I was almost blown up." I tried to laugh it off, but it sounded forced even to me. Going with the truth was easier. "I've been having migraines and some blurred vision, which is common with the level of concussion I sustained. The doctors over there assured me it'd get better with time as long as I don't reinjure myself."

He looked at me long and hard then leaned forward, bringing himself closer. "You're not going back there."

He said it as a statement, but I answered anyway.

"No, I don't plan on it. I'm not sure what my next move is, but I use my brain too often to risk fucking it up permanently."

It killed me to acknowledge that. To give up in the middle of a story was almost unthinkable. I'd never done it, no matter how dire the conditions. But things had changed, and when it came down to it, my choice had been taken from me.

Caleb took this in with a level stare and slow, steady breathing. When he was ready, he spoke again. "You didn't know Graham was dying."

"No, I didn't. By the time I had a new phone and the wherewithal to listen to my messages, he was already gone." I pressed the heel of my palm into my temple. "I would've been here. It wasn't Hannah's or anyone else's burden to take on."

"She never saw Graham as a burden."

"Right." I nodded, even though, to me, that was all he'd been.

"You had different experiences with him," Caleb explained. "The old man cleaned himself up. Got right with the town, changed Hannah's life for the better. When I say she didn't see him as a burden, you need to understand I mean it. Her Graham wasn't your piece-of-shit dad. He waited until it was too late to change, but he did, Rem. He did."

I didn't know what to say, so I just sat back and took a long swallow of my beer.

Caleb, who'd been with me all the way to the end, who understood who Graham had been with me, reached out and squeezed my arm.

"Shame he couldn't get it together for you. I think your leaving was the wake-up call he needed."

I chuffed. "The irony isn't lost on me."

"Yeah." He took out his phone, swiped the screen for a minute, and passed it over to me. I picked it up, looking at the picture of a little boy with chocolate eyes and shaggy chestnut hair atop a horse. I knew it wasn't Caleb, but it could've been from how much this kid resembled him.

"Yours?" I asked, already knowing the answer.

He nodded. "That's my boy. Jesse's ten."

Two tons of loss downpouring directly on my chest. "Christ. You were twenty-one when you had him?" I glanced at his bare left hand. "You're not married?"

"Nah. His mom's a good woman, but we both knew it never would've worked. Luckily, we do well co-parenting."

I shook my head, staring down at the picture of his son. "I should've been here for this."

He chuffed. "Would've been nice, but we're calling it water under the bridge now. You stick around long enough, you can meet him."

I swallowed hard as I handed the phone back. "That'd be great. I'd like that a lot."

I turned my head, my eye catching on a woman leaning over the bar, laughing with the bartender. Even from a distance, there was no mistaking Hannah Kelly, her endless, muscular legs encased in worn jeans and all that long, dark hair spilling down her back. It was good seeing her with a smile since she'd been scowling the times I'd seen her.

The smile suited her. It was more natural than the scowl. I hoped she got a lot of use out of it.

While she stood there, a man in a dirty T-shirt and backward cap approached her. She straightened and rotated her body, one elbow on the bar, leaning casually. He was shorter than her despite her not standing at her full height.

As he spoke, her smile dimmed until it was barely there.

Caleb grunted, and I wrenched my focus from Hannah to find he'd been watching the same thing.

"She's had it rough," he uttered. "Not just losing Graham. The last guy she was with did her dirty. He was a piece of shit, we all knew it, but he still managed to blindside her."

My gut clenched in a knot of barbed wire. I tensed, fingers digging into my thighs.

"The guy she's talking to?" I asked.

"Nah, that's not him. That guy has been circling around for a few months."

I raised a brow. "You going to intervene?"

"Nope." He chuckled. "Han can take care of herself. If I tried, she'd go off with him just to spite me."

That had me chuckling with him. "You Kellys and your obstinance."

A commotion drew my attention back to the bar. Dirty Shirt was hopping on one foot while Hannah clapped with delight. Without warning, her eyes flicked up, finding mine. Her teeth dug into her bottom lip, but she couldn't get rid of her grin.

"What'd I tell you? My sister's a different kind of beast."

I snorted, not taking my eyes off the strange scene. "Something tells me she wouldn't like you calling her a beast."

"She's heard it before. Almost broke my nose the last time."

"She punched you?"

"Worse. She threw an apple at my face."

"Guess I got off easy with the muffin," I muttered. Caleb might've asked me to repeat myself, but my tongue became useless as Hannah Kelly sauntered over to our table.

She stopped beside her brother, bumping his arm with her hip. "You're out late, old man."

He kicked an empty chair out. "Take a load off and tell me what you did to that guy."

She spun the chair around and straddled it backward, her arms resting on the back. "Who, Mark? All I did was doubt he could sing the national anthem while hopping on one foot. He chose to prove me wrong."

Caleb shook his head. "And did he?"

She rolled her eyes. "Come on. Do you think he knows the words to the national anthem even in the best circumstances?" She glanced at me. "Some company you're keeping, by the way."

"Be nice," Caleb drawled. "Rem and I had a long talk and settled what we needed to settle. We're cool."

She wasn't facing me, but I didn't miss the rigidness in her shoulders and press of her fingertips against her arm. Hannah Kelly wasn't anywhere near my good side, and from the looks of it, she wasn't too happy her brother had crossed that line with me.

"That's a choice," she bit out.

"Yep. You could make the same one." Caleb was relaxed as ever but kept a watchful eye on his sister. He'd always been protective of his family. But then, he had a good one worth protecting.

"Really think I'll pass," she chirped.

"Han…"

"Well, thanks for telling me about your night, Cay, but I have plans." She did some trick with her legs, rotating her whole body so she was sitting with her back to the table, poised to make hay.

"Oh yeah? What might that be?" Caleb challenged.

The quiet little waitress, Alice, appeared from nowhere with a basket filled with chicken wings and handed them off to Hannah before hurrying away. Hannah lifted the basket up like a prize.

"Tonight's plans: this basket of wings and a round of pool before I walk myself home and tuck myself into bed." She hopped up, cradling her wings like a little baby, and ruffled Caleb's hair with her free hand. "See you around, Cay."

"Be good, Han," he called after her.

She waved as she walked away, singing out, "Always am!"

Caleb shook his head and looked at me with pity. "Think that's going to take some work."

"You tell no lies," I agreed.

After a moment, his expression grew serious, thoughtful. "How long are you planning on sticking around?"

I tapped my head. "A while. I don't have an exact timeframe. I can't risk getting hurt again, and I need to give my brain time to heal."

"Mmm." He tossed back a couple fries. "It might be too physical, but if you're at loose ends, we can always use help at the ranch. The upside is you've done it before, and I won't have to go through the trouble of training you only for you to leave."

The idea instantly excited me. But Caleb was right; I wasn't too sure about my physical limitations. Doing a long day of work outside probably wasn't my doctors' idea of resting and healing, yet it was impossible to turn him down outright.

"I've missed mending fences with you." I rubbed the scruff on my chin. "I'd probably need to be on light work..."

He chuckled. "I'm not planning on paying you. Whatever you do it's strictly volunteer."

That had me laughing. "All right then. I'll keep you posted."

He rapped his knuckles on the table. "You do that. Take it easy on my sister while you're at it—even if she doesn't take it easy on you."

I glanced at Hannah. She was in the back of the bar, eating a chicken wing with abandon, a pool cue tucked under her arm. I shifted uncomfortably. This woman had taken on my burdens all alone—whether she recognized them as such or not. It wasn't fair or right.

"You don't have to ask. I wouldn't dream of hurting Hannah."

"I know you wouldn't." I had a second to feel good about his confidence in me despite him only just forgiving me for the hurt I'd caused. It didn't last when he added, "Not on purpose, anyway."

That stung, but he wasn't wrong.

When it was time to leave, I would. That might have meant never seeing Caleb or his family again, but I didn't belong here, and I wasn't going to be staying.

Chapter Ten

Hannah

MY REGULARLY SCHEDULED PROGRAMMING was once again interrupted by the necessity of paperwork. It truly sucked the joy right out of life. Even more so now that Remi was lurking about Graham's house.

I got the sense he was giving me space, though. Since our unexpected encounter at Joy's last week, where my traitor of a brother had decided to leave the past in the past, I'd only seen Remi in passing. I'd spied him hanging out with Henry around the property and had narrowly avoided a run-in in the kitchen one afternoon, but we hadn't exchanged a word, and I was pleased with that.

But his presence loomed.

He was annoyingly, distractingly...*there*.

I did not have time to think about Remington Town. Not when I had calls to make and bills to send out.

I was currently on the phone with Keith Levinson, a grizzled old rancher who was ninety if he was a day, hard of hearing, and stubborn as a mule—a fantastic combination.

"You want change? Did I not pay you the right amount last time?" he hollered into my ear.

"No, Mr. Levinson. You paid the correct amount. I need to switch your appointment," I shouted back. "Can I come out Wednesday?"

"I'm sorry to hear that," he answered.

I banged the heel of my hand against my forehead. This was what I got for trying to make my life easier. Keith's property was a sixty-mile drive from Sugar Brush. It wasn't an out-of-the-ordinary distance, but I'd agreed to a standing Wednesday appointment for a new client who lived near Keith and hoped to consolidate my driving time and do them both on the same day.

"Would it be possible to turn the volume up on your phone?" I asked.

"Sure, you can come by my home. When were you thinking?"

I closed my eyes, deciding to let him guide the direction of this conversation. Maybe that'd make things easier. "Does Wednesday work?"

"My shirt's blue. Why do you ask?"

Oh boy. I carefully enunciated my next words and basically yelled this poor man's ears off. "Can I come on Wednesday?"

He chuffed. "You know I never go anywhere, young lady. Any day of the week is fine by me."

Success. Time to be done while we understand each other.

"Great. I will see you next Wednesday."

"Well, all right. Wednesday is fine. You didn't have to shout."

He hung up without saying goodbye, and I tossed the phone on my desk. Letting my head fall in my hands, releasing the frustration burbling in my throat in a high-pitched yowl.

I didn't want to do this. If Graham were here, he would have taken care of these calls. He loved chatting with the folks who'd been his clients for years. He'd been good at it.

I *really* missed him.

I couldn't stop the second cry from spilling out, another frustrated, angry keen. That was why I shouldn't have been surprised when the door to my office pushed open moments later and a deep voice interrupted my spiral.

"Hannah...are you okay?"

My surprise was the only reason I grabbed the object closest to my hand—a stress ball shaped like a cupcake—and lobbed it straight toward the voice.

My aim was true. The cupcake collided with the center of Remi's forehead and bounced off with panache. But my heart was thudding too hard for me to really admire my accuracy.

"What the hell?" I screeched, pushing back in my chair, rolling into the far wall. "You can't just barge in like that! You shaved a hundred years off my life, Remington!"

He rubbed his forehead, stooping to pick up the squishy cupcake. "You were yelling. I thought you were hurt or in trouble."

"Well, I'm fine, as you can see." But I was panting. This man wasn't small. Normally, his footsteps sounded like a herd of elephants on the old floors, but he'd managed to sneak up on me.

He held up the cupcake. "I guess I should be grateful this wasn't a letter opener."

I narrowed my eyes at him. "Unfortunately, I don't have one. It could've been my phone, though."

"Glad it wasn't." He stepped into my office and placed the cupcake on my desk. "Everything okay in here?"

"Why wouldn't it be?"

"You *were* screaming, Hannah. Making sure you're not hurt isn't coming out of left field."

He had a point. I could've done better at moderating my reaction, but Remi's presence hadn't been on my mind. I'd felt the urge to scream, so I did. And for that one moment, however brief, it had made me feel marginally better, but then *he* appeared, and I was right back where I started.

"I hate making calls." I gestured toward the phone. "And sometimes I need to release some steam when I hang up. Is that a problem?"

His mouth twitched, and it was as annoying as it was kind of cute. Then my annoyance quickly redirected to myself for finding anything about this man cute.

"A warning would have been good." He tapped his temple. "I'll remember that. Anytime Hannah goes into her office, expect loud screeching to follow."

"I don't screech. If anything, I groaned."

"Don't think I'd call the noise you made a groan." He leaned on the doorjamb, crossing his arms. "If I had to name it something other than a screech, it'd be a howl. A pained one. Like an animal caught in a trap."

I picked up the cupcake. "You're really asking for another stress ball to the forehead, aren't you?"

He chuckled, one hand raising in defense. "I'm not. I only came to make sure you weren't buried under a bookcase. Glad to see you're uninjured."

"I'm fine." On the outside...

On the inside...well, I was a little battered, and my emotions had a limp, but he didn't care about that.

Not that I *wanted* him to care.

"I appreciate you checking on me. That was nice."

He lifted a shoulder. "Anyone would've."

"I don't know about that."

He didn't reply, and that was fine. I didn't need to have a conversation with Remi about the good and bad in the world. But he didn't leave. He stayed in the doorway, leaning and looking around, his arms folded over his chest. I took note of the golden tone of his corded forearms. Since arriving over a week ago, he'd spent a good amount of time outside, and it showed. Henry must've really been putting him to work.

I had my own work to do, but I wasn't going to attempt it with him standing there, watching. I arched a brow, waiting for him to speak since there was clearly something on his mind.

"Anything I can help with?" he finally asked.

"Did Henry run out of tasks for you?"

He hmphed. "Told me I was getting in his way."

I cracked a grin. "Sounds like him. He prefers doing things his way, on his own. That's why his cabin is a ways off from the house. I think he likes to pretend no one else exists."

He nodded, lapsing into silence again. I wondered why he wasn't leaving when we'd run out of things to say. Maybe he was bored and needed some direction. Being here instead of on the front lines of the conflict had to be a massive adjustment. He'd probably lived on adrenaline rushes, and now the most excitement he could get was me throwing things at his forehead.

The silence stretched for an uncomfortably long time before Remi finally broke it. "Are you doing okay?"

"I told you I was."

"No." His arms fell, and he tucked his hands into his pockets. "I know you're not hurt. I mean, since Graham—"

"Oh." My spine went ramrod straight. "Do you really care?"

I said this without ire. It was a legitimate question. A few minutes ago, I'd been sure Remi didn't give a single damn about how I was faring internally.

"I wouldn't have asked if I didn't," he replied. "Caleb really imparted how much Graham meant to you. He was more than just a boss."

I nodded. "A lot more than a boss. Family," I choked out. God, I hated how tight my throat was and how badly my eyes burned. I didn't mind crying. Hell, I'd cried rivers over the last few months, and there was an ocean of sadness still churning inside me. But I liked to save my tears for those who might understand. Remi wasn't one of those people.

"I don't know how to make things better for you, Hannah, but I'd like to make them easier. Tell me what I can help you with—the tasks you don't want to do or don't have time for—and I'll take care of them."

"I don't need help," I replied automatically, though it wasn't strictly true. I did, but not from him.

"Not from me," he murmured.

"Are you a mind reader?" I blurted.

His laugh was soft. "No, and gotta say I'm thankful for it right now. Your face is pretty easy to read, though. Right now, it's telling me to piss off."

I picked up the cupcake on my desk and squeezed it hard. "Well, you're wrong. I was actually calling you a dick in my head."

This time, his laugh was more like a roll of thunder, full-bodied and echoing off the walls.

"That goes without saying."

The corners of his hazel eyes crinkled into starbursts, and I wished I didn't find it as mesmerizing as I did. I also wished he didn't laugh so easily—especially when I was trying to be mean to him. It made it difficult to hate him. I still managed, though. Reminding myself he wasn't the slightest bit sad about losing Graham while I was still devastated did the trick.

I stood and walked toward him, taking the doorknob in hand. "I have a few calls to make. If that's all…"

He hesitated, but only for a moment before backing up a step. Once he did, I swung the door closed, breathing a sigh of relief.

Hopefully, it wouldn't be long before Remi got the itch to hit the road again.

I just had to wait him out.

Chapter Eleven

Hannah

A WEEK WENT BY, and Remington was still around.

I knew this because his footsteps were driving me crazy. I couldn't concentrate on anything with him tromping back and forth over my head. If I hadn't known any better, I would've said he was dancing up there.

He'd picked a bad day to take up two-steppin'. After a busy morning of clients, I was sweaty and tired. I wanted to get my paperwork done and get home, but not before I grabbed a treat from Sugar Rush.

My stomach rumbled at the thought. If Phe ran out of donuts before I got there, I was going to be pissed.

"Okay, concentrate, Hannah Kelly," I mumbled. "Surely he'll stop soon."

I picked up my phone to call a client, but before I could dial their number, I forgot who I was calling and why. My attention had been diverted by a sudden bang right above my head, followed by more of those torturous footsteps.

"That's *it*." I pushed back from my desk and yanked my office door open. "Whatever he's doing up there is going to stop. He can't just show up here and disrupt everything."

I stormed up the stairs, murder on my mind. No, I wasn't homicidal in real life, but my inner thoughts could get pretty damn bloody when I was on a tear. And *boy*, was I on a tear.

Graham's bedroom door was shut, but I didn't let a little thing like that stop me. I threw it wide open but didn't barge in. Not when I was faced with a sight I didn't know how to decipher.

Clothing was piled high on the bed, worn flannels and faded jeans. Graham's boots were lined in a row on the floor at the foot of the bed, and his hats were stacked atop one of the spindles on the footboard.

Remi turned from the closet, a couple sweaters bundled in his arms. His *bare* arms. He wasn't wearing a shirt. In fact, all he had on was a pair of low-slung athletic shorts.

"Hey." Dumping the sweaters next to the flannels, he straightened, his hands going to his hips. "I didn't know you were here."

I tried not to take him in but failed, my annoyance and hunger falling by the wayside as I got a good look at this man. He wasn't naked like he'd been the first day. Then, I'd been too distracted to focus on all that was Remington Town anyway. He wasn't buff like a gym rat, but he was very clearly strong, with broad shoulders and trim hips. Dark hair nestled between lightly defined pecs and trailed down an abdomen just soft enough for me to be tempted to rest my head on. Solid and real, Remi was so physically my type, it was almost painful.

"I got here an hour ago," I uttered. "I've been listening to you stomp around up here the whole time."

He winced, sucking air between his teeth. "Sorry. I would've done this another day if I'd known you were in the office. This house has good bones, but sound carries like nowhere else. I'd forgotten about that."

I walked into the room and picked up Graham's black flannel Stetson. "What are you doing with Graham's things?"

Remi scanned all of his piles then flicked his gaze to me. "Thought I'd bag it all up to donate. It's wasting space here, and there's bound to be someone who could use it."

I clutched the hat to my chest as my stomach bottomed out. "You're...getting rid of everything?"

He gestured carelessly to the piles. "Unless there's something you or Henry want." He tipped his chin toward the hat in my hands. "That Stetson? You want it?"

"Yes. Of course I do." My teeth dug into my bottom lip to keep it from quivering.

This room...it still smelled like Graham. A little bit of tobacco, fabric softener, and something unnamable that was strictly him. And Remi wanted to strip it bare, to erase every trace, when that was all I had: traces.

"Hannah..." Remi's voice softened. He came closer, though the bed was still between us. "I don't have to do this today. It was on my mind, but if you don't want me to, I can—"

"What's the rush?" I bit out, my grief rolling out in waves of anger. "He won't know his things are gone. He's gone, hopefully somewhere better, but if not, at least he's at peace. You're not gonna hurt him by tossing his things out. The only ones who are going to be hurt—"

I started to say "us," but that wasn't right. Henry had given a damn about Graham, but things weren't important to him. If all this stuff was gone by tomorrow, he wouldn't notice.

"You," Remi uttered. "I'm going to hurt you by getting rid of it. *Shit*, sweetheart, I wasn't thinking."

I shielded my eyes so he wouldn't see if they betrayed me and let the welling tears drip.

"Half this house is mine. I'm claiming this room and all the things in it. These are my clothes, my boots, my hats." I swiped the back of my hand over my wet eyes. "Just go out and close the door. Pretend it's not here."

He looked around the room for a long time, surveying everything in it, which wasn't much. Graham had had a pretty spartan decorating style. He hadn't cared for knickknacks or clutter. But there was a picture of him holding little Remi on his shoulders on his nightstand. The last book he read was dog-eared beside it, along with his reading glasses. Signs of his life were in this room, and I wasn't ready for any of it to be gone.

Remi finally nodded. "I can leave it, but if you change your mind and want to clear it out, tell me. You don't need to do it on your own."

He was so casual about this, and it didn't compute for me. No matter how fractured his relationship with his father had been, I couldn't comprehend how he could have no feelings about his death.

"This really doesn't affect you, does it?" I set the hat down to pick up a flannel and lift it to my nose. Then I glanced up at Remi, who was watching me. "Even now, surrounded by his things and his scent, you feel nothing?"

He rocked back on his heels, his jaw tensing, though his eyes were soft on me. "I am sad, Hannah. Seeing you missing him, mourning him...it hits me square in the chest. You holding that flannel, searching for something you can hold on to...? Your loss is palpable, and I'm sorry as hell for it." He touched the place over his heart with his fingertips. "I don't feel what you feel. Looking for it in me is a waste of time. My father abandoned me when my mother died. He was here, in this house, but only in body, and even that was touch and go when he went on such extreme benders, he forgot his name, let alone the son he had at home. I mourned the father I once had for years while he was still alive, but I got tired of it. These days, I'm all out of grief. That well is dry as a bone, and there's no bringing it back."

I clutched the flannel tighter. This wasn't new information. Graham had been honest about why Remi had wanted nothing to do with him. He'd known the kind of father he'd allowed himself to be. But hearing it from Remi...well, it was hard to reconcile his description of his father with the man I had known, though I understood it was nothing short of the truth.

"I won't look for it anymore." I blinked at him and sighed. "If you want to get rid of anything else, run it by me first, all right? I'm not a hoarder, and I know someone else can use these clothes, but...not yet. It's too soon."

He bowed his head, his lids lowering. "Okay, Hannah. I hear you, and I get it."

Tossing his hands out, he let them fall heavily to his sides.

"Is it hard for you to relax and stay in one place?" I asked.

He groaned lightly. "You have no idea."

"No, I do. Relaxing isn't in my wheelhouse. If I don't have a task, I go out of my mind."

"Yeah." He glanced at the piles again. "Cay offered me work on the ranch."

I didn't hesitate. "You should do it."

His eyes lit on me, sparking with amusement despite the heaviness we'd just shared.

"Trying to get rid of me?"

I scoffed. "Absolutely. I don't think I can bear another afternoon of you tromping around up here. If we're being honest, I'm not sure the floorboards can take it either."

That got him laughing. His head tipped back, revealing the pointy Adam's apple in his golden throat. My lips twitched with the urge to smile. I'd always found it difficult not to laugh when others were, but managed to suppress it by burying my nose in the flannel. His laughter petered out, and he gazed at me, those starburst crinkles around his eyes.

"This house has withstood many storms. I think it'll be standing long after I'm gone."

I swallowed hard, wondering when exactly that would be. I didn't ask, though. I wasn't certain I wanted the answer.

"I'm sure it will be."

Soon, I was back in my office, Graham's flannel over my tank top. When I heard heavy footsteps on the back porch, I peeked through the blinds. Remi and Henry were outside, and it looked like the old man was bossing Remi around.

Only then, when there wasn't a chance he could see, did I let my lips curve into a full grin.

Chapter Twelve

Hannah

TEDDY PLAYED FAST AND loose with his kisses. A little salt on my skin, and he was all over me, licking my neck and shoulder while I tried to smooth his hoof with my rasp. He had to practically break his neck to get to me, but he wouldn't be deterred.

I laughed as his big tongue dragged over my skin again. "Teddy, darlin', I'm trying to do my job here."

He nuzzled my head, his hot breath blowing my ponytail around. "You're a goofy boy, aren't you? Goofy and troublesome."

In my line of work, I spent time in close quarters with a lot of horses. They were all good boys and girls, even the troublemakers. I didn't pick favorites, but if I did, Teddy would be it. He was a sweet, affectionate stallion whose tongue dangled from his mouth when he was happy—which was often. It was simply impossible not to like him, even if his affection made my job take twice as long as it should have.

Once I finished with all four hooves, I gave him a good snuggle and a nice pat, then I packed up my tools and got back on the road. Teddy had been my last of the day, and I was looking forward to a stop at Sugar Rush. I was debating the merits of a muffin versus a donut, which was why I didn't notice the truck coming up behind me until it was on my ass.

This stretch of road was long and empty. There was no reason for a vehicle to be this close. If he wanted to pass, there was nothing stopping him.

I eyed him in the mirror, making out a vague outline of a man in a ball cap, one arm dangling out his window. I gestured for him to go around me, but either he couldn't see me or felt like being a dick because he stayed right where he was, about a foot from my bumper.

My stomach twisted. I tried not to jump to catastrophizing, but we were miles from anything with no cell signal. I did not like this. Not one bit. If I drove off the road, I'd have to hoof it a long way to get help. Not my idea of a good time—especially when my stomach was growling for my sister's baking.

Rolling my window down, I stuck my arm out and waved him past me. Without warning, he slowed down, putting some distance between us. Guessed he'd wised up.

Before I had the chance to breathe a sigh of relief, he sped up again, coming so close I braced myself to be bumped.

My sweaty palms clenched the steering wheel. Instinct urged me to put the pedal to the metal, but the less impulsive part of me told me to keep it steady. The last thing I needed was to lose control of my truck.

I tried to wave him around me again, but he didn't seem to like that. The asshole laid on his horn and swerved to the side. Holding my breath, I waited for him to pass, but he jerked back into my lane, kicking up dust and gravel.

Pounding heart lodged in my throat, I took the chance to glance at my cell, but it was useless. I'd already known what I would see. No signal out here in the prairie. My brothers had been hounding me to invest in a satellite phone, but I hadn't bothered. Right about now, I was feeling silly for not listening to them.

The truck swerved in and out of the lane, honking aggressively, before going back to silently haunting me.

"Come on! Just pass me!" I bit out between tightly clenched teeth. "Go around, you idiot."

Like he'd heard my pleas, the other truck swerved into the left lane and pulled up beside me, giving his horn a jaunty beep. I slid my eyes his way. We were right next to each other.

Cleve Jones.

There was no mistaking the jackass laughing his head off as he finger-gunned me. The man had to be in his forties but behaved like a stupid teenager.

My pulse firing out of control, I flipped him off and mouthed, "Loser," as clearly as I could so he'd know exactly what I thought of him.

He threw his head back in laughter and slammed his foot on the gas, speeding off down the road. I slowed down, letting him disappear ahead of me.

It took me the rest of the ride to calm down. For a minute or two, I truly believed I'd been in trouble. The darkest part of my mind had even considered I might've died out there. And for what? To amuse Cleve—a gray-haired, snaggle-toothed, second-rate farrier who had it out for me because several of his clients jumped off his shoddy ship to climb aboard mine?

If I told my brothers or my father about this incident, they'd be out for blood. There was no way they wouldn't be. And as much as I'd like to see Cleve taken down a few pegs, I didn't want any of my family members to wind up in jail. I could take care of myself. If

Cleve did anything like this again, I'd contact the police. I doubted it would come to that, though. Cleve had his fun, and now he'd move on.

The asshole.

By the time I parked my truck outside Sugar Rush, I thought I'd gotten ahold of myself, but as soon as my feet hit the pavement, my knees wobbled, and I had to clutch the door to keep from falling.

"Crap," I muttered, bringing my shaking hand to my face. "Stupid Cleve. I'm not letting that man get to me."

Slamming my door, I crossed the sidewalk, my focus solely on the entry to the bakery. As I approached, I reached for the handle, but it was pulled open before I could get to it.

Without looking up, I yanked my hand back and blurted, "Sorry. I didn't see you."

"That's all right, Hannah. You can go ahead in."

Startled, my gaze whipped up at the low, gentle voice, landing on a pair of lively hazel eyes. In the face of Remington Town being a gentleman, I normally would have come up with something snappish, but I wasn't my best self at the moment.

I attempted to brush by him, but of course my knees betrayed me once again, giving out as my shoulder grazed his chest. He caught me before I could go down, his grip warm and firm on my elbow.

"Careful," he murmured, far too close to my ear. "Steady now."

I would have yanked myself free, but the truth was, I needed the support, at least for a second or two. Fortunately, my pride was more powerful than my fear. I carefully extracted myself from Remi, willing my legs to stand on their own.

"You okay?" he asked.

"Yeah. I'm good."

My gaze darted around the shop. For once, it wasn't busy, with only a few people scattered around, sipping coffee and eating sweets. Phoebe was chatting with Camille behind the glass display case, and suddenly, I knew exactly what I wanted.

I felt Remi's eyes on me as I beelined toward my sister. I did not stop at the counter. Rounding it, I walked right into her, wrapping my arms around her. Luckily, she didn't have anything in her hands and was able to return my embrace.

She laughed softly. "What's this all about, Banana?"

"I missed you." That wasn't a lie. Phoebe smelled like sugar and everything good and sweet. Her hugs were always warm and fierce, and this one was no exception.

"I saw you this morning. What's up with you?"

I sighed, letting my head fall on her shoulder. "I got spooked on my way home. Cleve thought it was funny to pretend like he was going to drive me off the road. There for a minute, I thought he was actually going to do it."

She pulled back, holding my arms. "What do you mean? Cleve Jones?"

Damn. I shouldn't have said anything. I hadn't intended to, but the warmth of Phoebe's hug had loosened my lips. Now, she was worried, and I didn't want to lay that on her.

"It was his version of a prank...I think. You know he thinks he's funnier than he is."

Her brow crinkled. "This doesn't sound like a prank. What he did was dangerous."

"Who's Cleve Jones?" Remi asked with an edge I didn't recognize.

I guess I'd been so distracted I'd forgotten he was lurking about.

Jerking away from Phoebe, I stared at Remi, my mouth slightly agape. Then I moved to the counter opposite him, leaning on my palms.

"It's rude to eavesdrop, Remington."

He cocked his head, his jaw rippling. "I walked in with you. I wasn't hiding behind a corner; I've been here the whole time. Now, tell me about being run off the road."

Again, my mouth flopped like a fish, no sound exiting it. Phe stood next to me, linking her arm through mine.

"He's an idiot," Phoebe explained. "Hannah's success has emasculated him, so he takes it out on her by trying to steal her clients and being a general nuisance. This is the first time I know of him doing something dangerous, though."

Remi's nostrils flared as his narrowed gaze slid from Phe to me. "You're going to the police, right?"

I shook my head. The thought of doing that was exhausting. "It was a prank."

Before I knew what was happening, he snagged my hand and lifted it in front of my face. "Is that why you're trembling? Doesn't sound like a prank to me."

I wanted to argue, but my sister squeezed my arm. "He has a point. Cleve may have thought he was being funny, but he went too far. You should make a report, let the cops give *him* a scare. Maybe he'll think twice about harassing you next time."

"I—" Any argument I could have had was eaten up by Remi's fierce glare and Phoebe's pleading eyes. I blew out a breath in defeat. "Fine. I'll go to the station. But not before I eat two donuts."

Making the report wasn't as terrible as I'd thought it would be. It had taken less than an hour to recount the incident and leave my contact information. Not that I'd really needed to since the officer had been in Caleb's graduating class, but I appreciated him doing things the official way.

I made my way outside, exhausted to the bone from my long day of working and everything that had come after. A scorching shower followed by vegging on the couch were my only plans for the rest of the evening, and I couldn't wait.

My steps came to a halt when I spotted Remi leaning against the brick wall next to the station entrance. He saw me at the same time and straightened, eyeing me expectantly. I drew in a breath, prepared to bustle by him, but he easily fell into step with me.

"How'd it go?" he asked.

"Fine." I glanced at him then faced forward, heading in the direction of my apartment. "You didn't need to wait."

"Felt like I should since I was the one who insisted you do this. Are they going to do anything about it?"

I shrugged. "They'll give him a visit. I'm sure Cleve will deny it happened, and since I don't have any proof, that'll be it."

"They tell you that?"

"They didn't have to. It's why I hadn't wanted to bother in the first place. I don't want anyone going out of their way for me."

"Hannah, you deserve people going out of their way for you."

It was such a Graham thing to say; I sucked in a sharp breath. Too sharp to be disguised. Remi's head whipped my way, his gaze boring into me. When I didn't look back, he must've decided I'd answered enough questions and didn't press for more.

I pointed toward the building down the block. "That's my place. I can get there on my own."

"I guess you didn't read the fine print when you signed the contract. This is door-to-door service."

My lips twitched, almost smiling. "Funny, I don't remember signing anything."

"You did. Talk to Dell Rivers about it."

I snorted a little laugh. "I'll put that on my to-do list."

He continued strolling with me, his arm casually bumping into mine. "Phoebe seems like she's doing well for herself."

"She's a goddess." I winged a brow when he didn't immediately agree. "I saw you eating one of her lemon bars. I know you get it."

He chuckled. "Absolutely. I've been a lot of places, eaten a lot of different food, and that lemon bar was top tier. It's no wonder she always has a line."

We were in front of my building now, so I jerked my chin to Phe's place. "This is her apartment. Mine is upstairs."

He tipped his head back to look up at my windows then swiveled to catch my gaze. Those crinkles appeared like a hidden weapon, and dammit if I wasn't defenseless against them.

"Nice to live close. You two watch out for each other."

It wasn't a question, but I answered him anyway. "We do. It's what us Kellys have always done."

"Yeah. You were always good like that." He stepped into my space and placed his heavy hands on my shoulders. "Are you doing all right now that you've had sugar and time?"

"I'm fine. It was the adrenaline before, that's all."

Hazel eyes darted all over my face as if searching for the truth. I wasn't sure what he saw, but he nodded like he was satisfied.

"I'm glad I was there to catch you this time, Han."

The way he was looking at me now was worse than the crinkles. Concerned and tender, like he truly cared and meant what he was saying—exactly the kind of thing that was dangerous to me. My dopamine-deficient brain would latch right on to this good feeling and mix it up into something more than it was. I was self-aware enough to recognize my own patterns, but somehow, I kept repeating them anyway.

Well, that wasn't going to happen with Remington Town.

"If you could avoid telling my brother about this, that'd be great." I retreated toward the steps, away from Remi. He slowly let his hands drop to his sides. "Good night, Remington."

The crinkles appeared again, along with a ghost of a smile. "Night, Hannah Kelly."

I wasn't going to catch feelings for Remi, but that didn't mean I wasn't human. Standing there, I watched his very fine, muscular ass encased in a pair of snug blue jeans as he walked away. When he turned the corner and disappeared, only then did I head for my door.

But I didn't get off scot-free for that little sneaky peek. As soon as I passed her door, Phe stuck her head out, a wide grin on her face.

"You and Remi had a moment."

I rolled my eyes. "I don't know what on earth you're talking about."

"I know what I saw, Banana, and since my windows were open, I know what I heard too. That was a moment."

If she were anyone else, I would have flipped her off. Since she was Phoebe, I pretended to gag myself.

"No moments were had, nor will any ever be had between me and Remington Town. And you can take that to the bank."

At most, it had maybe been half a moment, but there was no need to admit that out loud.

Chapter Thirteen

Remington

STIFF AND MORE THAN a little sore, I slid off my saddle with a groan. My boots hitting the ground sent a jolt through my head I couldn't disguise. Caleb hopped off his saddle and was next to me in an instant, concern crinkling his brow.

"Shit, did I push you too hard?"

I tried not to wince at the sound of his voice. The past couple hours, I'd been out in the sun with him, mending fences and checking the property. It'd felt good. Like I was back where I belonged. I'd been the one to push myself beyond my limits.

It'd been a long while since work had been anything close to pleasurable, and I'd been enjoying myself so much I'd ignored the way the sun had been getting to me to have more time in the saddle, riding next to Caleb. Now that we were back in the barn and I was off my horse, there was no denying I'd fucked up.

"No. This is all on me."

He patted my shoulder and led me to a hay bale set against a bare wall. "Sit. I'll get you an ice pack and fresh water."

Sitting wasn't a choice but a necessity. My vision was blurred, and there was an ice pick lodged in my skull. When my ass touched the hay, I winced. Eyes slamming shut, I let my head fall into my palm and put pressure on my temples.

Jesus, I was out of practice. I hadn't been on a horse since I'd left home, and I was paying for it.

Footsteps approached, but they were too light to be Caleb. I cracked an eye open, spotting the outline of a boy coming toward me. He stopped a foot or two away, his hands on his hips.

"Who're you?" he asked.

"I'm Remi. Who might you be?"

"Jesse Kelly. This is my ranch, you know."

"Ah. You're Caleb's boy." Jesse nodded, confirming this as fact, though there was no denying it. Even with my vision gone to crap, I was able to make out Caleb's face duplicated on his son. "I've known your dad since we were younger than you are."

"That's crazy. I've never even seen you before." Despite his doubt, he plopped down on the hay bale next to me.

I let my eyes fall closed again. If this kid thought it was strange I wasn't looking at him; he didn't point it out.

"I've been gone," I explained.

"Where'd you go?"

"All over the world. I take pictures for a living."

"Like...for magazines—models and stuff?"

"Some of my pictures are in magazines, but they're not of models. I document events in the world, like wars, famines, natural disasters. It's a type of journalism."

"So you take pictures of sad stuff."

Damn. He'd whittled my career into the simplest of terms, but he wasn't wrong.

"Yeah. It's not all sad, but there are a lot of bad things that happen in the world, and it's important everyone knows about them."

I opened an eye again to see his reaction. He was thoughtfully nodding.

"Ms. Clark—she's the librarian—has a quote hanging behind her desk. It goes, 'Those who don't learn from history are doomed to repeat it.' It's kinda like your job is to make sure people don't repeat the sad stuff, right?"

Before I could figure out how to answer his profound observation—in an age-appropriate way—Caleb's voice cracked the air.

"Tell me you're not talking that man's ear off, Jess."

Jesse shook his head. "Nope. He was talking to me. Is it true this guy's your friend?"

Caleb laughed as he tossed me an ice pack. "Kid, if you doubted what he was telling you, why're you sitting so close to him?"

Jesse shrugged. "I don't know. He looks pretty harmless, and I was ninety percent sure he was telling the truth."

"Always good to double-check. Did he tell you how long we've known each other?"

"Since you were younger than me," Jesse replied.

"That's right."

Cay passed me a chilled bottle of water, and I took it gratefully, rolling it over my forehead before taking a long pull. The ice pack on the back of my neck was bringing me the relief I needed, but getting to know Caleb's son hadn't been half bad either. He'd been a good distraction from the throb in my skull and a vivid reminder of what I'd missed out on being gone so long.

Jesse nudged me. "You're back now? What kinda sad things are you taking pictures of around here?"

"Jess..." Cay warned, but I didn't have a problem with his question.

"It's all right. The truth is, I'm not working right now because I was in a bad car accident a couple months ago. The even bigger truth is I'm a little burned out from all the sad stuff, so I'm taking a break."

This was the first time I'd voiced that aloud. I wasn't just in Sugar Brush to heal but to figure out how I wanted to move forward. Thoughts of flying into a war zone didn't fill me with adrenaline like they used to. It might've been a temporary thing; I couldn't be sure. But I finally had the time, space, and desire to really think things through.

"Yeah, that makes sense. Maybe it's time for someone else to record history," Jesse replied.

Caleb crouched in front of his son and ruffled his hair. "You're too damn smart, you know that?"

Jesse's chin rose proudly. "No such thing."

I chuckled. "He's got a point there, Cay."

Caleb's grin grew serious after a moment of surveying me. "Have you been to the doctor lately?"

"I actually have an appointment in Denver tomorrow. I was thinking I'd return the rental car while I'm there. You know if there's any kind of shuttle that'll bring me back? I'll drive Graham's truck the rest of the time I'm here, but—"

"You don't need a shuttle. I just talked to Hannah while I was in the house getting your ice. She's seeing clients out that way tomorrow. She can bring you back."

I winced. "It's more than a two-hour drive. I doubt she is going to volunteer to do me any favors, let alone this one."

"Aunt Hannah's nice. She'll do it," Jesse assured me.

Caleb clapped a hand on his son's shoulder, jostling him. "Aunt Hannah is a little mad at Remi right now, but you're right. We ask her, she'll do it. She's too nice to say no." He shot me a crooked smirk. "I can't guarantee you'll get much polite conversation out of her on the drive, but she'll do it."

Not a chance he was wrong, but I was looking forward to whatever Hannah Kelly had in store for me.

Chapter Fourteen

Hannah

I COULD NOT BELIEVE my ears. "No. Absolutely not."

"I wouldn't ask if it wasn't important," Caleb replied.

My fingers curled around my steering wheel. If I didn't hold on tight, I might've ripped out my speakers to silence Caleb's nonchalant voice coming through them. "Convenient of you to wait until I'm already across the state line so I can't drive over there and strangle you."

My brother had the nerve to laugh. "Wasn't too worried about that. Figured I'd ask you last minute so you couldn't find another solution. If you don't drive him back, he'll be stranded down there."

I flipped on my turn signal harder than necessary, steering my truck down the hard-packed dirt road leading to my client's ranch.

"I really can't believe you, Cay. You expect me to chauffeur Remington around after he...what—does some big city shopping? I just don't know what could be so important—"

"He's seeing a neurologist, Han."

That brought me up short. "Why? Is something wrong with him?"

"He didn't tell you about the accident?"

Cold prickled my skin all over. "No. I have no idea what you're talking about."

"Seems like something he should've mentioned to you." Caleb sighed. "Guess I'm left to be the one to tell you everything. At least, what I know."

"Go on. Tell me."

By the time Caleb got through describing what had happened to Remi, I'd been parked on my client's property for several minutes. A low spark had lit in my belly, burning brighter with every detail, but I had to tamp it down. Now wasn't the time to process any of this. It was much too big, and I had a job to do. My mind had to be on my horses—not the fact that Remi had almost died on the other side of the world while his father had been living his final days.

The ranch owner walked out of his barn, giving me the side-eye, no doubt wondering why the hell I was still in my truck and not tending to his horses.

"I gotta go, Cay."

"All right. I'll let you get to work. You'll drive Rem home when you're done, right?"

"Yeah." I blew out a heavy breath. "I'll drive him home."

Remi didn't keep me waiting outside the hospital. As soon as I'd texted I'd arrived, he came out, taking long, confident strides directly to my truck. I couldn't stop myself from looking for signs of injury, but he was just as sturdy and in one piece as he'd been the last time I saw him. As he drew closer, my attention got caught on the scar on his temple. I'd noticed it, but I'd been too caught up in my anger to really process how fresh it was.

He climbed into my truck, a grin on his face, and held out a bottle of Sprite. "Tell me you still drink these."

"I—" I glanced from his face to the bottle. "Yes, I still drink them."

"Good." He handed it over, and I let it rest in my hand, unsure how I felt about...well, anything. "I owe you for giving me a ride. A soda's not gonna cut it, but it's a start."

"Don't worry about it. Caleb's the one who owes me anyway." I placed the soda in a cup holder and wrapped my fingers around the wheel. "Ready?"

"Whenever you are."

We were miles down the road, leaving the outskirts of the city and heading northwest toward home, the radio playing low. Remi's head had fallen to rest against the window as soon as I'd started driving, but he picked it up now, turning toward me.

"I'm surprised you take care of horses all the way down here."

I shrugged. "They were Graham's clients. I took them over when he...retired. But you know this area. Everything's far. I don't mind driving, though. I'm used to it."

"Yeah. It's easy to forget how far apart things are. With enough distance, this whole place got smaller."

My laugh was soft and a little bitter. "There's nothing small about Wyoming. Well, except the population. Still the lowest in the country."

I caught the twitch of his mouth out of the corner of my eye. "The way Wyomingites like it, huh?"

"Some of us, sure. I wouldn't want to live in a crowded area, but I don't mind being around people."

"Guess you always had that at the ranch—enough tourists to make it interesting and enough space to never feel hemmed in."

"Yep. Just how I like it."

The flame in my belly was rising, each breath giving it more life. If I'd laid a hand on my abdomen, I bet it would've sizzled. I couldn't keep talking to Remi like everything was normal and okay. If I did, I'd turn into a fire-breathing dragon and burn this truck to ashes. Reaching out, I turned the radio up, signaling in no uncertain terms I was finished with the idle chitchat.

Remi, for his part, took my hint graciously. After a minute of looking at me, he went back to leaning his head against the window. We spent the rest of the drive that way, Remi relaxed, and me...well, I was *not* relaxed.

This man had almost died. He'd been in a coma due to a traumatic brain injury. Yet he'd allowed me to be angry at him. Not only that, he'd allowed me to take that anger out on him as if any of what had happened had been in his control.

That made me...so, so mad. I couldn't even aim my rage at him anymore since this wasn't his fault. He was a *victim* who needed to rest and heal. But instead of telling me that, he'd just let me be a bitch to him. He'd played the bad guy for me, and I'd enjoyed giving him his lashes because I hadn't been bogged down by grief while railing my frustrations at him.

Each mile that he gave me room, allowing me silence, was so goddamn considerate, the flame in my belly grew until it was almost too big to contain.

Luckily, we reached Graham's house before I exploded.

Except Remi didn't hop right out like I'd expected him to. Instead, he turned the radio off and twisted in his seat to face me.

"Thank you for the ride, Hannah."

I nodded. "It isn't a big deal."

"Maybe not, but you helped me out, and I appreciate it." Silence stretched between us, the burning continued, and still, he didn't leave. "I'm planning on driving Graham's truck."

Blood swished through my veins like a wild, rapid ride, making my ears buzz.

"Are you?"

"Yeah. It's my plan, but the truck's half yours, so I wanted to make sure it's all right with you. I get that it might not be. If you want, I can pay you your portion of the value. Just let me know what you're thinking."

Considerate. Again. Gah!

"Are you even supposed to be driving? Did your doctor okay you?" I asked.

"I'm good, Hannah. Doc said I'm recovering fine. My scans looked good. I still need to be mindful about too much light since it tends to bring on migraines, but I don't plan on taking any long drives."

"You drove yourself here. I mean, when you first came back to Sugar Brush."

"I did." He let out a long sigh. "Probably shouldn't have, but I took it slow and steady. I didn't want to put anyone out having to come to pick me up."

That fire burned all the way up to my chest, but I swallowed it down.

"Makes sense." I drummed my fingers on the wheel. "I have to get home, so..."

"Right. Think about the truck." He put his hand on the door. "Really appreciate you driving me back. Anything you need, I owe you."

"You got me a Sprite. We're even."

He needed to stop being so damn nice, so I could get back on the road and scream in the privacy of my own vehicle. If he didn't leave soon, I might not be able to contain it.

He stayed where he was for so long I turned to see what the hell he was doing, only to be met by soft, gentle eyes and a curved half smile.

"What?" I snapped.

That half smile turned full on. "Nothing. You're just a really good girl, Hannah Kelly. *Really* good."

Then, as if he hadn't shattered my bones, ground my lungs to dust, and combusted my brain, he hopped out of my truck and strode off with a casual wave over his shoulder.

I didn't make the decision to follow him; it just happened. He'd barely gotten his front door open when I stormed onto the porch, my fists balled at my sides.

This man was going to get it.

He'd lit the spark. Now, he'd have to deal with the consequences.

Chapter Fifteen
Remington

Pounding footsteps had me turning around, shocked as hell to see Hannah coming at me like a hurricane. She didn't stop until we collided in my doorway. She bounced off my chest, and I grabbed her shoulders so she didn't fall, but she shrugged me off.

Cheeks blazing cherry red, she shoved me. "How could you not tell me?"

"What? What's going on, sweetheart?"

"Pfft, don't *sweetheart* me, Remington!"

"Okay. You want to come inside and talk?"

"No."

She shoved me again, and I let her move me so I didn't wind up on my ass, where I suspected she was fully capable of sending me. The woman was strong.

"Tell me what's going on."

She tossed her arms out. "I threw a muffin at you—at your *head*."

"A cupcake too," I added.

"It was a stress ball." She gave me another shove, though it wasn't as hard as the first few. "Right at your head. How could you let me do that?"

"I didn't have a lot of say in it, Hannah."

Oh, her face lit up even more. She'd been pissed before. Now, she was a ball of fury.

"You're so...so...gah!" She clawed at my T-shirt until she had a good grip with her fingers. "I called you heartless for not being here when you almost *died*. At any point, you could have told me why you hadn't picked up your phone, but instead...why? Why didn't you say anything?"

I took hold of her wrists, rubbing my thumb over her racing pulse. I allowed her to push me around more if I didn't think she'd hate herself for it when the dust cleared. So I steadied her, keeping her still to give her the chance to calm down and get back to herself.

"'Cause I could see you needed to be mad at someone and let it be me. And let's be honest, had I gotten the calls in time, I still don't know that I would've come. I can't say with any certainty."

Her eyes narrowed. "You would have. I'm certain of that."

I cocked my head, studying her. She was still boiling, but it had gentled.

"I might be as heartless as you thought, sweetheart."

That earned me a groan. "Don't talk nice to me now, Remington. I'm not ready for that."

I laughed and let go of her wrists to hold my hands up in innocence. "I wouldn't dream of being nice to you. Last thing I'd do."

She didn't laugh with me. Instead, her gaze locked on my mouth, and her body tensed. That was the only warning I had before she crashed into me, her lips meeting mine in hot, wet anger.

It was the underlying sweetness that had my mouth moving against hers before my brain caught up to what was happening. But even when it did, I kept kissing her because it felt too good to stop.

It'd been a long time since I'd had a woman in my arms, and that was where she was. I wrapped her up, pulling her flush with my chest, one hand bracing the base of her skull, the other at the small of her back. She was warm and solid, smelling like sunshine and sweat. And she fit against me like she was made to be there. Tall enough I barely had to bend. Strong enough I could hold her tight without worry she'd break.

The moan she unleashed when our tongues touched was both carnal and...pained. It was the pain that brought me up short as the reality of what was happening barreled back to the forefront.

Caleb had warned me she was fragile. Told me how rough she'd had it, and I'd promised to be careful. I'd seen her grief, had practically felt it, sharp as a knife, when we'd stood in Graham's room together. I couldn't hurt her any more than I already had, yet here I was kissing this woman without any thought to the consequences.

But *fuck* did she taste like the best dream I'd ever had. Wrenching my lips from hers wasn't easy. It was picturing the tears I'd seen in her eyes that allowed me to pull myself away.

Hands on her shoulders, I put some space between our bodies, and it was crazy how unnatural it felt when I hadn't known what it felt like to hold her until minutes ago.

"No, baby. We can't do this."

I really didn't want to say it, but it had to be done. I wasn't in a place to make promises to anyone, and Hannah deserved someone who was. I just hoped I wasn't around when she found that guy. Now that I'd had a piece of her, it was going to be difficult to shake off.

Her hazy eyes met mine, slowly clearing. When they did, they went sharp, and the flush in her cheeks deepened.

"Right. I shouldn't have—I'm sorry." Her lips rolled over her teeth as she roughly shrugged me off. "I have to go."

She spun away from me so fast she stumbled over her feet. I caught her elbow to help her straighten, but she yanked her arm from me, running down the porch steps.

"Hannah—"

She tripped again but managed to catch herself on the railing before throwing herself toward her truck. Swinging the door open, she flung herself inside and backed out in a cloud of dust and fury. I would've worried about her driving in this state, but once she got turned around, she maneuvered down the long driveway carefully.

She'd just needed to get away from me.

I stood on the porch long after she'd disappeared, my hands locked on the back of my neck, my heart lodged in my throat.

The last ten minutes had felt like a fever dream, but the lingering sweetness on my lips reminded me it had been very real. I'd had Hannah Kelly in my arms and her mouth on mine.

I didn't know how it happened or what it meant.

What I did know? I'd fucked it all up, and it was on me to make it right, some way, somehow.

Chapter Sixteen

Hannah

I covered my face with my hands. "I've never been so embarrassed in my life."

Phoebe's fingers paused in my hair. "Really? I was there when you were a teenager. You did some pretty embarrassing stuff."

I moved my hands to glare up at her. Since my head was currently in her lap while she stroked my hair, it didn't have much of an effect. Still, I was fragile, and she didn't need to point out how much I'd made an ass of myself in the past.

"I came to you for comfort."

"And I'd love to do that, Banana. But without knowing exactly what happened, I can't properly tailor my comforting."

I shifted my hands back over my eyes, unable to bear knowing I was being perceived, even by my sister.

"I gave Remington Town a ride home from Denver this afternoon."

"I know. Caleb told me about his accident when he stopped by Sugar Rush. That was nice of you." I huffed, and she carried on like I hadn't made a sound. "By the way, I love how you say his full name like there's another Remington I would mix him up with."

"Please. Let me be formal about him to create some much-needed distance."

"Hmmm, and why do you need distance from Remi?"

"Because…when I brought him home, I had some things to say to him about not telling me he'd had a TBI. I'd thrown a muffin at him, Phe."

"You did? One of my muffins?"

"Yes, not that it matters."

"Well, at least I know it was soft. Some of those grocery store muffins are like rocks."

I groaned. "The point isn't the muffin. The point is I threw things at him while he had a brain injury. I was also a mega-bitch to him about not getting here in time and needed to know why he'd let me. Do you know what he said?"

"What did he say?"

"He said he could tell I needed someone to be mad at and let himself be that person."

She sighed. "That's really sweet, actually."

"I know," I cried. "So that's why I did the dumbest thing possible."

"Did you punch him?"

"No, worse. I kissed him."

"Oh," she whispered. "Did he kiss you back?"

"He did, but it must have been an automatic, shocked reaction. Once he had his wits about him, he pushed me off and told me no."

"Oh," she repeated, softer this time. "Did he say anything else?"

"Just that we couldn't do that while holding me as far away from himself as he could." I pounded my forehead with the heel of my hand. "I've been so good about not giving in to my impulses, but I had all these big feelings about everything and all I could think about was kissing him. I should have left, but you know me. I don't like to do the things I should, and now I've made a complete fool of myself."

"I'm sure it's not that bad. You're making it worse in your head."

Phoebe knew me. She understood perceived slights and minor rejections had the potential to cut me deeply. While most people would have probably been embarrassed about throwing themselves at a man who wasn't interested, they'd brush it off and move on, and here I was, contemplating how I could disappear into the ether so no one could see me again. I felt gross and undesirable, and worse, I'd pushed myself on Remi without his consent. Coming back from this seemed insurmountable.

"I'll just never see him again. I'll have Dell send him a letter telling him he can have the house."

"Hannie, no. You love that house." She grazed her knuckles across my forehead before gently knocking me there. "Remi is a nice guy. I'm sure he won't hold the kiss against you. He probably won't even bring it up."

That did nothing to comfort me. I didn't want Remington Town to be a nice guy. His being an asshole would have made all this so much easier.

"I'm going to disappear."

She snorted. "No, you're not. Just stay away from the house for a while. You'll get over it."

"I doubt that. Remember when I dropped my entire soda down my shirt on my first date with Kyle?"

"Um...no. You dated a Kyle? Which one? Kyle Thompson?"

"Yes, Kyle Thompson. I was thirteen. It was my first date."

"Okay...sorry if I forgot Kyle. Why are we talking about him?"

"Because"—I swung my legs around to sit up—"whenever I remember that date, I get nauseous. He laughed for a split second before helping me clean up. It was so sweet, but all that stuck with me was his half-second laugh. I barely remember anything else about that date."

She puffed up her cheeks to slowly blow out a breath. "Okay, so we accept you'll be mortified forever. Remi most likely doesn't have that problem. I bet he's already forgotten all about it."

I sprung to my feet, incensed. "Am I so forgettable? Is that what you're saying?"

She giggled at me—it was the only thing to do in the face of my irrationality—and I couldn't stop myself from laughing with her. It stopped me from spiraling further despite already twisting myself pretty deep in a pit of despair.

"You're so dramatic, Banana," Phoebe chimed sweetly as she made her way to her small kitchen. "I have a few extra pistachio macarons. Would you like one or five?"

"You know the answer to that."

She came to me with a pink box in her hands. "Five."

"Exactly."

I let her distract me because this was Phoebe's baking. It could cure any woe for a while, and since actually becoming incorporeal wasn't going to happen, I'd take it.

A week later, I had almost returned to normal. There were moments when it all came rushing back and I had to pause what I was doing so I could melt with shame, but for the most part, I had moved on.

Spending next to no time at the house had helped a lot with this. I'd still had to drop by to pick up my tools and do a few things in the office, but I'd breezed in and out. And by "breezed," I meant I snuck in like a thief in the night.

It might not have been the mature solution, but it was what I'd needed to handle the rejection, still blazing quietly in the background.

Tonight was family dinner night. They were something I always looked forward to, but this one even more than the rest. My grandparents had finally gotten back from their month-long European cruise, and I absolutely couldn't wait to hear the tales they had to tell.

Well, my grandmother would do most of the telling while Granddad watched her. It was his way and what worked for them. They were cute as pie.

I kicked my boots off at the door and hurried into the kitchen. Dad and my grandfather were at the table, shucking corn like always. I beelined for Granddad first, throwing my arms around his neck before he could even put the corn down.

He chuckled beside my ear as I sucked in his scent, not realizing how much I'd missed everything about him until now. Our house was right beside his. Growing up, I'd see him pretty much every day, and he'd always been at the center of my life, truly the heart of our family.

"It's good to see you too, darlin'," he cooed gruffly.

"Don't use up all her hugs, Connell."

With a wide grin, I let go of my grandfather and straightened just in time to be embraced by Lily Smythe-Kelly, my glamorous, worldly grandmother. She smelled expensive, and her skin was soft as velvet. Like Mom, she didn't seem like the kind of woman who lived on a ranch, and for the first ten years of my life, she hadn't. But she and my grandfather had made their way back to each other and had been inseparable ever since. I got the sense she'd live in a trash heap if he were there with her.

She pulled back, her hands on my shoulders. "Oh, *gorgeous*. How have you been, my love?"

"Good." I nodded. "But we don't need to talk about me. I want to hear everything about your cruise."

She waved me off. "I hardly have the energy to tell the same story multiple times. Let's wait until those siblings of yours arrive. For now, I want to hear about you. You don't look as sad as you did when we left, but you've always been good at hiding things from us."

"Mom," Dad warned softly, "let her be."

She glanced at my father over her shoulder, unbothered by his admonishment. "I'm asking the questions that should be asked, Lachlan." She faced me again, her rose-colored lips curving into the gentlest smile. "Now, tell me."

I sucked in a breath then let it all out. "The sadness comes in waves, but it's not all the time, and it doesn't drag me under. I miss him terribly, but I'm relieved he isn't suffering or in pain. Going into his house when he's not there still feels unnatural, and I hate that."

"Oh, my sweet girl." She pulled me into another hug, hard and fierce, exactly what I needed. By the time she let me go, I'd been fortified, ready to face what came next.

After giving my mom a squeeze and kissing the top of my dad's head, I sat at the table, chatting with everyone about the horses I'd seen over the last week. Soon, Phoebe arrived, followed shortly by Cormac. Both were given the same bone-crushing hugs from our grandmother and all-encompassing embraces from Granddad.

Caleb and Jesse were the last to arrive. My nephew led the way, carrying a stack of books in his arms, as usual. Caleb came in behind him, and much to my horror, he was not alone.

Remington Town strolled into my parents' kitchen, a big bunch of flowers tucked under one arm and a six-pack of beer in the other.

My mother paused over the chicken she'd been seasoning at the expansive, marble-topped island, her brows diving like lightning. Only Jesse, wrapping his arms around her waist, softened her.

She gave him her full attention. "This is entirely unfair, Jesse-boy. I can't hug you back with my hands coated in raw chicken, and I have this strong need to squeeze you."

He tipped his head back, grinning. "You squeezed me yesterday."

She leveled him with a stare. "Are you implying I'm not overdue for more?"

"No," he giggled.

"Mom," Caleb interrupted, "I brought Rem. Figured since you always make more than enough food, it wouldn't be a problem."

Her gaze flicked to Cay. "A call would have been nice." Then she looked at Remi. "But you're right; we do have enough. Are those flowers for me?"

Remi cleared his throat and stepped forward, placing what I now saw was one of multiple bouquets of wildflowers on the island. "They are. Sorry for just showing up. I didn't know you weren't aware."

Caleb, for his part, scuffed his socked foot on the floor while Mom washed her hands at the sink. "My fault. Slipped my mind."

"Sure, Cay." Her brow winged. "Or you didn't want me to say no."

Dad had gotten up when Remi arrived and now slid an arm around Mom's waist, tugging her into his side. "Which you wouldn't have, right, Ellie?"

She patted his chest. "Of course not. The more the merrier."

Though my dad hadn't mentioned it to me, I knew he'd spent time with Remi while he'd been working the ranch. They exchanged a simple handshake, while my mother's greeting was more layered.

She broke away from my dad to take Remi by the shoulders and stare at his face, slowly shaking her head.

"You've gotten older" was her first observation. "For a long time, I never thought I'd see your face again. It's good to see the lines around your eyes and the shape you've become, but I wish I could've seen it happening."

Something in Remi collapsed. His shoulders rolled forward, and his chin dipped to his chest.

"I thought you'd forgotten me," he replied, his voice thick, almost hoarse.

"Yes...well, I'm not happy with you for leaving for so long, but forgetting you was never a possibility. You were my Cay's shadow. I was always surprised when he was alone; it was so rare."

He shifted, his eyes sliding to the side. "Yeah. Sorry about that. I—"

"Don't be sorry. You were like a fifth child. As I said, the more, the merrier. It's just when you left, there was a hole where you'd once been. Perhaps I was a little pissy about that and took it out on you in the grocery store." She patted his cheeks and smoothed his hair off his forehead the same way she did with Cay and Mac. "That's all in the past. You're here now, and we're all happy for it."

"Than—" He stopped, clearing his throat. "Thank you. For saying that. For all of it."

Stepping back, she waved his words off. "Don't insult me by thanking me for caring about you, Remington." Then she spun away, going back to her chicken, leaving Remi shell-shocked.

I caught Phoebe's eye when she turned my way after watching the whole interaction. She patted her chest like her heart was fluttering, and I crinkled my nose. Her eyebrows popped, so I flared my eyes.

Mac laughed, which was nothing new. "Stop the silent communication. It's creepy."

Granddad playfully swatted Mac's head. "Leave your sisters alone."

He held his hands up. "All right, all right. I've lived with their creepiness this long; why change?"

My grandmother's cry of happiness jerked everyone's attention back to Remi. He'd given her one of the bouquets and had received a rosy kiss on his cheek in return. His gaze found mine, and the warmth in it had me looking away. Then, within two heartbeats, he was at the table, handing Phoebe a bouquet, which could have only meant—

"Han," he gruffed, standing before me, "these are for you."

The flowers were shoved toward me, and dammit, they were beautiful, but the gesture even more so. I couldn't, in good conscience, bat them out of his hand and stomp on them, even though that was what he deserved for being so outrageously thoughtful.

So, I took them, even managed to politely thank him, but I did it all without looking at him once.

And that was exactly how I planned to spend the rest of dinner—avoiding Remington Town with every fiber of my being.

Chapter Seventeen

Remington

I DIDN'T KNOW HOW it had happened, but somewhere in the shuffle of the ten of us crowding around the oversized farmhouse table, I ended up in the last empty seat, right beside Hannah. I knew she didn't want me there. She'd done her best to stay away from me over the last week and had barely acknowledged my presence in her family's home. But me getting up and asking someone to switch seats wasn't an option.

First of all, she'd be mad if I caused a scene.

More importantly, I didn't want to.

The truth of the matter was I didn't like being ignored by Hannah. It pissed me off even though I knew I didn't have any right to feel that way. After all, I'd been the one to draw the line between us. And I'd done a whole decade of ignoring.

Under the table, my knee hit Hannah's. When I didn't move away as quickly as I should've, she reached down and shoved my thigh.

"Stop manspreading," she uttered through gritted teeth. "It's rude."

"Just sitting here eating my dinner," I murmured back.

On Hannah's other side, Jesse surveyed us both. "What are you two whispering about? Something boring?"

"We're not whispering," she blurted. "Remi is talking to himself."

Jesse eyed us skeptically. Since our first conversation, we'd shared a few more, and I'd learned this kid was seriously smart. He read non-fiction from the adult section of the library for fun and knew a lot more than the average ten-year-old. He wasn't buying the made-up story Hannah was trying to sell.

My shoulder bumped Hannah's as I tipped my head toward Jesse. "Your aunt's mad because I was taking up space, that's all."

"You were taking up *too much space*, Remington." She elbowed my bicep, though it was more playful than anything. "You're doing it again, by the way."

Elena's head swiveled our way from across the table. "Are you two fighting?"

"Nope." Hannah sat up straight. "Just having a chat."

Memories of sitting at this table as a kid rushed in. Two or three of the Kelly siblings bickering. Their mother asking if they were fighting, them immediately denying it. I'd never let myself be swept up in their troublemaking for fear I wouldn't be invited back. But seeing how easily I'd been accepted into the fold tonight, those worries seemed far away.

Though, I wasn't sure they'd like me too much if they found out I'd had my mouth on their beloved daughter's. Or that I was thinking about doing it all over again while sitting here beside her.

"Remington's taking up too much space," Jesse chimed in. "That's what Aunt Hannah says."

Elena arched a brow. "Really, Han? You come from a family of giants. You should be used to it."

Hannah huffed. "I'm sure you enjoy being crowded by Dad."

"I sincerely doubt it's a real burden to have Remi close to you." Hannah tensed at her mother's comment, but Elena didn't notice and continued. "By the way, Rem, Caleb told us you had an appointment with a doctor last week. How'd that go?"

"Well," I started, "he said it's hard to predict the long-term impact of my injury, but I'm doing the right things by taking it easy and avoiding possibly dangerous situations. I'll go back in a few months for a follow-up."

"You'll still be here in a few months?" Hannah asked.

"I intend to be."

"I bet you're itching to get back on the road," she pressed. "I bet you can't wait to break out of here."

"Hannah..." Lachlan shook his head at her but didn't say anything else. The way she slumped in her seat, it didn't seem necessary.

"Will you be doing that, Remington?" Hannah's grandmother, Lily, asked. "Once you have clearance, will you be returning overseas?"

"I don't know. I'm at a crossroads at the moment, not sure what either direction holds."

"There are plenty of things to photograph in the US," Elena added. "You could spend the rest of your life capturing beauty."

"It's important to document the sad things," Jesse chimed in. "But Grandma's right. The beautiful things are just as important."

"I agree." I caught Caleb's eye across the table. "Your son is something else. You know that, right?"

He nodded. "Amazes me every day."

Jesse beamed. "Ms. Clark, the librarian, says I should have her job because I know the books just as well as her and the county could get away with paying me in candy to save money."

That got a laugh from just about everyone, even Hannah, but as soon as I looked at her, she bit down on her bottom lip and focused on her plate.

Now that she wasn't talking to me, not even bickering, I wanted it back. If she'd allowed it, I would've asked her about the rough time she'd gone through recently. I might've even asked how she'd become so close to Graham. I was deeply curious where Hannah Kelly was concerned, but she wasn't giving anything away.

Seeing how she was with her family only added to it. The Kellys had always been tight, and not a single one bit their tongue when they had an opinion, but Hannah was a little cyclone, sweeping down over each of them to leave little doses of teasing, encouragement, advice, and commiseration. I'd always wanted to be an official member of this family, and that hadn't changed, but I now had a hankering for Cyclone Hannah to sweep over me, and that was brand new.

Lily and Connell took over the conversation the rest of the meal, recounting the countries they'd been to and friends they'd made. When Connell got talking about taking Lily dancing in the disco, he looked a lot younger than his seventies, and Lily blushed like a new bride. Which, in a way, I guessed she was.

Hannah's grandparents had been divorced when I'd first started coming to the ranch. Lily had lived in California while Connell had been right here. I didn't know what had happened to tear them apart or how they'd managed to come back together. Lily just showed up one day and hadn't left Connell's side since.

As a kid, I hadn't been able to grasp the magnitude of these events. Looking at them now, remembering Lily's absence from this table for a lot of years, I was starting to get it.

I leaned into Hannah, bumping her shoulder. "Your grandparents are a whole lot of good, aren't they?"

Her brow furrowed as her gaze slid to me. "What?"

"Them, together," I murmured. "It's not just good for them. It's the entire family, whole again. I feel it. Don't you?"

She rubbed her lips together and stared at me for so long I didn't think she'd respond. Then her gaze flicked to Lily and Connell. They were laughing, their hands joined on the table, their faces flushed with life and contentment.

"They are a whole lot of good," she agreed quietly. "That's what can happen with second chances. Fences mended, hearts repaired."

The double meaning was clear. She wasn't just talking about her grandparents.

"Funny, I don't remember you being particularly forgiving, sweetheart," I rumbled as close to her ear as I could get without my lips brushing her skin.

"Especially since I don't think I have any reason to be."

Her chair ground against the wood floor as she shoved back from the table with sudden force. Everyone stopped what they were doing, heads whipping in her direction.

She waved a dismissive hand. "Sorry. I'll be back. Excuse me."

Dinner went on, but Hannah didn't return until plates were being cleared. She immediately pitched in with the other Kelly kids while Jesse got the privilege of loading the dishwasher, which he did meticulously. Hannah tried to sneak a dish in herself, but he grabbed it from her, lining it up where he wanted it.

She ruffled his hair, and he promptly smoothed it out, grinning back at his aunt. It was cute. *They* were cute. I found myself chuckling as I observed them from the other side of the kitchen.

Caleb came to stand beside me, watching the scene. "Feels like old times, doesn't it?"

"It does. Strange how fast it happens, becoming part of the fabric of this town. Didn't think I'd fit here anymore."

He raised a brow, reminding me of his mother. "You think you fit now?"

I shook my shoulders and arms out, flexing my hands. "Feels like I could. The question is: do I want to? And that, I do not know."

"Hmmm. You ever find a place that fit you better?"

"That wasn't what I was looking for, Cay."

He made a rumbling sound and turned to me, his arms crossed over his thick chest. "And that wasn't what I asked."

The places I'd called home base over the years flashed across my brain like a slideshow: Chicago, Prague, New York, Seoul. Cities I'd liked, had spent months at a time, formed friendships, relationships, a life in, but I couldn't say any part of me missed them, and I'd sure as hell never stopped to wonder how I'd weave through those particular tapestries.

"No. Never found it," I admitted.

He clapped me on the shoulder. "That makes me sad for you, Rem. Maybe it's time."

I sucked in a deep breath, the scent of home filling my lungs from corner to corner. When I exhaled, it felt like losing something. "Maybe it is."

Chapter Eighteen

Hannah

MY WEEK OF AVOIDING Remington had come to an end the night at my parents' house. After that, he kept popping up everywhere I went. Had he not seemed as surprised as I was, I would have suspected he was following me. Our carts had collided in the grocery store. I'd almost run him over while he'd been crossing Main Street. He'd been walking out of the house as I'd climbed the porch steps at Sugar Rush for an afternoon caffeine fix.

Sugar Brush was a small town. Running into people was inevitable. But my run-ins with Remington had exceeded the norm. Tonight, it was happening again at Joy's Elbow Room, and I was beginning to think some nefarious force was pushing us to be at the same place at the same time.

Cormac was running late for our pool date, so I parked myself at the bar, sipping on a Shirley Temple. Running the length of the bar was a mirror, reflecting the action going on behind me, distorted and somewhat warped as it was.

I hadn't noticed the table for four when I'd arrived, but once I found the group in the mirror, I couldn't stop watching.

Tina, Teller, and her husband, Brady, were sharing a table with Remington. I couldn't quite read Remi's expression, but his folded arms and tilted body read like a man who would have rather been anywhere else.

Oh, if they were reciting poetry to him, I would need to be carted away since I'd be laughing too hard to stand. I was already snickering into my drink at the very idea.

"What's so funny, Banana?"

I grinned at my baby brother. For once, he was dressed in a T-shirt and jeans instead of his ubiquitous suit and actually looked his age.

I patted his scruffy cheeks. "You're late. I had to start the party without you."

He took a sip of my drink and smacked his lips. "Not spiked. Doesn't explain why you're sitting by yourself, cracking up like a lunatic."

I yanked my glass from his hand and slammed it on the bar. "Of course there's no alcohol, Maccie. I'm pretty damn insulted you had to check."

He grabbed the back of my neck, pulling me off my stool and into his side. "I'm just teasing you, Han. I know you're not drinking."

Alcohol and I didn't mix. Since it had led me to make destructive choices one too many times, I'd given it up before I was even legal to drink. I had plenty of vices and habits, but that wasn't one of them.

"I don't like that kind of teasing." I shrugged him off. "I'd ask for an apology, but I'll just kick your ass at the pool table instead."

Drink in hand, I led the way to the back of the bar, making sure to weave past Remi's table. As we drew near, Tina's voice rose above the music and din of conversation.

"His tender heir might bear his memory," she recited somberly, one hand raised in front of her, shaking with each word, "but thou, contracted to thine own bright eyes, feed'st thy light'st flame with self-substantial fuel…"

For one fleeting moment, I met Remi's panicked gaze, and I couldn't stop myself from barking out a laugh so loud everyone around us turned to look. Poor Tina lost her spot in the poem, her hand hanging impotently as she scanned the printout in her lap.

"What's happening?" Cormac muttered from behind me. "Why're Double T reciting Shakespeare? Is this hell?"

I lost it, cracking up so hard my brother had to take my drink from me so I wouldn't spill it. With the back of my shirt gripped in his fist, he guided me like a naughty puppy to the rear of the bar, away from Sugar Brush's version of the Globe Theatre. I could practically feel the eye daggers Tina and Teller were throwing at me and hid behind a post until I could get a hold of myself. Luckily, it was the middle of the week. Joy's wasn't packed, but Kayla from the grocery store and her boyfriend Brian were at the next pool table over, casting plenty of side-eyes my way.

Mac stared at me, the corner of his mouth hitched. "Something tells me you've been up to no good."

I swiped the tears from the corners of my eyes and grinned at him. "I may have implied Remi's a big fan of poetry. Tina and Teller apparently took that little tidbit and ran with it."

Hands on his hips, he shook his head at me. "I don't know what you're trying to do, but I can't in good conscience leave Remi alone with those two—not when you set him up like that."

"What?" I swiped my hair from my face and waved to Kayla. When she finally looked away, I turned back to my brother. "Come on, Maccie. If he didn't like the sonnets, he wouldn't be sitting with them. Besides, he's got good ol' Brady over there with him.

Surely his tales of glory on the football field have balanced out all the Shakespeare."

"Nope. Nothing you can say will convince me he's at that table by choice. I know a hostage when I see one." He straightened and ran his hand down his front, smoothing out his tee. "I'm going in."

Cormac was too nice for his own good. And *mine*. As kids, if I thought up a devious little prank and he found out, he'd always rat me out. Not because he thought it was wrong. It was because his empathy well was too deep to see someone even mildly uncomfortable.

I peeked around the column, displeased to find Cormac had extricated Remi. They were now at the bar together, ordering drinks. I was so busy watching them, I failed to notice Tina and Teller approaching until they were in front of me, looking pretty damn put out.

"You think you're so funny, don't you?" Teller hissed.

"Yeah." Tina stomped her foot. "You've been jealous of us since high school. Like we can help that we're prettier than you."

Teller raked her beady little eyes over me. "Maybe if you made an effort, you wouldn't be so bad. But then you'd be like other girls and little Miss Tomboy can't have that, can she?"

I looked down at my fitted black tank, jeans, and favorite cowboy boots. I'd showered and changed after work. Had even swiped on lip gloss and mascara.

"I thought I looked cute." I snapped my fingers. "Dammit. I'll have to try again next time."

These women were out of their minds if they thought I should get frilly to play a round of pool with my damn brother. Then again, I wasn't sure either of them would be caught dead outside without being fully made up. Lip gloss and mascara were so far below their bare minimum they couldn't even see it.

Tina stepped into my space, poking her finger at me. She was a good eight or nine inches shorter than me, so it lost some of its threat, but I sure didn't appreciate her aggression. If she didn't back her ass up, I would have no problem putting her in her place.

"You're a bitch, Hannah Kelly. Someone's going to teach you a lesson one of these days."

Teller grabbed Tina's bicep, pulling her back. "She's not worth it, T. She thinks she's funny, setting us up to make fools of ourselves, but she's the one who looks foolish."

I folded my arms over my chest. "If you're here expecting an apology, the possibility of that flew out the window when you called me a bitch. Why don't you move along? I'm not interested in reliving high school with you."

Teller's eyes narrowed on me, spite pinching her mouth into a pucker. "Tell Watt hi for me. Oh, that's right, he dumped your ass, didn't he?"

Tina snorted, her eyes raking over me. "No wonder he stepped out on her. Sleeping with her has to be like sleeping with a dude."

My mouth fell open as her words landed in my chest. Damn her for hitting me exactly where she knew it would hurt. I couldn't give a shit about her insulting my style, but I hadn't quite recovered from the way my ex had screwed me over, so this didn't roll off my back as easily as I wished it would have.

My fists balled at my sides, though I couldn't say what I'd planned to do with them since I didn't get the chance to figure it out.

"All right, all right." Remi slid in front of me, blocking me from view. "You said what you had to say. Time to move along."

Tina huffed. "I don't know why you're sticking up for her. She did this, you know."

Teller crowded Remi, poking her stubby finger around him. "You're a bitch, Hannah."

"You already said that," I replied.

A low, guttural squeal emanated from between her gritted teeth. "God, I'm gonna—"

A thick arm banded around her middle, dragging her backward. "That's enough, Tell." Her husband, Brady, held her firmly in front of him, a scowl crinkling his doughy face. "Let's go."

She tipped her head back, her painted lips pursed. "But, babe, Hannah—"

"Don't care, babe. You're not makin' a scene in the bar I frequent. Time to go home." He jerked his chin toward the other angry blonde. "Tina, you too. Out of here. *Now.*"

Brady had never been good for much, but he cleared Tina and Teller out of Joy's in less than thirty seconds. Only when they were out the door did Remi turn around to look me over. He reached out like he intended to run his hands down my arms, but I stepped away and swiveled my head, trying to spot Cormac.

"He had to leave."

I whipped around to face Remi again. "Mac left?"

"He did." He picked up a pool cue, passing it back and forth between his hands. "Got a call while we were at the bar ordering. Some big, important guest showed up at the resort a day early. He had to head back to work to deal with it. Told me to keep you company, so that's what I'm going to do."

"I"—could not believe my brother had ditched me without a goodbye—"think I'll head out too."

"Stay." He used the cue to block my path. "Let me beat you at least once."

"I see what you're doing. It's not going to work."

He cocked his head. "Isn't it?"

"Nope."

His mouth slid into a slow, easy grin. "I get it. No one likes to lose."

Damn him. He already had my number. There weren't many challenges I had the willpower to walk away from.

"Fine. You want me to sweep the floor with you; that's your decision." I popped my hip, tipping my head toward the table. "Rack 'em up, Town. Let's do this."

Chapter Nineteen

Remington

HANNAH INSISTED WE FLIP a coin for who took the first shot when I'd tried to be a gentleman and let her have it. No matter where I'd traveled, there always seemed to be a pool table, so I'd played a lot over the years. I wasn't a world champion by any means, but I held my own. Yet, despite what I'd said, I wasn't out to beat Hannah. Giving her the first shot had been my olive branch, which she'd rejected soundly.

Then she won the coin toss anyway, the goddamn menace.

"I can't believe you sicced Tina and Teller on me."

Her eyes flashed to me as she chalked her cue. "I don't know; it seemed like you were enjoying your time with them. Looked like you were on a double date."

"You believe I was there willingly?"

She smirked, the little shit. "I can't imagine any other reason you'd be sitting at a table with those three, listening to Tina perform Shakespeare."

"Too bad you missed Teller reciting Cummings."

Her brows rose. "Moving, was it?"

"Oh yeah." I tapped the table with my fist. "I came in for a drink. Maybe some conversation if anyone worth talking to was around.

Then those three showed up, sat at my table, and there was no escape—not until Cormac took pity on me."

Tina and Teller had been less than amused when he'd revealed Hannah had been joking about my love for poetry. Not that I had anything against it, but I'd never had the burning desire for it to be recited to me ad nauseam.

"My brother"—she shook her head—"barely remembers you, you know, so he doesn't hold a grudge."

I didn't need to point out she seemed to be the only one keeping hold of her grudge against me. She knew it as well as I did. But her family's anger was a decade old. Hers was a lot fresher, more painful. If she still needed to be mad at me, I'd let her use me as a target. I understood what it was like to carry a load of anger. If it didn't come out somewhere, it'd tear her apart, and I wasn't going to stand by and let that happen. I could withstand her anger when it manifested into poetry and potshots.

And the best fucking kiss of my life.

She leaned over the table, lining up her shot. Standing slightly behind her, I allowed myself a meandering look at her long, leanly muscled body. Legs that went on for days and days. An ass that filled out her jeans in all the right ways. A waist that curved in just enough for a pair of hands to fit on either side. Hannah was well made. Sturdy enough to face down stallions and Wyoming winters while painfully feminine in her little movements, her scent, sweet laughter, and all the details that made up the rest of her.

The luxurious, thick, shiny hair cascading down her back was a contrast to the simplicity of her style. She'd worn it down tonight, and my fingers twitched to trail through it, to bury themselves in the depths, to know if it felt as soft and silky as it looked.

She'd made the first shot and was lining up her second when she spoke. "I feel your eyes on my ass."

"Think I'd be insulting you if I didn't look. It's a mighty fine ass."

Her shot went wide. She whirled around, her cheeks flushed. "You did that on purpose."

I lifted a shoulder. "You brought up your ass. I just told you what I thought of it."

Hair whipping behind her back, she groaned. "Don't be cute, Remington. Unlike my brother, I can hold a grudge until the end of time."

"I thought we were past that."

"We were, until that kis—forget it. Just stop looking at my ass and take your turn." She stalked over to the high-top table we'd set our drinks on and took a long swallow of the bright red concoction she called a drink.

The next two shots were mine. I took my time with them, drawing out the game as long as I could. After this, I had no doubt Hannah would hightail it out of here, and I'd drive back to the house. To the quiet and solitude I didn't think I'd ever get used to again. Too many years at the center of the action had me seeking a piece of that. It was how I'd ended up at Joy's the last few nights. That, and I'd suspected I'd eventually run into Hannah again since our paths seemed to be on a collision course lately.

We traded places when I missed. I took a pull from my beer while Hannah bent over the table again, her ass angled away from me this time.

"When did you leave the ranch?" I asked.

She straightened, holding her cue in one hand. "A few years back. Maccie moved to one of the staff cabins when he came back from college, and Phe rented the apartment below the one that's now mine to be close to Sugar Rush. It was just me, Mom, and Dad for a while. I hadn't really considered moving, but Graham had told me it was time to go."

Surprise and mistrust tightened my gut. "What gave him the right to tell you that?"

The curve of her mouth was bitter, but her eyes turned wistful and distant. "You ever work with anyone day in, day out for years?"

A few faces ran through my mind, catching on one. Logan. He hadn't made it out of the crash that almost killed me.

Yeah, now wasn't the time to think about Logan. I'd save that for when I was trying to go to sleep and all I could do was stare at the ceiling, imagining his final minutes.

I cleared my throat, shaking off the memories. "I'd always end up in the same places with the same people."

"You bonded?"

"It wasn't an office situation where we sat around during our lunch breaks and shot the shit."

She cocked her head, waiting for me to answer her. I dug deep, thought about what a bond meant. I couldn't say I'd been friends with most of the journalists I'd spent time with, but there were shared experiences that had made us understand each other in a way outsiders never could.

I blew out a breath. "We bonded."

Her nod was decisive. "That was me and Graham. He rode with me to see my clients, helped me out when I needed it. That put us in my truck every day on long, open roads. We talked. A lot. Eventually, he knew me as well as my blood family. So, when he told me it was time to move on and give my parents the privacy they deserved after raising four and a half kids—you're the half, by the way—I listened. Besides, he'd been right. Lucky for me, the apartment above Phe's was put up for rent, so I snagged it and have been there ever since."

I swallowed a thick shard of rock. My father had never given me a lick of advice. I'd never given him the opportunity. For the first time since returning to Sugar Brush, a sense of loss crept in. Doubt over my choice to never look back dimmed my edges. The version of Graham Hannah spoke of was so foreign I couldn't even begin to fathom the kind of advice he would have given me if he'd had the chance. Would I have taken it? I couldn't say, and now, I'd never know.

Hannah released a light, airy giggle, bringing me out of my thoughts. "I don't want to even think about what my parents are doing with the house to themselves. One time, I showed up without calling first, and...well, let's just say those two crazy kids are still very into each other."

I had no choice but to laugh with her. "Good for them. Don't wanna think about it either, but I'm happy they have something rare like that."

"Rare is right." She emptied her glass and slammed it down on the table beside my beer. "Take your shot, Remington."

I grinned. "Every time you say my full name, I hear it as a cuss word."

"Good." She returned my grin. "That's my intention. But out of curiosity, which one?"

A laugh from deep in my chest shook my shoulders as I released it. I couldn't remember the last time I'd laughed so hard or loud. Maybe never. Hannah had a way of chipping away at me, cracking open parts I'd abandoned long ago.

"Starts with an *f*, sweetheart," I finally managed to say.

She giggled. "The right one, then." Then she reached for her glass, frowning when she found it empty, like she'd forgotten she'd drunk it all.

I nodded toward the full beer beside mine. "Take that one. It was meant for Cormac before he cut out early."

She yanked her hand away from the table like she'd touched something hot. "Oh no. I'm good. Thanks for the offer."

"Not a beer fan?"

"Nope. I prefer to get drunk on the sugar in my Shirleys."

"Ah. Not a drinker?"

"I'm not," she confirmed.

We kept talking and playing. I ordered her another Shirley Temple and drank Cormac's beer myself. I won the first game, but Hannah trounced me in the second. She was just as sore of a loser as she was a terrible, gloating winner, and both fucking delighted me.

I wasn't ready for the night to end, but she hung up her cue, stretching her arms over her head. Her jaw cracked, she yawned so wide.

"I'm going to hit the road."

"You look like you're slumping." I hung my cue next to hers on the wall rack and slipped my hands in my pockets. "I'll drive you home."

"That would be silly. It's a five-minute walk."

"Then I'll walk you home." She opened her mouth, no doubt to protest, but I held up a finger. "You can say no to me for most things, and I'll listen, but this is not one of them. I'm walking you home, Hannah."

"I wasn't going to say no."

I winged a brow. "Really?"

She chucked me under the chin with her knuckle. "Guess you'll never know, Remington."

I groaned, following behind her as she started for the door. "You're a menace. You know that?"

The sway she added to her hips was answer enough. She knew exactly what she was doing—and she was having fun doing it.

Once we were outside, I fell into step beside her. The sidewalks along Main Street were pretty empty, only illuminated by intermittent streetlamps. When we'd put a little distance between us and Joy's, our boots hitting pavement and Hannah's soft exhales became the only sounds I was aware of.

To my surprise, Hannah didn't seem in a big rush to get home. As we walked, my hand brushed against hers. She didn't pull away, so I let my pinkie slide over hers.

She turned her head, squinting at me. "Are you flirting with me right now?"

I curled my pinkie around hers. "I don't know what I'm doing."

She wiggled the finger I had hooked but kept it where it was. "Feels like you do."

"Guess I'm good at faking it. I haven't had a clue what I'm doing or where I'm going in a long while."

"Hmmm. It feels like wherever you're going, you're gonna take me with you." Soft, lilting words placed into the starry night by her sweet mouth had me reacting viscerally.

"Christ, Hannah." I took her hand in mine and dragged her under the awning of the building we were passing, cloaking us in shadows. "All I know is I can't stop thinking about the taste of you. It's wrong,

I know it. I need to walk you home and let it be. That would be smart."

Her face was mostly hidden in the dark, but I made out her long, slow blinks. "You told me no, Remi. You pushed me away."

"You were upset, sweetheart. I would've been taking advantage of you in that state if I had let it continue. I may not be perfect, but I'm not that kind of man."

Her soft exhale brushed my chin. "And you want to kiss me now?"

"Hell yes, I do." I brought my hand to her face, cupping her jaw. She leaned into my touch and shuffled closer, her breasts skimming my chest.

"Then what are you waiting for, Remingt—?"

I was on her before she could finish, wrapping my arm around her back and covering her mouth with mine. The rest of my name—her curse—became muffled as we collided.

That was what it was. A crash of two bodies, an explosion of tongues and lips, a detonation of hands feeling, clawing, clinging. We twisted until Hannah's back hit the building, her chest flush with mine. I dug my fingers into her hair and gripped the ass that had been driving me to distraction all night with my free hand.

Time and place ceased to matter. There was only the solid, sexy warmth of the woman in my arms, the feel of her hand snaking up the back of my shirt so we were skin to skin, her tongue tangling with mine. Her shape and height fit like we'd been formed for this—for each other.

She broke the kiss first, laughing breathlessly against my lips. "Come on, Remington. I have to get home."

My forehead rolled along hers. "Yeah? You're still tired?"

"Exhausted." She shoved me away but snagged my hand. "Walk me home like you promised."

"Fuck, Hannah," I gritted out. My zipper was making imprints on my dick as it tested the sturdiness of my jeans, but I managed to move along with her.

We got half a block before she whirled around, her palms flat on my chest, her eyes dancing over my face. In the circle of light from the streetlamp above us, I made out Hannah's swollen lips and tangled hair. Never considered I'd be seeing her this way, nor that I'd be the one responsible, but I was proud as hell and so turned on by her I couldn't think straight.

That was all right. In the next second, she pressed up on her toes and slotted her mouth with mine. This kiss was teasing, light and airy. A little nip and suck, her tongue dragging along my lower lip before she pulled it between hers. Then she was gone again. Her fingers still woven with mine, we continued toward her place.

"You're not going to regret this tomorrow, are you?" she asked.

"I'll have to see how tomorrow pans out. Are you going to go back to avoiding me?"

She shrugged. "I doubt it, but I'm somewhat unpredictable—even to myself." She turned to look at me. "I don't do well with rejection. It always feels bigger than it is."

"I was trying to do the right thing last week. You get that? It had nothing to do with whether I liked kissing you."

I stopped, yanking her against me. We were almost to her place, and as much as I wanted to, I wasn't going inside with her. But I wasn't done with her mouth yet. Not by a long shot.

Holding the base of her skull, I tipped her head back and lowered my mouth to hers. A high little whimper escaped her lips as we made contact. This kiss was slow, gentle, stretching the time we had out in long strokes of my tongue over hers. Little by little, she melted like wax, draping her body against mine.

That hand of hers snuck up the back of my shirt again, and her fingertips dragged along my spine. Up and down, up and down, sinking me into this moment with her. In the recesses of my thoughts, I remembered why we shouldn't have been doing this, but everything about having Hannah in my arms, our mouths joined, felt too right to care.

Then her hips rocked against me, and I forgot everything, even my fucking name. My dick was angry, hard, wanting inside her, to be touched by her, any of her attention. All she'd given was a little friction. And dear god, I was on edge.

Her lips curved into a smile against mine. "We're probably on every business owner's security cam right now."

I growled, pulling my face away from hers. "Damn this town for finally becoming high tech."

She snorted a laugh and slowly slid her hand out from under my tee. "I think you were walking me home."

"That's right. Let's do that."

I shook my hand free so I could wrap my arm around her waist and tuck her into my side. Now that the thought of someone seeing her, watching her, had been put into my head, I was pissed, mostly at myself. For not considering anything like that, but also at the imaginary prying eyes who'd be playing back the footage.

We arrived at her place in no time, and Hannah once again twisted in my arms. Reaching up, she cupped my face in both hands, her eyes dancing between mine, only visible under her porch light.

They came to a standstill, gazing directly at me, and I braced myself for what she had to say. I had no idea what was going on in this girl's mind. To be honest, her unpredictability was part of her appeal. She kept me on my toes.

"I had a good night with you," she finally said.

"I did too." I gripped her waist, stroking my thumbs against the skin just above the waistband of her jeans. "Great night."

"I want to invite you in, but I'm not going to."

I shook my head. "I wouldn't take that invitation."

Hannah dimmed in an instant. Like someone had taken a vacuum and sucked all the light from her.

"Oh. Okay." She tried to turn, but I wasn't letting go. Not yet.

"I want to. You have to feel how badly I want to." I pressed forward, prodding her belly with my cock. It was supposed to be a demonstration of my desire, but I couldn't stop the groan from traveling out of my chest or suppress my need to rock against her a couple more times. "You feel that, sweetheart? That's all for you."

Breath hitching, she looked at me through her lashes. "I feel it."

"But you and I just came to a truce tonight. So even if you would've invited me in, I would have been a gentleman and resisted because it's the right thing to do. I don't want you waking up tomorrow with regret. I don't want that for either of us."

Her eyes narrowed. "You assume I would have asked you to stay."

"I assume one time wouldn't be enough for either of us and we'd fuck until we both passed out. That's all I assume, sweetheart."

Her puff of breath was warm and frustrated. "I've never fucked all night, but yeah, I think I probably would with you." She gave me a shove, which was becoming her signature, though this one had very little force behind it. "Well, you better get gone then."

I let go of her hip to tap my lip. "One more, then I'll get gone."

With a sigh, she rolled her eyes. "Oh, all right. If it'll get you leaving sooner."

Her lips were on mine in the next breath, her fingers tangling into the back of my overgrown hair, kissing me sweet. We took our time, exploring the feel of lips and skin that had been entirely foreign before tonight. As soon as things turned heated, we cut it off, both taking a step away at the same time.

I jerked my chin toward her steps. "Get in there. I'll wait here until I see your light flick on."

She retreated backward, her swollen lips hitching into a smirk. "Night, Remington."

I barked a laugh. "Glad I didn't kiss the sass out of you." I shooed her away. "Get out of here, Hannah Kelly."

With a laugh of her own, she ran up the steps and disappeared out of sight. I held my breath until light spilled from her apartment then started my walk back to Joy's. It wasn't nearly as interesting, but it was quiet, giving me the space to think. Too bad that was the last thing I wanted to do. Not right now, when I was feeling better than I had in a long while.

I didn't come out of that headspace until I reached my truck and noticed a slip of paper under my wiper. Grabbing it, I unfolded it and froze when I read the message someone had left behind.

Hannah Kelly is a slut. Stay away.

My head whipped around, searching for anyone who might've been watching, waiting for me to receive this, but there was no one nearby.

I crumpled the note in my fist, enraged anyone would think that about her, let alone leave me a message with these words on it. As if I'd heed this feeble fucking warning.

I felt it then. The walls of this town closing in around me, squeezing my shoulders tight. This was what I'd hated about living here. Everyone watching, thinking they knew other people's business when they had no clue what went on behind closed doors.

The old, familiar urge to run far licked at my heels, but I tamped it down.

This was one note. One jealous, idiotic person.

No one was going to force my hand.

I'd leave Sugar Brush when I was good and ready and not a second before.

Chapter Twenty

Hannah

MY MIND WAS ALREADY on my next stop as I packed up my tools. Today had been one of my busier days, but I only had one more client, then I could take a long, cold shower. The sun had been brutal, beating down like a hammer. My mother had instilled the importance of skincare from a young age, so I'd slathered on sunscreen every couple hours, but I was still soaked in sweat.

This job wasn't for the weak, but that was why I loved it. Not many things were better than spending my days taking care of horses, moving my body, and rarely having to sit behind a desk. If I had to work in an office—well, I'd probably be fired on my first day for spacing out. Luckily, I didn't have to worry about that.

I approached my truck, not noticing the flat tire until I was already upon it.

"Shit."

This wouldn't do. I had a spare, but driving on a spare wasn't ideal when my next job was forty-five miles down the road.

Circling the rear, I put my tool bag on the ground and went back to check out the tire, realizing the front one was flat too. A pit of dread swelled in my stomach as I bent down to look at it. There was no mistaking the wide, jagged puncture in the tread. I trailed around the truck to examine the other tires, swallowing down bile as I confirmed all four had been slashed in the same way.

I hadn't run over something sharp. Someone had done this on purpose.

Wind knocked out of me, I fell into my front seat, my legs dangling out the door. I needed to get to my next job. That wasn't a question. The "how" was what was stumping me. I'd call Cay or Mac, but they were both working. Phe was too. I also needed my truck towed. I couldn't exactly leave it at my client's ranch, and it wasn't drivable.

Calling a tow was my first step. Once that was arranged, I sucked it up and made another call.

"Hello?"

"Hey, Remi. It's Hannah."

"Hannah," he breathed, and my toes curled. He had a way with his mouth, and my name uttered from it sounded better than ever. "Good to hear from you. Been a while."

He wasn't pleased with me, and he had every right to be pissed. Since he'd walked me home from Joy's Elbow Room, I'd gone back to avoiding him. I hadn't wanted to, but being near him, I would've had to fight myself from jumping into his arms—and that was exactly why I'd kept my distance. The fact remained, getting close to Remi wasn't going to end well for me. He wasn't here for long, and I knew myself well enough to predict how this would go. I'd get attached like always, and he'd break my heart in one way or another.

"I hate to call you like this, but I need help. Are you busy?" I asked.

"Not with anything I can't put off 'til later. What do you need?"

I rolled my eyes skyward. This man, contrary to what I'd originally thought of him, was a good one. I'd known before I'd called he would drop what he was doing to help me. And that was why I had to say away. He might not have wanted to admit it, but he was Graham's son, and the apple didn't fall far from the tree.

Before I could finish telling him where I was, he was already on the move, coming for me.

All I could do was brace myself and wait.

Remi was spitting mad. He kicked the hell out of my tires, spewing a litany of curses as he paced.

"Who the hell did this?" he snapped. "Where's the owner of this place?"

"I don't know, and the owners are working."

Hands on his hips, he scowled at me. And goddamn if he didn't look good in a ball cap, maroon T-shirt with the sleeves rolled all the way up, and a pair of faded blue jeans. When my eyes reached his face again after checking him out, his scowl deepened.

"Hannah," he growled, "you don't seem to be taking this seriously. What the hell?"

I shrugged. "It's a pain in the ass, but I don't have time to throw a hissy fit over it. I need to load my tools in your truck and get to my next job." Tipping my chin toward the house, I went on. "I talked to Jacob, the owner of this property while waiting for you to get here. He's going to check his cameras but said he'd be surprised if anything was picked up with where I'd parked."

"Don't have time for a hissy fit," he muttered, pacing in tight circles next to my broken-down truck. "Dammit, Hannah. Who did this? An angry ex? Someone else?"

"Don't have any angry exes." I bent to grab my tool bag and started toward Remi's truck, his heavy footsteps nipping at my heels. "If I had to guess, I'd say it was Cleve. He's been trying to poach my clients. Jacob told me he'd been out here last week, looking for work, and that he'd informed him I'd be out this week to do the job. Cleve was well aware I'd be here."

As soon as I put my bag in the bed of his truck, he gripped my bicep and whirled me to face him.

"Why do you sound so nonchalant about this?" he demanded.

"Oh, I'm mad, Remington, but I don't have time to dwell on it. I'm already late for my next client—which is where I need to keep my focus. Once I'm done, I'm gonna kick Cleve's ass."

His glare could've set me on fire; it was so hot. "You're not kicking anyone's ass. We're going to the police."

"Of course." I looked down at his hand. "Can you let me go? I can drive if you want."

His grip loosened, and he slid his hand down my arm all the way to my fingertips. He held them, rubbing his thumb over my knuckles as he frowned at me. The two actions were so incongruous I almost laughed but held it in. I didn't think Remi would appreciate it very much.

"You're not driving." He pulled me toward the passenger side and yanked open the door. "Get in, Hannah."

I must've been too slow to comply because he grabbed me around the waist and lifted me clear off the ground, plopping me in the seat. Then he leaned in, stretching the seat belt across my body, and latched the buckle. His head was right at my chest. Without thinking, I stroked my fingers along his nape, where it met his T-shirt and ventured just beneath it.

He turned, his eyes landing square on mine. "What are you do-ing?"

"Saying hi to you. Maybe trying to calm you down."

"You think touching me is going to calm me down?"

I dug my teeth into my bottom lip, nervous at how fiercely his brow dipped over his stormy eyes.

"Let me roll with this, Rem. I need to work right now. When I'm done, I'll deal with it all."

"Including me?"

I nodded once, letting my hand glide out of his shirt, down his neck, to his chest.

"Yes. Including you."

The starbursts around Remi's eyes had returned, but he wasn't grinning at me. He was laughing his ass off at the miniature pony poking me in the back of my head with her muzzle while I was trying to trim her sister's hooves.

I snarled at him, my upper lip curling. "You're supposed to be assisting me."

He held up the rope I'd given him, keeping Penny in place. "I am. You didn't tell me I'd have to keep the other ponies away."

Reaching behind me, I patted Nickel's flank. "Get on, girl. It's not your turn yet."

She chuffed, hot air blowing my ponytail around, but she did not budge, leaning her body against mine.

Normally, the owners or a caretaker helped me while I was trimming, but that wasn't happening today. It was my fault for agreeing to come while the owners were on vacation and their teenage son had been left in charge. He was too busy playing video games to get his lazy butt out here, and Remi was too busy laughing to be much use.

To be fair, the ponies were tiny, ornery, and adorable. If I didn't have one leaning her entire body weight on me while I was trying to tend to her sister, I would've been laughing too.

"Don't think she's listening," Remi remarked.

"Nope. Nickel does what she wants."

It didn't take me long to take care of the ponies' hooves. I got through all four and their two mini-donkey friends as quickly and efficiently as I could. My efficiency had been tested by Nickel needing snuggles, but it was an inconvenience I didn't mind too much.

The donkeys were enamored with Remi. At one point, they tag-teamed him, both nipping at his jeans and nuzzling his stomach and back. He took it well, letting them do their donkey thing and giving them both plenty of head scratches.

I almost wished he wasn't such a natural with the animals. It only made him more attractive, which was annoying. If he'd hated the horses or had been bothered by the donkeys, it would have made the pull I felt toward him much easier to resist.

Damn him.

He was sitting in the dirt now, Calliope's head in his lap, scratching behind her ear. His lips were moving as he spoke to her quietly. Once I packed my tools away, I crouched next to them.

"What're you guys talking about?"

He grinned at me. "That's between us."

"Oh, I see. First you steal my pal then you keep secrets with her? This is the last time I bring you on a job with me, Remington."

He cocked his head. "Seems to me I brought you."

"I've already got Cleve trying to hijack my jobs. I don't need you doing it too." I gave Calliope's dusty flank a good pat and rose to my feet. "I'm ready to hit the road when you are."

I started for the truck, and it didn't take long before Remi's hurried footsteps sounded out from behind me. He caught me easily, hooking me by the belt loop.

"You need to take this seriously, Hannah. You can't let this slide."

"I'm not letting anything slide." We reached the truck, and I turned to face him. "I'm going to have to pay for four new tires and a tow truck, and that pisses me right off. If Cleve pulled this nonsense, he's going to be the one who fixes it."

He stepped into me, and there was nowhere for me to go once my ass hit the truck. Taking his ball cap off, he spun it around to put it back on backward, and my breath lodged in my throat.

I'd already been through a lot. I could not handle Remington Town with his sleeves rolled up and a backward baseball cap. It was too much. Too damn much.

Then he braced his arm beside my head, taking his torture farther, and brought his face a couple inches from mine. His glare could have melted glaciers.

Never one to back down, I tipped my chin up. "I like your starbursts better than this frown." I pressed my lips against his down-turned mouth, and he stilled, neither responding nor pulling away. "Kiss me back, Remington."

He took my chin in his hand, keeping me still. "As sweet as your lips are, I'm not going to be distracted. What someone did to your truck is a whole hell of a lot more than nonsense. It's malicious and violent. I can't stand the idea of anyone coming near you or your property with the intent to destroy, and I won't be idle while that happens. I'm taking you to the station to report this. If the cops won't deal with it—"

I kissed him again, hard and fast, and all I got was another glare. "I never said I wasn't going to report it."

His exhale was heavy and warm as his forehead fell to roll over mine. "That's right. You didn't."

"Remington," I whispered. "Let's go. It's hot, I'm tired, and I want to get this over with."

He stayed like that for another minute, his sweat mingling with mine. It wasn't gross, though. It was him, and the closeness felt too good to complain about.

He took my hand in his and stepped back, giving me a thorough once-over. "All right, sweetheart. Let's get you cooled down and taken care of."

The drive back to town was pretty quiet. But for every one of those long miles, Remi kept hold of my hand with the air blasting.

Cooled down and taken care of. Exactly as he promised.

Chapter Twenty-one

Remington

IT WAS DÉJÀ VU seeing Hannah walk out of the police station. She hadn't let me go inside with her, but that hadn't been a surprise. Frustrating fucking woman. Her streak of independence was a mile wide, and as much as I liked the hell out of her confidence, in this situation, I would have appreciated her letting me in. Leaning on me a little. 'Cause seeing those slashed tires had carved a deep pit of uselessness in my gut, and I needed to feel useful right now.

She walked up to me, her tired eyes darting between mine. "You waited."

"Where else would I be?"

"Back home, so you don't have to deal with any of this."

"Nah, the house is too quiet, and I don't mind dealing with your complications. Especially when it means keeping you safe." I nodded toward the station. "They have anything helpful to say?"

She shrugged, looking exhausted. "Same as last time. They'll talk to him, check out Jacob's security footage. I don't know if anything'll come of it. We'll have to wait and see."

That answer wasn't even slightly good enough. I wasn't sure how long I'd be able to wait and see, but for now, I was willing to drop it. Hannah didn't look like she could deal with much more, and I wasn't about to be the one to pile more burden on.

I took her hand in mine and squeezed. "Let's get you home."

She arched a brow. "You're coming with me?"

"You surprised?"

She sighed a little laugh. "No. Not really." We started toward her place, leaving my truck parked along the curb. "You know, I was doing a really good job keeping away from you."

That that was exactly what she'd been doing hadn't escaped me, but I couldn't put my finger on the why. We'd called a truce, had come to an understanding. And I knew I wasn't the only one feeling the pull between us.

"You were. Why is that?" I asked.

"I don't think we should get mixed up."

I held up our joined hands, scoffing. "I think we already are."

"Yeah," she sighed. "Seems like it."

When we got to her place, I didn't stop at the bottom of her steps like I had the times before, and she didn't question me following her. Once she unlocked the door, she opened it wide, inviting me in without saying the words.

Inside, Hannah bent down to unlace her boots, and I looked around. Her living room and kitchen were one cozy room. The furniture looked comfortable and lived in. Framed Wyoming landscape photos made up the art on the walls. Long velvet curtains flanked the tall windows, and matching pillows rested in the corners of the sofa. The kitchen took up one wall with aged white cabinets, a stove and refrigerator. A small, two-seater table divided the spaces.

It was nicely decorated. Anyone would feel at ease here. But it wasn't Hannah. She didn't belong in a small apartment. She needed space. A place to run, to have horses of her own, to spread out and be free. This apartment didn't suit her.

Hannah had grown up on the largest ranch in this part of Wyoming, surrounded by animals and acreage. That was the kind of place where she belonged.

"It's small," I said.

"Is it?" She straightened and looked around. Like she hadn't noticed the size before now. "Guess it is."

"No yard."

"Nope." She pointed to my shoes. "If you're staying, take those off please."

"I'm staying."

Her gaze flicked to mine. "Good."

While I was kicking off my boots, she sauntered away from me, peeling her tank top over her head. Tossing it behind her, she continued toward a doorway at the other side of the room.

Hooking her fingers in the waistband of her jeans, she pushed them down her hips and wiggled them off her legs, discarding them just as carelessly, leaving her in black cotton underwear and a black sports bra.

"What're you doing?" I gruffed.

She glanced at me over her shoulder. "Taking a shower. My skin's like a salt lick. Isn't yours?"

I got caught on the long line of her spine as she moved away from me and the round curves of her ass cheeks peeking from the sides of her underwear. It was the shower turning on that brought me out of my stupor and the realization that I'd been given an offer to join her dawned.

I followed her, shedding my clothes on the way. She'd left the bathroom door open, confirming I was welcome. Kicking off my briefs, I approached the shower curtain and peeled it back. Hannah was under the spray, facing me. Her eyes flared for a heartbeat before she stepped back, giving me space.

I took it without hesitation, climbing into the small tub with her.

"Hey," she murmured.

I took her by the waist, gently pulling her toward me. "Hey."

Rivulets streamed down her face, gathering in the hollows of her collarbone. Her small breasts, capped in tight cherry nipples, grazed my chest, and her skin was warm and smooth under my palm.

"Hey," she repeated, barely a whisper.

"Can I wash your hair?" I asked.

Her brows popped. "You want to?"

"I do." I smoothed my palm from the top of her forehead, over her crown, to the base of her skull. "Prettiest hair I've ever seen."

Her lips parted before she nodded. "Okay. If you really want to."

"Told you I did, Han."

I grabbed her shampoo, poured it into my hand, and slowly worked it into her hair. Eyes fluttering closed, she released a long breath and leaned into me. I took my time, massaging her scalp as I lathered her hair. With each pass of my fingers, the tension in her expression eased. I watched her, taken by the droplets of water caught in her feathery lashes and the single drop caught above the upturned bow of her lips.

I'd seen a lot. More than my fair share, truly. But without a doubt, I'd never seen anything as beautiful or wondrous as fierce and feisty Hannah Kelly giving herself over to me, even if it was temporary. No matter where I went or what I saw after this, I'd hold this image of her tight in my mind.

She rinsed the shampoo from her hair, and I repeated the same process with her conditioner. Taking my time, stretching it out as long as I could. By the time I was done, she was loose and pliant, her head on my shoulder, arms draped around my waist. And throughout it all, she'd turn her head every once in a while, pressing her lips to my skin.

"This is really nice, Rem," she murmured.

"Anytime," I promised, meaning it down to my depths. I'd fly from the other side of the world if she asked me to do this all over again with her.

She shuffled closer, her arms tightening. I dipped my head down to rub my cheek against hers. Pressed against her, I couldn't miss the tremble that quaked her body.

"You doing okay, sweetheart?"

A sniffle followed by a nod. "I think it's hitting me now. Someone really wants me to fail, huh?"

"Doesn't matter what they want. It's not going to happen."

She tucked her face into the side of my throat. "I really don't want to deal with this, Rem. Not on top of everything else."

"You don't have to. I'll take over. If I need to, I'll bring your family in. But you don't need to worry about it. I have the room and time to take it on for you. Will you let me do that?"

"I don't know. I don't want to get used to you."

Her admission struck me in the gut, but she had every right to that feeling. I couldn't give her any assurance. My plans were so up in the air, my next step was a mystery to me. But damn, I wished I could be the person Hannah could count on to be there when she needed someone to lean on.

I only had the present, and that was what I gave her.

"All I'm asking is for you to let me take this on. You can do that for me, right, sweetheart? Give it over."

I didn't get the response I was looking for, but I forgot all about it when Hannah lifted her head and pressed her lips to mine. She went searching for something, licking at the seam of my lips like a test. I let her in, gathered her tight, and soaked her up.

A naked, wet Hannah Kelly was in my arms, kissing the hell out of me.

She'd gone through a hell of a day, so I'd set aside our circumstances—naked, wet, close—to take care of her needs. I'd made my dick shut up and cut off my desire for this woman so I could focus on her and pull her through her troubles. But the meeting of her tongue against mine sparked me awake and every nerve in my body was aware of every inch of hers.

Whirling around, she shut off the water, and I followed her out of the shower, holding her hips and kissing the back of her neck and shoulders. Shuddering, she paused her movements and reached up to grip my nape.

"Oh god," she moaned. "Look at us. I can't—Remi, I can't..."

Through the fog, our distorted image reflected back at us in the mirror. Me behind her, one hand braced on her hip, the other traveling up her ribs to cup her breast. Her skin was like peaches and cream, soft and flawless. Mine was brown from too much time in the sun without concern for sunscreen.

I rocked against her, my dick seeking her heat and finding it between the valley of her round ass. Her lips parted on another moan, and her head lolled on my shoulder.

"Remi, dammit," she uttered. "I wasn't gonna like you."

I grinned against her wet hair as I passed my thumb over her nipple. "Does that mean you do?"

At her pause, I searched for her face in the mirror. She looked pissed.

"Tell me, sweetheart," I ordered lowly. "Tell me what you mean."

She shook her head, her spine arching as she sought me out the same way I had her. "I don't know, but I need you to fuck me."

"Christ, Hannah, you have no idea how badly I want to give in to you."

She tipped her head to the side, bringing her lips to my throat. That was all the warning I got before her teeth sank in, biting down so firmly my eyes rolled back. Then she let me go and dragged her tongue along my stinging skin.

"Give in then," she rasped, severing the last of my self-control.

My palm moved to her throat, cupping her with enough pressure to get her attention. Our eyes met in the mirror and became locked together in the heat passing between us. She saw me. Saw what I was feeling. And she did not flinch.

I tapped her fluttering pulse and lowered my mouth to her ear.

"Remember, baby, you asked for this."

On her gasp, I pounced.

Chapter Twenty-two

Hannah

REMINGTON TOWN TOSSED ME onto my bed like a sack of potatoes, and I'd never been so turned on in my life. Then he wrapped his fingers around my ankles and yanked me to the edge of the mattress without an ounce of tenderness—exactly what I needed.

Dropping to his knees, he pried my willing thighs open, uttering curses when I was all spread out before him, bare and slick with desire. I pushed up on my elbows to watch him, but he only had eyes for my pussy.

"What do you think?" I asked, breathless. "Like what you see, Remington?"

He cursed again and dipped to bite my inner knee. "You're a goddamn menace, Hannah. I'm going to eat every last drop of you."

"Oh god." My hips rose, seeking him out. "Do it. Touch me, fuck me, do something before I get mad at you."

He clamped down a little harder on the meat of my thigh, sending electric shocks through my body. It was a struggle holding myself up on my elbows when my bones were melting, but I had to see him, to watch him work.

Against my live-wire skin, he growled at me. "You're gonna get what I give you. That might be a spanking, or it might be getting your pussy licked." His eyes found mine from between my legs, and damn, did he look good there. "Are you going to be a good girl for me, Hannah? Are you even capable of that?"

"What if I'm not?" I panted. "What if I can't help being bad?"

He dragged his thumbs over my lower lips, hovering right above my clit. "Either way, I'm going to get my mouth on this pussy and my cock inside you. How soon that happens depends on you. Now, let me ask you again, are you going to be a good girl for me?"

I nodded frantically. "I'll try."

The corner of his mouth hitched as he lowered his head, getting closer to where I needed him. "Not gonna promise me?"

"I can't promise not to be bad. Not until I know how well you can make me come. If you do that right, I'll be anything you want me to be."

He leaned in, swiping his tongue along my seam. "Mmm...you are something else, sweetheart."

"You like me," I accused.

He held my gaze for a long beat. "Every bit of you."

There was no more talking from either of us after that. Holding my legs open with both hands, Remi buried his face between them. I was so turned on it didn't take much for me to start writhing under his ministrations.

I fell back on the bed, my eyes slammed shut, closing out everything but his tongue laving my flesh. He was unhurried and precise, lapping at every solitary inch. When he got to my aching clit, he did some kind of magic with his tongue, pressing and wrapping around it. My hips launched off the bed, and my hands shot into his hair to hold him there.

Exactly there.

That spot he'd found like instinct had led him to it.

I cried his name, cried for mercy, begged for him to never stop. If he did, I would die; that was how dire the situation was in my pleasure-addled mind.

My ecstasy crested, careening into an orgasm to end all others. Belly so tight, it was unbearable until I unraveled, loose and free-falling. My grip stayed on his hair, needing to tether myself to something real and tangible when everything else had become blurred and ethereal.

"Rem, oh my god, Rem. I can't, I won't…" My head thrashed as he continued with his evil plans to rob me of my brain, my will, my entire body. It evaporated with each lash of his tongue. Then he had the audacity to slide a thick finger inside me as if I wasn't already delirious. "Evil," I panted.

He hummed and licked, plunged and curled his finger.

I asked for more, or maybe I thought it and he read my mind. Either way, he added another finger and drove deep. So deep my legs vibrated and toes curled. Pleasure leaked from my pores. It was never-ending as he pressed on a spot in my inner walls and sucked on my clit. My muscles quaked and bones danced. Skin on fire, nerves alight. Too much. Not enough. I needed… I needed…

"Remi, I need you inside me." The realization poured out of me in an almost panicked shout. I had to have this man in me, and there was not a second to lose.

He must have felt it too. One moment, he was on the floor, and the next, he'd shoved me up on the mattress and positioned to kneeling between my legs. I reached blindly for the condoms in my bedside table, but he took over, pulling out a foil packet and making quick work of sheathing himself.

Then he had my thighs open and pushed toward my chest, his thick cock pointing right where I wanted him to be. His eyes met mine, a question in them.

I nodded vigorously. "Yes. Please, yes."

Wrapping his fingers around his length, he guided himself to my entrance. Despite the two orgasms he'd given me, I was shaking with need. There was no relief as his blunt tip breached my entrance, marking the final moment of Remi being careful with me.

"Goddammit, Hannah," he growled, driving into me in one smooth, hard thrust. He held himself there, nearly at the end of me. "Fuck."

His fingers dug into the back of my thighs, and his eyes, full of anger and accusation, latched on to mine.

"What?" I cried, desperate for him to move, though I was still trying to adjust to the way he'd filled me to the brim and stretched me to capacity.

"You know what." His damnable hips pulled out only to plunge forward, lodging himself in the spot he'd now claimed at his. "You feel that too."

"I feel it too," I agreed. "Give me more of it. All of it."

He lowered his face, the tip of his nose grazing mine. "Remember you asked for this."

It was the only warning I got before he let loose. Scooping up my ass, he elevated my hips, angling me so he could fuck me into the mattress. Powerful thrust after powerful thrust, he took my breath away. I was at his mercy, unable to respond to his ruthless pounding.

It was fast, harsh, frenzied. I clawed at his shoulders, nipped at his sweaty throat, licked his fluttering pulse. Remi cursed me over and over, and I kissed him just as many times.

Even though I had him, I craved him. When he hit the end of me, I wanted him deeper. He wrecked me, and all I could think about was putting myself back together so he could do it again.

"Hannah," he gritted between clenched teeth. "Oh god, my god, Hannah."

His wet lips found mine in a sloppy, needy kiss as he slid one hand from beneath me to glide over my torso. His palm was hot and rough as it moved up my ribs to my breast before pausing at my throat. I moaned, and his fingers flexed around the vibrations.

My brain tried to stutter on why Remi had to be the one to bring me here—to a place I'd never been. Why was this man, who I'd only just come around to liking, capable of giving me what I needed, like he'd studied a manual on my inner workings? Why was I having the most carnal sexual encounter of my life with a man who wasn't sticking around?

Then he found my clit with the pad of his finger, and all my questions washed away with a wave of pleasure.

We rode it together, kissing and clawing. My leg hooked around his back, his hand around my throat, our eyes locked, and I couldn't look away. It was too intense. Too much for the first time. Maybe for the thousandth time. But Remi had me in every sense. I was caught up in him, in how his body made mine feel, in his weight on top of me, his breath mingling with mine every time he made me gasp with wild, reckless abandon.

I came in an explosion of heat and desire, and still, he fucked me. That finger on my clit was as determined as the thick cock planted in my belly. His hand on my ass squeezed tight, teetering on too much without crossing the line. Nips at my lips and jaw and throat were soothed with wet kisses.

He never relented, driving into me with a force that had me bracing my palms against the headboard above me. And dammit if I didn't love every brutal second of it. It hurt—in the best way possible. The kind of pain that made me remember I was alive and renewed the blood pumping through my veins.

Through all this, there wasn't even a heartbeat where I wasn't aware Remi was the man giving me this. And when I looked at him, watched him watching *me*, I knew he felt the same. What we'd discovered tonight was strictly ours.

That made it easy to let go. To let this happen, consequences be damned. I lost count of my orgasms and the time. This haze we were trapped in made the rest of the world far away.

"Hannah, you're killing me." Remi shook his head, sweat raining from his forehead onto my chest and lips. He dragged his fingers through the salty drops and over my lips. "I want to come on you. Can I?"

"Please," I whined, frantic for something I hadn't known I wanted until now. "Do it. I need it."

He pulled out of me, and I mourned the fullness he'd given me, but not for long. Ridding himself of the condom, he moved to straddle my middle, placing his knees on either side of me. I plumped my breasts, giving him a target. With a harsh groan, he jerked his red, angry cock in his fist. I was enthralled. His stomach rippled. The corded muscles in his thighs clenched. I held on to his thrusting hips and wound my hands around to his ass.

"Give it to me, Rem." My neck arched as I moaned, utterly breathless with anticipation.

"Here you go. All for you."

His ass flexed in my hold as he stilled, his head thrown back in agony. Hot spurts landed on me, dotting my breasts and chin. There was so much of it, thick and heavy, running in streams to my throat and collarbone, and I loved every ounce of it.

"Yes," I whispered. "Exactly that."

His head hung low, and under heavy lids, he surveyed the masterpiece he'd painted on me.

Brow crinkling, his eyelids fluttered. "Jesus, Hannah, if you could see what I see."

I slid my palms from his ass to his front, smoothing over his hips and stomach. "If *you* could see what *I* see."

With a shake of his head, he fell forward, bracing most of his weight on his forearms. Our chests pressed together, making us both messy, but Remi didn't acknowledge it. He didn't say anything, in fact. Instead, he kissed me, giving me long, lingering licks as he stroked my hair from my face. After everything, it was incongruously sweet, and I melted into it.

Eventually, our kissing slowed, and we rolled to our sides, still wrapped in each other. Our lips made light passes here and there, and I let my fingers trail down his spine as he held me close, his palm on my backside.

"I should take another shower," I murmured.

"I should join you."

"Probably."

"This might start all over again."

I pulled back, blinking at him. "Would that be a problem?"

His mouth hitched. "Only if it's a problem for you."

I pressed my thighs together, finding tenderness but no pain. "Not a problem at all, Remington."

He laughed against my lips. "Absolute menace."

At first, I didn't understand why I had woken up. My room was pitch dark, and my glowing clock read 3:17 a.m. This was sleep time. But movement beside me put me on red alert.

Remington. That's Remington.

I turned my head, seeking him out in the dark. He was asleep on his back, his breath coming out in sharp bursts, his head thrashing back and forth. Fists bunched the sheet at his chest, and his legs were drawn up, bent at the knee.

For a few seconds, all I could do was watch him struggle. Then my brain kicked in. He was having a nightmare, and from the looks of it, it was torturous.

I reached out, putting my hand over his fist. "Remi," I whispered. "Wake up, Rem. Wake up."

His head whipped in my direction, but his eyes remained shut. His face was warped with pain, pulled down at the corners, slashed with lines on the planes.

I rolled toward him, throwing my arm across his chest. "Remi," I said closer to his ear. Not loud, but more than a whisper. "Wake up, honey. It's just a dream. I'm here with you."

Without warning, his eyes sprung open, wild and frantic. They bounced over my face and to the ceiling as if he was placing himself.

"It's okay," I soothed. "You were having a nightmare, but you're okay."

His eyes returned to me, staring for several pounding heartbeats before his breath released in a heavy whoosh.

"Hannah," he rasped. "I'm—what—"

"You're okay." I brought my hand to his face, surprised to find wetness on his cheeks. If I tasted it, I knew it would be salty. Whatever he'd been dreaming about had made him cry in his sleep. A little piece of my heart broke, and the caretaker in me sprung to life. I scooted over, pressing my body against his. "Look at me, Remi. You're okay. You're here with me. Everything is fine."

"I'm here with you," he repeated. "I was back there, I think, in the car. This time, I saw it coming. I tried to stop it, but I was moving through mud. Slow motion. Nothing I could do, but I saw it coming. I knew it was going to happen. Everyone else...they were singing along to the radio. And I think—"

I shut down my emotions, swallowing the lump in my throat. It wasn't my turn to be upset, even though hearing him talk about the accident that had almost killed him made my heart race with panic.

"What do you think, Rem?" I asked.

"I think that really happened. I was dreaming of a memory." He took my hand from his face and held it on his chest. "We were singing together. Having a minute of happiness in between all the stress and horror of working in the field. Then...nothing. We were blown up. Two of us died singing."

"Maybe they really didn't see it coming. Maybe their last memories were the happiness you were feeling."

He nodded slowly. "God, I hope so, but I don't know. I don't know..."

"Then hang on to that hope, baby." I pressed soft kisses to his bicep and shoulder. "Keep it close. That's all you can do, right? Hope it didn't hurt and they didn't know. Hope they died singing."

"Yeah," he answered tightly. "Gotta have hope."

I kissed his overly warm skin again. "Have you been having nightmares often?"

Another heavy breath, then he rolled to his side and gathered me against him. "Since I was a kid. It's where I work out the things I'm not able to during the day. I had issues before I went abroad. I've seen a lot, Hannah. Heavy things most people would rather not know about. I carry them with me, even in my sleep."

"That makes sense." I leaned toward him, touching my lips to his. "Just so you know, if you want to work things out with me, you can. I'm strong enough to carry some of it. Or I can just hold you through it."

His eyes darted between mine, and I felt his breath hitch as he held it. Then, he nodded, letting it all go.

"I'll keep that in mind, sweetheart."

He didn't say anything else, but he kept his arms wrapped around me, and when he fell asleep, he was finally at peace.

I stayed up until sunrise, watching over him. When light slanted through the cracks in my blinds, I finally gave in and let sleep take me away.

Chapter Twenty-three

Remington

Least I could do after being a burden of a guest was have coffee waiting for Hannah when she woke up.

She padded out of her bedroom a quarter past nine, hair a mess, yawning, wearing an old flannel shirt that barely cleared the tops of her thighs, and I froze on her couch, too stupefied to spring into action.

"'Morning," she chirped sleepily. "You let me sleep in."

That got me moving. Crossing the small space, I took her by the shoulders and shifted her to the side so I could pour her cup.

"What do you take in your coffee?" I asked.

She snorted a laugh from behind me. "Did you just move me?"

I turned, mug in hand, eyes wide. "Uh...yeah. Guess I did."

She took the mug from me and set it on the counter. "This is too much commotion for me when I just woke up. Is this how you are every morning?"

"Uh, no. Not really."

Winding around me, she went to the sink, filled a pink plastic cup with water, and grabbed the pill bottle sitting next to it. Shaking one into her palm, she tossed it into her mouth and downed the entire cup of water, slamming it onto the counter. She wiped her mouth with the back of her hand, then laughed, finding me staring at her.

"Surely me taking my ADHD meds is not that interesting, Remington."

I rubbed my nape, off-kilter already. "I—feel like crap for keeping you up last night. I had big plans of making it up to you by fixing you coffee and taking you out for breakfast."

"You don't need to feel like crap." There wasn't much space in the kitchen, so it didn't take much for her to come to me and loop her arms loosely around my neck. "If I wake up at night, it takes me a while to fall back to sleep. Don't think for a second I minded being there for you. You don't need to make up for anything."

I winced. "No matter what you say, I don't like being the cause of you missing sleep. Glad you could catch up a little this morning."

"You were quiet as a mouse out here. I almost thought you went home."

"Nope. I wouldn't leave without saying something." I spread my fingers across her back and trailed down to her hips. "I called the station from your porch. They went out to see Cleve last night. He denies any involvement. Jacob's footage didn't pick anything up either."

She nodded. "That's what I expected. I appreciate you taking care of it for me, though. One less thing for me to think about."

"Told you I would," I reminded her.

Her pretty brown eyes softened on mine. "That's right. You did. Thank you for being a man of your word." Her lips grazed mine once then went in harder for a second time. "You know, I wouldn't object to being taken out for breakfast. But you should be aware if people see us out together, tongues will wag."

"You think I care what anyone in this town has to say?"

She lifted a shoulder. "Gossip has a way of filtering back to my family. You might care about that."

"And you imagine they'll have a problem with me treating you to breakfast?"

She speared her fingers into the back of my hair and shot me a little grin. "Okay, Remington. If you don't care, neither do I. Just thought I should give you fair warning."

I slid my hand down her back to cup her bottom, which was smooth and bare. Blood rushed due south to my groin, but I ignored it. I'd fucked Hannah six ways to Sunday last night, now was the time for me to be a gentleman.

"Noted." I gave her butt a light smack. "Why don't you get your pretty little ass dressed, sweetheart?"

"All right." Her fingers left my hair, and her palms came to rest on my chest. "I put a new toothbrush out for you in the bathroom. I had to choose between a red one and a blue one. I decided on red. Hope you like it."

I grinned at her, pleased as hell to experience Hannah Kelly in the morning. "Red's my color. You chose well."

"Good." Teeth digging into her bottom lip, she stepped away from me. "Give me ten minutes. No—fifteen. You wrecked my hair last night. I have to deal with the consequences."

She whirled away, and it took all my willpower not to follow her to her bedroom.

Saturday mornings, half the town of Sugar Brush converged at Grey's Diner, and for good reason. The pancakes were steaming, and the bacon was crispy. I had early memories of coming here with both my parents, back before life went to hell. And later, memories of accompanying the Kellys here for breakfast, and *later* later, when I was in high school hanging here with Caleb and our friends after Friday night football games.

Even with how busy it was, old man Grey ran a tight, efficient ship. We were led to a booth after waiting no more than five minutes. Along the way to our table, Hannah was stopped several times to greet neighbors and people who knew her family. I received nods and some looks of wariness, but I got that. I was somewhat of a stranger to this town now.

We finally slid into a two-seater, and though there were plenty of eyes on us, my focus was on the woman across from me. She'd tamed her hair into some kind of complicated braid draping over one shoulder, a few tendrils grazing the sides of her face. Her cheeks were rosy, lips shiny, lashes dark and sooty. There were light freckles sprayed across the bridge of her nose, and one had gone rogue, landing just below the bottom corner of her mouth.

She looked up from her menu and caught me staring. "What? Why are you looking at me like that?"

"You're nice to look at," I said. "Pretty as hell."

The rose in her cheeks bloomed, but she quickly covered it up with a groan. "Aw, Remington, don't go soft on me now."

My brow winged. "It's Remington again? What'd I do to deserve that?"

She chuffed. "The googly eyes and compliment. I can't handle it."

"You think you don't deserve a compliment?"

"I don't know." She waved me off with a casual flick of her hand. "I'm not good at taking them, I guess. But...thank you. Sorry I'm such a weirdo."

"You're not a weirdo, but I do think you haven't been complimented enough in your life." I picked up my coffee-filled mug, warming my hands with it. "I'll make it my goal while I'm here to get you inoculated to hearing how utterly gorgeous you are."

She puffed up her cheeks and blew out a breath. "Please don't. If you do, I'll get used to it, and when you're gone, I'll be bereft of the praise you took with you. Let's just keep on how we were, all right? That was working fine."

There was more behind her request, but this wasn't the time or place to dig. Besides, she was right. Did I even have the right to dig when this was temporary?

"If that's how you want it," I conceded.

Our orders were taken, then one of our high school teachers stopped by the table to catch up. Mrs. Shepherd had taught art and photography. She'd lent me her Nikon, and through her, I'd caught the bug.

"I've followed your career, Remi," she said. "I have to admit, I tell anyone I can that I was your mentor at one time."

That made me smile, knowing I'd been remembered so fondly. "Well, that's the truth. Without you giving me your camera, I don't know where I'd be."

She was pleased with that and squeezed a promise from me to come visit her photography class once school started up again. When she left, Hannah raised an eyebrow.

"Won't you be gone by September?"

Sudden dread weighed down my gut. "I keep telling you I don't have plans. Well, I didn't until now. I said I'd be here, so I'll be here."

Her eyes narrowed. "Where did you live before your last trip overseas?"

"With an ex-girlfriend in Seattle. It was her place. When I left for my last job, that was that."

"Hmmm." She rested her chin on her fist, her gaze lively and inquisitive. "In all these years, where did you consider home?"

I shook my head. "I didn't have one. Not really. Seattle was off and on for two years, though a lot was off with me traveling. When I first left here, I ended up in New York. I crashed there, worked, took some classes. Then I met a freelance journalist headed to Central America, where a war was breaking out. He asked me to go with him to document it. I wasn't attached to New York. When it came down to it, I wasn't attached to anything, not even my own life, so I went."

"How old were you? Nineteen? Twenty?"

"Twenty," I confirmed. "Got my eyes opened real fast. This world we live in can be brutal. More than most of us lucky ones can even imagine."

Our food was delivered, bringing a pause to our conversation. Hannah had gotten a stack of chocolate chip pancakes while I'd ordered fried eggs, bacon, and biscuits with gravy. The way Hannah's face lit up as her food was placed in front of her made me wish I had my camera. Strange, considering I hadn't picked it up since the accident. But if anything deserved documentation, it was this, now.

She didn't dig in as quickly as I'd expected. After cutting a few pieces, she looked up at me. "I lied to you, you know."

With a mouthful of biscuit, I cocked my head in question.

"Well, it wasn't entirely a lie. I told you Graham was the one interested in your career, not me. I tried not to be, but...your work is too compelling. I have an alert set on my phone for when anything of yours is published." She wagged her fork over her pancakes. "You take photographs that make me feel things. It makes me wonder how you've witnessed what you have and are still able to get up, go out to breakfast, and live a normal life."

"First, I'm honored to know that despite your disdain for me, you appreciate my work."

She snorted. "Disdain is a little extreme."

I raised my brows. "Is it?"

"For the most part, I was indifferent to you until Graham was dying. Then...okay, yeah, you could say I felt disdain. But I'd already been following your career for several years by then. I'd gotten hooked on how you tell a visual story."

Warmth coated the inside of my chest. She may not have been good at taking compliments, but she was pretty brilliant at giving them. And I'd heard a lot of praise for my photos over the years. I'd won awards, had them hung in museums, but nothing had ever made me feel as tall or proud as I did now. Hannah Kelly wasn't easy to impress, and I'd done it without being aware. Now that I knew, every photo I took in the future would be done with her seeing it in my mind.

"I learned on the job," I explained. "A big lesson I took from the vets I met was I was there to work, to document, not be part of the narrative. The only way I was able to do my job was to learn how to detach myself through my camera lens. I met journalists who were so weighed down by what they'd seen they were never the same. The frequency of PTSD amongst the people who cover conflicts is really high."

"Not you though?"

I inhaled slowly, considering my answer. "I had a pretty volatile childhood, Hannah. I got good at compartmentalizing the bad stuff and locking it away. That helped me in being able to do the same with my work. That's not to say I haven't been changed by my experiences. I undoubtedly have. My worldview is a hell of a lot darker than it once was. But at the same time, I think I'm able to understand there's no black and white. Sometimes, the bad guy is just a scared teenager forced to hold a gun. Sometimes, the guy who looks like a suicide bomber is a distraught husband walking for miles and miles to find medicine for his dying wife."

She rubbed her lips together, nodding. "You're going to go back? Once you're healed, you're going to put yourself back in danger?"

I bit off a piece of bacon and slowly chewed. "I don't know how to do anything else."

"Right." After a beat, she perked up and stabbed her fork into her pancakes. "Well, maybe you should break out your camera while you're here so you don't get rusty."

"Maybe I will. Your mom and nephew reminded me it's just as important to document the beauty in the world too."

She smiled at me around a mouthful of pancakes, and my fingers twitched. For the second time this meal, I wished I had my camera to document the beauty across from me.

Instead, I dug into my food, the flavors richer than I remembered. That might've been the company affecting my taste buds, but it didn't matter. All I knew was I was enjoying being here with Hannah—talking to her, answering her questions, looking at her. For the time being, there was nowhere else I'd rather be.

Until a shadow crossed our table. Right before an excited voice called our names.

"Aunt Hannah! Remi! What are you doing here? Why are you guys having breakfast together?" Jesse bounced on his toes at the end of our table. "Dad, look who's here. Weird, right?"

Hannah put her fork down to grab her nephew's hand. "Hey, dude. You convinced Dad to treat you to breakfast?"

"Yep." Jesse nodded proudly. "I had to drag him out of bed."

Caleb put his hand on top of his son's head. "Think it was the other way around, kid." Then his gaze swept from his sister to me, his expression unreadable. If he was pissed, he wasn't giving it away.

Hannah didn't seem alarmed at her brother's presence. Then again, she hadn't been the one warned to stay away.

"I'd invite you guys to join us, but I don't think you'd fit," she said.

"That's okay. We're having guy time," Jesse proclaimed.

Hannah held her hands up. "Oh, excuse me. I would never intrude on guy time."

Caleb's eyes were locked on me. His nostrils flared as he sniffed. "So, this is happening?" he gruffed.

I nodded, bracing myself for what came next. There was no use denying it. I was too old to sneak around. More than that, I didn't want to.

"Yeah. It's happening."

"You're gonna heed what I told you?" *Take it easy on my sister...*

"I will."

"All right then." For Caleb, that was that. He was a man of his word, and he was taking me at mine. I appreciated that about him. Plus, the last thing I wanted to do was let him down again. Actually, no—the last thing was letting Hannah down. Caleb came in a close second.

Jesse shuffled closer to me. "Are you going with Aunt Hannah to the rodeo?"

I glanced at Hannah then back to the boy. "She hasn't invited me. Think that means she doesn't want me to go?"

Jesse's head whipped to his aunt. "You don't want Remi to go to the rodeo?"

She rolled her eyes. "Maybe I haven't gotten a chance to ask him."

"Well, you should," he declared.

Caleb interrupted, rapping his heavy knuckles on the table. "Come on, kid. Let's go get some grub."

When they left, Hannah smirked at me, clearly amused. Something told me it had nothing to do with my lack of rodeo invitation.

"What's got you smiling, Hannah Kelly?"

"Did you just perform some manly passing of the baton—me being the baton—with my brother right in front of me?"

Laughing, I reached across the table to nab her fork. It happened to be loaded with pancakes, so she tried to steal it back, but I managed to get it in my mouth before she could. To make up for it, I returned the fork along with a piece of my bacon.

She ate it, but she did so with a deep scowl aimed right at me.

"A while back, Caleb asked me to take it easy on you. That was him checking in, making sure I was keeping my promise."

"Hmph." She folded her arms across her chest. "I guess you lied then."

My brow dipped. "What? In what way?"

A devious curl started at the corners of her mouth. "Do you call what you did to me last night taking it easy? I don't remember it that way, but—"

Barking a laugh, I tossed my napkin at her. "Fucking menace," I muttered. "You had me worried."

She grinned. "Good. Can't let you get too comfortable."

"Always on my toes with you."

Her teeth dug into her bottom lip, biting back a smile. She really was pretty. I was glad I hadn't noticed back when we were teens. Caleb wouldn't have been as easygoing if I'd been crushing on his fifteen-year-old sister. That, and it would've been a lot harder to leave.

"I meant it, you know." Locking eyes with her, I grew serious. "I know you've had a huge upheaval with Graham passing, and Cay said there was an ex who did you wrong. I'm not going to be another cause of you hurting. I need you to tell me if you see that happening and I don't notice."

She swallowed hard. "We're just having fun, aren't we?"

It didn't feel like the right word for what we were sharing, but I didn't know what else it could be.

So, even though my skin pricked with unease, I agreed. It was all I could do. "For as long as you want to, sweetheart."

Chapter Twenty-four

Remington

I SHOWED UP AT the Kellys for dinner once again. This time, it was Connell Kelly who'd extended the invitation. We'd run into each other in town, he'd treated me to a cup of coffee like we were old friends, then told me what time the meal would be served. The Kellys weren't much for ceremony, and I liked that about them. I never questioned where I stood with any of them.

When I'd met Caleb back in kindergarten, he'd told me his grand-dad lived right next door. With a couple acres between the two houses, his definition of next door definitely hadn't fit with what I'd imagined. First time I'd visited, he'd taken me for a ride on his side-by-side to his granddad's house, showing me how *close* it was.

For a kid who had thousands of acres to his family's name, I guessed two or three was nothing.

I was sitting on the back patio, sipping a beer while Connell grilled, when Hannah and Phoebe arrived. Hannah marched straight up to Connell and laid a kiss on his cheek. He squeezed her shoulders and told her he'd missed her. No doubt they'd seen each other in the last few days, but I also didn't doubt he'd genuinely missed his granddaughter.

She spun around, alighting on me, seated on a padded bench. "Well, look who's here. Remington Town."

I raised my bottle. "Hannah Kelly."

It'd only been a day since I'd dropped her at home after having breakfast, but it felt longer. She hadn't known I was going to be here tonight, and I wondered how long she would've gone without seeing me if it had been up to her.

Crossing one foot over the other, she considered me, and I did the same right back. She had on her brown cowboy boots, her long tan legs bare and smooth under a cream, gauzy dress that floated over her figure and stopped midthigh. That thick wave of hair I'd formed an obsession with spilled over one shoulder, a barrette holding it off her face on the opposite side.

Crickets chirped, the earth spun, her family moved about in the background, but the space between us was suspended, separate from gravity and time.

Until Jesse darted between us, his dog chasing behind him. Hannah grinned, and I had no choice but to answer with a wide smile of my own.

She sauntered over, stopping right in front of me so the tips of her boots met mine. "Fancy seeing you here, Remington."

"I received a personal invite from your granddad." I patted the cushion beside me. "Sit here. Tell me a thing or two."

Her hesitation was brief before she flopped down on the bench, crossing her legs toward me. Boot hooking on the back of my calf, she trailed her fingertips down my forearm to my hand, giving it a squeeze.

"I have a confession," she whispered.

I caught the tips of her fingers in my grip and idly ran my thumb back and forth over her short nails. "What's that, sweetheart?"

"I'm pretty glad you're here."

From another woman, that might've sounded lukewarm. From Hannah Kelly, I took it as she'd said it. She was happy to see me, and I sure as hell was pleased to see her.

I tipped my head toward hers, close enough to get a dose of her warmth and scent without touching. "Me too."

Caleb walked out onto the patio, hands on his hips. He turned, spotting us sitting next to each other. We were barely touching, but I had to imagine our intimacy was unmistakable.

That was why when he shook his head and walked back inside, I chuckled under my breath and Hannah rolled her eyes.

"He thinks the idea of me kissing boys is gross, like I'm twelve."

I had to laugh. 'Cause yeah, that was true. "Probably worse that the boy is me."

"Mmhmm. You're Cay's. I'm surprised he's sharing."

"Unfortunately, I have no interest in kissing Caleb."

Her lips pursed, tempting me, but I wouldn't go there. Not here, with Jesse running around in the yard and her granddad a few feet away.

"Only you, Hannah." I moved my thumb along the edge of her hand to the pulse in her wrist. "You look gorgeous tonight, by the way. I like your dress and the thing you did with your hair."

Dipping her head, she smoothed her dress out over her legs then touched her barrette. "Thank you. It's not anything fancy, but—"

"Nope. You're gonna let me tell you how gorgeous I think you are. All you have to do is say 'Thank you, baby.'"

Rearing back, her eyebrow arched. "I have to call you baby?"

I grinned at her. "Why not? It's better than asshole."

Giggling, she tilted toward me, her head falling on my shoulder. Then, so quiet I almost missed it, she whispered, "Thank you, baby."

182   JULIA WOLF

And yeah. I liked that. I liked it a whole lot.

During dinner, conversation landed on the topic of the rodeo. The cowboys descended on Cheyenne through the month of July. Along with the rodeo, there was a fair with rides and games and a concert series, some big stars, some smaller musicians.

"Remi's coming with Dad and me next weekend," Jesse announced.

Hannah shook her head. "Nope. How can he go with you when he's going with me?"

Lock let out a deep chuckle. "Hard to believe, considering the two of you don't get along."

Caleb groaned, and Elena patted her husband's hand. "I think they're getting along just fine now," she murmured to her husband.

Lock's brow pinched as his attention shifted from his wife to his daughter before finally landing on me. Hannah and I were beside each other, our shoulders brushing, her foot hooked behind mine beneath the table.

"Oh," Lock intoned. "I see."

"What?" Jesse leaned forward to examine us. "What do you see?"

Caleb tousled his son's hair. "Grown-up things, kid."

Jesse groaned. "You always say that. It's so freaking annoying."

"It's a rite of passage," Connell stated. "One day, you'll get to say it to your children."

"Pfft. I'm not having kids," Jesse declared.

"That's what I said and look at me now." Caleb pointed his fork at his chest.

Jesse crossed his arms. "Yeah...well, if I *do* have kids, I'm not gonna have them with just anyone. I'll make sure I'm married first." He shot his dad the side-eye.

Before Caleb could argue, Lily interjected. "Remi, darling, since you're going with our Hannah to the rodeo next weekend, I should let you know there's a band playing after, and she always enjoys dancing to their music."

"I didn't know that," I replied. "That's good information to have."

Cormac put his fork down. "So, we're all just accepting the two of them?"

Everyone looked around at each other before giving a chorus of yeses. Then Elena spoke for the family.

"We adore our Hannah, and we love Remi. That's really all we need to know in these early stages." She flicked her manicured nails. "When it's time to know more, I trust you two will tell us. Especially if you intend to have more breakfasts at the diner where I have to hear about it from Mae Whitaker and not my own daughter."

Jesse pushed up on his knees and threw his arms out. "Will someone just tell me what we're talking about?"

Caleb nudged his shoulder. "Butt in the seat, kid."

Lily was a little more forthcoming, leaning into Caleb as she put a roll on his plate. "It's romance and kissing. Do you want to talk about that?"

"Oh no." He covered his mouth like he was gagging. "That can stay grown-up stuff. No thank you."

Grinning, I turned to Hannah once the topic moved on again. "You know, you never did ask me to go with you."

Her tongue darted out to wet her lips. "I was hoping it had been implied."

"And you were hoping I'd say yes?"

"If you want to go..."

"Hannah"—I took her hand under the table—"you don't need to worry about me turning you down. That isn't going to happen."

She sucked in a sharp breath and shot me a narrow-eyed look. "I wasn't worried, I—"

"Think you were, sweetheart. So, even though you didn't ask, I'll give you an answer. I'd love to go with you. Even more, I'd love to take you dancing after. I have to warn you, though, my moves are pretty rusty. You might want to make sure your toes are covered up for your protection."

Her scoff was soft and amused. "I think I can manage that."

Cormac's laughter drew us apart. We both turned in his direction at the other end of the table.

"How in the world did you convince Hannah to let you drive tonight?" he asked Phoebe.

Phoebe shrugged. "It wasn't hard considering her truck's in the shop and I'm not going to let her get behind the wheel of Greta."

Lily clucked her tongue. "I still disagree with you naming your vehicle Greta. If anything, she's a Maryanne."

Phoebe's nose scrunched at her grandmother. "Greta is definitely not a Maryanne."

Lock stared down the table at Hannah. "What's going on with the truck?"

Hannah stiffened next to me before blurting out a half-truth. "It needed new tires. I was overdue."

If she felt me boring a hole in the side of her head, she didn't react. I didn't agree with keeping what happened a secret from her family. If Cleve or someone else was out to get her, they needed to know. The more people who were aware of the situation, the safer she would be.

Lock scratched his jaw. "Correct me if I'm wrong, but didn't you replace your tires less than six months ago?"

Hannah's shoulders bunched. "It must've been longer than that. I—"

If she wasn't going to tell them, it had to be me. She could be pissed at me for doing it, but I'd rather her be safe and angry than...yeah, I wasn't going to think about the alternative.

"Her tires were slashed on Friday when she was out at Jacob's ranch. We think Cleve Jones did it."

Color rose on Lock's face as a flurry of exclamations went around the table. His eyes darkened, locking onto me.

"Why do you think it was Cleve?" he asked tightly.

Hannah shook her head. "I'm handling this. You don't need to worry."

"Why would you not tell us?" Elena breathed out. "Why—?"

Lock put his hand on her arm, taking over the questioning. "You think it was Cleve, which leads me to believe this wasn't the first incident. I am going to need you to be honest with me, Hannah. We don't hide things in this family—not when it comes to personal safety."

Hannah shifted uncomfortably, moving her fork around on the table. "For a while now, he's been trying to poach my clients. That's not a big deal. I can handle it—and his comments."

"What kind of comments?" Caleb barked.

She held up her hand. "I said I can handle it."

I squeezed her thigh. "Tell them what he did on the road."

"What did he do?" Lock asked lowly.

Hannah flicked her hand like what she was about to tell them was no big deal, but the quiver in her chin gave her away. "I was driving down Happy Jack Road, and he came up behind me. Got right on my bumper and wouldn't let up. This went on for miles, him on my ass, no one around. I admit, it scared me, especially because I didn't know it was him. I thought he was going to push me off the road. He finally moved past me, laughing his head off like it was all a big joke."

After a beat of silence, Caleb asked gruffly, "You go to the cops?"

She nodded. "I did. I went about my tires too. They have no proof. All they could do was talk to him."

Lock shoved back from the table, murder burning in his gaze. "This won't stand. It's obvious he wasn't spoken to in the right way."

Caleb rose with his father. "I'm going too."

Cormac was next. "I need to see his face when he hears what'll happen to him if he doesn't back off."

Hannah hopped to her feet, her napkin balled in her fist. "Absolutely not. You're not going after Cleve Jones."

It was obvious to me they'd made their minds up and nothing Hannah could say would stop them. The three men were already heading toward the door.

There was also no way I wasn't going with them.

I got up, following Elena out to the foyer. Throwing open the coat closet, she produced a baseball bat and handed it to her husband. They exchanged a long look that needed no words. The intensity between them was enough.

"I'm in," I said firmly. "I need to be there."

Hannah whirled on me, her jaw tight. "Don't you dare. This is ridiculous."

I pushed her hair away from her face. "It needs to happen. Cleve has to see how many people are in your corner. He can't keep coming after you. We'll put an end to it."

She jerked away from me, her mouth set in a scowl. "I'm going to be so pissed if I have to bail any of you out. And don't even think about getting yourselves hurt."

Cormac patted her shoulder as he headed out the door. "No one's getting hurt. Eat your dinner. We'll be back by dessert."

"Shut up, Maccie," Hannah gritted out.

Elena went to her daughter and wrapped her arm around her waist. "Shhh, darling. Let them do what they have to do. Sometimes, all it takes is a little threatening with a bat to set someone straight. Let's hope Cleve is smart enough to heed this warning and leave my girl alone."

I was the final one out of the house. The last thing I saw before I shut the door was Hannah's flushed, pissed-off face.

Chapter Twenty-five

Remington

CLEVE JONES LIVED DOWN a dirt road on a patch of dead prairie. The junk covering his dried-out grass was prettier than his post-war brick ranch-style house.

Lock's truck came to a stop in his crumbling driveway, dust kicking up in a cloud around us. The four of us climbed out, Lock and Caleb both with baseball bats hanging loose from their hands.

Like he'd known we were coming, Cleve was sitting on his concrete slab front porch in a worn-out lawn chair. In a pair of stained sweats and an undershirt that had been white once upon a time, he hadn't dressed up for guests. He was swigging a beer, several empty, crushed cans strewn around his feet.

"You're on private property," Cleve shouted. "Turn right back around."

Lock's steps didn't stutter as he strode up to the porch. "Like to have a word, then we'll be on our way."

Cleve let out a loud belch and crumpled his beer can, tossing it on the ground in front of Lock.

"I already know what you have to say. Just because your kid doesn't have a sense of humor doesn't give her a right to sic the cops on me." He clucked his tongue. "That's some petty bullshit."

Lock knocked the end of his bat against the porch. "Seems you need to work on your comedy routine if you think trying to drive a woman off the road is the height of hilarity."

Cormac stepped forward, his arms crossed. "I don't think it was funny. Maybe you should explain the joke to me."

Cleve rolled his eyes, but he was so blitzed they bounced around his skull until he got them set straight again.

"Not explaining anything to you, baby Kelly."

Caleb slapped his bat against his meaty palm. "Let's talk about you messing with my sister's tires. You're gonna be paying for those repairs, Jones."

Cleve reached into the cooler beside him and took out another beer. When he popped the lid, fizz spilled over his hand and onto his sweats. He didn't seem to notice, and if he did, he didn't care.

"Yeah, I'm not paying for shit," he stated. "Cops were already out here. I'll tell you what I told them: I wasn't there. Didn't touch her tires. Don't know anything about it. To me, it sounds like someone doesn't like that girl. Can't imagine why that would be."

Then he started laughing like he'd said the funniest thing he'd ever heard. Caleb stepped forward, but Lock put his arm out, holding his son back.

It took a lot to make me angry, and right now, my blood boiled with fury. I'd seen Hannah after he'd scared her on the road. I'd held her through quaking trembles after her tires had been slashed. There was not one thing funny about any of this.

"You piece of shit." I only got one foot on the porch steps before Cormac grabbed the material of my shirt and dragged me backward.

"Gotta stay calm as you can," he muttered. "Hannah won't be happy if you get arrested, remember?"

Knowing he was right, I sucked in a heaving breath, my fists balled at my sides. I needed to get back to Hannah, make sure she was all right. I couldn't do that if I was locked up.

"Let me," Lock ground out, stretching his bat to touch Cleve under his chin. "Listen up."

Cleve's laughter ceased, and his hazy eyes grew wide. "You can't touch me."

"Not your turn to talk." Lock jerked the bat, pushing Cleve's head back. "I don't care what you admit. You went after my girl. That's a fact not up for debate. I can't prove you slashed those tires, but I don't need to. You're going to be paying for the repairs to make up for trying to run her off the road."

"I—" Caleb's bat came down hard on the scattered cans, cutting off Cleve's protest.

"Time for you to listen," Caleb barked.

Lock pressed his bat a little harder. "You come near Hannah again, you so much as look at her or breathe in her direction, I'll be back, and next time, it won't be with a bat. You hear me, Jones?"

Before he could answer, the front door swung open, and a skin-and-bones woman wearing a dingy housecoat stepped out, a shotgun cradled in her arms. I went on red alert, focused on the gun, bracing for her to make a move to use it.

"Time for you to leave our property." She sounded like she smoked three packs a day, raspy and older than her true age. "My husband answered your questions. He spoke to the police. You have some gall coming around here and waving around your fancy-ass Kelly threats. I'm not your employee anymore—you made sure of that—so you can't boss me. And you might think you own this town, but you don't."

Lock slowly backed off, his bat dropping. "Don't think I own the town, Christine. Cleve's crossed the line. Maybe he didn't slash Hannah's tires, but he freely admits to trying to run her off the road, and that's unacceptable."

Christine stood next to her husband, the gun still loose in her arms. "He heard you. You said your piece. Cleve's got no reason to interact with your precious princess anymore, so you can get that idea out of your big head. Now, this is the last time I tell you to leave before we have a real problem."

I hadn't taken my eyes off that gun. Cleve was an asshole, but there was something about this woman that led me to believe she'd have no problem using her weapon on us. If her yard ended up littered with four dead bodies, she'd probably just shove our corpses under the rest of the junk and go about her day like it was nothing.

Without warning, Christine's beady gaze landed on me. "You're not a Kelly, are you?" Her eyes pinched before rounding. "I know exactly who you are. You're a Town. Surprised you're taking up for the Kelly girl considering word was going around that she wasn't just working for your daddy, if you know what I mean."

"Enough," Lock bit out. "Keep my daughter's name outta your mouths and we won't have any more trouble."

He looked at the rest of us, jerking his head to the side. "We're done here, boys. Let's go."

Not trusting either of the Joneses as far as I could throw them, I backed my way to the truck. Cleve was too busy getting wasted to care that we were leaving, but Christine kept a close watch until we were all loaded up and pulling out of her driveway.

As soon as we were on the road again, Lock found my gaze in the rearview mirror. "That wasn't true, you know. There were never rumors about Hannah and Graham. She made that up on the spot."

I nodded. "I didn't believe it for a second."

My father had been a lot of things—a womanizer wasn't one of them. And Hannah...yeah, I wasn't going to let my mind go there. It was clear to me her feelings for him had been purely familial, and I knew that without ever seeing them together.

Cormac leaned over, speaking quietly. "Christine's an angry woman, and she's not a big fan of our family. Used to work at the resort, cleaning rooms."

From the front, Caleb filled in. "They caught her stealing."

Caleb sighed. "She was the first person I had to fire. It didn't feel great, but..."

"Had to be done," I filled in.

"Yep," Lock agreed. "Had to be done."

The drive to the ranch was mostly silent. Seemed like the rest of the men were just as eager to get back and have this all be over with. For my part, I wanted to see Hannah and make sure we were all right—that *she* was all right.

I shouldn't have been worried about Hannah. She was standing on the porch, one shoulder against a post, her arms crossed, all attitude. As soon as we were out of the truck, she made her way down the steps, peering at each of us.

"Looks like you're all in one piece." She raised her chin. "Did Christine bring out her gun?"

Lock chuckled. "You know it." Then he hooked her around the neck and planted a kiss on her forehead. "It's over, Hannah. What's done is done. You've no cause to be mad. Let it go."

She frowned at him. "And what if today had been the day Christine decided to unload that shotgun?"

"It wasn't," he said steadily. "No reason to live in the what-ifs."

Caleb walked by, tousling her hair. "Granddad better not have eaten all the pie."

She hmphed. "It would serve you right if he had."

Cormac gave her shoulder a squeeze. "Sorry, Han, but that prick needed to be put in his place."

She rolled her eyes, and by the time she straightened them, we were the only two still outside. I was beside the truck, waiting my turn, ready for whatever she had to give me.

Her arms were still folded tight as she focused on me. "Did you flex your big muscles and intimidate the weaselly little man?"

I cocked my head. "All I'm hearing is you think my muscles are big."

She scoffed and sauntered over to me, stopping when her boots hit mine. "You *would* hear that. I don't love you charging into danger for me, Remington."

I held up a finger. "One, there's no world in which I wouldn't charge into danger for you. I've been in the middle of riots. It takes a lot to spook me. Two, this situation wasn't dangerous. Cleve doesn't strike me as a man who would willingly take on another man, let alone four."

"That may be true, but you had to have noticed Cleve's wife is a little unhinged."

"Hard to miss." I ran my hands along her arms, slowly unfolding them, then placed her palms on my chest. Mad as she might've been, she left them there, and I took that as a good sign.

"It's best not to poke a hornet's nest, you know." Her nose crinkled. "Last thing I want is Christine Jones putting me on her list."

I raised a brow. "She has a list?"

"Yep. It's said she keeps it in her purse. The second you cross her or even annoy her, she writes your name on it. Kayla from the grocery store saw it firsthand when Marvin Tennison neglected to put a separator on the conveyor belt at checkout, causing their groceries to get mixed up. Kayla said Christine took her list out and wrote Marvin's name in big block letters, and there were plenty of other names above his."

I had to bite back a laugh. Hannah was telling me this story in earnest. "Anything happen to Marvin?"

She nodded. "All his flowers wilted almost overnight. And Marvin takes his flowers seriously. His neighbor said he'd cried in his garden for a solid hour when he came upon the horror show. Everyone suspects Christine had something to do with it, but of course, no one can prove anything."

I curled my arm around her waist, tugging her a little closer. "It's a good thing you don't have a garden. Christine Jones doesn't like you very much, but I'm not sure she's a fan of many people based on our short acquaintance."

A cute little line formed between her brows. "You're probably on the list now too."

"Good. I wouldn't want you to get lonely on there."

She let out a little laugh, smacking my chest. "Stop it. This isn't funny."

"Oh, I think it's hella funny." I walked her backward until she met the door of Lock's truck, then I reached down and scooped her up from beneath her ass. Her legs locked around my waist, and her hands slid up to hang over my shoulders. "I'd been prepared to get things thrown at me when I got back."

Her eyes narrowed. "There's still time."

"Hmmm." I dipped down to kiss her throat. "Then maybe I'll just stay close so you don't have enough room to wind up a pitch."

"Maybe that's a good idea." She latched on to my bottom lip and gave it a tug with her teeth. A growl traveled up from my chest, making her giggle.

"Menace," I whispered against her smile.

"I'm not mad at you, Remington," she stated.

"I'm glad for it, even if I'm surprised."

"I get why you might be. The fact is, I'm Lachlan Kelly's daughter, and I have two brothers who grew up in his image. They can't help putting themselves in front of women—especially women they love. It's in their blood. If you hadn't gone with them, my granddad would have been the fourth one in the truck. So I'm not surprised you all went to confront Cleve. The men in my life are protectors. That's all there is to it."

"I'm a man in your life?" I asked.

Her legs tightened around me, putting her warm core in contact with my growing erection.

"As long as you're around, yeah. I haven't gotten you out of my system yet. Have you?"

"Hannah..." I kneaded her round, tight ass. My head was spinning, trying to catch up to where we were. I was still a mile behind. At the place I'd assumed we were going to be—and that place didn't include her pussy grinding on me and her lips whispering against mine. "Does anyone ever get you out of their system? Seems impossible."

Her laugh was breathy with a tinge of bitterness. "It's possible, but good to know I've tricked you into thinking it's not." She pressed her lips to mine in a quick, hard kiss. "You want to take me home?"

"I do. Just know I'm coming in."

Her eyebrows waggled. "Oh, I know you are, Remington."

With Hannah wrapped around me, I carried her to my truck, laughing the whole way there. How this woman had managed to make me laugh while my dick was hard as steel was a mystery, but damn if I didn't intend to try to unravel it piece by piece for as long as she'd let me.

Chapter Twenty-six

Hannah

MY CHEST WAS FLUSH with my headboard, fingers curled tight around the top. Remi was behind me on his knees, working me hard, driving into me like he was desperately searching for something.

His grunts next to my ear made my eyes roll back. We didn't need words. Those noises were the most erotic sound he could make. They were his reaction to me, my body, being inside me.

We'd been at this all week. Every spare minute, we'd attempted to find out if our first time together had been a fluke. So far, the results were inconclusive, so we were forced to keep experimenting.

Tonight had started on my couch while watching a movie. We'd both reached for the last Twizzler. Remi had grabbed it, but growing up with two brothers who'd had a habit of stealing my food, I'd become a scrapper. I'd lunged for the licorice, trying to take it from his hand. That had ended with us on the floor, going at each other like animals.

Once I'd had him naked and his mind on other things, I'd stolen the Twizzler and ran for my bedroom, but Remi had caught me before I'd reached the bed. Then he'd distracted me by spanking me, followed by his mouth between my thighs. He'd devoted himself so thoroughly to the cause—the cause being my orgasms—I'd given him two-thirds of the Twizzler as a reward.

And while he'd been eating it, I'd dropped to my knees, taking him deep in my throat. The sounds he'd made were feral. I couldn't decide if I liked his breathy moans or wild grunts most.

Remi had a lot more control than I did. I liked the feel of him on my tongue far too much to want to stop. He'd been the one to pull out of my mouth and throw me on the mattress. Then he'd positioned me how he'd wanted me and went to town, fucking me with brutal precision and strength. I hadn't started smashed against the headboard, but he'd shifted my entire body with his forceful thrusts, pushing me forward until there was nowhere else to go.

One week of this sweaty, needy fucking, and I was addicted. All my worries, troubles, and grief were still present, but they were faded by the bright Technicolor of Remi's attention.

My head fell back on his shoulder as I moaned my pleasure to the ceiling. His palm slid from my hip to my belly and traveled up my torso, stopping to play with my breasts for a long while before settling on my throat. He held me in this position, my head back and against him, feeling each moan he pounded out of me.

I covered his hand with mine, pressing on his fingers to add a little pressure. Just enough to feel dangerous, bringing me to another height. So high I was breathless and panting.

His hips slapped my backside, and I used my hold on the headboard for leverage as I pushed back to meet him, taking more.

I turned my head to look at him, discovering he was already staring down at me. His hazel eyes had gone dark, pupils blown wide. A red tint traveled from his throat to his cheeks, and a sheen of sweat glistened on his forehead. This man was gorgeous and carnal, and I could say for sure I'd never been this attracted to anyone. He had learned my body and desires and played into them like an expert on the subject.

"Need to fuck you, Hannah," he gritted next to my ear.

"You are," I replied shakily. "You so are."

"More."

Pulling out, he gave me no opportunity to feel his absence before he flipped me onto my back and fit himself between my legs again. He spread me open, hooking his arms under the backs of my knees, and lined himself up with my opening. I nodded, and he drove forward, sliding all the way to the hilt.

Never once did he take his eyes off me. He held my gaze from inches away, watching me like I was fascinating. Like I was the center of everything. It was a heady feeling, having Remi's entire focus.

He dipped down to lick my lips and touch his tongue to mine. "You taste so damn good."

"Thank you," I breathed, and his reply was a loopy grin.

Oh, I was spiraling, losing myself to him, and I had no inclination to stop. Instead, I wrapped my legs around his back and pulled him deeper.

"Fuck, Hannah." His forehead dropped to mine as he surged into me with desperation. "Oh, fuck, baby. Oh god, oh god, oh god."

I clawed at his shoulders as his hips made short snaps, those last moments of us teetering at the edge together. My belly tightened, pressure building in my core, so close to bursting.

"Hannah!" he exclaimed, his neck arching as spurts of liquid heat coated my inner depths. I raised my head, latching on to his exposed throat, sucking as I ground against him, taking myself to where I needed to be.

He held my head against his like I was a little vampire, and he was my willing victim. I didn't let go until my pleasure crested and crashed, receding like the tide. Then I fell back on my pillow, without breath or bones.

Remi carefully pulled out and flopped to his back, a possessive hand splayed on my stomach. He was quiet, catching his breath. I liked that. We never had to have some big analysis of what we'd done. We both knew how good it had been.

After a minute of staring dazedly at the ceiling, Remi's soft laughter pulled me back to the present.

"What's so funny?" I asked.

"I'm just thinking how pissed Caleb's going to be when I show up with a massive hickey on my neck."

"What? It can't be that bad." I pushed up on my elbow to examine his neck, and my mouth fell open. "Oh."

He was already bruising, right in the center of his throat, and it wasn't small by any means.

He laughed again. "Yeah, oh. You wrecked me, you little monster."

I shoved at his shoulder. "You should've stopped me."

He pulled me on top of him, circling his arms around me. "Did I say I didn't like it? Nope. I'm just gonna catch shit from your brother."

I gasped. "And come up with an explanation for Jesse when he sees you at the rodeo tomorrow."

"I'll tell him his aunt throat punched me."

I snarled. "If you do, I'll throat punch you for real."

Snickering, he palmed the back of my head, pushing it down so I lay on him fully, my cheek on his chest. It was...nice. Sweet even.

Remington Town was leading me straight into the danger zone, and I liked it so much I closed my eyes and followed him.

I had my truck back, but Remi drove us to Cheyenne anyway, his hand resting on my bare leg the whole way. Well...at times, it roved under the hem of my sundress, but mostly, he seemed to want contact with my skin, his palm cupping my knee, his thumb rubbing small circles on the outer curve.

I spent a lot of time on long, empty Wyoming roads, and I didn't mind it, but I had a feeling the next time I drove alone, I'd feel the ghost of Remi's hand on my leg and miss it.

When we parked, Remi circled the truck and helped me out. I thought he'd try to hold my hand, but he hooked me around the waist instead. Still clinging to this being nothing more than sex, I wasn't sure I'd wanted him to hold my hand, but I also wasn't sure if this was any better.

I went with it anyway. There were so many people heading to the stands we might've gotten separated if we weren't attached.

It was how I excused it in my head.

Though, I still hadn't come up with an excuse for sleeping with him every single night. It just kept happening, and it hadn't occurred to me to stop it. I'd always been a thrill seeker and I had yet to discover anything more thrilling than being taken roughly and thoroughly by this man.

Caleb and Jesse were in the stands waiting for us. Since my brother was a head taller than most people, we found them easily. They'd chosen prime seats behind the chutes where the riders mounted their broncos and bulls.

Caleb rose to greet us, took one look at Remi, shook his head, then shot me a death glare. "Dammit. Really, Hannah? You had to do that?"

I looked at the hickey peeking out of the collar of Remi's button-down then swung my attention back to my brother. "He tripped. Ran into a doorknob."

"A doorknob...with his neck?" Caleb grumbled.

"Yep." I cuffed his shoulder as I passed him. "He's really clumsy."

I greeted Jesse, who was peering at Remi with a scrunched-up expression. "Did he really trip?" he asked dubiously.

I sat down next to my nephew and squeezed his shoulders. "Not really. I'm pretty sure it's a bad reaction to an insect bite. City boys like Rem are sensitive to the great outdoors."

Remi took the seat on my other side with a sigh. "Really, Hannah?" he groused, almost as grumpy as Caleb. "*Really?*"

I had to snicker at how annoyed he sounded. If he hadn't wanted to walk around with a big hickey, he shouldn't have let me suck the soul out of his neck. It wasn't my fault he was so delicious and made me act out. He should've been more careful with his big dick.

I patted his leg. "It's okay, Remington. Once you've been in Wyoming a while longer, you'll toughen up."

Jesse was still eyeing Remi, doubt pulling at his brow. "I've never seen a bug bite that looks like that. You sure that's what it is?"

Remi covered his smile with his hand, but I kept my composure, nodding seriously. "Absolutely. I think it was from one of those invasive species. You know, the ones that came from Asia on a cargo ship?"

That was all the distraction Jesse needed as he dove into telling us about the book Ms. Clark had shared with him. With anyone else, my mind would have wandered, but Jesse was pretty much my favorite person in the world, so I gave him all the attention his big brain deserved.

Once he got through summarizing the entire book—in great detail—Remi draped his arm around the back of my seat and tugged me into him.

"You're lucky he bought that," he murmured into my hair.

"He probably didn't, but he's sweet enough to let me off the hook." I crossed my legs toward him, our feet getting tangled how I liked. "He's too smart for his own good. Mine too."

"But you're good with him."

"Yeah. I think he's grand. Don't you?"

His mouth hitched in one corner. "Yep. Pretty damn grand. I'm still getting over Caleb being a dad. Think you'll have one or two of your own?"

"I hope so. I've always wanted to remake my family—two boys and two girls. But compared to most of my graduating class, I'm an old maid and my ovaries are dried-up husks." I scoffed. "With my career, I'm going to need a solid partner who'll go fifty-fifty on parenting, and I haven't found that person yet."

His fingers curled around my shoulder. For a beat, they were too tight, but then they loosened, and he slowly stroked my skin. "There's no rush, sweetheart. No need for you to settle."

"I won't." I hooked my pinkie around his free hand. "Pinkie promise."

He chuckled, his gaze surveying the dirt-floored arena. "I haven't been to a rodeo since I was a kid."

"You're in for some fun. Dell Rivers' granddaughter, Kennedy, rides one of his horses to race the barrels. She's like the wind."

"Can't wait."

Cay and Remi got us drinks and junk food before the show started. I was about to bite into my loaded hot dog when there was an announcement about a change in programming. There was a replacement rider tonight, and according to the MC, we were in for a treat.

Watkins Simms.

Every drop of blood drained from my face.

"Aw, damn," Caleb crumbled. "There goes the night."

"What?" Remi swiveled back and forth between us. "Who's Watkins Simms?"

Jesse piped up. "That's Aunt Hannah's ex-boyfriend. We don't like him because he went out with another girl and broke Aunt Hannah's heart. My grandpa said he's a real prick."

Caleb plopped his big hand on top of his son's head. "That was too much information—and don't say 'prick.'"

Jesse's eyes rounded. "But he is a prick, isn't he? Or did I use that word incorrectly?"

While Caleb explained to Jesse he had indeed used the word the right way, but it wasn't appropriate for a ten-year-old boy to say, Remi turned my way.

"You want to leave?" he asked.

I sucked in a deep breath and shook my head. Last I'd heard, Watt was supposed to be in Texas all summer. I definitely wouldn't have shown up had I known he'd be riding, but I wasn't going to let him ruin my night. He'd ruined enough. "No, it's fine. Knowing him, he'll be out there all of five seconds."

Of course, he'd be in the chute right below us, getting his bull roped up while waiting for his turn. That didn't mean I'd have to watch him, though. I could enjoy my night without forcing myself to sit through Watt putting on his show.

"Say the word and I'll get you out of here," Remi vowed.

I leaned in, touching my lips to his. "Thanks for being the best, Remington."

Starbursts bloomed around his twinkling eyes. "Amazing how you tell me to fuck off so sweetly."

"Maybe me saying Remington means something else now."

He chucked my chin with his knuckle. "You're not going to tell me, are you?"

My eyes twinkled right back at him, amazed and grateful at how quickly he was able to turn my mood around.

"Not even a chance."

Chapter Twenty-seven

Remington

WE HAD FUN THROUGH the broncos, barrel racing, and stock roping. Hannah was on her feet half the time, cheering loudly and clapping her hands over her head. She gave zero shits about anyone's opinion. She was enjoying herself with her whole damn chest.

And I was enjoying being here to see it.

To tell the truth, I could take or leave the rodeo, but she made it a good time and dragged Jesse into the spirit with her, doing a little dance each time one of the girls successfully roped a calf. I caught Caleb watching his kid and sister. There was a calmness to him he didn't always have. His mouth was curved into a soft grin as he brought his beer can to his lips.

I thought I got it. Jesse was bright and inquisitive, but from what I'd seen, he spent a lot of time buried in books. Caleb let him do his thing, but it must've been nice for him to see his son busting loose and simply being a silly kid for once. It probably only added to Caleb's happiness that Hannah was dancing alongside him.

Once again, a sense of loss struck me in my chest. I wished I could picture Hannah dancing with baby Jesse in her arms or Caleb toting him around on his shoulders, but I'd missed out on all that. Walking away from my life hadn't been a mistake, but leaving these people behind had been. I couldn't regret who I'd become outside the confines of Wyoming, but I'd always be wistful over what I'd missed. There was no chance of getting that time back. All I could do was make better choices going forward.

The change in Hannah was swift and obvious. Down below, a new set of cowboys had emerged, and bulls were being loaded into the chutes. Hannah stiffened next to me, her jaw set tight.

One of those guys had to be her ex. I scanned them, each one cockier than the next. When I landed on the man at the end, dressed in black all the way up to his hat and thick mustache, instinct told me he was the one. It was the way he stood, wide and arrogant, his hands looped in his belt, emphasizing the massive buckle. And the way he scanned the stands, like he was looking for someone.

I saw it when he found her. The man lit up, and a slow grin spread across his face. Hannah made a little growl, and two seats down, Caleb muttered an expletive.

Jesse perked up and craned his neck. "Is the prick here? I see him. There's the prick!"

Caleb groaned again, reminding his son not to use that word. Though, he wasn't very convincing since that guy was most definitely a prick.

"All right." I laced my fingers with Hannah's. "Ready to head out? I heard something about dancing."

Her eyes flared. "You're going to take me dancing?"

I nodded. "I was listening when Lily mentioned the band you like playing tonight. I'm not an idiot. I take hints."

We said goodbye to Cay and Jess, and I pulled her up with me. Before we left the aisle, I glanced down at the chutes again. This time, Watkins Simms was focused on me, and his mustache was turned down, framing his heavy frown.

Maybe it was a dick move, but I stopped Hannah, took her chin between my fingers, and planted a firm kiss on her lips. I didn't have to check if Watkins was watching. The daggers in my back were enough evidence. For Hannah's sake, I hoped he choked on bitter regret. It pleased me to no end to be the one to remind him of what he would never have again.

"Was that for me?" Hannah swiped her thumb over my bottom lip. "Or him?"

"Me," I told her. "All for me."

Then I slipped my arm around her waist and got her out of there.

I appreciated Hannah's taste in music. The band played covers—classics and newer hits. They kept it lively, bringing the crowd onto the dance floor.

And quite a crowd there was. A massive barn had been converted into a concert venue with lots of room to dance in the middle, seating around the sides, and a bar running the length.

Since we'd arrived and grabbed drinks, Hannah had been moving her body to the music. Whatever had happened with her ex had seemingly rolled off her back. At least, if it hadn't, she was good at pretending.

I couldn't say I was much of a dancer, but there was not a chance I'd leave her out on the dance floor on her own. She turned me into a pole, spinning and twirling around me, holding my shoulders and clinging to my chest for balance.

"Do you hate this?" she asked next to my ear.

"Not even a little." I let my hand slide to the upper curve of her ass. "How could I hate watching you when you're on fire?"

"I'm not on fire," she laughed. "This band just plays all the songs I like. I will never be a person who doesn't dance to my favorite music. It's just not gonna happen."

"I admire your conviction, sweetheart. I might not be a dancer, but if I'm alone in the shower, you'll catch me belting out some tunes."

"Remi"—she clutched the collar of my shirt— "you can't keep something like that from me. I demand you sing to me next time we shower together."

"Aw, Hannah." I gave her ass a squeeze, pulling her hips into mine. "You think I can remember lyrics when you're standing in front of me all naked and slick? Not possible."

"You can close your eyes." Her bottom lip poked out. "I want a serenade, Remington."

"You tell me what you saying my full name means now and I'll consider it."

Taking my hand, she raised it up above our heads and twirled away from me, laughing.

"Not a chance," she sang, whooping when I reeled her back in hard and fast, making her collide with my chest. "So rough."

I scraped her hair from her face, aiming a smirk at her. "I heard you like me a little rough."

Her eyes rolled, but I'd earned a smile, so all wasn't lost. "What kind of rumors are you listening to, mister?"

"Not rumors. I was referring to how loud you scream when I spank your sassy ass."

Groaning, her forehead knocked against my shoulder. "Good lord. Are you trying to get fucked in your truck? If you keep talking to me like that, it's going to happen."

This woman...my dick was thick and hard, pulsing against my zipper. There was no way she didn't feel it prodding her belly. I bet if I lifted the hem of her dress and checked her panties, I'd find them wet. She got off on teasing me. I didn't mind it since I'd come to discover she always followed through.

"Do you think I'd object to that, Hannah?"

"No, but I'm not done dancing yet, so stop saying sexy things to me."

"By all means, I wouldn't want to cut your dancing short. And that's purely for selfish reasons. I'm enjoying watching your moves too much to want it to end."

The crowd had gotten denser when the rodeo ended. Rowdy people pressed in on all sides, and soon, we were covered in a sheen of sweat. Hannah didn't seem to notice or care, singing and swaying with the beat of the band like she was all alone. Well, not entirely. She kept a hand on me at all times, at the least making it clear to those around us we were together. I appreciated that since there were a number of guys giving her the eye. I wasn't a fighter, not if I didn't need to be, but my fists had curled a few times when someone got too close, or their eyes drifted to parts of her they shouldn't have.

Eventually, we took a break and grabbed water from the bar. My back was against the rail, and she was leaning into my chest, facing away from me. Arm around her middle, my fingertips trailed over the thin cotton of her dress, feeling her warm stomach rise and fall with each breath.

We stayed like that for a while, relaxing with each other, listening to music, watching the world go by. Then Hannah tipped her head back and kissed the underside of my jaw.

"We should get going, huh?" she said.

"We can stay as long as you want."

"The drive home isn't short." She twisted to face me. "I'm ready; I just need to use the restroom first."

"Anything you want, sweetheart."

I walked her to the long hallway where the bathrooms were. As usual, the women's had a line, so I kicked back against an empty wall within sight of the door so she could find me when she was finished.

It wasn't long before a man came to a stop in front of me. The first thing that registered when I looked up from my phone was the oversized belt buckle then the coiffed mustache. Hannah's ex wasn't bad looking, but he bordered so much on the side of ridiculous I questioned her taste in men.

"You're with Hannah Kelly." He issued this as a statement and then offered me his hand. "Watkins Simms. You can call me Watt."

I didn't bother shaking his hand. "Don't think I'll be calling you anything. We'll be gone in a minute."

He shook his hand out and slid his fingers along his mustache. "She tell you she was my girl?"

"Funny, we didn't talk about you at all."

He grinned, though it didn't reach his eyes. "I had her for a little more than a year. Things didn't work out, but I'll always hold a special place in my heart for her. She's a good girl, even if she is...a lot."

"I know what Hannah is. We don't need to do this. You can walk away."

He held up his hand that wasn't holding a beer. "I'm just being friendly, bud."

"I have enough friends," I intoned, but he wasn't taking the hint.

He chuckled like he amused himself. "All right. I get it. You'll see for yourself. Girl's gorgeous, but she's too needy. It got suffocating after a while. But hey, you might like that."

I wasn't a jealous man. Had never felt particularly possessive. In past relationships, I'd trusted easily and given miles of freedom without question. Never cared too much about them having guy friends or texting their exes. Looking back, that probably said more about the state of my feelings for them than anything else. Standing here in front of Hannah's ex, I wasn't the least bit calm. Knowing he'd touched her and carried intimate memories of her made my blood boil. But what really drove me to the edge was the way he casually disparaged her, like I needed a warning from a man like him.

I remembered what those women had said at Joy's the night we'd played pool. This guy had cheated on her yet had the audacity to point out her perceived flaws. Made me spitting mad.

"Heard you stepped out on her."

He cocked his head. "I thought you didn't talk about me. Sounds like you did."

"Nope. That was the word around town. And not only did you step out, you didn't have enough care or respect for Hannah to be discreet about it."

"Nope." He breathed a laugh, his hand raised. "No way. I may have been a dick and went somewhere I shouldn't have, but Hannah was the one who'd brought it to the public forum. She didn't have to put me on blast at Joy's. And the crazy bitch definitely didn't need to dump a beer on my head and lodge a fuckin' dart in my ass. But she did. Right in front of half the town. If people are talking, that's on Hannah, not on me."

Before I could tell him he'd gotten what he deserved, Hannah came blazing up to my side, her face flushed with anger.

"I'd do it again in a heartbeat, Watt. How about you beat it before I beat *you*?" she snapped.

He laughed even harder. "You're pretty when you're mad, firecracker. Damn, I missed you, girl. Kinda sad you didn't stay for my ride tonight. Remember when you were my good luck charm?"

Her hands flew to her hips. "You don't miss me. Only thing you miss is having my adoring audience. I think you know I'm not stupid enough to ever let you have that again."

He smirked at her, and there was nothing kind about it. "Funny you think I'd want you back. Yeah, you're pretty, but you're too fucking much, Hannah. Always have been, always will be. Good luck to this new guy. Hope you don't smother him too."

"That's enough. We're outta here." I hooked her around the waist and pulled her against me, meeting Watt's beady little eyes. "You and your mustache are gonna have a nice life together, Watkins. Hope he keeps you warm at night."

I guided Hannah out of the barn into the cool night, not stopping until I had her strapped in my truck. Once the seat belt was secure, I leaned in and covered her mouth with mine. Lips parting on a whimper, she let me in. My tongue found hers, sliding over and winding around it. Her fingers tangled in my hair, and her body arched toward mine.

I kissed her breathless, then I kissed her some more. I could've offered her words, let her know I didn't agree with anything he'd said, but instinct told me to show her. There was no world in which

Hannah Kelly was too much. Yeah, she was a lot, but no more than I could handle. That was because I actually liked this woman. Her strength was a turn-on, not a threat, and I was happy to hand the spotlight over to her. That way, I got to see her light up the way she deserved.

I didn't know if I got that message across with my lips, but by the time I pulled away, Hannah was wiggling in her seat, and her lips were puffy and swollen.

Closing her door, I rounded the truck. With one hand on her knee, I drove out of the parking lot, getting us on the road home.

We were miles out of Cheyenne when Hannah's legs fell open. With her hand over mine, she guided it up her inner thigh to the warm spot between them. There, she made me cup her over her panties. The wetness was unmistakable.

"Hannah..." I warned.

"Pull over, Remi. I need you to pull over."

Unlike the last guy, I didn't have any inclination to deny this woman when she was needy. The next turnout we crossed, I did exactly as she'd asked.

I pulled over.

Chapter Twenty-eight

Hannah

I think I've lost my mind.

It felt like it when I vaulted across the cab of the truck to straddle Remi's lap. But he didn't laugh at me or tell me to slow down. Instead, he slid the seat back to give us room and braced his hands on my hips.

I wasn't as controlled. Anger fueled me, but that wasn't what had me scrambling with the zipper on his jeans and grasping his thick cock. It was the kiss he'd given me. How he'd handled me after god knew what Watt had told him about me. The reassurance he'd given me in his solid touch. The passion he'd fed me without me asking for either.

He'd said I was on fire when I was dancing, then he'd thrown gas on my blaze. Now, I was an inferno. Desperate for him. No way I could make it home. Not without finding the relief I knew he'd give me.

Remi's thumb hooked my panties, pulling them aside. I held his length in my fist, rubbing my aching clit against it—back and forth. His fingers tightened on my hips, and he grunted. It was the sound I longed to hear from him, pushing me over. Rising on my knees, I guided him to my entrance and sunk all the way down until my ass met his thighs.

We were alone in the dark, our panting breaths and distant sound of the highway to keep us company. His features were only hinted at by the pale light of the moon finding its way in through the windows, but his eyes were shiny and locked on mine.

"Remi," I whispered, unwilling to break the quiet spell. "I need you."

"I'm here," he murmured. "Need you too, sweetheart."

I clung to him, my arms tight around his shoulders, my face buried in his neck. I rode him, hard little pumps, slamming myself down again and again. His wide palms slid up and down my back, one gripping my nape, the other on my bottom. He kneaded my flesh, venturing between my cheeks to touch where we were joined, then higher, teasing my other opening with his index finger.

A sharp cry wrenched from deep within me when he breached me there, his fingertip pressing on sensitive nerves. If I thought he'd do it in this setting—unprepared, on the side of the road—I would have begged him to take my ass too. It wasn't something I'd ever wanted, but I was wild for this man. He made me want him in every way.

"Remi," I panted against his throat. "I'm going to come, baby. That feels so good."

"Let me feel it." He slammed me down on his cock as he arched into me. "Give it to me, Hannah."

Sharp, colorful pleasure racked my body. Trembles emanated from my belly, spreading along my limbs until I was shaking all over. Remi held me tight, his upward pumps shorter, faster, hitting a spot that made my eyes roll and my brain go blank.

I came hard, my inner walls clenching around his length. Remi rode me through it, moving me when my bones became too melty and my muscles gave out.

He leaned me against the steering wheel and took my hips in his hands. It was too dark to see much, but he was watching us come together and slide apart, lip caught between his teeth, tendons stark in his neck.

My belly tightened once more, pressure returning, building. He was too beautiful, too fierce in his desire for me, too determined to fuck me deep and raw. I couldn't help myself. Pleasure raced through me, embarking from my mind and pussy at the same time, meeting in a fiery collision at my center. I was set off, crying, scraping my nails along his sinewy forearms, grinding down on him, taking him as deep as he would fit.

"Mouth, Hannah." He gathered me close, cupping the back of my head. "Want your mouth on me when I come inside you."

"Okay," I breathed.

I planted my lips on his. It wasn't so much a kiss as it was an exchange of breath. Panting back and forth, his lungs filling mine and giving it back.

Remi grunted, vibrating my lips as he bucked into me in wild, short, frenzied strokes. Then he went still, his fingers digging into my ass, tangled in my hair. My insides were coated with heat, filling me and overflowing.

"Yes," he murmured into my mouth. "Yes, Hannah. So good."

"Yeah," I sighed, rolling my forehead along his. "So good."

I was messy and wet, a little sore too, but my body was sated, and my mind was satisfied. Remi kissed along my collarbone and held me sweetly. He seemed in no rush to put me back in my seat, and I wasn't eager to go.

I turned my face into his hair, inhaling the sweat and sun from his skin. Vine-like tendrils reached from my heart, threatening to twine around his. Alarm bells should have been ringing in my head, but I was too relaxed to notice if they were.

Remi broke me from my treacherous thoughts. "I don't want to say it, but we need to get back on the road, sweetheart."

"We do." I nodded lazily. "That means I'm going to need to climb off you."

"Probably, yeah."

Remi helped me back into my seat and offered me a few tissues to clean up. We'd stopped using condoms after the first time, mutually agreeing we didn't need them since neither of us was sleeping with anyone else and I had birth control covered. And while I liked having him bare in me, I could have done without the mess he left behind. But Remi was a gentleman. He'd noticed I had a sensory issue with squishiness between my thighs and always wiped it away for me.

"Sweet man." I grinned at him as I cleaned up what I could.

He tugged a chunk of my hair. "Don't ever say I didn't do anything for you."

"I would never."

Silence descended once we were driving again. Flashes of tonight's events—coming upon Watt talking to Remi, hearing a snippet of what he'd had to say about me—tumbled around my head. I hated that Remi had to meet him, let alone speak to him. And god, did I hate Watt. I wished he'd never flashed his cheesy smile at me. I'd always been a sucker for a cowboy, and as awful as I now knew Watt was, he was the physical embodiment of my type.

I had terrible taste in men. The more volatile, the more my brain wanted to latch on and never let go. My attraction to Remi was an anomaly. Then again, he wasn't exactly a safe bet. Sure, he was calm and collected, but he was a rolling stone. There was not a chance he'd stick around long term, and I was deeply rooted in this town.

My sigh was long and heavy. Remi reached for my leg, taking his spot just above my knee.

"You okay?"

"I am." I let my fingers trail between the bones in his hand like railroad tracks. "So, that was my ex. I'm sorry you had to meet him."

He chuffed and flipped his hand over to capture mine. "No skin off my back. Only thing I regret is not shutting him down before you came back and had to hear him running his mouth."

"I've heard it all before from him." I puffed up my cheeks, blowing out a long breath. "I had this friend, Sarah. We weren't besties, but I'd hung around with her since high school. When I got with Watt, she kept telling me rodeo guys weren't loyal. It wasn't in their nature. I brushed her off, fancying myself in *love*."

I let my head fall against the cool window, and Remi squeezed my hand, showing me he was listening.

"Then Graham got sick and needed more of my time. Of course, he didn't ask for it, but I wanted to be there for him. I admit I asked Watt for support. The prognosis hadn't been good, and I'd been falling apart a little. Maybe I leaned on him too hard, I don't know."

Remi grumbled, his fingers tensing slightly. Otherwise, he remained quiet, concentrating on the road in front of us.

"One night, Graham forced me out of the house so I could go watch Watt ride. I didn't tell him I was coming, wanting to surprise him, and walked into the locker room to Sarah blowing him."

"*Fuck*," Remi snapped. "Fucking idiots."

"Yeah. Sarah apologized but basically said I told you so." I scoffed at the memory. Sarah had definitely told me, then she'd given me a live and in-person demonstration of just how right she'd been. Of course, she could've mentioned she wouldn't have known what loyalty was if it had slapped her in the face, but that was neither here nor there. "And Watt...well, he'd tried to get me to forgive him, but when it became clear my interest in him had ceased the second I saw his dick in my friend's mouth, he turned it all around. Said I'd driven him away by clinging too hard and making him uncomfortable telling him I loved him all the time. Said I talked too much, asked for too much attention, spent too much time with my family, wanted too much sex...I was *too much*. He wasn't the first person to say that sort of thing to me, so it's probably true, but he was a nasty bastard about it. His ego is too big for him to be the villain, so he laid the blame on me. As if my personality deficiencies had guided his dick into Sarah's mouth."

For a while, Remi didn't say anything. I didn't know what I wanted him *to* say, but the quiet after I'd finished explaining the details of my sordid relationship was deafening.

Silly me, I felt the need to wipe away the discomfort between us. "Anyway, it's not a big deal. I'm over him, and I haven't spoken to Sarah since. The only thing I have left from that relationship is a boatload of trust issues, but th—"

"Hannah," he gritted out, "I'm glad you're over him. He isn't good enough to be the dirt under your boots. And he lied to you, sweetheart, along with whoever else told you you're too much. It's a deficiency in them. They don't know how to handle a strong woman with a big personality. It's not anything wrong with you."

I sucked in a sharp breath. "I don't know if that's true..."

"It is. Think about your family. They get you. They adore you. None of them have ever tried to change you, have they?"

A lump balled in my throat. "No. But they have to love me."

"What about Graham? Did he have to love you? Take you under his wing? Spend all his days with you?"

"I...well, no." I could still hear him laughing at me when I went on one of my rants, or he caught me dancing around his kitchen or singing to the horses. "I don't think I'm too much for everyone, Rem. I don't hate myself or anything like that. I've accepted this is who I am. But I get I'm not everyone's cup of tea."

"You don't need everyone to like you, Hannah. Just the important ones."

"And...you like me, don't you?" I wanted to slap my fool mouth as soon as the question snuck out. What the hell was I—

"Of course I do. If you need to ask, I'd best do a better job showing you."

"Oh." I sunk into my seat, a silly little smile spreading across my face. It was a good thing the cab was dark and Remi couldn't see me. I'd already embarrassed myself enough for one night. "I like you too, Remi."

"Good to know, sweetheart."

He said it like he truly meant it, and more than anything, I wanted to believe him.

I must've dozed off because the next thing I knew, the truck had come to a stop and Remi was unbuckling my seat belt. I glanced around his hazy eyes, surprised to see the house and not my apartment.

"You forgot to take me home," I croaked.

"Oops." He pulled me out of the truck, his arm around my waist, guiding me to the porch. "Guess you'll have to spend the night with me."

Butterflies launched in my stomach. After the heaviness of earlier, I was surprised he didn't want a break from me and more than a little pleased to be wrong.

I laid my head on his shoulder, my smile kept secret under the cover of darkness. "I guess so."

I woke in the morning tucked against Remi, my face in his underarm. I had no clue how I'd gotten into that position, but I wasn't upset about it. He was so warm there, and his natural scent was even stronger. I nuzzled my nose into him, his soft hair tickling me, and took a deep whiff.

His low chuckle alerted me I wasn't the only one awake. "You're sniffing my armpit?"

"Mmhmm." I tugged on his pit hair and pushed up on my elbow, grinning at him. "I like how you smell."

His hand came to the side of my face, cupping me gently. "That's sweet and cute and a little gross."

I laughed. "You just described me on a daily basis."

"Nope." He rolled us so he was half on top of me. "You smelling my pits is only a little gross—nothing about *you* is. You're funny and alive. You sleep like the dead except when you're invading my personal space and my armpit. But you're so cute about it, I don't mind. Plus, you're incredibly hot."

I blinked at him, my cheeks flaming and heart going pitter-patter. Those tendrils that had been a threat last night were back in full force, clawing at my chest to attach themselves to Remi.

"Holy wow, Remington. I'm going to want to wake up to you every day if all these compliments are included."

"You say that like it's a bad thing."

"It will be when you're gone and no one's telling me I'm hot at—I checked the time on his digital clock—"nine in the morning."

His fingers flexed in my hair, and something dark and stormy clouded his eyes for a moment before he shook it off.

"I don't think you'll have to worry about a shortage of compliments, sweetheart." He dipped down, pressing a firm kiss to my lips before sitting up and rubbing his face with both hands. "Let me make you breakfast. Waffles?"

"I like waffles." I knifed upright and shifted to my knees behind him, my chin on his shoulder. "Fair warning—I don't have my medicine with me. The chances of me spacing out or saying something before thinking it through are high. Don't be alarmed if it happens."

He turned, rubbing the side of his face against my nose. "Got it. We'll get you fed then home for your meds. Anything you say or do will not be held against you."

I kissed his shoulder, my chest so very warm. "Thank you, baby."

He left the room, and while I got dressed, I glanced around at the decorations. This had been Remi's childhood bedroom. There were still relics from that era scattered around. A football trophy. Ribbons from the county fair where he and Caleb had shown a few cows. Framed drawings Remi had done when he was little. A poster from a band I'd never heard of. A piggy bank filled to the brim with coins.

He'd replaced the twin bed that had been in here with a queen-size one, but otherwise, this room had been frozen in time. I'd asked Graham about it once. In his typical, nonchalant style, he'd told me it wasn't his stuff and Remi would decide what to do with it when he came home. He'd been so sure Remi would return, and in the end, he'd been right.

As far as I was concerned, he could keep this bedroom the same. Maybe this would be his new home base where he'd land in between jobs. It would be nice for him to have that, even though the idea of him flitting in and out of Sugar Brush felt like an anvil dropping on my chest.

I had to stop thinking about the end when we were only just beginning. This thing between us might fizzle out on its own and all this worrying would be for nothing. Who knew?

I kept this thought clutched tight to my chest until I entered the kitchen. Remi was standing at the island, stirring the waffle batter. His hair was mussed, a few dark strands hanging over his forehead. He'd thrown on a T-shirt and sweatpants, both threadbare and barely stretching over his frame. Like he'd pulled them out of the drawers from his high school days. When he moved just right, a sliver of his stomach was revealed. I could have stood where I was and watched him all day.

How dare he call *me* hot when he looked like *this*?

"How do you feel about sprinkles?" He held up the spatula covered in batter and colorful sprinkles. "I hope positively because it's too late."

I swallowed down my heart currently trying to leap out of my throat. Not only was he obscenely attractive, but he did cute things like put sprinkles in our waffles.

"I feel great about sprinkles," I managed to answer.

"Good." Remi patted the island beside him. "Now, put your pretty ass right here and keep me company. It's been a while."

I shuffled forward, giving him a wobbly little grin. "All of five minutes."

His eyes danced over me. "Like I said, a while."

Oh...I was screwed. But I hopped up on that counter anyway. If I was going down, I was going to enjoy every damn second of it.

Chapter Twenty-nine

Hannah

REMI AND I WERE at the diner having dinner. I was trying to be a good companion but failing miserably. There were things I wanted to talk to him about that I wasn't sure he'd want to hear. Like how I'd caught myself picking up my phone to dial Graham several times throughout the day, and I was frustrated with myself for forgetting I couldn't do that anymore. If it were Phoebe, I would have told her how I was feeling, but with Remi, I'd tucked it away for later.

Except...even buried, my frustration was lurking, taking my attention from him.

He chuckled. "Guess I need to choose a less boring topic."

Startled I'd let my thoughts wander so far he'd noticed, my spine snapped straight, and I tipped toward him.

"No—it's not you at all. It's my damn brain."

He glanced around the diner, taking everything in. For a Thursday evening, it was fairly busy. Teller and Brady were a few tables away, Teller throwing eye-daggers my way every few minutes. Plenty of other familiar faces were scattered around, as well as tourists passing through our pretty little town. Enough to distract me, for sure, but on a normal basis, I found Remi so compelling my focus locked on him and stayed there.

Today had just been so crummy, my need to vent was overwhelming everything else.

"Is there too much going on?" he asked gently, without judgment.

I loved that he was aware of our surroundings and understood why it might be difficult for me to give him my full attention. He'd hate to hear me say it, but in this instance, he reminded me of his dad.

"No. Not really." I blew out a heavy breath. "One of my horses has chronic laminitis—inflammation of the tissue connecting the hoof to the bone."

He winced. "That sounds painful."

"It definitely is, but it's not uncommon. I've treated many horses with it, but this one mare, I can't seem to help. I've been working with her vet and owner to get it figured out, and it's like we keep taking one step forward and two steps back."

He reached across the table to squeeze my hands, and it was nice. "I wish I had some advice." That was nice too.

But it wasn't what I needed.

I sighed. "I do too."

Remi watched me, a deep crevice between his brows. "That's not it, is it?"

I shook my head. "Not all of it."

"You need to talk about it?"

"Yeah, but I don't think you're the right person for me to talk to."

Hurt rippled over his expression. He fell back against his seat, our hands losing contact. "All right. Then...uh—"

"It's not you, Rem."

He huffed a short laugh. "Still not me?"

"It isn't. I just—" There was no way out of this, and honestly, we couldn't keep dancing around the topic of his dad. I still ached for him every day, and not being able to express that to Remi was untenable.

So I told him.

"Here it is. I spent the day wishing I could call Graham and ask for his advice. And every time I wished it, grief struck me like a bolt of lightning to the chest. I'll never be able to have his advice again. I miss him in a way I can't explain to you because you *don't* miss him. I understand why, and you have every right to those feelings, but right now, I'm thinking about him. I'm missing him, and I can't talk to you about it."

He blinked a few times then took a deep breath. "Why not?"

"I'm not going to do that to you. It wouldn't be fair."

"You can talk to me about anything. I'll try to understand. It'd kill me knowing you had a bad day and are holding it all in to make me comfortable. You don't need to do that, sweetheart. I sure as hell don't want you to."

"Oh." I pressed my lips together, struck by the vehemence in his voice. "Okay."

The corner of his mouth twitched, and he leaned forward again, reclaiming my hands. "You know what I've always wondered?"

"What?" I whispered. "What have you wondered?"

"How you ended up working with him."

I raised my brows. "It's a sordid tale involving me getting arrested. You sure you want to hear it?"

"You think that would deter me? I'm all the way in. Tell me how sweet Hannah Kelly got arrested."

"I'm sweet now, but in high school, I was a bad, bad girl."

He laughed. "I don't believe it."

I grinned. "I was a little thrill seeker. When I was younger, Caleb would speed with me in his little ATV, zipping over the hills so fast we went flying. I loved it. Craved it. When I got older, I spent more time testing limits than studying for actual tests. Anything dangerous, I went for it—including boys."

He groaned. "Always the boy's fault."

"Nope." I shook my head. "All the trouble I got into was absolutely my fault. I had this boyfriend, Richie Slater. You remember the Slaters?"

His eyes narrowed. "The Slaters? You mean the meth heads who lived on that broken-down compound outside town? One of them was your boyfriend? How did your dad let that happen?"

I flipped his hand over to follow the lines on his palm with my fingertips. "My dad didn't know. Keeping my bad, bad boyfriend a secret was even more thrilling. I was good at being sneaky. My parents didn't catch me. Well, not until I was arrested. I was the passenger in a car Ritchie stole. We were both high as kites when he crashed into a fence in front of a state trooper."

Remi flinched like the news of my delinquency was a slap to the face. "Jesus, Hannah. Were you hurt?"

"Luckily, I'd had the wherewithal to put on my seat belt and only got a little bruised. What hurt more was seeing how disappointed my parents were."

"Can't even imagine the ride home with Lock and Elena."

I snorted. "They didn't have to say a word. I wanted to shrivel up and die from the look in their eyes."

"I bet." His brow quirked. "How'd this lead you to Graham?"

"I got probation and was ordered to go to five AA meetings in addition to seeing a psychiatrist. Graham was at my first meeting. He'd been sober for over two years by then." My eyes flicked to his, gauging his reaction. "For what it's worth, he stayed sober until the day he died."

He nodded, his jaw working back and forth. "Good for him. Wish it didn't take me leaving for him to care about anything but the bottle."

"Believe me, he wished it too. I think that's why he took me under his wing in the first place. He never said it, but he knew I had a connection to you. I guess he felt if he couldn't do right by you, he'd try to help me."

"He succeeded in that, didn't he?"

"Yeah, he did. He had me assisting him at Town Hoofcare, going on client visits, taking care of the tools. Around that same time, I got my ADHD diagnosis and was put on meds. They were absolutely life changing. I finally understood why I'd been behaving the way I had and why some aspects of life were just so damn hard for me. Everything came into focus. Graham encouraged me to go to farrier school. I'd been this floating feather, going wherever the wind blew me, and he gave me direction."

My parents had been pretty devastated they hadn't known how badly I'd struggled, but I'd been a master at hiding it. It took me crashing and burning for all of us to wake up to how badly I had needed help.

That felt so long ago now. I wasn't that lost girl anymore.

I threaded my fingers through Remi's. He'd missed everything Graham had freely given me. Graham had made no bones about what a shitty father he'd been to his son. He knew he'd turned himself around too late. But he *did* turn himself around.

"I feel like I'm rubbing the way he was with me in your face, and I don't want to do that. I just miss my friend a lot, and days like today are even worse. But I don't want you to feel bad, and I—"

"No, Hannah. You're not rubbing anything in my face. The man you just told me about...it's like hearing about a stranger. I'm glad as hell you ended up where you did, and I'll never begrudge you the support he gave you just because I never had that." He lifted my hand to his mouth and kissed my knuckles. "I understand what you're missing now, sweetheart— someone who was an integral part of shaping who you are. And who you are is incredible."

My heart, which was already a tender little thing, softened even more. It shouldn't have been possible, but there was really no way for me not to fall for Remington Town, and it terrified the hell out of me.

I waved him off. "You can't say things like that to me in public."

"Fine." He huffed a laugh. "I'll say it again in private."

Once we paid the check, we walked to my place hand in hand. Remi pulled me to a stop at the bottom of my steps, cupping my jaw in his warm hand. His eyes darted between mine for long moments before he leaned in to place a sweet kiss on my lips. Then he wrapped his arms around me and planted more kisses in my hair. And I melted, the tension I'd been holding on to falling away as I took the comfort and care he was offering—that I needed after my hell of a day.

The loud rumbling of an engine interrupted our peace. Both of us turned to see the source, but the street was relatively empty. Seconds later, the rumbling grew closer, and an oversized dark-colored truck came into view, the beam of bright lights approaching. They were going much too fast.

"Someone needs to—"

What I'd been about to say was cut off when the truck veered toward the sidewalk. Remi yanked me backward, practically throwing me onto my porch steps. A scream lodged in my throat when I landed. Remi stood in front of me, blocking my view, but the truck's lights spread around him as it continued toward us.

My body locked, and my eyes slammed shut. I needed to see. I had to know. But my eyes refused to open. I braced myself for impact, and when it came, I finally moved, flinging my arms out and screeching in terror.

Except it wasn't a truck on top of me. Remi cradled me with his body, his cheek against mine, his arms around me.

"Hannah, baby, it's okay. You're safe. They're gone. You're safe, sweetheart," he chanted next to my ear.

My eyes finally fluttered open, and Remi was there, above me. "What was that?" I croaked.

"Someone being a dick and trying to scare us. They got close, but if they meant to hit us, they could have." He stroked my hair away from my face. "Ready to stand up?"

"I think—" I wiggled my toes and bent my legs. "Yeah, I'm ready."

Remi got me up to my apartment. Once he closed the door and locked it, he had me in his arms again, holding tighter. His breath was heavy in my ear, chest rising and falling in rapid waves against mine.

"*Fuck*," he gritted out. "Fuck, fuck, fuck. That was too fucking close."

"But we're okay. We're not hurt. It was probably just some idiot kids entertaining themselves."

He drew back, a scowl pulling at his features. "What color's Cleve's truck?"

My eyes flared in realization. "Navy blue."

"What color was that truck just now?"

"Dark. It might've been navy, but it could've been black or gray."

I didn't know why I was trying to explain this away, only that Cleve had been quiet since my dad, brothers, and Remi had paid him a visit. I'd been hoping that had been the end of it.

He strode to my windows, peering out as he took his cell from his pocket. "I'm calling it in. We're not letting this go, Hannah."

Swallowing hard, I nodded. "Okay. Do what you think is right."

After everything that had happened today—the mare, missing Graham, making a police report for the third time this summer—sleep eluded me. Remi was crashed out hard beside me, but it was two in the morning, and I was still staring at the ceiling. I considered getting up and doing some exercises in the living room to rid myself of the excess energy, but I knew myself well enough to know that wouldn't work. Besides, the last thing I wanted was to wake Remi.

So I lay beside him, a ticker tape of endless thoughts scrolling through my brain. That was why I noticed when the nightmare started. Remi twitched and released a deep, guttural groan. His hands flew up beside his face, balled into tight fists.

"No," he moaned. "Oh no."

I laid my hand on his heaving chest, rubbing in gentle circles. "Remi," I said softly. "Wake up, baby."

He shook his head, thrashing back and forth against his pillow. "No," he cried. "I can't—*stay*. Stay!"

I moved closer, patting his cheek. "Wake up, Remi. You're having a nightmare. Come back to me."

With a sharp gasp, his eyes opened. At first, they were unfocused and wild, but the more I stroked his cheek and murmured reassurances, the haze cleared.

"Hannah," he rasped. "I'm so sorry, sweetheart."

"You have nothing to be sorry for."

He reached for me, his fingers threading through the side of my hair. "I woke you up and now you have to deal with my shit in the middle of the night."

"I wasn't sleeping." I rubbed my nose back and forth along his. "I was wide awake, dealing with my own shit."

"Dammit," he breathed. "Then I'm sorry for falling asleep and not being with you while you were struggling."

My mouth twitched. "You're apologizing for falling asleep now, Remington? Come on. We don't need to be so formal with each other, do we?"

"Not formal, no. But I need you to know I care about you, and if I fall down on the job, I'm going to make up for it." He pulled me down to his chest, tucking me snug against him. His fingers trailed up and down my spine in a slow, rhythmic motion. "What were you thinking about, sweetheart?"

"A lot."

"Give it to me. I want it."

He didn't know what he was asking for, but I took a deep breath anyway and laid out the wild roller coaster that was my mind. "The mare, Graham, my clients I'm seeing tomorrow—well, today...the cowboys who drool over Phoebe, my grandparents getting older, worry about Jesse having enough resources for his big brain in this small town, trying to remember when I changed my sheets, the tag in my shirt, the blueberry muffin I'm going to have for breakfast, how long you're going to be in town, why Cleve hates me so much, what snack I'm going to pack to eat while I'm on the road, the contents of my pantry, if this winter will be as bitter as the last, and...well, I think you get the picture."

He heaved a sigh. "You're right. That is a lot."

"Once I get going, it's difficult to stop." I shoved my face into the side of his throat, feeling the stress of the day slowly dissipating. "What were you dreaming about?"

"I think...I think it was about my dad. Me chasing him and him walking away. I kept getting close, trying to reach out, but every time I did, he'd slip away." He cleared his throat. "Sometimes my brain's a little on the nose. I don't need Freud to analyze the meaning of that dream."

"You said you work things out in your dreams. Did you? Work something out, I mean?"

"I don't know." His arms tightened around me. "Seems like it's too late to work out what I needed to with my old man. He's gone now, and the way we left it is the way it'll always be. Maybe that's what I need to be working to accept."

He rolled me onto my back, his hands bracketing either side of my head as he loomed over me. "I want to help you fall asleep. Can I make you come—ease some of those thoughts out of your head?"

I reached for his face, dragging my fingers along his rough scruff. "Please, Rem. And let me ease some of those thoughts out of yours."

Remi undressed me slowly, gently, then himself. His mouth trailed down my body, stopping at my breast to taste then roaming lower, leaving wet, warm kisses as he went. He settled between my legs, stroking my inner thighs and belly as he lowered his mouth to my flesh.

I slid my fingers through his hair, sinking into his touch. My eyes fluttered shut. In the dark, the silence, my senses were pared down to the basics, and *he* was what filled them. Remi's sunshine scent on my sheets. The wet sounds his tongue made against my sex. My light, feathery breaths. His palms on the backs of my legs. His rough stubble rubbing my inner thighs. The silk of his thick hair running between my fingers.

I sighed out my pleasure, my exhale expelling the harsh awareness of everything outside these walls. With Remi, I did not have to think about any of that. He made it impossible to. There was only us, Remi giving me pleasure, me allowing my tendrils to curl around him just a little.

He rose over me, sliding his length into my body. For once, he took his time sinking all the way inside. Inch by inch until we were deeply connected. Our hands intertwined above my head. Our eyes locked in a span of time that was so stretched, it was like gossamer. I could have stayed like this with Remi forever. There was no grief, no troubles, and the impossibility of us didn't exist. It was just us, ebbing and flowing in time with each other.

Remi watched me with soft intensity. I freed one hand to trace his expression with my fingertips. His starbursts were mere echoes, only faintly visible, but I knew them. In one summer, I'd grown to know the planes and lines of this man's face like no one's before him. I dragged my knuckle along his cheekbone and the pad of his chin. Lifting my head, I kissed along his jaw and the tip of his nose.

"Hannah," he murmured. "You feel so good. My beautiful girl."

This thing between us was special and quiet and carnal. I was so drawn to him, I wondered how it was possible we'd known one another most of our lives yet had only just discovered *us*. We'd filled in the cavity left by a great loss with tender knowing and tentative, delicate feeling.

I reached for Remi. Reached and reached and reached. He answered with deeper slides and open hands. Focused eyes and soft lips on my skin. We lapped and receded, again and again, until there was nothing but pleasure spilling like lava over and around us.

When it was all over, our legs tangled, with me tucked snugly against Remi's broad, smooth chest; I closed my eyes and inhaled his scent mingled with mine.

"Thank you, sweetheart."

"For what?" I whispered.

"Mmm." His chest vibrated my cheek. "For being mine tonight."

Tonight. Tonight, tonight, tonight.

I didn't have to think about the limits of that one word. Not now. Not when it was three in the morning and sleep was so close I could taste it.

I snuggled closer, winding my arm around his middle. "Good night, Remington."

He kissed my forehead, lingering there for several moments. "Night, Hannah."

There was more to say. So much more. But not now.

Not now.

Letting myself have this, exactly what I wanted right now, I gave in to the pull and fell asleep to the steady beat of Remi's heart.

Chapter Thirty

Hannah

Maybe it was telling Remi about Graham, or it could've been enough time had passed, but a week later, I woke up in Remi's bed with a burst of energy. He was still fast asleep, and I wanted him to stay that way. His sleep had been so fitful lately he'd developed dark smudges beneath his eyes. There was a lot he needed to work out, and I wondered if he should have been doing it during daylight hours instead of relegating it to his unconscious mind.

But I wasn't sure it was my place to say that, so I did the best I could to take care of him when we were awake and soothe away his troubles during the night.

Moving carefully, I slipped from our bed and padded down the hall to Graham's bedroom. His clothes were still on the bed, exactly where Remi had left off in his task.

Shutting the door, I sat on the edge of the bed, closed my eyes, and inhaled deeply, nearly whimpering at how faint Graham's scent had become. He'd been gone for months now. An entire season. It felt like yesterday and forever at the same time.

The task of cleaning out his room was past due, but I needed to be the one to do it. I hadn't been ready until this morning. Now that I was in here, looking at the piles that were just things and not at all who Graham was, I couldn't remember exactly why I'd insisted on keeping all this stuff.

Once I got going, I was a whirlwind, stacking bags filled with old T-shirts, worn-out jeans, sweaters older than me. I set aside a few flannels and tees I wanted for myself. A few belts I thought Remi might want to keep, but the rest was prepped to go. Someone would make good use of it. Sitting here, it was wasted.

I had no idea how long I'd been at it when the door squeaked open, startling me out of my hyperfocus. In my surprise, I let loose the item in my hand. When it connected with Remi's forehead, I thanked my lucky stars I'd been holding a pair of socks and not the paperweight I'd had minutes before.

"Holy shit!" I exclaimed, my blood racing in my ears. "Give a girl a warning, why don't you!"

Remi, smooth operator he was, caught the socks as they bounced off his head with a laugh. "I was looking all over for you, calling your name. I would've had to be a herd of bison to make more noise."

Pressing my hand to my thrashing heart, I looked around the room, shocked at all I'd gotten done. "I was in the zone. I didn't hear you at all. Sorry for throwing things at you again."

He approached, circling his arm around my waist to haul me into him. I earned a kiss on the cheek, then the corner of my mouth, followed by my lips.

"I thought you left," he murmured.

"I wouldn't leave without saying goodbye." I laid my hands on his bare chest. It was warm and solid. "You should know by now, when I wake up, I'm really awake. I got the idea in my head to come in here and finish what you started, so that's what I've been doing."

"I missed having you in my armpit when I woke up." He looked around his dad's bedroom, landing on the garbage bags I'd stacked in one corner. "You're clearing it all out?"

"Yeah. It's time. I set aside a few things. He wore in his flannels to perfection, so I'm stealing them. There's nothing softer than a flannel that's been worn and washed three hundred times, you know?"

"It's not stealing, sweetheart. They're yours. He left them to you."

"Half mine, but I figured you wouldn't want them. You're not really a flannel guy."

"You figured right."

I separated from him to show him the belts I thought he might want. "These were handmade by a leather artisan in Laramie. They're heavy duty and in really good shape. And while you're not a flannel guy, you are a cool leather belt guy."

He took the belts from me, running the length of one along his palm. It had a basket weave pattern with a wolf embossed on the sides. "I remember him wearing this one when I was a kid. My mom was the one who'd discovered the artisan. She gave this to him for one of his birthdays. Since I can recall it, it must've been the last one before she died." His fingers curled around it. "It'll be more a part of her than him, but yeah, I'd like to keep it. Thank you for knowing that, Hannah."

I smiled, soft and sad. "He told me his bride had started his collection."

Remi's gaze jerked to me. "His bride? I'd forgotten he'd called her that. I guess that's because he stopped talking about my mom when she died. Hell, he stopped talking to me at all."

Tingles ran along my skin from the strange detachment in his voice. But then, he sounded the same way every time he spoke about his father. Even when I'd spilled my history with Graham, he'd been caring and gentle, but like he'd said, it was as though I'd told him a story about someone he'd never met.

He'd been the same when talking about his ex. *Seattle.* Two years together, and she'd been relegated to the city they'd lived in. Would I become Sugar Brush when he talked about me one day? Another one in his long line of temporary home bases?

Well, there was no sense in fretting about that right now. I couldn't see the future, and I liked Remi far too much to snatch my heart away now.

I probably more than liked him, but I *definitely* wasn't going there. Not yet. Not until I knew the ground we were on was steady.

Once bitten, twice shy and all that.

Remi hooked his arm around my neck, hauling me into him again. I earned a firm kiss on my forehead.

"We'll take these bags out to my truck later, drive them into town to the donation center." Another kiss, this time on my temple. "You did a good job, sweetheart. You got a lot of work done before the sun even knew it was daytime, and some of it was with me on your mind. Now I have you on my mind, and I want to make my girl breakfast and spend our day together."

Oh yeah. I definitely more than liked him. I let my body lean into him but tried my mightiest to keep my heart from doing the same.

"Sounds like a really good plan, Remington...as long as there are sprinkles."

He smiled into my hair. "Of course. I'd never short you on sprin-kles."

"You know, before you came along, I ate a blueberry muffin every single day. Deviating from that would have thrown me off the rest of my day. But now I'm eating waffles with sprinkles sometimes, and my days are...well, let's just say they're not bad."

"Not bad? Guess I'll take that as a compliment." He laughed softly.

"I meant it as one."

"My days with you are...not bad either, sweetheart. I'm glad to be the one to add sprinkles into your life. A colorful girl deserves a colorful breakfast."

I squeezed my eyes shut. "That's sweet. Real sweet."

And that was why my mightiest wasn't even close to good enough. My heart was Remington Town's, damn the consequences.

As much as I would have liked to be the kind of woman who lazed about on a rare Sunday with no plans on the horizon, that wasn't me. After breakfast, Remi and I finished clearing out Graham's bedroom. I boxed up the few things I wanted and secretly suspected Remi might have liked to have in the future, and we loaded the rest into Remi's truck to drop off in town.

There, we stopped in for a cup of coffee and a treat at Sugar Rush and got the latest gossip from Phe. Apparently, Brady and Teller had been in earlier, whisper-yelling about Brady texting some girl from his work. It ended with Brady getting a cup of—iced—coffee dumped in his lap and Teller storming out.

I wished I could have seen that, but my sister's animated recounting of the events was almost as good as being there—especially the bit about Brady chasing after his wife, leaving a stream of coffee and ice cubes down the sidewalk.

It was pretty hard to feel sorry for two people who so thoroughly deserved each other.

When we got back to the house, I started for the porch, but Remi grabbed my hand, weaving our fingers together.

"Let's go for a walk, sweetheart."

I nodded. "That sounds like a good idea."

Henry kept a path cleared around the property. We trailed along, nowhere in particular to go, letting the sun warm us. Soon enough, the wind would become bitter, and spending long lengths of time outdoors would be pretty unbearable.

Remi might not be here by then. I couldn't say I'd blame him if he left before winter fully set in. I always thought I was used to Wyoming cold, but when it hit every year, the brutality came as a shock. It'd be even colder this year without Remi, though.

"What's the deal with Teller and her husband? Brady?" he asked.

"Oh god, what *isn't* the deal? They've been together since we were in high school, and Brady's been cheating on her ever since."

His brow dropped. "Does she know that?"

"I couldn't fathom her not knowing. Feels like the whole town knows. Of course, that's because they like to air their dirty laundry out in public. It might be some kind of kink."

He sputtered. "A kink thing? Expand on that."

"Yeah, like Brady gets off on being degraded by his wife. I can't think of any other reason he'd go along with having a fight in the bakery on a Sunday morning where half the town is going in and out, picking up their pastries and coffee."

He made a gurgling sound in the back of his throat. "I don't want to think about what they went home and did."

"No—gross!" With a pained groan, I knocked my head into his shoulder. "Don't put that idea in my head, Remington."

"You brought up their kink. This is all on you."

We fell into laughter, which led to a short make-out session, thoroughly wiping every gross image of Brady and Teller away before continuing our walk. When we came upon the stables, Remi steered us that way. I went with him, even though I knew what we'd find inside.

Emptiness.

He pushed open the creaky door and flicked on the lights. For a building that'd been abandoned for years, it didn't have a haunted feel and that was because Henry kept it in such good shape. He hadn't allowed nature to take over or vermin to move in. If we had a horse who needed a place to stay, it could have been moved in today.

Remi sauntered down the row of six vacant stalls, his hands on his hips. Stopping at the end, his back to me, he stated, "He sold my horse when she died."

"You had a horse?" I asked, still by the entrance.

He wrapped his fingers around the metal grill at the top of the stall door. "He was my mom's. She declared him mine when I was seven or eight. A sorrel gelding named Huck. I learned to ride on him. Spent most of my early years with him. Then, one day, my mom was gone, and a couple weeks later, so was Huck. He sold all the horses, but losing Huck gutted me."

He was telling me this devastating story while once again sounding removed from it all. I couldn't say I felt the same. Pressing my hand to my topsy-turvy belly, I breathed through a wave of nausea. I'd known Graham had sold his horses when he couldn't bring himself to take care of them properly, but he'd never told me about Huck.

"We could track him down, Rem. See what kind of life he led after—"

"No." He shook his head and turned around. "It was a long time ago. Nothing I can do about it now besides let it go."

"Yeah," I whispered. "That's true."

He crossed the room, curving an arm around me. "Wipe that sadness away, Hannah. I don't want you to feel sorry for something I got over years ago."

"A boy and his horse should never be separated. It's just a fact of life." I slapped his chest. "But fine, I won't be sad if you're not. Well, not about that at least. I'm sad these stables are empty. They should be filled with life and the pastures outside should be grazed. That's what's a real tragedy."

"You think so?" He skimmed his nose along mine. "You'd fill this land with life?"

"I would. If you were a horse, wouldn't you want to live here too? It's gorgeous and has so much room for roaming and grazing."

Remi hummed noncommittally and flipped off the lights. We continued on our walk, quiet this time. He seemed to be deep in thought, and I decided to enjoy the golden glow of the prairie grass and push away the ache deep in my belly.

Out of nowhere, Remi said, "You could do that, you know."

I turned my head to look at him, but his focus was on the sprawling landscape ahead of us. "What?"

He finally looked at me, and the care in his hazel eyes was devastatingly lovely. "Fill these stables up again. After all, all this is half yours to do what you want with it. You want horses; you should have them."

"Maybe," I hedged.

We walked on. A lighter topic and a few make-out sessions. It seemed we couldn't go long periods without kissing.

In the back of my mind, though, I kept asking myself the same question. How could this man be so tender and careful with me and, at the same time, speak about this place and my future here like it had nothing to do with him?

The answer was right there, shouting at me and waving ten blazing red flags.

Because Remington Town knows he won't stick around to be a part of my future. When it comes down to it, he probably won't even be a part of my winter.

And still, we walked on, hand in hand.

Chapter Thirty-one

Remington

THE FIRST TIME I'D been in Hannah's apartment, I'd had the thought that she didn't belong in a closed-in space like that, nice as it was. But it wasn't until we roamed Graham's property, seeing her wistful for what it once was and what it could be, that the thought struck me. *This is where she belongs.* Ten acres was a postage stamp compared to the Kelly ranch, but if all this was hers, she could have her space, her horses, anything she wanted.

I wanted that for her.

I set up an appointment with Dell Rivers the first chance I got, which ended up being a week later. He'd questioned my decision but, in the end, had agreed to prepare the paperwork.

Walking out of his office, the preliminary paperwork in hand, I felt lighter than I had in some time. That was how I'd known I'd done the right thing. Hannah would have her land, her horses, room to run and be free, and I'd get to give all that to her.

Yeah, I'd definitely done the right thing.

I couldn't wait to see her face when I told her—just as soon as Dell finished filing what he needed to and not a second longer.

After my meeting with Dell, I drove back home. Since Caleb was still limiting my time working on the ranch until his stubborn ass decided I'd fully recovered and Hannah was off at work, I was at loose ends. Sitting around, doing nothing, wasn't me. I was accustomed to being on the move, having a goal, but I still hadn't uncovered what that looked like since coming back to Sugar Brush over two months ago. I was in the middle of considering what I wanted to do with my day when Henry rapped on the screen door and called out, "Got you a package, kid."

I pushed the door open and took the small but heavy box out of his grizzled brown hands. "Thanks. Do you want to come in, have a glass of water or tea?"

Henry had been living on this property for as long as I could remember, and he'd always been old. His skin was leathery from his years spent in the sun, and the crags on his face were deep and weathered. His white hair was almost always covered by a trucker hat, and his wiry frame was beginning to stoop, but he could still lift a bale of hay over his shoulder without flinching. He could've been fifty or ninety. I couldn't guess, and asking was out of the question. It didn't really matter anyway. Henry was as much part of this property as the yellow grass covering the land and the lone pine tree that had sprouted up out of a slab of granite I'd been fascinated by as a kid.

"Nah." Henry waved me off, already shuffling away from the door. "Too much to do to spend time chitchatting."

With no other fanfare, he tromped down the porch steps.

I took the box into the kitchen, noting it'd come from North Carolina, but no name. I didn't know what I expected to find, but a scratched and beaten leather camera bag wasn't it. There was a folded piece of paper on top of it with a note inside.

Dear Remi,

You were always part of Logan's stories. He admired the work you did, and his private goal was to match your skill and ability to tell a story through a picture. As his mother, I thought he was brilliant, but he always strove to be better. You inspired him.

This camera was his most treasured possession. He had no use for other material things. I'm sure you understand.

I think Logan would be honored for you to have his camera. Keep it or give it to someone else who will treasure it. I have a feeling you'll know what to do.

I'm sorry we were never able to meet, Remington, but I'm glad I have the chance to tell you how highly my son thought of you. Live well. As you know, life is far too short.

In gratitude,

Rebecca Adamski

Knotted emotions clogged my throat as I lifted the bag out of the box, picturing it where I'd last seen it, slung across Logan's chest. I couldn't remember if he'd had it in the car the day we wrecked. It would've been a miracle if it survived in one piece. Maybe he'd been carrying his second camera that day.

Unzipping the top, I held my breath as I slid out Logan's Nikon. It was pristine, well taken care of. Some of my colleagues primarily used their phones to capture images, but Logan and I had agreed nothing touched what we could get with a high-quality professional camera.

With a clenched gut, I powered on the camera and brought the viewfinder to my eye. My finger twitched on the shutter release, and something shifted in me. This camera was mine now, and I would make good use of it.

Instinct drove me outside into the fields, and my feet didn't stop until I reached the tree in the rock. There, I raised the camera again, and for the first time since I'd arrived in Wyoming, I was truly, fully myself.

I was sitting on the porch steps when Hannah pulled up. She waved as she drove past me, parking in front of the detached garage. Hopping out of the truck, she sauntered over to me, her thumbs hooked in her belt loops.

The sun was behind her, glinting off her hair, casting a golden hue on her bare shoulders. With each step she took, her lips curved a little more. I raised the camera in my hands and snapped a series of pictures of her.

She stopped right in front of me, hands on her hips. "You'll have to talk to my agent before you take any more pictures. I'm expensive, you know."

Grinning, I lowered the camera to rest on the step beside me and walked down to meet her, looping my arm around her waist to draw her in.

"That's why I had to steal those shots. I knew I couldn't afford you." I touched my mouth to hers, soft and slow. Her fingers curled into my shirt, gripping the fabric in a fist. "Prettiest pictures I ever took," I murmured.

"Shut up and kiss me, Remington."

With a laugh, I banded my arm beneath her ass to lift her and walked her over to the post holding up the porch, pressing her back against it. Her long legs wrapped around me, ankles locking behind me and her fingers delved into the sides of my hair. I took a beat to drink in her face, a little smudged with dirt from a long day at work. Sweat beading in her hairline. Freckles dusted the bridge of her nose and fanned out along her cheeks. Since we became an *us*, I'd seen her nearly every day, but there was no getting used to this. Her beauty nearly dropped me to my knees every damn time.

I covered her mouth with mine, giving her the kiss she'd requested. Long and deep.

Her lips parted, letting my tongue sweep inside to explore. Her legs tightened around me as a soft moan spilled free. Once I'd started, it'd become impossible to stop. I slipped a hand under the back of her tank to get to her warm, smooth skin.

"Remi," she murmured, "I'm so dirty. You don't wanna touch me."

"Says who?" I continued under her shirt, trailing my fingers along the edge of her sports bra. "I don't mind dirt."

Laughing, she unlocked her legs and gave me a gentle shove. "Well, I do. And it's not just dirt on me, you know. There's a good blend of sweat and horseshit."

"All right." I let her drop her feet to the ground but kept her close. "I like your sweat, but I could do without the horseshit."

"Figured." She took my hand in hers. "Come keep me company while I unload my tools."

Grabbing the camera, I followed her to her truck. I didn't try to help her. I'd made that mistake once. Hannah had a system, one I couldn't grasp, so she'd forbade me from touching her tools. I couldn't say it didn't bother me just standing by while she worked, but I knew when to stand down, and this was one of those times. I'd learned Hannah had come up with ways to cope with having a somewhat chaotic brain. Her after-work ritual was one of them, and my interfering really threw her off. That meant I sat in a folding chair, staying quiet and watchful.

The view was nice, and I sure as hell didn't mind the company, so I had no problem with it. This time, I took pictures of her, her tools, the garage. The textures and lighting made for some interesting images. I was looking forward to editing them on my laptop. The excitement stirring in my gut was familiar and had been sorely missed.

Once Hannah had finished, we went into the house. She took a quick shower while I sat at the kitchen table, loading the pictures onto my computer. I was engrossed in the first edit when she reappeared in one of Graham's flannels and nothing else.

"What are you up to?" she asked.

I patted my knee. "Come here, I'll show you."

She made herself at home in my lap, her solid weight both a comfort and a visceral turn-on. Then again, this woman could breathe and my dick would take notice.

I scrolled through the unedited pictures I'd taken today. There were...a lot. Hundreds. I'd been out for hours roaming the property, even catching Henry from a distance.

"These are all from today?" she asked.

"They are."

"They're incredible, Rem. What made you decide to break out your camera?"

I touched the Nikon sitting beside my computer. "This isn't mine. It belonged to Logan Adamski. He was one of the photographers in the car with me that day."

She sucked in a breath. "He's the one who didn't make it?"

"Yeah. His mother sent me this. She said he'd want me to have it and make good use of it. How could I put it back in the box? It seemed disrespectful not to take it out and grab a few photos. But once I got started, I didn't want to stop. I remembered what it was like to look at the world through my lens and find interesting in the mundane. Beauty in devastation. Magic in nature."

She twisted in my lap to face me, her eyes roaming my face, surveying me. "You're really happy."

"Yeah, maybe? Having a camera in my hands was like...like regrowing a missing appendage. I can survive without it, but now that it's back, I feel whole again."

"I'm glad you have it, then." She brushed her nose along mine. "Was Logan your friend?"

"He...I'm not sure I'd call him a friend. He was younger. Early twenties. He reminded me of myself when I first started. Full of adrenaline and vigor. Ready to change the world with his pictures, you know? We met in Thailand a few years ago, after the tsunami. I'd only been there a couple days, and it had been his first time working overseas. I saw him off and on after that. When we'd met again a couple days before the wreck, I'd noticed a big change in him. Some of his light had dimmed. It's impossible for it not to.

Being on the ground in the middle of a disaster—and the disasters we documented were more often man-made—hearing the sounds, the smells, witnessing firsthand what desperation drives people to, I think it rewires our brains. The only way to get out of this job whole is to detach. I'm not sure Logan ever conquered that skill. He'd told us he'd been thinking about going home, maybe staying put for a while. Then..."

She curled into me, her face in my throat, her arms tight around my shoulders. I held on to her, probably a little too hard, but she let me take the comfort I needed.

"Sometimes it's too late to go home," I rasped past the grief clawing at my throat. "You never know until it's too late."

Hannah rubbed slow circles between my shoulder blades and pressed light kisses along the column of my throat.

"Lucky for us, you came home," she whispered, so soft I barely made it out. Then she moved her mouth next to my ear and said, "He was singing, baby. Remember that?"

A wave of tenderness crashed into me, and I clung more tightly to this woman. Alive and solid and real. Untouched by so much of the ugliness that was out there. Hannah Kelly was like coming upon a pure, crystal-clear stream after I'd been wandering the desert, unaware of just how damn thirsty I'd become.

We stayed like that, the two of us wrapped in each other, for a long while. Eventually Hannah returned to her original position in my lap and began peppering me with questions about the camera, then sat with me through the editing process. She seemed interested in all of it, curious about my career and art, so I spilled. Telling her about the places I'd traveled, where I'd want to go back to given the chance, and countries I would never set foot in again.

I missed her questions petering out because once I got going, I wanted her to know everything. This was me sharing a big part of my life with her, something I generally kept compartmentalized from the people I'd spent brief periods of time with over the years. With Hannah, I had an all-encompassing urge for her to know me and for me to truly know her. She'd let me have these beautiful glimpses of her internal life, but I craved the wide-open picture.

After a while, Hannah got to her feet and poured us glasses of juice. She brought me mine, then retreated away from the table to lean on the island, slowly sipping from her glass.

"You're far away," I said.

Her smirk was automatic but missing some of her normal sass. "I'm right here."

"Far." I got up and joined her at the island, cupping her nape to draw her near. "This is better."

She set down her glass to spread her fingers on my chest. "I'm really happy for you, Rem. Thank you for sharing your passion with me."

I cocked my head, alarm bells sounding in the distance. "You don't sound all that happy."

"I am, promise. I'm just tired and thinking about the drive home."

"You don't need to go home. Stay here."

She turned her head and yawned, but I could've sworn it wasn't real.

"If I stay here, we both know I won't rest. Plus, my medicine's at home, my clean clothes...I'm gonna go."

I tensed, prepared to fight her. "Why?"

"I just told you." She raised herself on her toes and pecked my lips. "I need a good night's sleep. When I'm here…"

She didn't need to say her nights with me were often interrupted by my nightmares. The thing was, they'd lessened over time and with having her beside me. But that wasn't her cross to bear; it was mine. If she didn't want to spend her nights comforting me, she shouldn't have to.

"I get it." I touched my lips to her forehead, then let her go. "Go home. I'll see you in the morning."

She untangled herself from me without a second's hesitation, gathering her things and stuffing her legs back into her jeans. With her hand on the doorknob, she turned back to me and offered a wave.

"Don't stay up all night editing pictures," she said.

"Yeah," I replied, gripping the edge of the counter hard enough to crack it. "Drive carefully, Hannah."

One curt not, then she disappeared out my door, leaving me wondering what the hell had just happened. How had we gone from being wrapped up like two octopuses to spending the night apart?

Hannah withdrew from me; I knew that much.

This was my first time opening up like I had, but maybe I'd come on too fast, too strong, and she wasn't ready for it. I'd be disappointed if that were true, because there was nothing Hannah could share with me I couldn't handle. I'd thought she was in the same place with me, but what did I know?

I guessed I read her wrong. And standing here in this quiet, empty house sure as hell didn't feel good. Not good at all.

Chapter Thirty-two

Remington

Two days had gone by, and I'd barely seen Hannah. I'd caught her at the end of her day yesterday. She'd been sweet as always, giving me kisses and winding her arms around me, and she'd come inside, but not for long. When I'd asked her to stay awhile, she'd claimed to have plans with Phoebe.

Maybe that had been true. Hell, given their relationship and how close they were, it probably was, but I was uneasy about her sudden absence. It was like she'd given herself over to me then stolen herself away without a single warning.

My thoughts kept coming back to me overstepping. That had to be what it was. I'd made her uncomfortable with how much I'd shared. Too much, too soon.

It hadn't felt soon. Sure, I'd only been in Sugar Brush a few months, but we weren't building this thing between us on nothing. We had a lifetime of history to mount our relationship on—shared roots I'd tried to kill but hadn't seemed able to.

The feelings I'd developed for Hannah were unexpected. Unprecedented for me when it came down to it. But I had welcomed them. Let them bud and blossom, sensing if I did, beauty would come of it. There was just no damn way I'd been wrong about her feeling them too. No damn way.

Either something else was going on, or I was being a needy, paranoid ass and would be better off taking a breath and relaxing. Two days without my girl wasn't the end of the world and sitting around going over and over what had taken place between us wasn't helping anything.

So I drove into town and parked outside her place. Her lights were on. She was up there and not with me. Didn't feel right.

I had no game plan when I got out, climbed her steps, and knocked on her door, but I wanted to see her, so I was here.

It took her a while to open up. When she did, she didn't look exactly thrilled. She still looked gorgeous, her long hair draped over her shoulder in a thick braid, wearing men's boxers and a white tank, but tired too. There was a blankness in her gaze that had alarm shooting up my spine.

"Hey." Her eyes flared on my face. "This is a surprise."

"I missed you at the house today. Wanted to see your face."

"I wasn't there long." She leaned her shoulder against the doorjamb, not inviting me in. "What's up?"

My brow dropped low at her lackadaisical response. I'd missed her enough to swallow my pride and seek her out and all I was getting in return was indifference. What the hell was going on?

"Like I said, I wanted to see you. I told myself you weren't avoiding me. That I was being needy by missing you. Seeing as you aren't happy I showed up here and you're not asking me inside, I don't think I was being paranoid, was I?"

Hannah sighed. "Maybe not. I needed a step back to think."

My jaw went rigid. Suspecting it and hearing it were two entirely different things. I'd never wanted to be so wrong in my whole life.

"Yeah? Care to share any conclusions you've drawn?"

Her fingers curled around the doorframe as she shifted her weight from one bare foot to the other. Tongue darting out to lick her lips, her eyes slid sideways, avoiding mine.

"I'm ready to call it a day, Rem," she uttered without much life.

I jerked back. "On us?"

"Yeah. I'm sorry, but I can't see this going anywhere, and it doesn't make sense to keep dragging the inevitable out." Her tone was flat. I couldn't say if she was upset, relieved, angry, or somewhere in between.

I felt like I'd been knocked flat on my ass. "Not going anywhere?"

"Mmm. My life is here, in Sugar Brush, and yours is out there. We can keep having fun until you leave, but it would be smarter to end it before one of us gets attached. It's for the best."

"Hannah...*Jesus*. I'm feeling a little fuckin' blindsided here." I dug the heel of my hand into my temple. "Just like that, you're ending us, no discussion?"

Her expression tightened, mouth pinching. "There doesn't need to be a big discussion. It only takes one 'no,' and I'm saying it. I don't want to do this anymore. Let's move on from it, all right?"

I looked at her but couldn't read her. Not a single thought or emotion. She'd locked it all down. Something like panic stirred in me. She was really doing this.

"Nothing about this is all right. There's no reason to end things. It's too good to stop it. I don't want this."

She sucked in a stuttered breath. "I do, Rem. It's too much for me. We shouldn't have gotten started in the first place, and that's my fault. I'm sorry, but I can't continue."

Putting my hand on the wall outside her door, I leaned in, getting close to her face. "This isn't right, you deciding for us without any warning or discussion."

"I get that, but it was going to end anyway." She took a step back, crossing her arms over her chest. "I'll stay out of the house while you're in town. Make it as easy on us as possible."

"How is this going to be easy?"

"I don't know. But it'll be harder later." She raised her fist to her chest. "Can we just let it be? I don't want to fight with you, I—"

"Want me to walk away?"

She didn't deny it, and I felt like a goddamn fool standing outside her door, not even given the courtesy of being invited off the stoop to be dumped.

"I'm sorry," she whispered.

"All right, Hannah. If that's what you want, I'll give it to you."

Even though it killed me to do it, I turned my back on her and walked away. I got two steps down when what sounded like a whimper made me pause and turn back. When I did, all I saw was Hannah disappearing behind her door as she closed it.

That was that.

Fuck.

How could that be that?

I stopped at my truck but didn't get in. Another night by myself in Graham's house sounded like hell, so I kept walking until the neon lights of Joy's Elbow Room beckoned me. It wasn't particularly busy, and I was grateful since I was in no mood for conversation. My only desire was a couple hours where I wasn't alone with my thoughts.

The quiet little waitress, Alice, came by my table and took my order. She moved efficiently, writing everything down on her notepad, then scurried away with barely a murmur. My beer came fast. My burger took more time, but that was okay. My mouth was filled with sawdust, and I didn't know if I'd be able to choke anything down anyway.

My head was on upside down. I couldn't make sense of what had just happened on Hannah's doorstep. I was certain I hadn't been alone in my feelings. Hannah had been right there with me, falling just the same. There was no way she hadn't.

And then...nothing.

"Hey there."

I looked up from my burger, my eyes landing on one of the blondes who'd read me poetry. Pretty sure this one wasn't Teller, but her name failed to come to me.

"Hello," I replied, dread pooling in my already soured gut. I really didn't want to fucking do this.

Her hands resting on the back of the empty chair across from me, she bent forward to give me an ample view of her tits. "My night's looking up now you're here," she slurred. "Are you all alone?"

Being as polite as I could without giving her room to work her way in, I answered, "Just grabbing dinner before heading home."

She pushed her lips out, looking duckish. "No Hannah?"

"Not right now, no."

"Seems like you two are attached at the hip. You should be careful, though. Her last boyfriend had to scrape her off like a barnacle, you know."

Stomach clenched, I cocked my head. "I didn't know that. He tell you that before or after he stepped out on her?"

Pink flared in her already flushed cheeks. "He didn't tell me anything. It was Sarah, Hannah's former best friend. She had a lot to say about her. I should probably tell you so you don't make the same mistake Watt did. She's pretty, but—"

I was through being polite. I didn't want to listen to another word this woman had to say. Not about Hannah or anything else. "Is there something you need?"

"I'd love your company, Remi. It's not too often we get new guys in town—" she flapped her hand haphazardly, "—well, you're not new, but same difference. Anyway, I'm sure you have fascinating stories to tell, and I'd *love* to listen to them."

I picked up my hamburger and brought it to my mouth. "Just having dinner. Not interested in talking tonight." I took a big bite to punctuate my point.

She didn't seem to get it though, giggling as she pulled out the chair. "I love a hungry man," she cooed. "Men with big appetites need to—"

I'd never know what she was going to say because she was cut off by the clacking heels of Lily Smythe-Kelly. With her coiffed silver bob, silk blouse, slim-fitting skirt, and what had to be a designer bag hanging from the crook of her elbow, she stood out in a townie bar like Joy's.

"There you are, dear," Lily announced in her own regal way, shouldering not-Teller out of the way. "Thank you for keeping Remington company, Tina. You can go now."

Tina's dark eyebrows popped in surprise. "Excuse me, Mrs. Kelly, but we were—"

Lily, who had to be in her late seventies but didn't look a day over fifty-five, shot Tina a look that would have made my balls wither and fall off.

Tina visibly swallowed. "Of course. Have a good night, you two."

She stumbled from the table, stopping a few times to steady herself on the backs of chairs. My attention returned to Lily as she took the seat across from me, putting her wineglass down beside her clutch.

"Thanks for the rescue," I said.

Lily sipped her wine. "Mmm. I've gotten used to most aspects of small-town living but having to see the same few abysmal people on a regular basis still gets under my skin. Fortunately, those types are few and far between in Sugar Brush."

"Lucky for you, living out on the ranch, you are pretty isolated from the Tina types."

"One would think, but I'm a people person, Remington. Connell is happy as a clam surrounded by horses, steer, and family, but I have to come into town several times a week, or no one would like the person I'd become."

Despite the storm brewing within me, I had to laugh. "Pretty sure Caleb is the same."

"And my Lachlan too. The Kelly men were born to be ranchers. Though we'll see about our Jesse-boy. He marches to the beat of his own drum, that one."

I nodded, wiping my mouth with my napkin. "He does. Smart as a whip. If he doesn't take to ranching, I'm sure there will be more Kelly grandchildren who will."

"Time will tell. I only hope I'm around to see it."

"According to Hannah, you'll live forever, so I wouldn't worry about that," I told her, even though saying her name and repeating words she'd whispered to me when her head had been resting on my pillow felt like rubbing salt into a gaping wound.

"My sweet granddaughter. She loves hard." She smiled, wistful and soft, before focusing her penetrating gaze back on me. "What about you, Remington? How are you handling being back?"

I answered carefully, conjuring up how I would have replied if I hadn't just been flayed alive on her granddaughter's porch.

"It's...not like I remember. I'm not feeling on edge every second of the day, so that's good. And I'm appreciating the beauty of the land a lot more."

"Mmm. There is a lot of beauty. I suspect a lot more than you've seen in your career?"

"I've been on six continents, Lily. Even when ugliness bled out into the dirt, there was always beauty."

"But your job wasn't to focus on that, was it?"

I exhaled slowly through my nose. "No. I'm not a nature photographer."

"But you could be, couldn't you? With your talent, you could take pictures of anything, and people would want to see them."

I tipped my beer toward her, flattered by her compliment. Something told me she didn't dole them out easily. "Maybe. I don't know. It's not something I've tried."

She folded her manicured hands on the table and leaned in. "Let's cut to the chase, darling. When will you be going overseas again?"

"I'm not sure. Doc said I needed to heal. I'm not ready to take a chance with an injury. Not yet."

"But eventually, yes?" she pressed.

I blew out a breath, picked up my burger, and looked at her. "It's all I know." But I didn't take a bite. My stomach dropped low, fast. I tossed the burger down and sat back in my seat, my hand on my twisted gut.

She picked up her glass, giving it a swirl. "Did you know Connell and I were divorced for almost fifteen years?"

"I remember hearing something about that. Didn't realize it had gone on for so long. I'm glad you and Connell found a way back to each other."

"We did, though it was me finding my way back to him. He'd always been in the same place." Her rose-colored lips curved into a slight smile. "We met young, you see. In college, at Savage University—the same school Lachlan and Elena attended. Cormac too. Connell has always been Connell, the son of a rancher who loved the land. I am the daughter of politicians, and I always knew that would be my path. My Connell loved me so very much, he married me and moved to Northern California so I could pursue my career. During that time, we had Lachlan and Saoirse, my daughter, and I worked my tail off. Before Connell and I got married, I'd promised him we'd all eventually move to Wyoming so he could take over the ranch, but I kept pushing back the date until he stopped asking. He took Lachlan and Saoirse to Wyoming for the summers while I stayed behind to work."

I found myself leaning on my elbows, drawing closer so I didn't miss her story. "You were a senator?"

"State senator, yes. Mind you, I'd paid my dues and worked my way up to that position, held my seat for the twelve-year term limit. I'm proud of what I accomplished, of course. It would be a crying shame if I wasn't since I lost my husband and alienated myself from my children."

"Connell left you because you wouldn't give up your career?" I asked.

Her lids lowered, long lashes sweeping over her finely lined, velvet cheeks. "Oh, my dear. Connell delayed leaving me for years because he loved me and our family. He wanted the life we'd promised each other, but he needed to be here, on the ranch, and I thought I needed to be in California. Like an idiot, I was so very mad at him for not staying by my side, when, in reality, it was me who didn't stand by him. I let the love of my life go because I didn't know how not to be anything but my career."

"There was no compromise?"

She lifted her glass, almost smirking as she brought it to her lips. "You're not listening, Remington. Connell did nothing but compromise while I...didn't. I thought we had time, and I was needed where I was. My ambition and my apathy convinced me I was right. We might have been married, but I'd broken so many promises, I'd made a mockery of our vows. Connell would say he was the one who put the nail in our coffin by getting plastered right here in this bar one lonely night and sleeping with some woman, and boy had I been angry when he'd confessed, but now, with hindsight, I don't blame him. We'd been dragging around the rotting corpse of our marriage for years, and that had pushed us to lay it to rest."

"For fifteen years," I stated, shocked at everything she was telling me. I'd been vaguely aware of some of this, but never the dirty details.

"Fifteen *long* years where I missed my husband every single day. Neither of us dated. We weren't interested in falling in love with anyone else when we were still very much in love with one another."

Her eyes pinched in a small wince, as if the memory was physically painful.

"But you're here now. Remarried."

"We are. It took me a long time to admit I'd screwed up and had driven not just Connell but Lachlan and Saoirse away. I made them all promises I did not see through." She sighed, weary and mournful. "They say you can never go home, and that is absolutely true, Remington. What you can do, though, is rebuild a new home. It isn't easy. It took learning humility and humbling myself. I'm lucky my husband is the forgiving sort. I'm lucky he never realized what a catch he is because he could have had the pick of the litter, but he only wanted me."

"I'm glad for you, Lily."

"Me too." She ran the tip of her manicured finger around the rim of her glass. "But I missed so many years, and I will have to die with that regret. There's no going back and fixing things now. If I could, I would have moved to Wyoming with Connell as I promised. I could have run for office here and left my mark. It could have been extraordinary. But I'd been so set on one path, I chose it over and over, no matter what I lost, instead of veering off and having everything."

I scrubbed the scruff on my jaw, mulling over the point of her telling me this story. I thought I understood it, but I needed her to say it.

Lily didn't wait for me to ask.

"When Graham passed, it snuffed out some of Hannah's light. He'd been a second father to her, a best friend too. But then you came back, and little by little, my bright Hannah-girl resurfaced. I've seen you together, Remington. It's clear to me there's something special between you, yet when I asked you when you were leaving, your answer was it's all you know. That may have been true before, but now you know what it is to be loved and adored by Hannah Kelly. Seems to me you'd be trying your damnedest to come up with a plan on what staying in Sugar Brush looks like so you can love and adore her back."

A vise tightened around my chest. I wanted to tell her she didn't know shit. I wouldn't have said it that way since she was who she was, but I still wanted to be able to tell her that. Except I couldn't. What she was saying rang true. That was why I'd been so fucking bowled over when Hannah ended things an hour ago.

I'd been loved and adored by her. She might not have said it, but hell, I hadn't told her I loved and adored her either.

I was only realizing that was the floating feeling I got whenever I was near her, or thought of her, or someone even mentioned her goddamn beautiful name.

"You don't have to say a word, darling," Lily went on as she rose to her feet, wineglass in hand. "I do hope you took in my story as a cautionary tale. Don't walk away and miss the beauty you could have had. If you do, I can guarantee you won't be as lucky as I was. Hannah won't be waiting for you when you finally come to your senses." She lowered her chin, giving me an imperious look. "That, I will make sure of, Remington Town."

Lily whirled away and strode over to the bar. She perched on a stool, her legs crossed, shoulders relaxed, as if she hadn't just eviscerated me for the second time tonight.

Damn these Kelly women.

Can't live without them.

I sat for a minute, trying to catch my breath and make up my mind on my next step. Once I did, I tossed cash onto the table to pay for the food I barely touched and my half-full beer and stood.

I could've let things settle, but if I'd taken anything from the story Lily had just told me, it was not to wait.

Hitting the street, I turned in the direction of Hannah's place.

She might've thought we were over, but she was wrong. I wouldn't be letting her go. Not when she didn't understand what we'd both be losing.

Chapter Thirty-three

Hannah

PHOEBE HAD FED ME homemade apple cider donuts. She'd rubbed my back and unbraided and rebraided my hair. She'd listened to me spill my guts.

Now she was giving me the strongest side-eye. So powerful, it cut through the tears blurring my vision.

"I don't think you get it, Phe. He's signing the deed of the house over to me. He's cutting all ties with Sugar Brush. He's gonna leave and never ever come back. I can't love that man. I won't do it to myself."

She sat in the armchair catty-corner from where I was sprawled on her couch and folded her arms. "Oh, I heard that, and I can imagine how you must have felt when you discovered what he was doing."

Like I'd been throat-punched. I hadn't been able to breathe or think straight.

That night Remi had shared his passion with me while I'd sat in his lap, I'd known. He came alive showing me his pictures. More than I'd ever seen him, and I truly loved that for him, even as my heart broke.

What I'd known that night had been confirmed yesterday. I'd meant to avoid him, to give myself space so I didn't fall any deeper, but he'd asked me to come in after kissing me silly, and I hadn't said no.

Silly.

He'd gone to get me a drink in his kitchen, and I'd spotted the papers poking out from under a magazine on the beat-up coffee table.

He was giving me the house, and the meaning could not have been more clear. Remi was leaving sooner rather than later, and he wasn't coming back.

"I felt stupid," I told Phe. "A complete fool."

"And so, instead of talking it over with Remi, you just...ended it? Without telling him the real reason? Without asking him a single question about the papers you saw?" She kicked my shin, a little harder than would be called gentle. "You're not one to hold your tongue, Banana. I don't get it."

"He was on my doorstep, Phe. If I would have let him in, I'd have caved, and I can't." I pressed my hand to my chest. Somehow, it was whole even when it felt like it was crumbling. "He was always going to leave. I let myself forget for a while, and it was so beautiful. I got attached when I promised myself I wouldn't. But I can't help myself. It's my cursed brain."

"Nope. I won't accept you belittling my sister's brain. Nor will I let you say the way you love is wrong. You do get attached, that's undeniable, but that's because you love with your entire being. Idiots like Watt don't deserve it. And that's their problem, not yours."

"It's my problem when I'm the one left behind." I swiped at the tears on my cheeks. "I don't want to feel this way. I already miss him, and he only left my doorstep an hour ago. If I love him more, I might let him use me as a way station between jobs, and that would be...soul destroying."

I felt her stare on me then heard her soft sigh when I wouldn't look. Phoebe didn't approve, but I knew in the end, she understood my need for self-preservation. I'd been in love a few times and had thrown myself into those relationships headfirst. I'd always landed with a thud then dusted myself off and recovered—it was what I did. Phoebe had been right there with me, putting me back on my feet.

With Remington...it was different. The fall was infinite. If I let it keep going, it wouldn't be so simple as dusting myself off. I'd have to figure out how to put myself back together again and I'd only just done that after Graham. I couldn't...just couldn't. Not again.

I sensed Phoebe before I felt her settle on the couch beside me. She pulled my head to her soft, warm chest. People saw us as the tough one—me—and the tender one—her—but when push came to shove, Phoebe was as sturdy as they came while my mushy feelings were only protected by a thin, brittle layer of steel. My sister had held me through crying jags, supported me when I'd fallen to pieces while Graham faded and after he was gone, and now, even though she didn't agree, she was comforting me through my sadness.

"I don't think he'd do that to you, Banana," she murmured, stroking my hair. "I wish you'd talk to him, at least one more time. I think it would make you feel better about everything."

I exhaled a shaky breath. "You're probably right. Today, when he showed up, I wasn't ready, so I shut everything down."

"I know, honey. But that wasn't fair to either of you."

"Yeah," I whispered. "I know that too."

I stayed with my sister a little longer, until my tears calmed and I wasn't quite so fragile. She asked if I wanted to spend the night with her, but she was already yawning at eight p.m. She'd be out like a light by nine, then I'd be sitting in her apartment, going mad. It was better for me to go mad in the privacy of my own place, where I could pace and wrap myself in Graham's old flannels while wailing old country ballads at the top of my lungs.

A container of donuts tucked under one arm, I let myself out and started up the stairs. I only made it up two steps before I saw him. Remington was standing at my door, knocking. My mouth went desert dry. A hundred different scenarios of what I should do exploded within my skull, leaving me immobile, watching him.

His shoulders collapsed after a moment, and his head fell forward, hitting my door. Defeated.

My muscles bunched, battling with my stubborn brain and the visceral need to go to him. Seeing him that way, the weight of the world pressing down on him, set off my primal instinct to protect him from it—even if I'd been the cause. Yet I couldn't move.

"Hannah, *please*. Just let me see you."

Remi didn't yell this plea. He'd barely pushed it from his throat, each word cracked and raw. So loaded with pain, tears sprung to my eyes. My body overpowered my brain, sending me up the stairs.

He heard me before I reached him, whirling around when I was two steps away. His eyes rounded in surprise, shining bright, then they laser-focused on me, scanning me from head to toe, stopping when he got to the tears trailing down my cheeks.

"You're crying," he uttered.

I stepped up to the landing, barely a foot from him. "I'm sad, but I have donuts."

"I don't like seeing you cry."

"Well, I don't like seeing you look defeated, so I guess—"

He took me by the elbow, scorching me with a light touch. "We're not doing this on your porch again. Let me in so we can have a real conversation. I feel like a door-to-door salesman trying to hawk encyclopedias."

"Do people even sell encyclopedias anymore?"

His brow dropped. "Hannah…"

I swallowed hard. "Okay. But you'll have to hold my donuts and let go of me so I can unlock my door."

He slipped the donuts from beneath my arm. "I'm surprised you locked it."

"I wouldn't have since I was only downstairs, but with everything that's happened…"

I didn't need to finish. He'd been there for the tire slashing and the truck almost running us down. Nothing had come from it, but that didn't mean it was over.

My hands shaking, it took me a couple tries to get my key in the lock. Once I did, Remi pushed the door open, holding it for me, then followed closely behind. I guessed he wasn't taking any chances of me locking him out.

Not that I wanted to. I didn't want any of this.

He kicked the door closed, locked it, and carried my donuts to the kitchen. Once they were out of his hands, he shoved his fingers through the sides of his hair and turned to me. I'd stopped on the other side of the couch, unsure what to do with myself—sit or stand or try to run?

One look at Remi's shimmering intensity, and I knew running wasn't an option.

He'd never let me get away.

Chapter Thirty-four

Hannah

REMI ROUNDED THE COUCH, putting us face to face. He was flushed, his scruff thicker than normal, the smudges beneath his eyes deeper. I wondered if he'd been having more nightmares. My stomach churned at the thought of him having them alone.

"First things first, we're not over. Not by a long shot." My heart stopped at his adamant declaration, and he didn't give me an opportunity to acclimate before going on. "You're unhappy, and I hear you. We'll work that out together. Get to the bottom of how I can make you happy."

I sucked in a sharp breath. "Remington...I know we need to talk. I'm sorry I blindsided you. That wasn't fair. But we can't continue. It's not good for me—not with you planning on leaving. I know you have your career, and that means you'll be traveling. I get how important it is to you. But I don't have it in me to wait at home for you to return. I don't even know if you'd want that, but I—"

"Hannah." He picked up my braid and wound it around his fist, drawing me into him. My hands flew up to his chest to brace myself. "I have no plans to leave."

"Maybe not right this second, but you will. I wish I was the type of woman to give you a kiss and send you on your way, but I'm not. I know myself. I need my man to be near. And that makes us incurably incompatible."

He shook his head. "You're saying a lot. Making a lot of assumptions. What you're not doing is listening to me."

"I've heard you, though." I shoved my shaking hands into my pockets. "You terrify me."

He froze, his eyes wide. "I terrify you?" He asked this so carefully, as if his words were footsteps over the thinnest of eggshells.

"I've watched you detach yourself. You shut off feelings you don't want. For god's sake, Rem, your father died after an incredibly long and painful illness, and you've barely said a word about him." He flinched like he'd been assaulted. I ached for causing him pain, but I couldn't see a way around it. "I'm terrified you'll detach from me just as easily. I think about it all the time."

"That's—" he cut himself off, shaking his head hard, like he was trying to knock the very thought out of his brain. "That's not going to happen. My feelings for my dad have no bearing on what I feel for you. If that's what this is about..."

"It's not. I mean, that's part of it, but not all. I don't see a way forward here, Rem, and I can't possibly invest more into us when I already know how this will end."

"How?" he exhaled on a harsh breath.

"You walking off and leaving me in the dust. I've picked myself up before, and I don't want to do it again."

His fingers went to the side of his head, carving furrows in his hair. It had gotten long since he'd come to town, overgrown. He needed a haircut, but it wasn't my place to tell him that.

Finally, he dropped his hand and pinned me with a liquid stare. "You're not asking me questions, seeing where I'm at. You made a unilateral decision, and you want the truth? I'm pissed at you, Hannah Kelly. You got your mind set a certain way and didn't give us a chance to work together to find a way for us to be possible."

He may have been mad, but he didn't sound it. All he was giving me was soft tenderness. It was almost enough to convince me he was right. That there was a way around these obstacles. Then I remembered how I'd come to the decision I made.

"I saw the paperwork for the house, Rem. You're accusing me of making decisions without you, but what about you giving me that house?" My chin quivered, the well of my sadness overflowing, but I choked back the threatening tears. "You're going to leave. Maybe you'll say you'll come back, but if you have nothing tying you here, why would you?"

"*Fuck*," he muttered, the tension in his jaw bleeding out to the rest of him. "That was supposed to be a surprise. A good one."

I sniffled. "How would you cutting all ties with this town be a good surprise?"

"No, Hannah. My ties to this town have nothing to do with a house or property. If that was the case, I wouldn't have been able to leave all those years ago."

"You had people who loved you then too."

He closed his eyes and lowered his forehead to mine. "I was really young, and so miserable, I couldn't see straight. I made a mistake, thinking I had to let go of everyone when I left. Lucky for all of us, I tend to learn from my mistakes. That's not one I'll make again."

"I can't be your Seattle," I whispered. "It would kill me."

"My Seattle?"

"I won't sit around and be your crash pad between assignments, Rem. I want a husband and babies. So, you see, we're at a crossroads and need to go our separate ways."

He jerked back, my braid unraveling from his hand. His eyes flashed with confusion then shimmered with anger.

"Goddammit," he gritted out. "What the hell, Hannah? Your stubborn little ass isn't hearing a word I'm saying."

"I heard you!" I argued, tossing my hands out in frustration.

"No, you didn't, but I'm going to set you straight right now. I'm giving you that house because you belong there. I want you to make it yours. Fill the fields with horses and the house with life. It needs that."

For a moment, I let myself drift to what that would be like. The rooms I would paint, what colors they would be. The horses... Maybe I'd steal my favorite gelding from the ranch...but no. I didn't want that. Not when I'd be there with nothing but Graham's ghost and my memories of Remi.

"That's nice and all, but—"

He strode forward, gripping the base of my skull. "You want me to stay?"

I nodded tightly.

"You never asked me to stay, Hannah. You know that? Never asked anything of me."

"I—" My mouth fell open then quickly snapped shut. "I can't."

He cocked his head, his gaze sweeping over me. "Are you scared I'll turn you down?"

I nodded again. I'd never ask that of him. Not unless I was absolutely sure he'd say yes, and I was the farthest thing from sure.

With a sigh, he wrapped his arms around me, hugging me tight. My arms moved automatically, embracing him with aching fervor. This didn't feel like goodbye, but what else could it be?

"I need you to let me talk while you listen." He smoothed his hand up and down my back. "Can you do that for me, sweetheart? Set aside what you've made up in your mind and really listen?"

"Okay," I wobbled. "I'll try."

He guided us to sit on the couch, pulling his knee up on the cushion so he could face me. Once situated, he took my hands and engulfed them between his.

"The god's honest truth is I dreaded coming back to Sugar Brush. I was gonna be in and out as quickly as I could. But things changed, and that happened pretty quickly. I remembered what I loved about being here. Not just the people, but the place. The blue, blue sky, the yellow grass, the openness, the air. But the people...the people are the biggest draw. I'd let myself forget what it had been like to sit down for dinner with the whole Kelly clan, to work myself to the bone alongside Caleb out on the ranch...and you, Hannah...sweetheart, you are everything good in this world. I've been around this globe, seen all the good and bad it has to offer, and I can honestly say that."

I had to bite my tongue not to say anything. Being quiet wasn't easy, but Remi wasn't done. I'd had my turn to run my mouth. Now, the floor was his.

"I didn't have plans on where I'd go after I left Sugar Brush, but I figured I'd be back overseas eventually. Until recently, it was all I'd ever known, and I had no desire to switch things up and lay roots. The thing is, though, it's been a while since I've thought about leaving this town. Instead, I've been wondering if winter will be as bad as I remember it. Thinking I need to order a new coat to get me through. It'd taken a talk with Lily to wrap my head around what that meant."

"My grandmother?" I blurted. "You talked to my grandmother?"

"Yeah. After I left you, Lily and I shared a drink at Joy's. She told me all about her divorce with Connell and how they reconnected."

I jerked in surprise. My grandmother was frank and open, but her divorce from my grandfather had always been a taboo topic. It still pained her to think about, so I was careful to never come close to mentioning it.

Remi continued, recapturing my attention. "She told me about her regrets, but the biggest thing that stuck out for me was when she said, 'you can never go home again.' Pulling into Graham's driveway the day I returned, I'd had that same thought. But Lily added something to it. She said you can't go home, but you can rebuild a new one, and that...well, it opened my eyes. I took a good, hard look at my intentions and actions and realized that's what I've been doing all these months. I'm nowhere near finished, but I've set the foundation for a new life in Sugar Brush."

"You have?" I croaked, my chin shaking violently now.

He saw it, and took care of me, cupping my jaw in his warm, firm hand. "You should know, sweetheart, since you're right in the center of it. I'm giving you that house because of everything I told you. You belong in the wide open where you can run and be free, and I want to give that to you. But, Hannah, I'm hoping like hell you'll want me to be there with you."

I found myself leaning toward him, drinking in his every word. "I didn't know you felt that way."

"I know you didn't. I've been working things out in my head when I should've been talking to you, but maybe...maybe I was scared too."

"Of what?"

"A number of things. Getting off the path I'd set for myself. Finding my way here in Wyoming. But I think my biggest fear is you not being as eager to build a life with me as I am with you."

"Well, you're dumb then, Remington Town."

He barked a laugh, and it vibrated all the way to my bones. "I might be, but I'm crazy, stupid in love with you, Hannah. I want to stay and figure out what life is going to look like together. Do you want that?"

I threw myself at him, hugging him so tight I would have worried about strangulation if my mind had been more present, but Remi just laughed and hugged me back. Because he was crazy, stupid in love with me and wanted to stay.

"Is that a yes?" he asked beside my ear.

"Of course it is." I rubbed my tear-soaked cheek against his scruffy one. "Yes, stay, Rem. Stay with me."

"I'm staying. It's gonna take a lot more than you breaking up with me to get rid of me."

I sob-laughed and pulled back so I could look at his beautiful face. "Don't let me break up with you again, all right?"

He gently brushed my hair from my face and looked at me like I was the center of everything...just like he'd said. How had I missed that? "I'll tie your stubborn little ass down and make you listen. How about that?"

I grinned through watery eyes. "I'm not going to break up with you again, but you can tie me down if you want to."

"Hannah..." he growled.

We stared at each other for a long moment. Slowly, my smile slipped, and I grew serious. Taking his face in my hands, I held his gaze.

"I'm really sorry for letting you walk away. I'm sorry for not talking to you like I should have. I hate knowing I hurt you, and I promise I won't do it again."

He let out a shuddering breath, then turned his head to kiss my palm. "Thank you for saying that, sweetheart. I'm sorry for letting you do it. I should have stayed and fought you."

"You needed Lily to set you straight."

He nodded. "I don't know how she knew to say exactly what I needed to hear, but she did."

"My grandma is amazing that way." I lowered my mouth to his, and there, with our lips brushing, I told him, "I love you too, you know."

"Yeah?" he rasped after a long pause.

"I do."

"Thank fuck, sweetheart."

After that, we didn't do much more than lie on my couch, tangled up in each other, periodically kissing, laughing, whispering sweet nothings. Mostly, we held on, making up for the days I'd pushed him away and he'd let me.

When I closed my eyes, letting exhaustion take me over, his heartbeat beneath my cheek, I was content and safe and grounded. Remington Town was mine, and I didn't have to let him go.

He wouldn't allow it.

Chapter Thirty-five

Remington

SOMETIME DURING THE NIGHT, I woke from something other than a nightmare. Hannah and I had fallen asleep on her couch. We were both too long for it—the crick in my neck evidence to that—so I carried her to bed and fell back asleep curled around her. My girl in my arms.

In the morning, I woke up rested for the first time in days. Hannah was still dead to the world, so I sat up and watched her. She lay on her back, her thick chestnut hair cascading over her white pillowcase, lips rosy and pursed. She was a sleeping beauty. I snatched my phone from the bedside table and took a few pictures of her. I couldn't help myself.

After a while, she started to stir. First, stretching her arms over her head, then rubbing her cheek against her pillow. With a soft gasp, her eyes fluttered open, darting around until they landed on me sitting above her.

"Morning, beautiful," I said softly.

"It's a good morning waking up to you," she replied. "I don't even mind knowing you were watching me sleep."

"Good, because I liked it."

She rolled into me, throwing her arm around my waist. "I hope you slept."

"I did. Just woke up a few minutes ago." I slid my fingers through her hair and curled my arm around her shoulder. "You still love me?"

She tipped her head back, a line carving between her brows. Maybe I was still feeling a little raw from the last few days, but I needed her to say it. Lucky for me, she gave it to me.

"Yeah, Rem, I love you. How about you? Still love me?"

"Love and adore you, Hannah."

Pushing herself upright, she planted her knees on either side of my hips and pressed her chest to mine. My arms moved on instinct, holding her to me.

"I fell asleep listening to your heartbeat," she said. "Now I want you to feel mine beating with yours. Do you feel that?"

"I do."

With her solid weight on me and in my arms, I settled. Closing my eyes, I cradled the back of her head, bringing her face into my neck and my nose in her hair. Soft, clean, sweet, I inhaled her until my lungs were filled. My Hannah.

Her lips grazed my neck, and her fingers stroked along my shoulders and down my bare chest. I touched her too, lifting her flannel to trail along her spine to the cleft at the base then back up again. Her skin was smooth, muscles rippling under the path I followed.

She lifted her face and brought it to mine. First to rub noses, then to roll her forehead along mine. I tipped my chin, she lowered hers, and our mouths met in a sleepy, languid kiss. Warm tongue against warm tongue, wet lips and hot breath. Kissing Hannah was an experience all unto itself. Sometimes frantic and needy, sometimes sweet and adoring. This one, though...this kiss was all about connection after a separation that hadn't been long in time but endless in the depth of our loss.

"Hannah," I whispered.

"Remington," she answered.

I cupped her bottom with both hands, pulling her closer. Her heat penetrated my briefs, aligning with my steely erection. She rocked against me, drawing her center along mine, two thin layers of cotton doing nothing to hide either of our need.

Pushing her panties to the side, I followed her seam from her back hole to her sleek little cunt and dipped one finger inside her. She shuddered, teeth clamping on my bottom lip as I explored her.

"That's my girl." I rested my head on her headboard to watch as I pushed my finger in deeper. "My gorgeous girl."

Panting, she ground down on me, rotating her hips to the slow, steady rhythm I'd set. Her fingers curled around my shoulders as she dipped down to move her mouth over me, nipping and suckling my neck, then shifting lower. Her tongue circled one nipple then the other. She laved my chest, taking her time when she reached the space above my heart. There, she kissed and kissed and kissed. Her lips roamed the parts of my body she could reach, leaving no skin unadored.

"Hannah, look at me."

Raising her head, she dragged her tongue along her puffy lips. "I see you."

I curled my finger inside her, pressing against her inner wall. "Do you feel that?"

"Oh yeah. I feel it."

"What do you want?"

She rocked against me, her breath stuttering. "I want you inside me. To feel all of you."

"Take my cock out."

She reached between us, and I raised my hips to help her as she shoved my underwear down. Once she'd freed me, her fingers closed around my length and pumped up and down. We stroked each other, watching, breathing in time.

"Unbutton your shirt. Show me everything," I said.

With her free hand, she worked to undo her buttons, revealing slices of skin until the sides finally parted. Everything stopped then—my breath, my heart, my thoughts. I'd almost lost this beauty. Had almost let her walk away from me due to both our fears. Now I had her, and there was not a chance I'd ever let her go.

"Give me your heart."

"You have it," she uttered as she leaned forward, allowing me access to her. I pressed my mouth over the flutter beneath her ribs. It beat in time to the pulse throbbing inside me, echoing her name.

I took one of her nipples into my mouth, sucking deep. Sweet skin and pebbled cherry nipples on my tongue and lips. Her pussy in one hand, round ass in the other. I was overwhelmed by my desire for this woman—to connect with her on every level I could for as long as she welcomed me.

She rose up on her knees, losing my finger, and quickly replaced it with my cock. She took me in a slow slide, her eyes on mine, her hands braced on my stomach.

"There," she murmured when her ass settled on my lap. "There you are."

"Right where I belong." I shoved her shirt the rest of the way off, needing to see more of her.

Once she was bare except for her scant panties bunched to the side, I spent a long moment taking her in. Long and lean. Pretty little tits that fit perfectly in my palms. A taut stomach, rounded hips, a waist designed for me to hold on to...my Hannah made up an ideal I'd never known I had until I'd laid eyes on all she was.

"You're so beautiful, baby," I told her as I gripped her waist. "I could look at you forever."

"Could you?" She rolled her hips, squeezing around me. "That's good because I like looking at you too."

I let her have her way, setting an unhurried pace. It was good to just be inside her and touch her all over with the knowledge she was mine. We had time now. There was no need to speed through this.

"I'm thinking about the winter coming up," I told her.

Her mouth hitched as she bounced on me. "Are you? That's what you're thinking about?"

"I am. I'm thinking of the long winter in store for us, where all we'll have is each other to keep warm. Roads will be snowy. We might get stuck inside for days and days."

"Hmmm." Her fingers crawled along my abdomen and up my chest, stopping to tease my nipples. "Whatever will we do with all that time?"

"I think"—I bucked my hips, hitting a new spot inside her—"we're going to have to get creative so we don't get bored."

An eyebrow rose, and her inner walls clamped around me. "You think you'll get bored with me, Remington? Is that what you're saying?"

I took her ass cheeks in my hands, kneading them before giving her a light swat. "I know I won't get bored with you. We're gonna have fun together, aren't we?"

Her breathing stuttered when I slapped her again, harder this time. "What do you want to do with me?" she asked.

"Make you come in every room of the house. Tie you up." My heels dug into the mattress, giving me the leverage to push deeper inside her. "Let you tie me up. Spank you for being naughty. Eat you out for being such a gorgeous, wonderful girl. Fuck your pussy until you scream. Fuck your ass until I can't see straight."

"More," she panted, her movements picking up speed and purpose. "Will you feed me your cock? Give me your cum for breakfast?"

"I will, then I'll make you waffles with sprinkles and lick syrup off your thighs."

"Yes!" Her head fell back, long ribbons of her hair grazing my hands on her ass. "I want you to take me outside when it's snowing. Pull my pants down just enough to get to me."

My eyes were like marbles in my head, rolling wildly from how hot this woman was. *My* woman.

"I'll have to fuck you fast, baby. I won't let you get cold."

"Yes. Fast and rough, Rem. Bend me over the porch railing and give it to me because you can't help it—because you need me right then and there."

"Oh fuck, Hannah." I surged into her, laziness replaced by urgency, needing to have more of her. "I have to have you."

"You have me." She brought her head back up, fiery eyes locking on mine. "I love you so much."

"Love you too," I gritted out as I flipped us around, putting Hannah on her back. Her long legs were draped over my arms, giving me the space to rut into her like the feral animal she always turned me into.

"Yes, Rem, yes. Don't stop." Nails dug into my shoulders, but I was only vaguely aware of the sharp bite. She felt too good, looked too beautiful, for anything other than *her* to enter my focus.

"Never, sweetheart. Never stopping."

Hannah released a long "Oooohhhhhh" as her neck arched and her body clasped around mine. It was too much. I couldn't handle how breathtaking she was, the offering of her throat, her tits, her entire being. Falling on her, I ravished her neck with my lips and teeth and took her breast in hand, the soft give of it pushing me over the edge.

Her racing pulse thrashed beneath my tongue as I spilled inside her, jerking and spurting over and over. My arms gave out from the strength of my orgasm, and I collapsed on top of her.

A breath whooshed out of her, then she laughed and circled her limbs around me, keeping me there.

"I'm gonna squash you." It was barely a protest since I wasn't moving. Not even if this building burned down.

Her hold on me tightened. "I like you squashing me. Don't you dare move."

Laughing against her skin, I realized a broken piece of me had mended. Finding her, this woman I never saw coming, had become my home.

I kissed her cheek with all the tenderness I held for her and sighed into her hair.

"I wouldn't dream of moving, sweetheart. Not even for a second."

Monday morning came fast. Hannah had to go back to work, which meant we were parting. A shot of panic struck my gut, but only for a second. Then her hand slipped into mine, and I settled again.

She was stopping in to see Phoebe before heading out to the house to grab her tools. I'd been invited to join her, but my woman needed a few minutes of sister time along with her customary blueberry muffin, so I declined.

"You're walking me to my truck, sweetheart?"

She grinned at me, resting her head on my arm as we strolled down the sidewalk together. "My mother taught me manners. I would never have my way with you without giving you a proper goodbye."

I laughed. "I'll have to thank Elena for teaching you so well."

"You do, and I'll never let you in my bed again."

I stopped abruptly and took her in my arms, jerking her against me. "That's never going to happen. Soon as I can arrange it, your bed will be my bed too."

"Are you asking me to move in?"

My brow lowered. "I thought I made that clear. Dell finishes the official transfer, and that house is yours."

She shook her head. "No. I don't want that."

My heart stopped. "You don't?"

"No. It's our house, Remi. Like Graham wanted it. Yours and mine. If I'm gonna live there with you, that's how it's going to stay."

Relief swept through me, and I dipped down to crush my mouth against hers. "You're a menace, sweetheart. Next time, lead with the good news, all right? I would love it to be ours—so long as you're planning on living there with me."

She giggled, holding me just as tight. "That's a deal. Now, let's get you back to the house so I can steal a muffin from my sister."

We made it to my truck, which had been parked in the same spot for two days. My eye caught something tucked under my wiper, and I figured it was a coupon or flier. Giving it a look, I realized it wasn't either of those things.

Hannah crowded in beside me. "Oooh, a love note? What's it say?"

"Probably critiquing my parking job," I joked, attempting to cover the dread pitted in my stomach as I unfolded the paper.

You lie with dogs, you get fleas.

Told you she's a slut.

Too bad you didn't listen.

Too late for you now.

"What the hell? Who would write something like that?" Hannah cried. "And what does it mean they told you?"

Carefully folding the note, I tucked it in my pocket and faced her. "I got another note like this a while ago and put it out of my mind. I'm sorry you had to see that, sweetheart. That was my mistake."

She glanced around us as if looking for the author. "I don't get it. Why would anyone—do you think this was Christine or Cleve?"

"I'd guess so, yeah." I took her in my arms and kissed her forehead. "You go ahead to Sugar Rush, be with Phoebe. I'm going to take this to the station."

"I can go with you."

"No. You don't need to be a part of this. I'll take care of it."

I was pissed off she'd had to see it in the first place. I would not allow her day to be interrupted by this ugliness. She'd done nothing wrong and in no way deserved this. My girl was strong, but she didn't need to be when she had me. I'd stand between her and anything or anyone who wanted to take her down. It would not happen on my watch.

Her agreement came easily, surprising me. "If you're sure. I'd fight you, but I have a loaded schedule and—"

"Don't want you to fight me." I took her chin between my fingers. "Hear me? I have the time and inclination to deal with this and shield you all I can, and that's what I'm going to do. Go eat your muffin and gossip with your sister, sweetheart. I'll let you know what's going on as soon as I can."

She sighed into me, her eyes closing for a moment. "I hate that we had such an amazing weekend and now this."

"Doesn't take away from any of the amazingness. You still love me?"

"Of course I do."

"I still love you. Falling deeper with every beat of my heart."

"Remington..." I would have called it an admonishment, but she smiled, "I'm falling deeper too."

"Yeah." I let her go, moving back a step. "Get on. I'll see you later."

"See you later."

I watched her until she disappeared into the bakery, then I got moving. I had business to take care of and my woman to protect.

Chapter Thirty-six

Remington

Tonight, I'd settled into my bed, my woman sprawled over me, whispering her love to me before she drifted off to sleep. More content than I could ever remember being, I should've drifted off with her.

After finding that note on my truck and not much help from the cops aside from filing another report, we'd moved on and ended up having a great week. Falling and falling and falling more each day.

Now that she trusted I'd be here in the future if she leaned on me, Hannah had cracked open her world to me. My woman hated doing paperwork, and I didn't mind it, so I took up that job. Taking part in Town Hoofcare, small as it was, only seemed right being the last Town standing.

It also meant Hannah had more free time, and I got to claim all those extra minutes.

And when she was out seeing clients, I sat in her office and started on my own work. I'd documented my travels extensively over the years, with the idea in the back of my mind to one day organize my thoughts and experiences into a book. It'd struck me that now was the time to do it. When I wasn't so far removed from that life, I could still draw from those feelings and memories.

I didn't know if anyone would be interested in what I had to say, but I'd cross that bridge later. For now, committing my words to the screen felt good and right.

Things were going so damn well, I should have been sleeping, wrapped around my woman, but I was staring at the shadows dancing on the ceiling above us.

Thinking.

"You terrify me."

Since Hannah had uttered those words last week, I hadn't been able to let them go. Not when I held her. Not when she told me she loved me. Not when I awoke to her nose in my armpit. Those words were always there, lurking in the back of my mind.

"I've watched you detach yourself. You shut off feelings you don't want. For god's sake, Rem, your father died after an incredibly long and painful illness, and you've barely said a word about him."

There was nothing to say about Graham, was there? He was my dad, but he'd failed me a long time ago, making it easy to cut him out of my life for good. I regretted Hannah having to take care of him alone in the end, but did I wish I'd had a chance to talk to him one more time?

Should I have been wishing for it?

I prodded at my feelings. The ones I'd had for Graham had been sealed behind a dam years ago and there was no longer anything there.

Was I even supposed to mourn a man who'd all but abandoned me? He'd been struggling when my mother died, but damn, so had I, and I was just a kid. How could I grieve a man who'd done that?

"You terrify me."

I turned my head toward my bedside table. Months ago, I'd stashed the letter Dell had given me. My father's final words to me. I hadn't considered reading it. Told myself what he'd had to say didn't matter. And yet, I'd kept it.

I loved the woman sleeping beside me, and I would be damned if I didn't give her my all. If she had even an inkling of fear I'd one day be able to walk away from her, I had to do everything I could to shut that down. Reading Graham's letter might not have been the answer to that, but there was a chance it was.

I carefully moved Hannah off me and sat up, swinging my feet to the floor. Sliding open the drawer, I slipped the envelope out and clutched it with both hands. Just holding it made my pulse pick up and stomach knot.

"You terrify me."

No way out but through.

Quiet as I could, I walked downstairs. Turning on the light next to the couch, I sat and stared at the envelope for another minute or two.

These were the last words my father would ever say to me. Once they were read, there'd be no more. And maybe, now that I was sitting here, finally ready to open this envelope, I was afraid I'd be let down by him once again.

I wouldn't have been surprised. Disappointed, on the other hand? Yeah, I thought I would be.

I ripped the envelope open and shook a folded piece of paper out. Breath stuck in my throat, I opened it, wincing at the sight of my dad's no-nonsense, block handwriting.

Never thought I'd see that again.

Holy hell. I rubbed my chest, but it didn't help ease the ache carving into me.

Already hurting, I took a deep breath and read.

Remi-boy,

If you're reading this, that means I'm gone. I hope like hell I got to say these things face to face and this is just a repeat for you. If you didn't make it back in time, don't let Hannah make you feel bad about it. I understand.

(If Hannah wants to lay a guilt trip on you, let her. She needs it. But don't take it to heart. She's the best girl I know, and somewhere along the way, she became the best friend I ever had. Maybe she can be that for you too. I'm taking that wish with me.)

Gasping for breath, I put the letter down to claw at my throat. Something had shifted inside me, compressing my lungs, making it almost impossible to breathe. What the hell was that?

Leaning over, head between my knees, I sucked in air, only getting a strawful at a time. Black spots danced in my vision, closing in on me, and the inside of my chest felt like gears and wheels were moving, clicking, grinding from disuse.

With a shaking hand, I picked the letter back up, reminding myself there was no way out of this but through. Had to read it, get it over with, move on.

This letter is for you, Rem, not me. No way to rid myself of my guilt for all the ways I failed you, so I want to leave you with things I learned to carry you through. For what it's worth, I'll go to my grave regretting the kind of father I was. I'm sorry, my boy. So damn sorry. That might not be worth anything to you, but it had to be said.

Now, on with it. Here's what I have for you:

1. *Stay with the people who stay with you. Give them your all. In the end, it's those connections that matter more than anything else.*

2. *Never be afraid to show your feelings. Good, bad, sorrow, joy. There's no shame in feeling what you feel. Let it out, or it'll rot away inside you.*

3. *It's never too late until it is. You regret something? Find a way to make it right.*

4. *Spend time in the sunshine every day, even when it's easier to stay in the dark. But wear your sunscreen, boy. You aren't gonna be young forever.*

5. *When you start your own family, love them through every one of your fears, tragedies, anger, disappointment. Love them no matter what.*

6. *That brings me to my final, most important point: see it through, Remi. Whatever you start, you see it through. Do not give up when it gets difficult. Don't tell yourself walking away would be better for everyone. The easy way out isn't the right way. No matter what, my boy, see it through.*

I'll leave this life knowing I failed as a father. After your mother died, I quit, but you know that. Getting lost in a bottle was easier than facing the job I had signed up for. And once I was lost, I was too ashamed to come back to you. I dug myself into a deep well of self-pity.

Only thing that got me out was you packing up and leaving. Too little, way too late.

If I do one thing right by you, Rem, it's teaching you from my failing. See it through. That's all you have to do. You'll get through darkness as long as you see it through.

I used to tell you the only way out was through, and that's the truest thing I ever said to you. You see it through, Rem. The other side might just be the most beautiful thing you've ever experienced.

I didn't deserve it, but I got some of that beauty my last few years in my friendship with Hannah. I'm leaving the two of you this house because I think you might be able to find that beauty in each other if only you spend time together. She's gonna be mad at you, Rem, but you see it through, you'll come out the other side to the best friend you ever had.

If that happens, I'll rest easy, knowing you're taking care of each other.

It's taken me a few days to write this. My end is coming at me like a freight train. I hope I get to see you one more time, but if you don't make it, I swear I understand. I want to tell you to your face how proud I am of you. Your mother's smiling down from Heaven, Rem, I feel it. When I get up there to see her, she's going to have some words for me, but I'm counting on her being the forgiving woman she always was and taking me into her arms after giving me the what for. Other than seeing you again, that's what I'm longing for now.

When you read this, I'll be gone. I'm dreaming of you hanging with Hannah, seeing each other through this wild and beautiful life while your mother and I watch from above. That's what I'm dreaming of.

Love you to the end, boy.

Your dad,

Graham Town

Wheels turned, channels opened, and the dam holding everything back burst. A sob ripped apart my tightly controlled emotions, letting them rage through me at once. Anger, grief, anguish, fury, loss—they all came together in a ball, rolling through my body, flattening everything else in their wake.

"Remington."

Her whisper came moments before her arms enveloped my shaking shoulders. Hannah, on her knees beside me, surrounding me in her embrace. I turned my head and buried my face in her neck. Not because I was ashamed of the rivers of tears I helplessly cried. I needed her scent, the feel of her skin and hair. Her weight on me to ground me when everything else was falling apart.

"He wrote me a letter."

"I know he did." Her arms tightened around me as her body shuddered from her own tears. "He so wanted to see you one more time."

"Yeah."

I'd known that. So why the hell was it hitting me so damn hard now? That letter should have meant nothing to me. Like I'd told myself Graham had meant nothing, but...I couldn't say that was true.

"I'm so fucking mad at him, Hannah."

"I know you are, baby." She moved, straddling my legs so she could get to more of me. Her forehead on mine, she dragged her fingers through my hair and down my neck. "Feel it, Rem. I'm here for you. You can say anything to me."

I let my head fall back so I could look at her through my tears. She gave me a sad, watery smile and used her thumbs to wipe the tears from my cheeks.

"He should've gotten better for me."

She nodded. "He should have."

"Why didn't he? Why the hell wasn't I enough of a reason for him to try?"

"I don't know, baby." Her voice was thick, filled with sorrow. For me, for Graham, for herself. "You were more than reason enough. He just couldn't get himself there."

"He should have tried harder to get in touch with me."

Another nod. "You're so very right."

"I thought he stopped loving me. Thought maybe he never had."

Her lips pressed together, and a sob racked her shoulders as she shook her head. "He loved you, Remington. He checked out on you. He screwed up in a way that can't be made up for. But he always loved you."

I took that in, felt the gears churning, clicking, moving. Tears I'd held inside for years rolled down my face in unending streams. Hannah would never lie to me, and she'd known my dad in a way I never had. If she said Graham had loved me, I'd take it as fact.

Knowing that didn't heal me, though. His love for me had been drowned out by alcohol and neglect for too long for it to make a difference now.

"That's not enough. Never was."

"No," she agreed. "But it's still important you know it. You were loved, and if Graham was right and there is an afterlife, you're still being loved by him. Even if he was wrong and this one life is all we get, things like love don't die. It's here in the grass, on the wind, in the bones of this house..."

"In you."

"Yeah," she croaked. "He thought we'd be friends."

"He was right about that." I blinked away the wetness coating my eyes, taking in the woman quietly crying in my arms. "I didn't want to grieve for him. Thought I got that out of the way a long time ago."

"You can't make your feelings go away just because you don't want them."

"I'm learning that." I touched my chest. Even though everything had changed, it felt the same somehow. "I should've been here. I'm so damn mad I got robbed of the chance to settle things with him. This letter...it's not enough."

"It's not." Her palms were warm on my cheeks, wiping my tears again and again as they flowed freely. "I'm so sorry, my love. I wish I had tried to find you earlier. I wish I could have given you that time. Oh, Remi, I'm sorry."

"Christ, Hannah, baby." I held her face in my hands the way she held mine, drawing my thumbs through her tears. "Don't be sorry. I have you, don't I? All the beauty and sweetness I never knew I needed in one wild, incredible person. I can't regret what brought me to you. You're the reason I read that letter, the reason I have a home, the reason I know I need to face what I feel so I can heal and be the man you deserve."

"Okay," she whispered, turning her head to kiss my palm. "I'm going to be here, seeing it through beside you. You hear me? We're gonna see it through together."

No way out but through.

In some strange, twisted way, walking downstairs to read this letter with my dad's words in my head was like coming full circle. Returning to a place where I was firmly rooted, loved, at home. Times had changed, and everything looked different, but the roots were what mattered. Every tear we cried together seeped into them, strengthening my tether to this place and this woman.

"I love you, Hannah Kelly. Thank you for not giving up on me."

"Never," she promised. "'Cause I love you too, Remington Town."

Two days later, Hannah took me for a drive. She wouldn't tell me where we were going, just that she had a surprise for me.

I'd be willing to walk to the end of the earth with her, so going on a drive was no skin off my back. Especially since I didn't have to have a hand on the wheel so I could put them both on her.

I was still raw from the letter, but riding with my woman, holding on to her leg while we sang along to the radio, was healing for me. It'd take time for me to get fully right, but I'd been denying my feelings for so long I was giving myself the grace I needed to do that.

Before I knew it, Hannah was pulling through the gates of a ranch, a little smirk on her lips.

"What are you up to?" I asked.

"You'll see."

She parked, and when we got out, she took my hand in hers, pulling me toward the stable. A few horses were out grazing, a man in jeans, a cowboy hat and a plaid shirt watching over them.

"Hey, Allen," Hannah called.

Turning, he tipped his hat to her. "Ms. Kelly. This your man?"

"Yep. Graham's son, Remington."

Allen strode over to us, his hand extended. "Nice to meet you. Knew your dad a long time ago. Got reacquainted with him when he helped Hannah out with my horses. My condolences."

I shook his hand, thanking him, even though I was still confused why we were here.

Allen winked at Hannah. "Follow me. I've got him in the smaller pin. The old boy gets cantankerous around others these days."

We trailed behind Allen. Hannah was practically vibrating. "What's going on?"

"Just wait, Rem. You'll see in a second," she promised.

Rounding the barn, we came upon a pen, holding one lone horse. He was a sorrel with a white muzzle and more white around his eyes. An old boy, as Allen had said.

Allen clapped his hands. "Come here, boy." The horse's ears twitched, but he didn't budge. Allen laughed. "He likes to pretend he can't hear, but watch this. Come on, boy. I've got a treat for ya."

The horse looked up, pinned Allen with his black eyes, and meandered over, nostrils flaring. I didn't know why, couldn't put my finger on it, but my stomach clenched as he drew near.

Allen fed the horse an oat ball from his palm and stroked his wispy mane. "Attaboy. You're just an old man, aren't ya? Earned your right to be cranky."

I cleared the knot in my throat. "What's his name?"

Hannah squeezed my hand, and Allen looked at me funny before shifting his gaze to her. "You didn't tell him?"

"No. I wanted it to be a surprise."

Allen's grin was slow, spreading over his whole face when he looked at me again. "Well, allow me to be the one to reintroduce you. This old man is Huckleberry Town."

My heart stopped as I got closer, looking into the eyes of the deeply familiar horse. "Huck? My Huck? He's got to be—"

"Twenty-nine years old," Allen pronounced proudly. "Slowing down, but he's got life in him yet."

Huck turned to me, giving me the stare down of a lifetime. There wasn't any way he remembered me, but when I stepped forward, my hand out to him, he pushed his muzzle against my palm and chuffed. I stroked his neck, the feel of his soft coat bringing to life memories of grooming him with my mother.

Hannah came up to stand beside me, her arm around my waist. "I've been trimming his hooves the last eight years, Rem. I always called him Huckleberry...but then remembered Allen calling him Huck and put two and two together. This is your guy."

For the second time in as many days, tears pricked my eyes. "You took care of him?"

"I did." She wiped a tear away. "I think he knows you, honey."

"Yeah?" Huck lowered his head to my shoulder, leaning his cheek against mine. "Seems like he does."

Allen let us stay for as long as we wanted, and I wanted to stay for a while, watching my old horse do nothing special but everything fantastical. Hannah remained right by my side, telling me little anecdotes about my boy over the years.

It didn't make up for my dad getting rid of him, but knowing he'd had a long, healthy life certainly eased that old wound.

Just another way Hannah helped see me through.

I gave Huck one last pat and turned to my girl, touching my lips to hers.

"You're good?" she asked.

"Better than good." I took her hand in mine. "Let's go home, sweetheart."

"Yeah," she agreed. "Let's go home."

Chapter Thirty-seven

Hannah

Cormac stole my phone out of my hand. "Nope."

"Hey! What's the problem?" I held my hand out, palm up. "Give it to me."

"Not happening." He tucked my phone in his pocket. "You haven't stopped looking at it since I got here."

"That's an exaggeration. I'm just replying to Remi. It would be rude not to." I picked up a dart and waved it at him. "Hand over the phone, bucko, and no one gets hurt."

My brother laughed, but he wasn't budging. And maybe he was right. I was more than a little bit enamored with my man. Like most things, when I was into something, I was all the way in, and everything else fell by the wayside.

Since the night Remi read Graham's letter, he'd opened up to me in a way I hadn't thought he could. We'd been raw, real, and honest with one another, and that had made me fall so deeply in love with him, I couldn't begin to know how I'd find my way out if I'd one day have to. But I trusted Remi through and through. In my heart, I knew I was safe to keep falling, and he'd be right there along with me.

After a couple solid weeks of living in coupledom bliss, it was time to come up for air and give some attention to the other people in our lives. So, when Cormac asked me to meet him at Joy's for dinner and a couple rounds of darts, I accepted. This had been our thing for the past few years. Even though peeling myself away from Remi had been torture, it was better to keep the balance. Besides, Remi was hanging with Caleb at the ranch, and that made me happy for them both.

"Fine," I huffed, setting down the dart to pinch Cormac's bearded cheek. "It's a good thing you're so adorable, or I'd be mad at you."

He swatted my hand away. "One, you gotta stop pinching my cheeks, Banana. You may have noticed I'm a full-fledged adult now."

"Pfft. You're a cute little baby."

My brother rolled his eyes. "Too far."

"You're the babiest brother I have," I countered.

"True. Caleb sprung out fully grown."

I giggled and played along. "With a beard too."

He slung his arm around my neck, grinning down at me. "I like you like this, you know."

"Like what?"

"Happy. You had a long, stormy year, but I think you turned a corner and found the sunshine. I can see it in your eyes. You're really happy."

I leaned into him, my chest a little tight and a lot warm. "I am, Maccie. I never would have predicted I'd find it with him, but..."

"Sometimes the best things in life are ones you don't see coming, huh?"

"I think so."

Shattering glass at the front of the bar grabbed our attention. I gasped as Alice fell down on her butt and Cleve went tumbling after her. By sheer luck, he splattered on the ground beside her.

Cormac moved before I could, hurrying toward the broken glass and sprawled bodies. But Christine got there first, and instead of helping her husband up, she gave him a swift kick to the ribs.

"You fuckin' drunk," she slurred. "Look what you did. Now we'll have to pay for all these glasses you broke."

From behind me came a bitter remark I did not need to turn around to recognize. "Oh my, how tragic. A drunk old man tripped over a mouse."

The accompanying laugh was just as recognizable. "So tragic."

"That's what *I* said, Tina."

"I know. I was agreeing with you, Teller."

Rolling my eyes, I walked away from the terrible twosome without giving them a backward glance and joined Cormac in helping Alice to her feet. She seemed dazed, patting herself to check for glass or wounds, maybe. Avoiding eye contact like it was her job.

Joy rushed over, bundling Alice in her arms and walking her away from the mess. "It's all right, honey. Don't worry your pretty little head about this."

Groaning, Cleve attempted to pull himself off the floor without much luck. His feet slipped out from under him, and even though Cleve was lower than scum, had tried to run me off the road, had potentially been harassing me, and had definitely been trying to poach my clients for months, Cormac was ever our father's son, offering the man a hand. Once Cleve was mostly steady on his feet, my brother wiped his hand on his jeans and steered me away as Cleve and Christine started hissing at each other.

We passed Tina and Teller sitting at a table with Brady, who was holding his head in his hands. I would have felt sorry for him if he wasn't just as bad as his present company.

Cormac tossed a dart at our target with a hell of a lot more force than needed. "That guy pisses me off."

I rolled my eyes. "I try not to think about him too much."

Especially since there was no proving he was behind the shitty notes left on Remi's truck. The cops had questioned him, but he'd denied it, as always, and since there'd been no witnesses, we were out of luck.

"Good idea." He held out a dart to me. "Ready to lose?"

I snatched the dart, giving him a dirty glare. "As if that's gonna happen."

Cormac might've been my baby brother, but that didn't mean I wasn't going to kick his ass. He had some tricks, but *I'd* been the one to teach them to him.

After two rounds of darts—both won by me—Maccie gave me back my phone and went to the bar to order another drink. He was currently flirting with a little redhead who had to crane her neck so far back to look at him there was no way she wouldn't have a crick by morning.

I smirked at her blush. So deep I could see it from the other side of the room. Maccie wasn't a womanizer, but he was smooth, and I'd seen him have this effect on women more than once. I was simultaneously proud and grossed out.

Lucky for me, my phone vibrated with a text from Remi.

Remi: *Hey, sweetheart. I'm gonna head over there in a half hour or so. Want me to stop by Joy's or meet at your place?*

I started typing out a reply when a sudden screech stopped me in my tracks. My head jerked up, stunned at what was happening on the dance floor.

Teller had Tina by the hair, dragging her away from a slack-jawed Brady. Tina stumbled back with her, swatting at her friend's hands, trying to disentangle herself from her hold.

"You bitch." Teller jerked Tina's head around like a rag doll. "How could you?"

"I don't know what you're talking about," Tina cried. "I swear it, T. I don't—"

"Oh yeah, you do. You think I didn't see you grinding on my fuckin' husband the second I stepped away to the bathroom? You think I didn't notice your lipstick in his truck's cup holder last week? I wasn't born yesterday, Tina!"

Brady just stood there like a dolt, his arms limp at his sides, his mouth agape, while Teller abused Tina's scalp. To be fair, pretty much every patron in Joy's had the same expression. Tina and Teller were thick as thieves and had always been that way. If they ever fought, it sure wasn't done publicly.

"You always were a slut," Teller shrieked. "I should've known you had no loyalty."

"I am loyal, crazy face." Tina batted frantically at Teller's arms, trying desperately to break free. "Let me go and maybe I'll think about forgiving you."

Finally, Brady jerked himself out of his stupor and vaulted into the fray, grabbing his wife around the waist. "Come on, Tell. Let's go home and talk this out."

"Don't you touch me!" Teller went wild, spitting and bucking, keeping hold of Tina with one hand and clawing at Brady with the other. "You did this too, you bastard. You really thought I didn't know? You're so stupid, Brady!"

Shame draped over me for gawking at Teller's clear misery like it was a sideshow. Sure, she was making a spectacle of herself, but that didn't mean I had to line up to buy tickets.

Spinning around in my seat, I tried to tune them out and replied to Remi's text.

Me: *Hey, honey. I'm going to head out pretty soon. I'll meet you at the apartment. xoxo*

His reply came almost instantly.

Remi: *We're finished here. I'm on my way now. Btw, I like that you didn't call your place home.*

Me: *My home is you, that's why.*

Remi: *Aw, baby, you're gonna get it. Love you. See you soon.*

Me: *Love you too, Remington.*

Cormac's shadow eclipsed the overhead lights, drawing my eyes up to him. "That smile can only mean one thing, Remi's coming soon."

Putting my phone down on the table in front of me, I snorted a laugh. "Soon, but not yet. I still have time to win another round of darts."

I stood and turned in time to see Joy directing a couple of ranch hands in the process of dragging Teller and Brady out of the bar. Alice put her arm around Tina's shoulder, guiding her to a barstool.

Mac shook his head. "Crazy, right?"

"Yeah." I scuffed the toe of my boot into the rough wooden floor. "I'm the last person to have anything good to say about the three of them, but it's pretty depressing to witness the implosion of a marriage and lifelong friendship."

"Right." He rubbed his nape and blew out a long breath. "Never thought I'd feel bad for Teller 'the Terror.'"

"Same. Makes me wish I'd passed her an anonymous note back in high school telling her what a dick Brady was."

Joy quieted the bar by banging the bell she kept hanging over the shelves of liquor. "All right, everyone. We've reached our quota of drama for the night. I don't care if it's a full moon. You behave yourselves, or I'm shuttin' down early!"

A round of applause scattered among the patrons. Most of us locals were the low-drama sort, so two outbursts in one night weren't what we were looking for.

"She means it," Mac said.

"Yep. That's why I love Joy."

"Me too." He jerked his chin toward Tina perched on a stool. Alice was fluttering around her, handing her an ice pack and something steaming in a mug. "Looks like Tina came out on top in this situation."

"I'm not sure she deserves that kind of care and sympathy."

Mac turned back to me. "I don't think there's even a chance Teller didn't know what was going on between Brady and Tina. The entire town knew. Teller is a lot of things, but she isn't stupid. No, I think that fight was because the two of them got sloppy and flaunted it. Teller could ignore it if they'd kept it quiet."

I put my hand to my forehead and squinted at him. "Great, Maccie. You've made an awful situation even more depressing. That's a rare talent."

He grinned. "Flattery won't get me to let you win the next round."

I grabbed a dart and waved it at him. "All right, bucko. Time to put up or shut up."

"You're on, Banana."

I bid Cormac farewell, leaving him at the bar to flirt with his petite redhead, and headed out to meet Remi. My stomach fluttered with excitement, which seemed silly since I'd only seen him this morning. But I could be as silly over Remi as I wanted since I was seriously in love with him.

As I passed the narrow alley between Joy's and the building next door, a crash and muffled cry drew me up short. *What was that?*

I turned on my phone and shined the flashlight into the thick darkness, taking a step forward. My beam landed on a bent figure, and it took me a moment to understand exactly what I was seeing. A million thoughts and suppositions raced through my brain in a matter of seconds.

Someone in a hoodie was...*oh shit*. Beneath them, on the alley floor, lay the body of a woman, her blond hair covering her face. Injured, probably. The person in the hoodie must've seen them lying there and were trying to help. Maybe the blonde was drunk and had fallen. Had Tina still been at the bar when I left?

No...she hadn't been.

The hoodie shifted, and my light hit them fully. Oh no, no, no, they weren't helping. White hands wrapped around the blonde's throat and—oh god, no.

"Hey!" I shouted, my feet moving faster than my mind could decide whether entering the alley was a good choice. "Get away from her! Let her go."

My boot skidded on something slimy, sending my shoulder into a brick wall. My phone flew from my hand, the flashlight blinding me. Covering my eyes, I leaned down to grab it, but before I could, something rammed into me. My back hit the ground with a thud, my head with a crack.

I blinked at the moon above me, whirling in a dizzying spiral. No, that was just my brain, jostled from impact. I couldn't lie here, not when—

Air left my lungs in a violent whoosh as heaviness landed on top of me. My arms moved with sluggish intent, clawing at the ground as I gasped for breath. It was no use. The next thing I knew, an iron vise wrapped around my throat.

Finally, my eyes cooperated long enough to focus on the weight compressing my chest. It wasn't some*thing*. The person in the hoodie straddled me, their knees on my arms, hands tight around my neck.

Not a person. A woman.

As my body struggled for survival, clarity struck. *I'm going to die. She's killing me.*

No, this wasn't happening. I couldn't die in a filthy alley and never see Remi again. It would break him. Break my family. And I was nowhere near ready. This beautiful life had just gotten started. I wouldn't be leaving it. Not tonight. Not for a long, long time.

Through crushing waves of dizziness, I bucked the woman on top of me and scrabbled for something to hold on to, coming up with nothing but sludge. I managed to get a handful of it and jerked my arm out from under her bony knee. With the last of my strength, I slammed it into her face, the force knocking her hood off.

The details of her shrill cry and the moon glinting off her blonde hair imprinted into my consciousness. When I could think more clearly, I would be able to home in on those two things, but first, I had to get away from her.

Her hands had loosened when I hit her, so I did it again, aiming the sludge at her eyes as I gasped for breath. This time, I landed on my target, and my attacker had no choice but to let go of me to protect herself. Once she did, I bucked hard enough to dislodge her.

Run.

My instincts screamed at me, but I couldn't seem to push myself upright. I knew I didn't have much time. She'd come after me again. This was my chance.

Drawing every ounce of strength my body still possessed, I flipped over, pushed up on my hands and knees, and crawled.

I was almost there. So close to the mouth of the alley. Streetlamps and voices of people walking down the sidewalk were just ahead. All I had to—

My foot was yanked out from underneath me, and what little breath I had whooshed out as my chest hit the pavement.

So close.

So, so close.

Chapter Thirty-eight

Remington

AFTER A DAY OF working on the ranch with Caleb and joining him for dinner, he and I were walking toward Joy's. He was meeting Cormac for a drink, and I was too antsy to wait for Hannah to get to her place.

"Think I'm ready for full-time work yet?"

"Nope," he replied.

I barked a laugh. "No? Am I ever going to get off the bench, coach?"

"Far as I'm concerned, nope."

"Hey." I pressed a hand to his shoulder. "I'm good, man. I only have the occasional headache these days. No dizzy spells. I'm healing."

"I'm glad, but the answer is still no. I like having you out there with me, but if I take you on full-time, when are you going to be able to work on that book of yours?"

"I—" didn't have an answer for that. We'd had a fantastic day. There was nothing like being in the saddle, doing hard work while shooting the breeze with the best friend I ever had. And because he was my best friend, he was looking out for me.

"No answer, eh?" He chuckled. "I'll take you on two days a week, but those other days, you're going to be working on your book so you have your evenings to spend with Hannah."

"I can't argue with that."

"I know you can't."

We were drawing close to the bar when movement from the alley caught my attention. Something big was on the ground—an animal?

"What's that?" Caleb's voice cracked like thunder in the otherwise quiet night. "What the hell is that?"

Before we could get a good look, a person wearing all black darted out, running in the opposite direction. Caleb and I exchanged a quick glance then moved in unison, booking it for the barely moving...it was a person sprawled on the ground, face down.

Caleb got to them first, crouching over the body. "Oh no. Oh no, no, no," he cried, falling back on his ass. "Hannah?"

My world stopped. Blindly, I fell to my knees beside Caleb—beside the body. "Is it—?"

"It's her," he rasped, moving the tangled, muddy hair off her bloody face. "Hannah?"

A ragged moan left her broken lips, her hand reaching out. I wrapped mine over hers, alarmed at how cold her skin was. But she was moving, breathing, alive.

"It's Remi, sweetheart." Somehow, the words came out steady, though I was a quivering mass of panic. "We're gonna get you help. You're safe now. You're safe."

The next couple hours were a living nightmare. Ambulance, cops, doctors, the Kelly clan, hospital, waiting room—all a blur of horror.

With my head in my hands, I leaned forward, guilt weighing me down like an anvil on my back. Elena was with Hannah, so all of us had to wait until we were allowed in her room. I'd never felt so goddamn helpless.

A heavy hand patted my back. "Get it out now, son."

I turned my head. Lock had taken the seat beside mine. He was watching me with warm brown eyes that reminded me so much of Hannah's. A knot lodged in my throat and refused to clear out.

He shook his head. "When you go back there to see her, you can't take any of this with you. She's going to be feeling bad enough as it is. You bringing your guilt won't help anyone."

"I should've been there," I rasped.

He jerked his chin toward Cormac, huddled up with Caleb on the opposite side of the waiting room.

"I just got through hearing my son say the same thing. I'll tell you what I told him, you did what you could with the information you had. Getting bogged down in the 'would haves' and 'could haves' will get you stuck in a world of hurt. Operate in facts. Hannah's injured, but she'll survive this. You got there in time, Remi."

I nodded, tears blurring my vision. "I just need to see her."

"I know, son." The weight of his big hand on my back brought me as much comfort as his words. "I have a feeling she needs to see you just as much. We'll get you in there soon."

Soon was relative, but a nurse eventually called us back to Hannah's room. I thought I'd gotten a handle on my emotions. But one look at my beautiful girl, bruised and battered in a hospital bed, and my knees threatened to give out. I had to brace myself on a wall, letting her family go ahead of me to see her first.

"Remi?" Raw and gritty, Hannah used her voice to call out to me. "Get over here."

Elena moved to the foot of the bed, giving me space to stand right beside Hannah. The bruises on her throat almost had me seeing stars, but losing it wasn't an option. Like Lock had said, she needed me. She was hurting, maybe afraid. The very least I could do was be a pillar for her to lean on, knowing I'd stay standing when she couldn't.

"I'm here, sweetheart,"

She reached for my hand, weaving our fingers together. Her eyes, bloodshot and filled with tears, found mine.

"I was trying to get to you," she whispered. "Kept thinking I needed to see you again."

My head fell forward. I took a deep breath, working hard to stave off the sheer panic.

"You did a good job, sweetheart. You fought hard. You made it to me."

Her split lips curved into the slightest smile as her eyelids drooped. Her doctor had dosed her with pain meds, but she was fighting them, trying to stay awake.

"I made it to you, Remington," she echoed softly.

I touched her unmarred cheek, cupping it as gently as I could. "You're safe now, Hannah. You need to rest. I'll be here when you wake up."

"Promise?" Her lids were already lowering.

"I promise. Wild horses couldn't drag me away."

"Okay," she whispered. "Just for a little while..."

Lock brought me a chair so I could sit by Hannah's side while she slept, her hand cradled in mine. Hearing her even breaths reassured me. Each one was precious, and I'd never take a single one for granted.

After a while, her siblings went home, but Lock and Elena stayed, snuggled together on the small couch under the room's lone window.

Elena had been there when Hannah had spoken to the police. Once Hannah had fallen asleep, she'd shared what had happened with Lock and me.

She'd gone down the alley to help Tina. It was no surprise she'd put her own safety aside to save someone else. But goddamn, if it didn't make me angry she'd been put in that position at all.

The police confirmed Tina hadn't made it, most likely strangled to death, and Hannah had been able to tell them Teller was the one who'd done it. Teller had gone after Hannah next, giving her a concussion and bruises all over, the worst on her throat. If Caleb and I had been a minute later, we might have been too late.

It took all my power to hang on to the fact that we'd made it in time. We hadn't been too late. Lock had been right. Spiraling down the rabbit hole of "could haves" would only lead me to a bottomless pit of misery. We'd been there, and Hannah was going to heal. That was what mattered.

I didn't know how, but I fell asleep sometime during the night, waking to fingers running through my hair. Jerking my head up from where I'd rested it on Hannah's bed, I was greeted by the most beautiful sight of my life, Hannah's smile.

"I woke you up," she whispered.

"I didn't mean to fall asleep." Scooting to the edge of my seat, I surveyed her bruises. They had gotten darker over the hours. "How are you? How's your pain?"

"Come closer." She'd barely pushed out any sound, but I'd heard. I pulled my chair as close to the hospital bed as I could, and she cupped my face, sweeping her gaze all over me. "I thought I'd never see you again."

"Not a chance."

"I kept thinking that...when she was killing me, I kept thinking I wasn't done loving you. We just got started."

I nodded, though each time I lowered my head, it became harder and harder to pick it back up with the weight of reality bearing down on me.

"You and I both had close calls; we both stared down death, but we turned back, and it brought us together. This is it, sweetheart. It's gonna be easy street from here on out."

She stretched her thumb to brush it over my bottom lip. "Your mouth to God's ears. I could use a little easy right about now."

"You'll get it. That, I can promise you. Your feet aren't going to touch the ground."

The door swung open, and Elena and Lock walked through. I must've been crashed out hard because I hadn't even noticed they'd left.

Elena stopped on the other side of the bed and bent down to kiss Hannah's forehead. "Morning, my darling girl."

Lock squeezed her foot over the covers and handed me a steaming cup of coffee.

"We spoke to Detective Cox," Lock started. "It looks like Brady and Teller are in the wind. Car's gone, clothes packed, cash withdrawn from their bank accounts. There's an APB out for them. Cox thinks they'll be picked up pretty quickly since neither are seasoned criminals."

"Your doctor will be in soon to check on you," Elena added. "If he thinks you're okay, you can go home this afternoon."

Lock folded his arms over his chest. "Not alone. Until Teller is brought in, you can't be on your own, Hannah."

"I've got her," I said. "She won't be alone."

His eyes landed on mine, staying there for a long beat. "I figured as much. She'll be safe with you."

"She will," I confirmed.

Hannah waved a hand. "I hate not being able to talk," she whispered.

Chuckling, I caught her hand and brought it to my lips. "Do you have any objections to staying at the house with me?"

Her eyes were round, worried. "Phoebe..."

Elena brushed her knuckles along Hannah's forehead. "Your sister is staying at the ranch for the time being. No one will be alone."

Hannah nodded then winced. "Moving is bad."

I kissed her fingertips. "Lucky for you, I enjoy being at your beck and call. You won't need to lift one pretty little finger until you're feeling better."

"Love you," she mouthed.

"Love you too, sweetheart."

The doctor came in to check on her soon after, and Lock and I waited outside. Resting his head against the wall, he blew out a long breath.

"Next time I see my baby girl in a hospital bed, it'll be after she's welcomed her own baby into this world," he stated.

My stomach clenched even as my heart picked up at the idea of that kind of future. "I'll make sure of it."

He cracked his eyes open and pinned me with a long, assessing stare. "I know you will, Remington. Just like I'm pretty sure you'll be the one by her side when she's having that baby."

"It'll be me. Hannah's my life."

"Good. Exactly as it should be." He straightened to face me and threw his tree-trunk arms around me for a tight, brief hug. "I'm trusting you with my girl, Remi."

"I've got her covered, Lock."

Another long pause where he held my gaze with a stony expression before breaking into a small but warm smile. "I know you do, son."

Having this man's confidence buoyed me. I would not let him down. Nothing and no one would come between Hannah and me. I'd keep that promise to my last breath.

Chapter Thirty-nine

Hannah

MY FEET HAD BARELY touched the ground since I'd left the hospital after lunch. Remi carried me to the bathroom, up and down the stairs, to the couch, to the kitchen. I was in pain, but walking wasn't a problem. I let him take care of me anyway. He needed it, and I did too. His tenderness and attention restored my security. In his arms, I was safe.

Still, as night drew near, I found myself staring out the living room window. Not because I was afraid, not really, it was just...the last time it was dark...

I shuddered, and Remi noticed. His head whipped toward me, and in an instant, he was on edge, poised to jump to my defense.

"What is it? Did you see something?" he asked.

"No." My throat was too sore to raise my voice higher than a whisper. But Remi hadn't left my side all day, so I didn't need to speak any louder for him to hear me. "I'm just—"

He took my hand between his, slowly rubbing. "Thinking about it?"

"Mmm. I think I must be in denial. I know it happened." I huffed. I couldn't even turn my head, the evidence irrefutable. "It doesn't feel real that Tina's gone and Teller...god, I can't believe her."

When I closed my eyes, I saw her face above mine. I wasn't certain if it was a memory or some horror my mind had conjured, but the fury twisting her features and reddening her skin wouldn't go away. I wasn't naive enough not to be aware of the evil in the world, but I never would have thought something like this would happen so close to home, much less by someone I had known most of my life. The reality was completely jarring as if my little world had been flipped upside down.

"They'll catch her," he soothed. "She's never going to come near you again."

"I know."

He squeezed my hand and brought his face closer to mine. "Give it to me, sweetheart. Lay it all on me. I'm here."

I touched his cheek, dragging my fingertips along the ridge of his cheekbone and over the thick scruff on his jaw. The sting began in my nose, working its way up my cheeks to prick at my eyes. Remi watched me with an awareness of a man who had found his woman strangled and near death the night before.

"I'm sad," I choked out.

He nodded. "I am too."

I flattened my palm against his jaw. "You're sad because I'm hurt."

"I sure as hell don't like it, sweetheart, but that's not it. I'm sad violence touched you—that you were a victim of it. I know what kind of life you've had here. Sure, it's been rough at times, but you could walk down the street without worrying, and now, that's changed. There's no going back."

"There isn't," I whispered. "I won't be the same."

"No. But I'm here to get you through it. I promise you can tell me anything. Give me the weight, and I'll help you carry it. If anyone understands, it's me, and there's nothing you can say that's too dark or bleak for me."

Tears trailed down my cheeks from sadness and relief. I didn't doubt he'd stand with me, but hearing the words, the acknowledgment and acceptance of my feelings, allowed me to exhale after I'd been holding my breath all day. With that exhalation came tears and trembles, and Remi was there, holding me through it. Soft murmurs beside my ear, careful strokes down my back, he let me cry but not alone.

"I'm sad for Tina too," I admitted. "She shouldn't be gone. What if she'd had more time? Maybe she could have turned her life around…"

"She might've, but let me tell you what your dad told me last night. Getting bogged down in the 'would haves' and 'could haves' will get you stuck in a world of hurt."

I sniffled, pressing my sore face into his throat. "That sounds like him."

"He's a smart man, and he's right. Tina could have been a lot of things, but if we focus on that, we'll get stuck. I don't want you stuck, Hannah."

"I don't want that either, but I think I need to be sad for a while."

"What happened to Tina is a goddamn tragedy. You feel what you need to feel. I'm here with you, and I'm not going anywhere."

"I know you aren't."

He kissed the top of my head. "If you're certain of one thing, I'm glad it's that. You've got me, sweetheart. No matter what, you've got me."

Despite my exhaustion, we stayed up late. I was worried what nightmares sleep would bring, and I couldn't stop staring at Remi. With the memory of those final moments in the alley when I was sure I'd never see him again still sharp in my mind, my eyes hungered for his face. He let me look without question or comment, reminding me, again and again, that I was safe and he wasn't going anywhere.

I believed him, I did. I'd always felt cozy and warm in Graham's house, and with Remi here, that feeling had only increased. But there was a chill in my bones I couldn't shake off. The rational part of me said it would take time, that I'd been through something traumatic and that didn't disappear overnight. Deep down, though, I worried this wasn't over.

I shoved those feelings ever deeper and let Remi carry me to bed.

Getting comfortable was an issue, but Remi surrounded me with pillows and the solid warmth of his body. Little by little, we both relaxed, fingers twined, his breath on my skin. When I finally let sleep take over, it was to his voice murmuring the sweetest of nothings in my ear.

Chapter Forty

Hannah

MY EYES SPRUNG OPEN, darting to the clock on my bedside table, 2:17 a.m. I'd only been asleep a little over an hour. What was I doing awake? My throat was sore, but the meds I'd taken before bed had dulled the pain enough to let me sleep.

My gaze shifted to the window across the room. At first, the otherworldly orange glow outside didn't register. It was strange, but I didn't understand what I was seeing. Not until I stared at the rippling air on the other side of the glass for a solid minute or two.

The fog of sleep finally lifted, and I shot upright, immediately wincing at the burst of pain in my limbs and throat.

Remi jerked away at my sudden movement, knifing into a sitting position. "What is it? Are you hurting?"

My arm felt like it weighed a thousand pounds as I lifted it to point at the window. "Rem...I think there's a fire."

He sprang to his feet, striding toward the window. When he turned back to me, his gaze was alert and panicked. "It's the garage."

I gasped. "No...Graham's tools."

He came back to me, handing me my phone, which had been charging next to my clock. "Stay here. Call the fire department. I'm going to see if there's anything I can do."

I shook my head, but I knew not to argue. There wasn't time. If the fire spread beyond the garage to the house...no, I couldn't even think it.

"Okay. Be careful, Rem."

He yanked on a T-shirt and shoved his feet in the boots he'd left beside the bed. "I promise you I will, baby. I'll be back soon. Don't leave this room."

He waited until I promised I would stay where I was then kissed my head and rushed out. I dialed 911 while standing at the window, watching the blaze overtake the garage in the near distance. My heart broke as the structure burned, the contents irreplaceable. Fear ratcheted up the beat of those crumbling pieces in my chest as I stood helpless while Remi raced into danger.

I couldn't see him, but he was out there, probably hooking up the hose to fight the flames licking the smoky sky.

Knees wobbly and weak, I backed away from the window until I hit the mattress and let myself fall. My body was done. My mind was so very tired. How much more could I take? If I lost Graham's house...no, that wasn't an option.

Footsteps sounded on the stairs, and for a moment, my heart lifted. Was Remi coming back to tell me the fire was under control?

Those steps were much too light and far too timid to belong to Remi. Panicked, I scooted backward on the bed until I hit the headboard and there was nowhere else for me to go. On instinct, I reached beside me, grabbing the bat I'd kept next to my bed since I'd moved out on my own at my mother's insistence. I'd never been so thankful for her paranoia as my bedroom door creaked open, revealing the hooded figure of a woman.

It's not over.

Teller took a step into my room, the light from the blaze outside catching on her face and—oh god. *No, no, no.* It wasn't Teller at all.

"Christine? What—what are you doing here?"

Pushing back her hood, her face became distorted by a heart-stopping, wicked smile. "Come on, girl. Thought you were smarter than that. Isn't it obvious? I'm gonna finish the job that blonde bitch couldn't."

Terror held me in place, the baseball bat held limply across my lap. "What? I don't—you don't have to do this. Remi's just outside. He'll be back any second."

"Nah, he's busy fighting that fire." She reached into her hoodie pocket, pulling out a handgun. "I don't plan on sticking around too long, though. Can't have anyone seeing me. That won't work."

Instinct told me to keep her talking. She obviously had something to say to me, a message she needed to get across. I'd let her pour out her vitriol until I could figure out how to get out of this.

"They'll suspect it's you. How do you think you'll get away with this?"

Her smile lifted. "I was never here. Teller was. She came back to finish the job." She waved the gun at me, her finger perched on the trigger. "Who do you think this belongs to? I should thank her for giving me this peach of a chance to finally get rid of you on a silver platter. Maybe now we can get ahead without the fuckin' Kellys coming in and ruining everything."

"How did you get Teller's gun?"

She laughed. "Walked right into her house and took it. Dumb bitch keeps it unsecured in her nightstand. Can't say I'm unhappy she's a dumb bitch since it worked out for me so well."

"There's no way this is going to work. Brady's with her. He'll know she didn't do this."

"Pfft." Christine rolled her eyes at me. "Like anyone will believe he's not covering for his wife. He's just as tangled up in this as she is."

My body came back online, fingers curling around the bat. I just had to find the perfect moment to charge her.

I kept her talking.

"If this is about my clients, I'll give them to Cleve. He can have them all. I won't tell anyone you were here. Everyone can win and—"

Her crazed gaze crashed into me, narrow and vicious. "You're not winning, Hannah Kelly. Your family thinks they rule this town, firing people without cause or warning, and I'm sick of it. It's time they lose, and you are the perfect starting point. How's Daddy Kelly going to feel when one of his precious princesses has a hole in her head?"

I moved, diving off the bed just in time. The next second, a shot rang out. With blood rushing in my ears, I charged Christine, slamming the bat into her. She grabbed on to me, bringing me down to the floor with her.

I landed on my back, my breath whooshing out of me, my head dazed. A strong sense of déjà vu struck me hard. I lashed my hands out at the ground beside me, scrabbling for something to hold. Unlike the night before, there was nothing but air, my bat lost in the scuffle.

With a wail of rage, Christine rolled away from me and started to climb to her feet, but I grabbed her ankle and yanked hard, bringing her back down. Dizziness kept me pinned where I was, but I refused to stop fighting. I had to survive this.

"You fuckin' bitch!" Christine hollered, pushing up on her hands and knees. "You're ruining everything. You Kellys always ruin everything!"

Swinging blindly, I managed to grab hold of her hair. If she succeeded in killing me, I'd make sure her DNA was all over the place so she'd spend the rest of her life in jail.

"Get off me." She wrapped her fingers around my wrist, twisting it back until I had no choice but to let go. Once she was free, she crawled away from me and got herself upright.

Still dizzy but not done fighting, I pushed myself up, only making it to a sitting position before Christine found her gun and had it pointed at me.

This is it.

I'm not ready.

I'm so sorry, Remi.

"Enough of you," she hissed. "Enough!"

Her finger moved to the trigger, and my heart thrashed, determined to beat as many times as it could before the end.

Before she could shoot, something moved in the hall behind her. White shirt, brown, wrinkled face, shotgun raised. Henry didn't look at me, but his mouth formed words I read clear as a bell.

Close yer eyes, girl.

This was Henry, who'd once said those same words to me when I found an injured pronghorn at the edge of the property and the only thing that could be done was putting it out of its misery.

Henry, who'd given Graham baths in his final wretched days.

Henry, who'd stood beside me at Graham's grave and had shed tears as his old friend was lowered into the ground.

My eyes snapped shut without a beat of hesitation.

Boom.

The shotgun blast deafened me, but I felt the fall of the body at my feet. Still, my eyes remained closed. I did not want to see. I'd already witnessed enough horror to bring me a lifetime of nightmares.

The scent of tobacco and dirt drew near before strong fingers dug into my arms. "Come on, girl. Yer safe now. Keep yer eyes shut. Let's get you out of here."

I let him lead me out of the bedroom, only opening my eyes once we made it to the stairs, and held Henry's hand all the way down them.

That was when the front door burst open. Remi rushed inside, sheer panic in his wild eyes, streaks of soot painting his face.

"I heard a gunshot," he panted. "Hannah, I—"

Walking straight up to him, he opened his arms and only then did I let myself fall apart. Without question, I knew this man would pick up my pieces and put me back together again, maybe even better than before.

Chapter Forty-one

Remington

THE NEXT COUPLE WEEKS were filled with confusion and action. Some questions were answered, but others might always remain a mystery. Our family and town rallied around us, showing support in the delivery of flowers and food, stop-ins, phone calls and, most helpfully, rebuilding the garage that had been destroyed.

There was no replacing the contents that had gone up in flames, but fortunately, not everything had been lost. Most of Graham's tools had been salvageable, which was really what Hannah had cared most about.

We were on our way to having a whole new structure. A dozen guys from the ranch had come out to demo the charred remains and returned this week to frame out the walls.

We'd gone through something ugly, and our town had answered in beauty. That beauty had helped heal Hannah and me, reminding us the universe tended to bend toward goodness even when it felt the opposite.

"Remington Town, come on, you slow poke. You're falling behind." Hannah laughed over her shoulder before urging her horse to go faster. The breeze caught her hair and the tails of her white eyelet bow as her horse galloped toward the creek beyond the crest of the hill ahead.

"Maybe I just like the view from back here."

Her laughter echoed off the endless sky, and my heart lurched. The night she'd fallen into my arms, fire blazing outside, dead woman upstairs, I'd wondered if I'd ever hear that sound again. But my woman rallied, and she did it quickly. There'd been tears, nightmares, new fears awakened, but Hannah had wanted to move on and get back to good, so she'd worked at it. And I'd been right there with her for all of it, no matter how hard going it got.

No way out but through.

I clucked my tongue, and Dynamite, the black mustang I regularly rode when working the ranch, gave chase, galloping over the rough, rocky terrain as easily as a fully paved path. His ears twitched as we drew closer to Hannah and her mare, the view opening to the true vastness of the Kelly ranch and all the wonders it held.

"There you are! I was wondering if you'd fallen asleep back there."

"Nope. My boy just likes to stop and smell the roses." I patted the mustang's neck and murmured, "Didn't mean it, Dynamite. You go at your own pace. Doesn't matter if our girl is faster. We like seeing her win."

Hannah watched me over her shoulder. "Are you gossiping about me?"

"That's between me and Dynamite."

Another throaty laugh, and she took off, her hair flowing behind her like chocolate streamers.

We finally caught up to her when we reached the creek. She'd already dismounted and was in the process of tugging her boots off. I let Dynamite graze with Hannah's mare and sat on the ground beside her to take my own shoes off.

She leaned over and pressed her lips to mine. "Hey."

I took her chin between my fingers. "Hey yourself."

Her smile came on slowly, curving the corners of her mouth then spreading to her cheeks and lighting up her eyes. "I'm happy to be doing this with you."

My heart thumped, and I pulled her closer, curling my arm around her shoulders. "Ah, Hannah-girl, how I love you," I crooned. "More and more every day."

"Yeah?"

"Oh yeah."

It'd been close. If Henry hadn't bypassed the fire to check on Hannah, I would've lost her. That weighed on me, and it would for a long time. How could it not?

Hannah hopped up and reached for my hand. "Come on. Soon, it's going to be too cold to do this. It's our last chance until summer."

I let her lead me to the creek, walking straight into the burbling water. We waded out to the middle, jeans rolled up to our knees. There we stopped, rocks beneath our bare feet. The cold, lapping stream hitting our calves. I took her by the waist and pulled her flush with me, her toes overlapping mine.

A smile broke free as I looked at her, the wind lifting her hair, sun glinting off her rosy cheeks, her chin quivering.

"I'm thinking we're too late, Han. There are fucking ice cubes floating past us."

She laughed. "What do you mean? It's so balmy."

"You lie, sweetheart. But if you wanna stay in here, I'll stay with you."

She poked my chest. "You've gotten weak. Don't worry; one Wyoming winter will toughen you right back up."

"You might be right about that."

She trailed her fingertip along the outer corner of my eye. "When you smile, you get these gorgeous lines that look like starbursts. I love your starburst smiles, Remington." She touched her lips to mine. "I'm ready to move back to the house. Are you?"

Since the night of the fire, we'd been staying at Hannah's apartment. Along with rebuilding the garage, work had been done inside the house too. I hadn't been sure Hannah would ever want to step foot in there again, but I'd needed to make certain there was no evidence of the violence that had taken place if she did.

Elena and Lily had put themselves in charge of redoing the bedrooms, moving our bed and belongings to the primary bedroom that had once been my father's. The fact of the matter was, even if Hannah was okay sleeping in the room where Christine had intended on ending her life, I never would be.

"I go where you go, Hannah. I know you love the house—"

She sucked in a breath. "I'm ready. I'm not letting one person take away the place that's always felt like home to me. She doesn't get that." She flattened her palm on my chest, right over my heart. "You had bad memories there, but we rewrote them together. We'll do the same now and make so many new ones the bad ones will be specks in our history. That house, that land, it's where we belong."

I kissed her forehead and stroked her silky, wind-whipped hair. "Like I said, I go wherever you go. If you think you'll feel safe, I'm more than willing to move back to the house."

"It's over, Rem." Her lashes brushed her cheeks as she exhaled a soft breath. "Those people will never touch us again."

The same night of the fire, the police had taken Cleve Jones into custody, and he'd sung like a canary. According to him, Christine had been the one who'd left the notes and forced him to slash Hannah's tires. He'd said she'd been behind the wheel when the truck had jumped the curb, almost hitting us. He claimed not to have known his wife had intended to kill Hannah, but we'd never know how true that was.

He wouldn't see the inside of a jail cell, but he'd left us alone. Last weekend, we'd gone grocery shopping and Cleve had turned down the aisle we were browsing. One look at us, and he wheeled around and went the other way. Legally, he'd had to, given the protective order Hannah had been granted against him.

There wasn't a lot of good about Cleve, but he was pretty much all bluster and very little bravery. I had a feeling he would do a lot to keep out of jail, and that meant staying far, far away from Hannah. Rumor had it his landlord was evicting him and he'd be moving to Utah to live with his brother.

Brady and Teller hadn't been so lucky. They'd been picked up outside a diner in Idaho and both were in jail, awaiting trial. Hannah would have to face that, but for now, it wasn't anything we were worrying about.

Hannah was safe, and we were together. We would see the rest of it through when it came time to face it.

"Then we'll move back to the house."

She shot me the sweetest grin. "And fix up the stables so we can get a few horses."

"I thought we were going to steal some from the ranch. I'm taking a liking to Dynamite over there."

"That's an option. I think I could sweet-talk my dad and Caleb into almost anything right now. I've got to milk the almost-dying-twice thing for all it's worth."

"Hannah," I sighed, resting my forehead on hers, "I'm not ready to make jokes about that yet. Maybe not ever."

Her fingers flexed on my chest. "I don't think I am either. I was testing it out, but it didn't feel great. Still, I'm sure we can work something out with Caleb if you're mad for Dynamite."

"Dynamite's a good boy, but I think he's firmly attached to the Kelly ranch. What if we start fresh?"

"I would love that." She laid her head on my shoulder and wrapped her arms tightly around me.

I had to close my eyes, inhale the scent of her hair, to feel the solid weight of her leaning against me. I'd been a hairsbreadth from losing this and the heavy knowledge of that had struck me in quiet moments like this over the past couple weeks.

Then, Hannah laughed, bringing me back to reality, where my woman was beautifully alive, colorful, and free.

"You're right, Remington. There *are* fucking ice cubes in this water. I think my toes now have frostbite. Get me out of here."

Grinning, I lifted her off her feet and carried her onto solid ground, where I collapsed to my ass, then my back, dragging her with me. Stretched out on top of me, she propped herself up on my chest, all smiles and sunshine as she tucked her icy feet between my legs.

"Better?" I laughed.

"So much better. I can always count on you, can't I?"

Meeting her gaze, I trailed my knuckles along the side of her face and gave her starbursts. "You can, sweetheart. Lean. I will always be there for you to rest on."

Her fingertip dusted over the corner of my eye. "Love you, Remington Town."

"Love you like crazy, Hannah Kelly."

Her grin slipped from adoring to mischievous. "Are you going to take me home and show me how crazy you can be?"

"All you had to do was ask." Taking her in my arms, I brought my mouth to her ear. "Let's go home."

No way out but through, and I couldn't wait to see it through with Hannah.

Epilogue

Hannah

One Year Later

My father took my hand and placed it on the crook of his arm. "Last chance," he whispered.

I laughed through the butterflies trying to work their way up my throat. "I'm not running away. You don't have to keep offering."

My mother rolled her eyes from my other side. "You love Remington."

He chuffed. "I do, but I'm not so sure about my daughter marrying him."

My father looked down at me, warmth radiating from his very core. Dad wasn't one to dress up often, but he was dapper today in a custom dove-gray suit with a bolo instead of a tie. His normally shaggy hair had been freshly cut and combed neatly away from his face. And his eyes, they shined on me, brimming with so much emotion, my own threatened to spill before I'd even walked down the aisle.

"Oh, Lachlan, yes you are," my mother chided, her arm looped through mine.

Dad slowly smiled and reached for my face with his free hand, patting my cheek. "You picked a good man, Hannah. I have no doubt about that. But you're still my little girl with a hundred bows in your hair. Give your old man a break. It's not easy wrapping my head around you becoming a wife."

I laid my head on his shoulder. "I still have a bow. It's just fancier now."

In lieu of a veil, Phoebe had taken the extra fabric from my ivory lace dress and turned it into an oversized bow secured on the back of my head. I wasn't much of a dress girl, but I had always loved my bows, and I loved that my sister had found a way to incorporate that into my wedding day.

Hell, I would have married Remington in cutoffs and a tank if my mother wouldn't have been mortified. But the truth was, now that I was standing in my pretty wedding dress, my hair curled and cascading down my back, awaiting my cue to walk down the aisle between my parents, I was glad I'd gone this route. Getting married to the love of my life wasn't any ol' occasion. This day deserved to be marked by getting gussied up in front of our friends and family.

"You're beautiful," my mother murmured. "Just glowing, my darling girl."

I told them I loved them and promised I was more than ready to make this commitment. After all, Remi and I had survived a lot, including one of the harshest winters in memory, and we still smiled when we woke up to each other and fell asleep tangled like octopuses.

Before I knew it, the doors opened, revealing my future husband at the end of the aisle. By his side stood Caleb and Cormac, and on the other side, Phoebe and Camille. Their smiles registered, but that was it. My focus was locked on Remington.

I glided to him, barely feeling the chapel's wood floor beneath my cowboy boots. Remi rocked on his heels, grinning, starbursts for days and days.

I laughed when I got to him, my father placing my hand in his.

Remi chuckled, his eyes darting over me like he couldn't drink me in fast enough. "What's so funny?"

"We're doing this." I lifted up on my toes. "I've never been so excited in my life."

"That's good, beautiful woman." Remi stepped closer, enveloping both my hands in his. "Because this is for keeps."

"No take backs."

"Nope." He grinned, bright and just as eager as I was. "Should we do this thing?"

"Never been more ready in my life."

"Me either, sweetheart."

Together, we turned to the chaplain, and on a lovely, clear afternoon inside the Sugar Brush River Ranch chapel with our family surrounding us—including Henry, who'd donned a suit for the occasion—we promised each other forever and became husband and wife.

We danced and celebrated into the night. My hair had gone up in a ponytail, and my dress had been switched out for a light, airy sundress. By midnight, Remi was down to his white undershirt and dress pants.

In the middle of the dance floor, surrounded by the most important people in our lives, we held on to each other. I tipped my head back, singing along to the music while Remi smiled down at me.

"My wife," he mouthed.

"My husband," I mouthed back, excited goose bumps blooming along my skin. "I've never, ever been happier."

He leaned down, his forehead resting on mine. "I haven't either, but I have confidence in us, sweetheart. We'll top this a hundred times over through our lifetime together."

My heart slammed and bounced inside my chest. "You...Rem...ahhh! This is why I married you—the things you say. You're right, though. You and me and the beauty we'll have."

"Our little family," he murmured, letting his hand drift down to my belly.

"Little bean." A surprise but so very wanted. The secret we'd found out four weeks ago and were keeping just between us. Although, from my mother's "glowing" comment earlier, I wondered if she had an inkling.

"Are you tired?" he asked.

"Yes, but I don't want this night to end."

"We'll have so many more of these nights, Han." Remi took my hand in his. "Right now, we're going to say goodnight to our guests and I'm taking my wife to bed."

I had no arguments in me, not when he said things like that. "I love when you call me your wife."

"Feels right, doesn't it?"

"So right."

The morning after our wedding, I woke to find Remi sitting up in bed, working on his laptop. I lay there quietly, watching him type, listening to the distant sound of our three horses neighing.

Over the last year, Remi had worked on his book tirelessly, and his agent had quickly found it a home with a publishing house. He was now on his second round of edits, and though he claimed it to be grueling, the spark in his eyes told me everything I needed to know. He loved it and found creative fulfillment in the process. I had a feeling he had more books in him after this one, but he always said he was taking it one book at a time.

He liked having the freedom to work with Caleb at the ranch a couple days a week and the time to take photos. Over the last year, we'd traveled to the surrounding states together, Remington capturing the natural beauty, me cheering him on. Watching him work filled me to the brim with satisfaction. And god, did it turn me on. My husband was so damn competent. And not just with a camera. He was an incredible writer, but he could also repair a fence on the ranch like he'd been doing it all his life and had retiled our powder room all on his own.

I'd yet to find anything Remington Town wasn't good at. So far, he was doing a bang-up job of being my husband, and in about seven months, he was going to excel at being a father. He'd had a brief moment of doubt, where he'd worried he'd screw up like Graham had, but we worked through it, just as we did every obstacle.

Our family motto was "no way out but through." We'd repeated it to each other during Teller and Brady's trial and sentencing, when we'd reached the one-year anniversary of Remi's accident, and a month later, losing Graham. During nightmares and moments of fear, we held on to one another and whispered those words. We always made it to the other side. All we had to do was see it through.

As if my thoughts whirled around him, Remi's gaze flicked down to mine.

"There you are." He set his laptop aside, slipped down and lay beside me. "Come here, wife."

I slid into his arms, tucking my head beneath his chin. "Good morning, husband."

He found my stomach beneath the covers and splayed his hand there. "How's our bean?"

"She's hungry and demands wedding cake."

He laughed as he kissed my forehead. "She does? You're so certain it's a girl?"

"I'm certain of nothing except cake." I tipped my head back to kiss his chin. "And my husband, of course."

"Well, if my wife wants cake, she'll have cake." His arms tightened around me. "Mind if I do this for another minute or two?"

I snuggled in closer, secure and at peace in his warm embrace. "I don't mind. If you want to extend it to five or six minutes, I wouldn't mind that either."

He squeezed me, exhaling a rush of breath. "God, I love you, Hannah Town."

"Oh." A knot lodged in my throat, and it took me a minute to swallow it down. "You haven't called me that before..."

"Like it?"

I let him see the tears pricking my eyes and the smile curving my lips. "It's just...so wonderful. I really love you too, Remington Town."

Bringing his lips to my forehead, he murmured, "Best morning of my life."

"Agreed," I sighed. "But...maybe cake would make it better."

Remi shook with silent laughter while holding me, and after our allotted time passed, he took my hand in his, his thumb rubbing my wedding band, and led me downstairs.

We spent the first morning of the rest of our lives eating cake in our pajamas, laughing and kissing the frosting off each other's lips.

And I knew, all the way down to my bones, this was only a preview of how wonderfully sweet our life together would be.

Sweet Like Poison

Curious about Hannah's parents' love story?

Meet Elena and Lachlan, before they became the Kellys in Sweet Like Poison:

https://mybook.to/SweetLikePoison

Acknowledgments

A few years ago, I dreamed up a young, cuffing season kind of man: Lachlan Kelly. He was a fish out of water—big, gruff guy who loved his truck and dreamed of his family ranch, going to college in southern California. There, he met the love of his life, the high maintenance, reformed mean girl, Elena Sanderson. Their love story was complicated and beautiful, and the epilogue made me want to know so. Much. More.

So, I took my family to Wyoming and soaked up everything I could about the state. What the land looks like, how the air feels and smells, and what the people are like. I pictured Elena and Lock there, and their childrens' stories bloomed in my mind. This is my first second-gen series, and I couldn't think of two better people to be at the head of the family.

When I was preparing for this series, I hunted down a Wyoming photographer, Madison Webb, who takes pictures of real couples in love. The cover photo is a real, beautiful couple in Wyoming, which I think makes it that much more special.

Thank you to my team who always bring my books to life: Kate Farlow, Monica Black, and my Fairy Proofmother, Rose. Shout out to my beta readers, Jen and Alley, and my wonderful PA, Amber. I couldn't do any of this without you guys!

I have to thank my family for humoring me when I said, "We're going on a research trip to Wyoming!" They hung in there with me when I dragged us all over the entire state of Wyoming. Sure, there were complaints from my tweens, but overall, we had a pretty damn magical time.

I hope *you* had a magical time reading Hannah and Remi's story, and will be sticking around for the rest of the Kellys!

About Julia

Julia Wolf is a bestselling contemporary romance author. She writes bad boys with big hearts and strong, independent heroines. Julia enjoys reading romance just as much as she loves writing it. Whether reading or writing, she likes the emotions to run high and the heat to be scorching.

Julia lives in Maryland with her three crazy, beautiful kids and her patient husband who she's slowly converting to a romance reader, one book at a time.

Visit my website:
http://www.juliawolfwrites.com